FORGET
ME
NOT

Also by M.J. Arlidge

DI HELEN GRACE

Eeny Meeny
Pop Goes the Weasel
The Doll's House
Liar Liar
Little Boy Blue
No Way Back *(an eBook novella)*
Hide and Seek
Running Blind *(an eBook novella)*
Love Me Not
Down to the Woods
All Fall Down
Truth or Dare
Cat & Mouse
Eye for an Eye

OTHER NOVELS

A Gift For Dying

M.J. Arlidge has worked in television for the last twenty years, specialising in high-end drama production, including prime-time crime serials *Silent Witness*, *Torn* and *Innocent*. In 2015 his audiobook exclusive *Six Degrees of Assassination* was a number-one bestseller. His debut thriller, *Eeny Meeny*, was the UK's bestselling crime debut of 2014 and has been followed by ten more DI Helen Grace thrillers – all *Sunday Times* bestsellers.

X @mjarlidge
/MJArlidge
@m_j_arlidge

FORGET ME NOT

M.J. ARLIDGE

ORION

First published in Great Britain in 2024 by Orion Fiction,
an imprint of The Orion Publishing Group Ltd.,
Carmelite House, 50 Victoria Embankment
London EC4Y 0DZ

An Hachette UK Company

1 3 5 7 9 10 8 6 4 2

A CIP catalogue record for this book is
available from the British Library.

ISBN (Hardback) 978 1 3987 0823 5
ISBN (Trade Paperback) 978 1 3987 0824 2
ISBN (eBook) 978 1 3987 0826 6

Typeset at The Spartan Press Ltd,
Lymington, Hants

Printed and bound in Great Britain by Clays Ltd,
Elcograf S.p.A.

MIX
Paper | Supporting
responsible forestry
FSC® C104740

www.orionbooks.co.uk

FORGET
ME
NOT

Day One

Chapter 1

'Darren, I'm begging you...'

The words tumbled from her, choked, heartfelt, desperate.

'Don't do this, *please*...'

Naomi's fingers were wrapped around her boyfriend's trailing arm, praying that he would stop, listen to her, change his mind. But her words had no impact, the muscular young man ripping his arm away and marching purposefully on. Marlands Shopping Centre was crammed with late-night shoppers, many of whom were casting sidelong glances at the couple, but Naomi ignored them, hurrying after her lover. Darren's blood was up, however, his pace relentless. Computer Exchange flashed by, then the pawnbrokers, then Rock Bottom Toys. The exit to Portland Terrace was only fifty yards away and Darren was making good progress in that direction. If Naomi was going to stop him, she had to do it *now*.

Lunging towards him, Naomi gripped Darren's shoulder, arresting his progress, spinning him around. Immediately, his features convulsed with fury, his mouth opening in a snarling curse, but the desperate fifteen-year-old got in first.

'Please, just tell me what you want from me. If I've done something wro—'

3

'There's nothing I could possibly want from *you*,' the junkie sneered, extracting his arm.

'But you *loved* me,' Naomi insisted. 'You said so a hundred times. I don't understand what's changed.'

'That was then, this is now.'

Angered, the twenty-two-year-old tried to turn away, but Naomi held fast to his arm.

'*No*, no,' she insisted, fighting tears. 'You *can't* just walk out on me. I've given up everything for you. My family, my friends. You *owe* me.'

'I owe you nothing,' he hissed in response. 'You knew full well what you were getting into.'

'So what was this all about? This whole bloody thing?'

Naomi's voice was piercing, shrill, tears staining her cheeks now, but she didn't care. It was as if the rest of the world didn't exist, her misery blocking out everything else. 'If you didn't care for me, why did you tell me you *did*?'

Darren said nothing, shaking his head witheringly, as if bored by her questions. With each passing second, Naomi felt more ashamed, more humiliated, but still she couldn't give up on him. He was all she had in the world.

'Please, Daz, it's *me*…' she pleaded, softening her tone.

Naomi chanced a step forward, then another. Taking encouragement from his silence, she slipped her slender hands inside his jacket, bringing them to rest on his hips.

'Your best girl.'

Standing on her tiptoes, Naomi raised her lips to his, kissing him.

'I'll be good to you, babes, I promise I will,' she whispered. 'You're everything to me, have been since the moment I first saw you…'

Her boyfriend stared at her for a moment, surprised by this

heartfelt confession. Then slowly the twenty-two-year-old lowered his face to Naomi's and whispered, 'You mean *nothing* to me, bitch. Get that into your thick skull.'

Naomi stared at him, lost for words. Then, before she could react, Darren placed a meaty hand on her chest and pushed with all his might. Taken off guard, Naomi tumbled backwards, tripping over her feet and crashing onto the polished floor. Pain ripped through her elbow as the wind was punched from her lungs, but before she could recover, Darren was in her face again.

'You were useful to me for a while, now you aren't. Got it?'

'Is that *all* I was to you?' Naomi cried, enraged. 'Some mug who'd steal for you, lie for you, just so you could get a fix...'

'Now you're getting it,' Darren smirked.

'But all those things you said to me, all those *promises* you made...' she moaned.

A broad grin spread across Darren's face, amused by her naivety.

'Jesus, you really *are* far gone. Do you think anyone could mean those things about *you*?'

He was laughing, cruel and self-congratulatory, his arrogance, his cynicism clear. How had Naomi not seen this? How had she fallen for this parasite? She wanted to rail at him, to vomit out her fury and disappointment, but no words came, her desolation total.

'Good luck, *babes*,' her ex-lover teased, rising. 'You're gonna need it...'

And with that, he was gone, sauntering out of the shopping centre and out of her life. Scrambling up onto her knees, Naomi watched him go, forlorn, disbelieving. All her hopes, all her dreams had suddenly gone up in smoke and she watched on in horror as her former boyfriend disappeared from view, before tipping her head back and howling out her agony.

Chapter 2

The sound that came from him was almost inhuman; an anguished, animalistic scream.

Detective Inspector Helen Grace crouched over the injured teenager, her hands clamped to the bloody hole in his stomach. She was working hard to convince the young man that he was going to be OK, but he was obviously terrified. Despite Helen's words of reassurance, the injured man cried out again, wild and desperate, appealing to his mother, God, *anyone* to end his torment, a thick belch of blood spurting out over Helen's hands as he did so.

'Jason, I need you to look at me. Can you look at me?'

'It hurts so bad,' the teenager moaned, his eyes scanning the heavens.

'I know, but I'm right here with you and I'm going to make sure you're OK. I'm a police officer, I know what I'm doing. You'll be fine...'

To her surprise, the teenager started to weep. Whether this was provoked by the pain racking his body or the realization that the best he could hope for tonight was to be arrested and charged, Helen wasn't sure, but it made no difference. Either way he was a pitiful sight. This boy, no more than seventeen years old, had wanted to play at being a gangster, but now faced the prospect of bleeding out in a cold, dark street.

'The paramedics are coming,' Helen added soothingly. 'Any minute now, you'll be on your way to South Hants Hospital. They'll have you patched up and back on your feet in no time.'

And then what? Helen knew that the teenager would be surplus to requirements in the criminal fraternity now, even if he *did* somehow manage to avoid prison. He had messed up big time, ambushed whilst ferrying a holdall of cash across town, and would surely pay for his failure, via exile or death. Helen sincerely hoped it would be the former.

Turning, Helen craned round, trying to see past the crowd of onlookers. Despite her comforting words, the teenager was dying in front of her, so it was to her immense relief that she now heard the squeal of brakes, the sound of doors slamming, then two paramedics hurrying into view, pushing through the crowds. Racing over, they crouched down next to the injured teenager, the lead medic slipping on a pair of latex gloves as he relieved Helen of her charge.

'His name's Jason Matthews and he's seventeen years old,' Helen reported, wiping the gore from her hands as she straightened up. 'Significant blood loss caused by two pistol shots to the abdomen. No other signs of injury. The shooters are long gone, so you're safe to move him whenever you like.'

'Let's get cracking then,' the paramedic breathed, nodding his thanks to Helen.

As he spoke, a third paramedic approached, pushing a stretcher, so Helen retreated, giving the emergency team the space they needed to work. Turning, she directed her steps towards the teenager's dented moped, which remained on its side, its engine purring. Slipping on her gloves, Helen reached down to switch it off, before turning her attention to the ripped holdall that lay close by, now devoid of its precious contents. A few twenty-pound notes had been lost in the struggle, fluttering around the hushed street as the wind picked up. Methodically, Helen chased them down, gathering and bagging the notes in the hope of shedding some light on the hidden faces behind tonight's bloodshed. As she did so, however, she noticed a young boy, no more than eleven, attempting to steal one of the missing notes, which had blown across to the other side of the street.

'I wouldn't if I were you...' Helen growled.

Startled, the child retreated swiftly, disappearing into the shadows, leaving the abandoned note behind. Helen scooped it up quickly, sealed the bag, and then turned once more to take in the scene. It was a sight that was depressingly familiar, the escalating feud between rival drugs gangs in the city becoming ever more blatant, ever bolder. This was the third such incident in as many weeks, all of them played out in heavily residential areas, all of them involving deadly weapons, be they zombie knives, machetes or pistols. People in the city were desperate, ground down by spiralling living costs, rising crime and family breakdown, and when people were desperate, the dealers thrived. Drugs were *big* business in Southampton right now and competition was rife, which meant only one thing – bloodshed. Helen had the sickening feeling that the gangs in the city were gearing up for all-out war, a development that would have serious consequences for everyone, not least her own unit, which often found itself chasing thugs who shot first and asked questions later. Helen had been quickly on the scene tonight, hearing gunfire as she drove home, the shooters vanishing moments before she arrived. What would have happened if she'd arrived seconds earlier? Would *she* have found herself in the firing line?

Pushing these thoughts away, Helen returned to the paramedics, who were gently lifting the injured teenager onto a stretcher. This was the human cost of people's desperation, the price of their addiction. Two years ago, this kid would have been at school, messing around with his mates, flirting with girls, behaving like an ordinary teenager. Now he was fighting for his life, blood seeping from his wounds, even as he screamed for his mother.

Would he live to see her again? Or would he die before he made it to the hospital? Helen couldn't be sure. She had done all she could for him, might even have saved his life, but was it enough? Was it *ever* enough? With the situation worsening day by day, with each new outrage presaging further bloodshed, Helen felt increasingly helpless and despairing, as the city she knew and loved prepared to plunge headlong into the abyss.

Chapter 3

'I'd love to help you, but we just *can't.*'

Naomi stared at the woman, unable to process what she was hearing.

'But this is a homeless shelter, right?' Naomi insisted, trying to keep her fear at bay.

'Yes, but—'

'And I've nowhere else to go. You've *got* to let me in.'

The manager, who called herself Tara, looked concerned, clearly affected by Naomi's distress. For a moment, Naomi allowed herself to believe that the gatekeeper would now soften and relent, ushering her inside, but as Tara looked Naomi in the eye, her expression crestfallen and guilty, the teenager felt the hope die within her.

'I want to, of course I do, but we don't have any beds available. We're completely full.'

Naomi stared at her dumbly. None of this made any sense. How many homeless people *were* there in Southampton? Yeah, you saw plenty of them on the street during the day, but surely there weren't enough to fill this *entire* building?

'There are another couple of hostels you could try,' the woman continued earnestly. 'One on Bridge Street, one on Thurlam Road.'

'I've *tried* those,' Naomi countered, her voice shaking. 'They told me to come here, they said you'd sort me out.'

'Do you have any family who can help?'

Naomi shook her head.

'Friends?'

Naomi dropped her head to her chest. She really didn't want to cry in front of this stranger, but she felt utterly desperate, as if the entire world had turned its back on her.

'Look, perhaps you could come back later?' the hostel manager continued. 'It may be that someone vacates their bed, decides they're better off elsewhere. These things *do* happen occasionally…'

It was a lie and they both knew it. Which is probably why she now reached out and squeezed Naomi's hand, whispering, 'Look after yourself, eh?'

Ten minutes later, Naomi found herself in Hoglands Park, trudging along the faded concrete paths. The skateboarders were out in force tonight, laughing and joking, as their boards clattered up and down the ramps. Their joy, their banter, seemed to mock Naomi, for whom every step was a struggle. The teenager felt robbed of energy, of resolve, of hope, as if nothing she did now would come to any good or make the slightest difference to her situation. Night was falling and she was alone in the city, with nowhere to go. Her misery was all-consuming, her fear palpable, yet the people who passed by seemed oblivious, hurrying to get back to their nice warm homes, as the rain clouds gathered above.

How had it come to this? Six months ago, Naomi had had a roof over her head, three square meals a day and someone to take care of her. It was just her and her mum, had been for years now, and even though they argued like hell, they'd been OK, or at least no worse than anyone else. Then *he* had come along – handsome, charming, manipulative Darren Haines. They'd met at a house party and he'd said all the right things, never leaving her side. She knew he was a bad boy, that he had a habit, but that only added to his allure. She knew better now, of course, having begged, stolen and borrowed to fund his grim addiction, having endured his vicious, drug-fuelled rages, having lived in that awful squat for over three months. But back then she was hooked – hooked on love, on rebellion, on proving to everyone that she could stand on her own two feet.

What a fool she'd been. What a naive, deluded, pathetic fool. She'd followed that boy – no, that *man* – to the moon and back and where had it got her? To Hoglands Park, with night closing in and the gunmetal clouds starting to spit on her. Perhaps it was all she deserved. Thinking back to the abuse she'd rained down on her mother, Naomi felt sick with shame. Her mum been trying to protect her only child, to warn Naomi off a boyfriend who was way older than her and who was obviously trouble. What had been her reward? Vicious rejection and vile accusations. Naomi shuddered now to think that she'd labelled her mother lonely, bitter, jealous, when she'd simply been trying to keep her on track, keep her in school, keep her from sinking into the gutter. Why? Why had she been so stupid? So cruel?

Naomi pressed on, avoiding the eyes of the men who passed by, seeing danger in every stranger, every movement, every shadow. Where was she supposed to *go*? Where would she be safe? She had lived in this city all her life, but now felt utterly bewildered, uncertain where to go or what to do. Should she head to the bus station? No, that was full of creeps and Darren occasionally dealt there. The train station, then? No, the police always moved people on there, she'd seen them do it. The Common? Just the thought of that made Naomi shiver, being out there alone in the cold, surrounded by those deep, dark woods...

Naomi was shaking now, fear mastering her. She'd have to

find somewhere outdoors to bed down, but the temperature was dropping fast and what if someone bothered her? How could she defend herself? She had nothing but her coat, a few pounds and her phone.

Her phone. Naomi paused, running her hand over the smooth surface of her Samsung. It was a mad idea, an outrageous thought given everything she'd done, but what choice did she have? Quickly, she scrolled through her contacts, until she located 'Mum'. Her thumb hovered, hesitant, guilty, then taking the plunge, she hit Call.

Naomi's heart was thumping as she waited for the call to connect, then suddenly it was ringing. Immediately, Naomi felt her whole body tense up. What was she going to say? What *could* she say after the way she'd behaved? Then suddenly, the call was answered, her mum's familiar voice punching through, urgent and fearful.

'Naomi? Is that you, love?'

Naomi was frozen to the spot, unable to move, unable to speak.

'Naomi, are you there?'

And now it hit home – the guilt, the all-consuming guilt. Naomi had turned her back on this woman, humiliated her, *destroyed* her. What right did she have to call on her now?

Naomi hung up without a word. Her chest felt heavy, tears were pooling in her eyes, and she hurried on her way, determined not to appear distressed or vulnerable in this nasty place. She'd barely taken three steps, however, before her phone started to ring – her mum calling back. This time Naomi didn't hesitate, rejecting the call and turning off her phone. She had made her bed and now she had to lie in it.

Pulling her coat up round her ears, Naomi continued on her lonely journey through the park, as the heavens finally opened and the rain cascaded down.

Chapter 4

'Is he going to make it?'

DC Paul Jennings' question was terse and to the point as usual. Crossing the incident room, Detective Sergeant Charlie Brooks stuck a picture of Jason Matthews on the board, before turning to face the rest of the unit.

'Honestly, I've no idea,' she replied. 'He's in theatre now and the surgical team are saying it's touch and go. All we *do* know is that if DI Grace hadn't happened to be close by, the poor boy would be dead already.'

'Poor *dealer*,' Jennings corrected her.

'Whatever his profession, he's someone's son, someone's brother,' Charlie retorted, an edge to her voice now. 'Moreover, he's a resident of this city and as such it's our job to find who was behind this attack. This seventeen-year-old boy was the victim of a premeditated attack, one which may yet cost him his life. Which is why I want you lot to drop whatever else you're doing and focus on this. DC Wilson, is there anything specific that links this attack to other recent gang-related activity?'

'Nothing obvious,' DC Japhet Wilson replied, rising to his feet. 'Generally it's dealers who've been targeted recently, warning them off other people's territory. This is the first time a cash courier's been attacked, so it's possible it was an inside job.'

'Or it may be an escalation in the conflict,' Jennings countered. 'All the recent attacks have involved two gangs – the Main Street crew and the Cobras. So far it's been minor league stuff, but we know that Matthews runs with the Cobras, so maybe this is the Main Street mob upping the ante, cutting off the Cobra's cash supply at source, using those funds to up their street presence, buy weapons, drugs…'

'But the MO, the weapons are different,' Wilson insisted. 'The other attacks were chance occurrences and in both cases *knives* were used. This seems to be a well-organized ambush, using a firearm.'

'Like I said, an escalation,' Jennings concluded, as if Wilson had just proved his point.

'Any news on the gun?' Charlie intervened, attempting to keep the conversation on track.

Now it was DC Malik's turn to rise, much to Charlie's relief. She was the most level-headed of their junior officers and unlikely to be drawn into a cock fight.

'Forensics are on it,' Malik replied. 'But the shell casings suggest it was a modified Glock. Not cheap or easy to get hold of and a very reliable weapon. Uniform haven't found anything in the vicinity, so we have to assume the shooter is still in possession of it.'

'Which is why he have to track them down ASAP,' Charlie declared, rapping the board with her knuckles. 'This attack took place in the middle of Freemantle, a heavily residential area. Plenty of families living round there, lots of potential for collateral damage. And the culprits are still at large, potentially planning more attacks, so we need to pull out all the stops. If our victim survives, obviously he's our first port of call, but in the meantime, I want you to reach out to any contacts you have on the street, anyone who might have information about a targeted attack on the Cobras by rival gangs. If you have any leverage, any minor offence that you might overlook in exchange for information, use it. DC Wilson, I'd like you to run the rule over firearms offences in the last six months, anything that might link this modified Glock to a specific individual or supplier.'

'Sure thing.'

'DC McAndrew, I'd like you to take point on triangulation. Find out what phone the victim was carrying, see if you can trace his movements over the last couple of weeks. Any repetitive patterns, any significant locations, I want to know about them.'

'Straightaway,' the experienced officer replied promptly.

'The rest of you, I want us to target anyone and everyone connected with Jason Matthews.'

Charlie picked up her marker pen, drawing spider lines from Matthews' mugshot to different circles of interest.

'Known associates. Family and dependents. Girlfriends. Anyone he's served time with. Anyone he's sold to. We'll target his known addresses, bank accounts and probation records tomorrow, but tonight I want us to be speaking to his *people*, seeing what we can glean about his movements, his loyalties, any specific problems he's had recently. Let's do a deep dive please. Any questions?'

Charlie scanned the sea of faces, but saw only purpose and determination.

'Right, then let's get to it.'

The unit broke up, heading off to do Charlie's bidding. As they did so, Charlie stole a look at her watch, depressed to discover it was gone nine o'clock. She had worked late every night this week, way past her overtime allowance, and another late finish beckoned. Sighing, she turned to her desk, only to find DC Paul Jennings blocking her path.

'Everything all right, boss?' Jennings asked solicitously.

'Fine and dandy,' Charlie replied evenly. 'Another day in paradise...'

She made to leave, but Jennings stepped forward, cutting off her escape route. He was a powerful presence, muscular, handsome and imposing, but tonight he wore a gentle, sympathetic expression.

'Only I was thinking, if you want to head off, I'm sure the rest of us can handle things here. You've done four straight lates as it is.'

'Thank you for your concern, but I'm not sure the new station chief would appreciate me going AWOL whilst DI Grace is still at the hospital.'

'But we know what we're doing and it'll take us the best part of the night to dig up Matthews' associates. Why don't you take a break, go home, see those lovely kids of yours?'

The offer seemed sincere, but Charlie knew it was nothing of the sort. She'd seen this countless times before – apparently well-meaning male officers laying traps for her to walk into. If a female officer clocked off early for 'family reasons', she would forever be dismissed as a part-timer, lacking in commitment and resolve. It had always been an unwritten rule that women in the Force had to work twice as hard as their male counterparts just to be taken seriously. It made Charlie's blood boil – it was so retrograde, so unfair – but that was the way the system worked and she was powerless to change it.

'Thanks for the offer, DC Jennings, but I'm good. Do you have anyone *you* need to get back for?'

Charlie knew the answer, which is partly why she asked it. Taking the hint, Jennings retreated, sharing a whispered comment with colleagues as he did so. Annoyed, Charlie marched back to her desk. There was no reason on God's earth why she should still have to prove herself to junior colleagues like Jennings, after all her long years of service, but it seemed a female officer could never do enough to confirm that she was worthy of her place on the team. Which is why Charlie would miss her daughters' bedtime tonight.

Again.

Chapter 5

She clamped her eyes shut, praying that sleep would come. But her heart was thumping, her mind racing, and it was impossible to banish her fears.

Naomi had walked for over an hour in the driving rain, desperately searching for a dry, sheltered space where she could hide away from the world. But she had no clue where to go and whenever she *did* manage to find a safe, secluded spot, she soon discovered that some other desperate soul had claimed it. She'd encountered wide-eyed crackheads, an elderly woman who was convinced Naomi was her sister, even a pregnant teen who'd told Naomi in no uncertain terms to move on. As each minute passed, Naomi's spirits had plummeted further. Her jeans were saturated, her hoodie too, and her resolve was fast dissolving. Part of her was fearful she'd have to keep walking all night, risking hypothermia or worse, whilst another part of wondered if that might be the best plan. At least she'd be on the move. At least she'd be safe. But then suddenly she'd stumbled upon the underpass which, though filthy and unsettling, provided shelter from the driving rain, and that had decided it for her.

For a moment, she'd felt a sliver of relief, as she stepped out of the deluge and into the dry. But this feeling soon evaporated as she took in the dimly lit flyover, which was haunted by the desperate and dispossessed – slumbering homeless, muttering junkies and shivering sex workers, plying their trade without hope or emotion. Tentatively, Naomi had picked her way past a sea of hostile faces, which turned to take in the new arrival with a mixture of curiosity and distaste. Normally, Naomi would have hurried through this gloomy space, keen to be back in the open air, but tonight she took her time, desperately seeking sanctuary. At first, her search seemed doomed to failure, but eventually she found a berth that appeared to be unoccupied. It was an old service door, allowing access to the tunnel's electrical and lighting systems, the large danger sign fixed to it urging pedestrians to keep clear. But the wide doorstep was large enough for her to bed down in, so Naomi claimed the vacant spot, trying her best to make herself comfortable. Curling up on the cold concrete, she'd pulled her coat tight around her, tugging the hood hard round her face until it pinched her skin, then closed her eyes, seeking oblivion.

It was a fruitless endeavour. Not simply because of the dull ceiling lights that cast a sickly glow over the dirty interior, nor because of the overpowering smell of car fumes from the vehicles that shot by without a second glance, but because of the noise. The rain continued to hammer down outside, water pouring from a broken pipe at the entrance to the underpass, and above that could be heard the cat calls, screams and banter of this forsaken place's occupants. Gradually this tumult had abated, as the traffic eased off, the junkies passed out and the sex workers called it a night, but even so, the unfamiliar noises, sudden, sharp and unsettling, kept Naomi alert and on edge. She desperately needed sleep, she was wrung out physically and emotionally, but couldn't quell the fear that twisted her insides, or the cloying cold of her saturated clothes. Never in her wildest dreams had Naomi thought she would end up here, shivering, desperate and scared. But this was her reality now.

She willed herself to relax, to get some rest, if only to ward off the light-headedness that gripped her. But her mind kept projecting forwards. What would happen in the next hour? Before the night was out? Tomorrow? Would she have to resort to begging to survive? Hanging around the homeless hostel in the faint hope that one of their occupants would be kicked out? Something worse? Naomi was pondering this, her mind full of dark thoughts, when she heard a new noise.

Footsteps. Soft and measured, approaching her hiding place. Instantly, she tensed up. Was this unfamiliar noise the staggering progress of a crazed junkie or click clack of a sex worker? No, these footsteps seemed confident, purposeful. Unnerved, Naomi scrunched her body up, trying to disappear into her hidey-hole, but her attempt to blend into her surroundings failed, as the intruder came to a stop directly in front of her.

'Hello, love. Are you all right?'

Naomi reacted, startled, but there was nothing hostile or alarming about the man's voice. In fact, he sounded warm, gentle, concerned.

'This isn't any place for a young girl like yourself to be. What on earth are you doing here?'

In spite of herself, Naomi craned round to see who this well-meaning soul was. But instantly she recoiled, the powerful beam of his torch blinding her.

'There's no need to be alarmed, I'd like to help you. There's all sorts of weirdos and dropouts down here, you don't belong with them. So what do you say? Shall we find somewhere better for you to spend the night? There must be hostels or B&Bs that can take you or at the very least a soup kitchen where you can rest up for a bit.'

It was a seriously tempting thought. What wouldn't Naomi give now for a dry, safe space and a hot cup of soup? So despite her natural caution, she turned to the man once more, hoping that her luck might be about to change. She wanted to see his face, to read his intentions, but the glare of his torch was still blinding and she could only make out a dark shape behind. Even so, she found herself responding to him now, as he reached out a strong hand to her, saying in a kind, encouraging voice:

'Come on, love. Let's get you somewhere warm.'

Chapter 6

Sheila Watson's heart pounded as she yanked back the corrugated iron sheet. She didn't know this part of town, had never set foot in a squat before and would never usually have ventured out alone so late at night. But Naomi's silent call had got her seriously rattled, hence her desperate mission to Portswood. This was a part of the city that had been slowly gentrifying, but there were still a few pockets of the suburb that harked back to the era when it was a haven for dropouts, criminals and junkies. The graffiti-daubed building in front of her was one such relic, a lifeless, sinister place, which promised only bad things. But Sheila had come this far – there could be no turning back now.

The front door to the old terraced house had disappeared long ago, replaced by a sheet of corrugated iron with a 'No Entry' sign crudely spray-painted onto it. Ignoring this, Sheila tugged on the barrier, determined to get inside. As she did so, the metal scraped on the concrete, emitting a nasty screech that set Sheila's nerves jangling. She didn't know who, or what, lay inside, but she certainly didn't want to announce her presence. Still, the damage was already done, so with a final yank, she dragged the makeshift door open, revealing a dingy hallway beyond. Summoning her courage, Sheila stepped inside.

Immediately, her left foot gave way, plunging through a rotten floorboard. Shocked, Sheila gasped in pain, her ankle twisting sharply, even as splinters of wood drove into her flesh. Wincing, she extracted it gingerly, running her hand over her leg to inspect the damage. As she did so, she was shocked to see that her hand was shaking, fear and adrenaline pulsing through her. Perhaps she was more nervous, more frightened than she thought. Even so, she had to keep going, to see if she could find the one person on earth that she truly hated.

How Sheila rued the day that Naomi had ever set eyes on Darren Haines. Sheila understood the attraction, she'd been a teenager once, but had never imagined that her daughter would become so obsessed with him, that Naomi's infatuation would tear their family apart. But it had done so and quickly, Naomi leaving home after a particularly violent argument to come and live *here*, amidst the other dropouts and wasters, dossing down on an old mattress. God knows what went on in this place, what people got up to in order to fund their habits, but if Naomi *was* still here, Sheila intended to drag her home.

At first, Sheila had been furious with her daughter following her departure from the family home, then deeply worried, then eventually resigned to a long battle to win her back. But Naomi's call tonight had shattered Sheila's resolve, her patient determination replaced by visceral fear. She was sure it was Naomi on the other end of the phone, she could hear her breathing, could sense she was about to speak, but then the call had suddenly cut off. Why? What had happened to her? When Sheila had tried to ring back, her call went straight to voicemail. Instinct told Sheila that something terrible had happened, that Naomi was being attacked, perhaps even fighting for her life. Terrified, Sheila had thought about calling the police, but she had butted up against their disinterested intransigence many times before, so had headed here instead, Naomi's home from home for the last three months.

Limping forward, Sheila poked her head into the front room, making out a couple of sleeping figures stretched out on the floor.

'Naomi, love, is that you?'

The figures stirred, but didn't respond. Peering more closely at them, Sheila could see that they were both large, male forms. She also clocked the discarded needles and scrumpled sheets of tin foil on the floor, so quickly moved on. There was no one present in the other ground-floor rooms, so grasping the banister, Sheila mounted the stairs. Immediately, pain seared up her left leg, her ankle protesting, but gripping the gnarled wood, she pressed on, finding her way to the first floor. Now she paused. There were three shadowy rooms off the main landing, all with their doors slightly ajar. Which one should she try? And what would she find inside?

Steeling herself, she laid her hand on the handle of the nearest bedroom and slowly, cautiously, pressed down.

'What the fuck are you doing here?'

Startled, Sheila spun round to find Darren Haines advancing upon her.

'You're not welcome,' he continued, crossing the landing to tower over her. 'So get out.'

'Where is she?' Sheila demanded, ignoring this intimidation.

'I said GET OUT!' Haines bellowed, grabbing her arm and yanking her towards the stairs.

Instantly, Sheila jerked herself free of his grasp. She was no match for Darren physically, but she had more to lose. There was no way he was tossing her onto the street like a sack of potatoes.

'I'm not leaving here without Naomi, so wherever she is, you go and get her.'

But the imposing junkie just shook his head, annoyed by her determination.

'Naomi? Where are you, love? It's me...' Sheila called out, ignoring him.

To her surprise, Haines took a step backwards, folding his arms and breaking into a smile.

'Naomi, please, where *are* you?' she persisted.

Now he started to laugh, cold and callous.

'Shout and scream all you like. She's not here.'

What do you mean?' Sheila replied, suddenly alarmed.

'I mean she's gone, vanished, vamoosed.'

'But why? I don't understand.'

'We're not together anymore.'

'Since when?'

'This afternoon. She was getting annoying, so I had to let her go.'

He cracked a huge smile, two gold teeth glinting at Sheila.

'Where's she gone?'

'Search me,' he shrugged.

'You tell me where she is,' Sheila demanded, advancing on her burly adversary and gripping him by his collar. 'I'm not leaving here until—'

'How should I know?' Haines responded, cutting her off. 'But odds on, she's probably flat on her back with some other fool. You know what she's like.'

Shocked, outraged, Sheila lashed out, her hand catching the unsuspecting junkie in the face, rocking his head back. He stumbled for a moment, surprised, then righted himself, feeling his left cheek where a thin line of blood bloomed, her ring having ripped his skin.

'Don't you dare talk about my daughter like that, you piece of—'

Sheila didn't get to finish her sentence, a meaty hand coming from nowhere and connecting sharply with *her* cheek. Taken by surprise, the middle-aged mum staggered backwards, crashing into the crumbling wall. Winded, she tried to right herself, only to see Haines advancing towards her, a murderous rage in his eyes.

Now Sheila didn't hesitate, grabbing the banister and propelling herself down the rickety stairs. She half stumbled, half fell, her left ankle giving out as she landed heavily on the ground floor. Pain consumed her, but she swallowed down her agony and stumbled on, barrelling out the doorway and into the driving rain beyond.

Desperate, Sheila limped away as fast as she could, terrified that Haines would fall upon her, and it wasn't until she reached the end of the street that she dared to pause and look back. To her relief, Haines was nowhere to be seen, clearly having thought better of his pursuit. But as she stood there in the worsening deluge, battered, weary and scared, any sense of triumph swiftly evaporated. Yes, she had escaped a violent attack but she had failed to find her daughter. Her beloved Naomi was still out there somewhere, alone and adrift. What was happening to her? Why had she suddenly called home? Was she even still *alive*?

Distraught, bereft, Sheila bellowed out her daughter's name, once, twice, three times. But there was no response, her anguished cry swallowed up by the darkness.

Chapter 7

What the hell was happening to her?

Naomi stumbled forwards, led on remorselessly by her attacker, who was dragging her down an uneven set of concrete stairs. She could barely take in her predicament, she felt nauseous, unsteady on her feet, her vision oddly blurred. She remembered getting a lift with her guardian angel, the strange route they'd taken through the back streets of the city, but after that everything was a blur. They'd stopped outside an unprepossessing building, which didn't look anything like the hostel he'd promised her, then he'd asked her to get something out of the glove compartment. His ID? A key? She couldn't remember. All she could recall was the horrible rag that he'd clamped over her mouth and nose as she leant forward – that awful smell, the burning in her throat, then the darkness that engulfed her.

She must have passed out because the next thing she knew she was here, being manhandled down dusty stairs that seemed to rear up to greet her, tripping her, impeding her. Her companion was swearing and cursing, angrily yanking her back onto her feet, marching her down, down, down. Despite her stupor, her alarm was growing with every step and Naomi opened her mouth to speak. She wanted to tell him he'd made a mistake, that she didn't want to be here, that she wanted to go home.

But as she parted her lips, no sounds came out. Her tongue felt thick, her mouth numb, and she was struggling to breathe. What had he done to her?

Naomi held her hand to the wall to steady herself, but her attacker pulled it away, pushing open a battered door and dragging her into the room beyond. Again, Naomi stumbled, struggling to take in her surroundings. They were in some kind of basement storage area, which was empty save for some old building equipment and a couple of discarded coke cans. What was this place? And why had he brought her here?

Naomi looked up at him, hoping to see some kindness, some explanation, some semblance of reassurance in his expression, but ignoring her, her captor forced her down onto her knees.

'Stay,' he barked, turning away from her and hurrying to the back wall.

Naomi did as he commanded, unable to move. She wanted to be sick, to scream, to pass out, but instead she just knelt there, watching as he got to work. Now Naomi was *sure* she was hallucinating. Her abductor seemed to be taking things off the shelves that lined the back wall, then removing the shelves themselves. What was he doing? She blinked once, twice, shaking her head to dispel these confusing images, but now things got stranger still. Reaching down, her abductor tugged at something and – incredibly – the back wall seemed to open, a joint in the middle releasing to reveal a secret chamber beyond.

Naomi felt bile rise in her throat. She couldn't see what was in there, but she didn't want to know. Moving one knee forward she tried to rise, something telling her that she needed to leave this building fast, that if she allowed herself to be manhandled into that dark space, she might never come out again. But she was still seriously disoriented and she fell sideways as she tried to right herself. Now her attacker was upon her again, dragging her up by her arm and pulling her towards the sinister opening. Once more Naomi tried to scream, to cry out, but managed only a dull murmur. It was too late and he propelled her into the gloomy, claustrophobic space. There was no air, no light down here, just an overpowering smell of crumbling plaster and stale urine. Naomi tried to jerk back, to free herself from his clutches, but her attacker was too strong, too determined, and she now felt herself forced down onto the ground in the far right-hand corner. Her back hit something hard and cold, a pipe of some kind, but before she could register the pain, her abductor had taken hold of her ankle, clamping something round it, binding her to the wall. Reaching down, he tugged at it a couple of times to make sure her bonds were secure, then he rose.

'Please...' Naomi gasped, finally managing a word of protest.

But he took no heed, pausing only to shove her roughly back down onto the ground, before turning and exiting the tiny, fetid space. Seconds later, he sealed the doors behind him, plunging the room into total darkness.

Which is when Naomi realized that she wasn't alone.

Day Two

Chapter 8

Yanking back the throttle, Helen roared down Western Avenue. Cranking up her speed, she tore through the city centre, weaving in and out of the traffic, before changing direction sharply to swing off the main drag into the car park of Southampton Central Police Station.

Parking up, Helen tugged off her helmet, pausing briefly to look up at the towering glass and limestone building which had been her lodestar for over three decades now. This place had saved her, had *made* her, and she always got the same tingle of anticipation when she arrived each morning. Life as the leader of the Major Incident Team was not without its challenges, especially as she had a new boss to contend with – the highly regarded, highly demanding Chief Superintendent Rebecca Holmes – but Helen nevertheless always looked forward to each new day. Her role here, the heavy responsibility she carried in investigating Southampton's most serious crimes, was one she gladly assumed. Indeed, in her heart of hearts, she knew she'd be lost without it.

Marching across the cold tarmac, Helen buzzed herself into the custody area. She knew the team would be hard at work and she was eager to find out if they had any new leads. Crossing the lobby, Helen unzipped her biker jacket, keen to change as fast as possible and throw herself into the fray. As she passed the main desk, however, she became aware of a heated exchange between the custody sergeant and a middle-aged woman, who appeared tearful and agitated. For a second, Helen was tempted to ignore them and press on, but something in the woman's anguished tone made her hesitate. She sounded desperate.

'Why are you not listening to me?' the woman complained bitterly. 'My daughter could be lying in a ditch for all you know. You've got to do *something*.'

The custody sergeant opened his mouth to let her down, trotting out the same tired excuse he'd used a thousand times before, so Helen nipped in first, before further damage could be done.

'Can I help at all?' she asked, her tone emollient.

The woman turned, looking up at Helen with tired, red-rimmed eyes. She was a handsome woman, with strong, chiselled features, but she seemed ground down and fearful today.

'I'm Detective Inspector Helen Grace,' Helen added. 'I run the CID unit here.'

'Well, I don't know...' the woman replied uncertainly. 'I was just telling your colleague here—'

'Why don't you tell me?' Helen interrupted kindly, ushering her over to a seat.

'I'm not sure where to start,' the woman said, sitting down, suddenly sounding very tired.

'Well, first up, why don't you tell me your daughter's name?'

The woman, who looked pleased that someone was finally listening to her, replied, 'She's called Naomi Watson. I'm her mother, Sheila.'

'And she's missing, you say?'

'Has been since late last night,' the middle-aged mum confirmed, anxiety creeping into her voice. 'She's been living with her dropout boyfriend in Portswood for the last three months, but he dumped her last night. She ... she called me just after eight o'clock, probably because she was upset and scared, but then just hung up. I don't know if something's happened to her, or she just couldn't face talking to me ...'

'You're estranged?'

'No, not estranged,' Sheila countered quickly. 'But we *did* have a falling out. Her boyfriend – Darren Haines – was a waster, a parasite, a junkie. Thanks to him, she dropped out of school, started stealing from me, from friends, ended up living in a horrible squat ...'

She was becoming visibly upset, so Helen laid a comforting hand on her arm.

'Sorry, it's just been really hard these last few months,' the desolate mother responded.

'I understand. So, last night, you rang Naomi back?'

'Hundreds of times, but it keeps going straight to voicemail. I spent the night driving around looking for her, always doubling back to Hoglands Park, but there's no sign—'

'Why there? Specifically?'

'Because I could hear the skateboarders in the background when she called me last night. I thought maybe she'd find somewhere to bed down nearby, but there was no sign of her ...'

Her voice shook, distress overwhelming her.

'I'm just so worried about her. She thinks she's a grown-up, but really she has no experience of the world, no experience of living on the streets ...'

'And how old is she, Sheila?'

'She's fifteen.'

She managed to get these last words out, then crumbled, sobbing bitterly as she dropped her face to her hands. It was hard not to be moved by her plight; though Helen had no children of her own, she knew this was every parent's worst nightmare. Sheila's daughter had been seduced by an older boyfriend then discarded like a piece of rubbish, left to fend for herself in a dangerous and unforgiving city.

'Sheila, I understand how upset you are, I really do. But Naomi's only been missing for one night and I'm sure she's sensible enough to keep herself safe. That said, I will make it a top priority to see if we can locate her. Has she got any friends she might have gone to? Other family members?'

Sheila shook her head dolefully.

'It's always been just her and me.'

'And is she likely to be using anything, something that might impair her judgement, her ability to identify risk? Booze? Drugs? Medication?'

'I don't think so. Her boyfriend was a dope fiend, but she never touched the stuff, didn't like the way it made her feel.'

'That's good. And do you think she'd know to go to a hostel or shelter if she was really desperate?'

'I don't know,' Sheila replied, wiping away her tears. 'It's a whole new world for her. I've made sure she's always had a roof over her head, food to eat, clothes when we could afford them ... She's never been on her own before and I just don't know how she'll cope. I've ... I've spent the night imagining the most horrible things. I was soaked to the skin myself walking through that storm, God knows what it must have been like for *her* ...'

She stared at Helen, hollow-eyed and desperate.

'Sheila, I know you're scared, but I want you to do something for me.'

The tearful mum nodded, seemingly relieved that Helen was taking control of the situation.

'I want you to go home. Hopefully Naomi will pitch up there, or call you back, but it's important you're there in case she turns up. In the meantime, I'm going to action a city-wide search, alerting every uniformed officer to look out for her, in the hope that we can have her back with you before the day's out. How does that sound?'

'It sounds...amazing,' Sheila whispered, looking surprised and tearful. 'I don't want to cause a fuss, but I wasn't getting anywhere with him...'

Sheila gestured towards the custody sergeant.

'Which was wrong,' Helen replied sharply. 'Naomi deserves our undivided attention and I'm going to do everything I can to get her back to you safe and sound.'

'Thank you, thank you,' Sheila intoned, clasping Helen's hands in hers. 'I know you must have a million better things to do, but it means so much to know you care.'

Helen took in Sheila's earnest, entreating expression, more moved than she could say.

'I do care, because I know what it's like. There was a time, years ago now, when *I* was living on the streets,' Helen confessed quietly. 'I would have given anything to have somewhere safe and warm to go to back then. So, please leave it with me and try not to worry. You'll need to keep up your strength for when Naomi returns home.'

Sheila Watson stared at Helen for a moment, then threw her arms around her, enfolding her in a fierce hug. Surprised, Helen nevertheless returned the favour, avoiding the eye of the custody sergeant who was looking at her with a world-weary, critical expression. Maybe he was right to be circumspect, maybe Helen *had* overpromised, but she sensed Sheila needed this certainty, this reassurance today. She just prayed she'd be able to deliver for her, that nothing bad had happened to the missing teenager. Life on the streets was a dark, dangerous experience, where the weak and vulnerable were often exploited. Helen hoped Naomi was safe and well, that she was even now building up the courage to call her mum, but she knew the teenager's welfare, her future, was far from certain. Naomi was out there somewhere, alone and adrift, and Helen knew from experience what she'd be feeling – lonely, disoriented and very, very scared.

Chapter 9

She pressed her back against the cold brickwork, unsettled, disoriented, but alert. Naomi had spent a terrifying night in total darkness, replaying the shocking events of her abduction, whilst imagining horrors yet to come. The water pipes groaned, insects scuttled past, and close by an invisible figure coughed, moaned and cried out in her sleep. Naomi had completely lost track of time, her phone and watch having been taken from her, and the night seemed endless. The minutes crept by, with no release, no relief, but now finally a dull light started to creep into the room, a sliver of illumination hugging the base of the hinged doors, its glow serving to give Naomi a murky view of her surroundings. It was such a tiny thing, but Naomi felt overwhelmed by the sudden appearance of light, confirming for her that the sun *did* still rise and fall, that the real world *did* still exist, that she hadn't been transported to some kind of underworld hell.

Screwing up her eyes, Naomi strained to see through the gloom. She was in a cell of some kind, chained to the wall in a space that was claustrophobic, cold and damp. The tiny space was ten feet by ten feet, low-ceilinged and compact, with nothing in the way of decoration or furniture. A water pipe snaked down her corner of the room, but other than that it was empty. Her companion lay on the floor not five feet from her, her face turned from Naomi. She was blonde, tall and slim, her delicate frame visible even through her stained t-shirt, which hung on her, baggy and loose. Tired joggers and stained, threadbare socks completed her sorry outfit.

Energized by the modest improvement in visibility, Naomi cast around her. She was searching for some means of escape – a hole in the brickwork, a weak point in the ceiling – but finding nothing, she turned her attention to her bonds. The chain attached to her ankle was heavy and robust, fixed to a wall plate via a solid metal hoop, but Naomi yanked at it now with all her might, determined to rip it from its moorings.

'Come on, come on...' she gasped, straining every sinew. 'Move, you little...'

She heaved and tugged for all she was worth, bellowing out her exertion, but her endeavour proved fruitless, the chain refusing to budge. Cursing, Naomi dropped it and made for the hinged doors instead. Could *this* be her route out? She launched herself towards the fake wall, determined to get some kind of purchase on it. But her captor had done his homework, the short length of the chain meaning she could touch the sealed doors with her fingertips, but not impact upon them. Exhausted, frustrated, Naomi rested her hands on her knees, fighting the sense of panic that was threatening to overwhelm her. She was determined to remain strong, defiant, but there was no escaping the bitter reality. This was her world now: four walls, a chain, and a mysterious companion.

Right on cue, the girl opposite started to cough; deep, racking coughs that made Naomi wince. They sounded brutal, painful, bloody, as if each eruption robbed her of a little more of her strength. Naomi had never heard anything like it before and it shook her to the core.

'Hey, are you OK?' Naomi asked instinctively, her voice rich with concern.

The coughing continued, but the girl didn't move.

'Is there anything I can do? Do you have any water down here or...?'

Now the girl managed to get a hold of herself, the coughing subsiding gradually, but still she didn't respond.

'My name's Naomi by the way,' she continued brightly. 'And you've nothing to be afraid of, I don't mean you any harm. Perhaps it would help if you sat up for a while—'

'Don't speak.'

Her companion hissed the words, terse and urgent. For a moment Naomi was speechless, stunned by her aggressive tone.

'What do you mean?' Naomi responded, finally finding her voice. 'I was just asking if—'

'He won't like it,' the girl interrupted firmly, ending the conversation.

Naomi stared at the girl, poleaxed. What on earth had this man done to her to make her so scared? So determined to avoid all conversation? Before she could ask, however, she saw the teenager move, rising from the floor urgently and moving swiftly to the opposite corner of the room. For a moment, Naomi was perplexed, but then she heard footsteps approaching, heavy purposeful footsteps. Their captor had returned.

Naomi retreated to her corner, only just making it there before the doors swung open. The effect was devastating, brilliant light flooding the interior, blinding Naomi and causing her to cry out. She kept her eyes clamped shut, waiting for her vision to acclimatize, but when she opened them once more, she found her abductor ranged above her.

'Take off your clothes.'

'Get lost,' she hissed back.

'Take off your clothes and jewellery and put this on,' he continued, ignoring her protests as he tossed a dirty tracksuit at her feet.

Naomi's body was rigid, her senses on full alert, as her abductor reached down, pulling her to her feet.

'Get off me,' she spat out, struggling.

'Do as you're told.'

'Go to hell, you piece of shit.'

Without thinking, Naomi spat in his face. For a moment, her captor appeared taken aback by this open defiance, but Naomi's punishment wasn't long in coming, the back of his hand connecting sharply with her cheek, sending her crashing back into the dusty brickwork. Her legs threatened to give way, but her attacker pinned her to the wall, taking advantage of her temporary disorientation to remove her bracelet, her earrings, the necklace that spelt out her name. Now he was tugging at the eternity ring her mum had given to her last Christmas, but Naomi's finger was too swollen for him to retrieve it and, cursing viciously, he gave up. Instead, he focused on her clothes, pulling off her hoodie and t-shirt, yanking down her jeans. Naomi tried to fend him off once more, but a brutal punch to her stomach robbed her of further resistance. Winded, Naomi slumped to the floor, letting him remove her Doc Marten boots and, having unchained her, pull off her trousers.

'Now get dressed.'

Sweaty, breathless, he watched on sternly as Naomi angrily tugged on the tracksuit. It didn't fit properly, it wasn't clean, but at least it meant she wasn't cowering beneath him in her underwear. Satisfied, he bent down and snapped the chain back onto her ankle, before rising and exiting the room.

Naomi lay on the floor, her heart pounding. What was he

doing? Where was he taking her things? And what did he intend to do next? Once more, Naomi moved back to her corner, determined to resist any attack, any outrage, but to her surprise, when her captor returned, he was carrying two battered metal bowls.

'Eat,' he commanded, placing his offering on the floor in front of him, before turning to do the same with his other captive.

Greedily, Naomi snatched it up. Her stomach was howling with hunger, but as she peered down into the bowl her appetite evaporated. The contents were repulsive – cold, lumpy porridge rising into a stiff, solid peak – and worse still, the bowl wasn't clean, the remnants of past meals mixed in with the grim, grey gloop. Sickened, Naomi pushed the bowl away, but looking up at her abductor accusingly, she was surprised to see him towering over her, intent on watching her consume it. But there was no way she could, not even if her life depended upon it.

'I'm not eating this shit.'

She'd hardly finished the sentence before he was her in face once more.

'You'll eat it, you stupid bitch. I'll make sure you do.'

As he spoke, he picked up the metal bowl, thrusting it into Naomi's right hand. As he did so, he grabbed her other hand, his strong fingers sliding around her wrist, gripping it tightly. Then he twisted, wrenching her skin round with all his might. Naomi howled out in pain, shocked by this sudden attack.

'Let go of me. Let go of me, you—'

She gasped, her words cut off, as he twisted still harder. It was agony, her wrist on fire, but her attacker didn't relent, shoving his sweaty face into hers, as he rasped, 'Now let's try that again, shall we? Are you going to be a good girl, Naomi?'

He was so close that their noses were almost touching, his eyes boring into hers. The pain was intense, his determination to break her will crystal clear, but still Naomi resisted. She had been tricked, she had been abducted, she had been imprisoned, but she had not been beaten. There was no way she was going down without a fight.

Chapter 10

Charlie Brooks pushed into the incident room, keen to start the day on the front foot. She'd arrived home late last night, enduring a few broken hours' sleep before rising to greet her girls. Despite some recriminations about missing last night's bedtime, Orla and Jessica nevertheless raised her spirits with their ebullience and humour, so having dropped them off at school, Charlie had headed to Southampton Central full of purpose and resolve, determined to seize the day.

Marching to her desk, Charlie became aware that most of the team were already in. Punctuality and professionalism were things that Helen insisted upon and Charlie was pleased to see her officers gathered in anticipation of another busy day. Surveying the early morning scene, Charlie noted that most of the team were gathered around DC Paul Jennings' desk, laughing and bantering over coffee. Camaraderie was to be applauded, good morale a prerequisite for a healthy, productive unit, but eyeing the group of male officers, Charlie suddenly realized that no one had turned to greet her. In fact, none of them appeared to have noticed that a senior officer had entered the room.

Frowning, Charlie abandoned her desk, making her way over. As she approached, she immediately picked up Jennings' strident voice.

'I don't want to say it was a foregone conclusion, but Alpha Boy just couldn't handle the Big Dog. And he lost his shirt because of it...'

Jennings broke into a deep, indulgent laugh, several colleagues joining in. But their mirth quickly subsided as they spotted Charlie approaching, several swallowing their smiles as they turned to her, sober, respectful and professional.

'What have I missed?' Charlie said brightly.

Nobody spoke in response. DC Jennings suddenly looked discomfited, the rest of his posse awkward.

'Something's obviously tickled you?' Charlie continued, wondering why she was bothering.

'It's nothing really, boss...' Jennings finally offered. 'Just that... that I won a bit of cash in a poker game on Wednesday night with a few of the lads... with some colleagues.'

Charlie noted his last-minute correction, an attempt to make his night out sound less exclusive. Irked by this clumsy clawback, Charlie replied, 'That's funny. I didn't hear about it. Is this a regular game or...?'

Now the junior officer really *did* look awkward.

'Now and again, you know. It's not a formal thing, just something we do from time to time down at the police social club at St Mary's.'

'Can anyone join in?'

Jennings forced a smile that didn't reach his eyes.

'Of course. If you're interested, we could always make room at the table...?'

Jennings was straining every sinew to appear welcoming, but the way his colleagues were staring at their feet signalled that they felt his discomfort too. Charlie let his question hang in the air for a moment, before deciding to put him out of his misery.

'Actually, you're all right. I don't know the first thing about poker.'

Charlie saw it straight away. A flash of anger in his expression as Jennings realized she'd been riding him, followed swiftly by a look of relief.

'Right, then,' she continued brightly. 'Let's gather round the board and get this thing started.'

Running a hand through his hair, Jennings tried to shake off his discomfort, following the rest of the team to the centre of the room. Reaching the murder board, Charlie turned to the assembled officers, speaking up loudly as she commenced the morning briefing.

'Right then, let's pull together what we've got. The media have had a field day with last night's shooting and you can be sure the new station chief will want to see progress today. So, let's start with known associates. DC Wilson, could you kick us off?'

The junior officer duly obliged and one by one the team members added their findings to the pool of knowledge. Charlie listened intently, writing up the leads on the board and challenging them where necessary. All the while, however, her mind continued to turn on the dynamic of the group. Despite her fun at Jennings' expense, or perhaps because of it, she remained unsettled and disquieted. There was something 'off' about it, something she couldn't quite put her finger on, which made her feel uncomfortable in a unit, in an incident room, that she'd happily inhabited for years. This had been her home from home, the scene of some of her happiest times and most difficult days. Only Helen knew the fabric of this place, the rhythm of the Major Incident Team, better than her, and yet for all that, Charlie felt the odd one out here, neither accepted or wanted.

Sometimes she thought she must be imagining it, but today that same feeling struck home with force.

She had been here longer, way longer than any of the officers in front of her. So why did she so often feel like an outsider?

Chapter 11

Helen stood in front of her superior's desk, like a student summoned to the head teacher's office. It was a profoundly odd dynamic, her new boss Chief Superintendent Rebecca Holmes fully ten years younger than Helen and the very image of fast-track success. Despite her relative youth, Holmes had presence, intelligence and dynamism, not to mention good looks, a winning package that had seen her rise through the ranks at impressive speed. She was known to be efficient, purposeful and politically astute, skilled in ensuring blame always landed elsewhere. Her record was spotless, her conduct exemplary, perhaps because she had had very little front-line experience during her meteoric career. This had worried Helen when news of Holmes' appointment had been confirmed, as had their very different outlook and methodology. Helen sensed the contrast keenly now, feeling like a grizzled old gunslinger in front of the shiny new sheriff. Holmes was a desk jockey, albeit a successful one, whereas Helen had spent more time in A&E than she had shuffling papers. Time would tell if this might prove a winning combination, but right now Helen felt ill at ease in Holmes' pristine office, in which everything was perfectly ordered, everything in its rightful place.

Holmes, by contrast, appeared relaxed and calm, dispensing

with the formalities and cutting to the chase. This was their first proper interaction, barring the official hand-shaking a few weeks ago, and she seemed determined to hit the ground running.

'So what do we know about last night's shooting?'

'We believe it's part of an ongoing turf war for control of the supply of illegal drugs in the Freemantle area,' Helen replied briskly. 'That part of town has always been under the control of the Cobras, but a new unit, the Main Street crew, want to muscle in. They've recently beefed up their numbers and seem more than happy to mete out the necessary violence to make their point.'

'A bad business,' Holmes replied, nodding thoughtfully. 'Which we don't want to spiral out of control. Do we have any leads?'

'It's early days yet, ma'am, but I'm confident we'll make swift progress. Whilst we're chasing down leads, I'm planning to pull in some of the main faces, put some heat on them, make sure they know that we will not tolerate the public being put at risk in this way.'

'Exactly so. Last night's shooting could have been significantly worse. A firefight could have developed, which would have been catastrophic in such a densely residential area. We will need plenty of uniformed officers in and around the area today, to reassure locals that they're safe and that we remain in control throughout the city.'

'I've already requested a doubling of uniformed presence there, and suggested we deploy as many support officers as we can, to answer questions and reassure the community.'

'Good. We need to calm and reassure, but we also need some results. This is the third such incident in as many weeks, something the police and crime commissioner was at pains to remind this morning.'

'No one's taking it more seriously than me, I can assure you,' Helen replied evenly, masking her irritation at this mild reprimand.

'Even so, we need *arrests*, Helen,' Holmes continued, flashing a smile. 'In situations such as this, it's my experience that what one needs is *visible justice*. News footage of thugs being dragged away in cuffs deters the bad guys and reassures the locals, not to mention our paymasters, so let's move as quickly as we can on this one. Some public arrests, some lengthy interrogations and then some solid charges – that's what's needed.'

Helen resisted the temptation to reply 'be my guest', instead nodding her head firmly.

'Excellent, then we're in agreement. I want all available resources redirected to this case, every member of your team working night and day to bring this one to a close.'

Helen was tempted to agree and depart, but something made her pause. She didn't like being told what to do, nor did she make a habit of lying.

'I would like to reserve *some* capability to explore other urgent investigations.'

Holmes looked up from her desk, having already returned her attention to her paperwork, clearly assuming the meeting was over. Frowning, she replied, 'Such as?'

'Anything important that comes in. We've got a missing persons case that's just been flagged, which I feel needs attention.'

'What are the details?'

'A fifteen-year-old girl who's run away from home. Been dossing down with a twenty-two-year-old boyfriend, a junkie and minor dealer, but they split last night. She was known to be in the Hoglands Park area around 8 p.m., but hasn't been seen since. Her mum was in reception this morning, very distressed.'

'So she's been missing for a matter of hours?' Holmes queried, surprised.

'Overnight, yes. It's obviously freezing, wet, and with the situation on the street as it is, I think it's potentially a very dangerous situation.'

'Well obviously I respect your instincts, DI Grace, but I think we'd need more evidence of an imminent threat before we deploy CID resources to this. Let uniform handle it.'

'Normally I would, ma'am, but I spoke to the mother personally and I think it needs a speedy and concerted follow-up. This kid's got nowhere to go and her chances of finding a safe space to bed down in are remote.'

'Even so, I think we should wait longer before making a decision on this. We don't even know that a crime's been committed,' Holmes replied, growing irritated.

'With respect, I don't agree. In cases like this, the first few hours are crucial.'

'Be that as it may, we have to make *choices*, Helen. And you know the rules – a shooting, an attempted murder, trumps a missing persons case every day of the week.'

'Try telling that to her mother.'

Holmes took a moment to respond, visibly taken aback by Helen's tart response, her refusal to roll over. Rising, she looked directly at Helen, as she replied, 'Helen, I would hate our first proper conversation to end in an argument, so let me be plain. Given our scant resources, we are forced to prioritize. It's not ideal, but it's the world we live in, hence why we have grading systems, protocols. Protocols which I expect you to observe. So let's background the missing persons for now and focus *all* our energies, *all* our endeavours on making the streets of this great city safe again. OK?'

'Yes, ma'am.'

Even as she said it, Helen knew she had no intention of obeying her superior's directive. Helen had the front-line experience, the nose for danger, the gut instinct that had saved many lives over the years. If she felt something needed urgent attention, she would double down on it, whatever the consequences. It was reckless, foolish and potentially damaging, but she knew no other way.

She had never been very good at following orders.

Chapter 12

From her vantage point at her desk, Charlie cast an eye over the busy incident room. Despite her misgivings about her position within this team, her words had certainly had the desire effect on the assembled officers, who were busy bashing the phones and running multiple lines of enquiry. They seemed energized, excited even, by the prospect of a major investigation. DCs Wilson, Malik, McAndrew and Reid were working flat out, setting an example to the others, especially DC Jennings. He had only been with the team a matter of months, but already Charlie could tell he was going to be a problem. Looking at him now, he seemed the very image of entitlement, going to his task with a marked lack of urgency, forever offloading unwelcome tasks onto junior colleagues, so that he could focus on more glamorous assignments. In Charlie's book, that kind of power play, that form of laziness, was completely out of order and she was even now considering marching over to him to remind him of his responsibilities, when she suddenly saw Helen enter. After a quick scan of the room, her old comrade-in-arms made directly for her, her expression serious.

'Everything all right?' Charlie enquired, intrigued.

Helen gestured to Charlie to join her at the board, out of earshot of the team.

'Probably,' Helen replied ominously, keeping her voice low. 'Just had a bit of a discussion with our new boss about priorities.'

'Oh dear,' Charlie teased, smiling. 'Are you still friends or...?'

'As much as we'll ever be. Anyway, I need you to do something for me, but we might need to keep it on the low down, as I'm not sure the chief super would approve.'

'Sure. What's up?'

'We've got a missing persons enquiry that I want fast-tracked. Naomi Watson, fifteen years old, missing since last night. I've sketched out the basic details here.'

She handed Charlie a sheet of paper, who ran a quick eye over it.

'And you want this done ASAP?' Charlie queried, failing to disguise her surprise. 'As in pull some of us off what we're doing here to pursue this?'

'Absolutely. I don't like the sound of it, so I want us to do some digging on the street. Perhaps you could talk to the hostels – Tara Bridges at Lime Street would be a good starting point – and maybe send one other officer to Hoglands Park, to ask around. We're pretty sure that was Naomi's last known location.'

Still Charlie paused, uncertain whether to comply.

'Is there a problem?' Helen asked, frowning.

'No, no,' Charlie responded quickly. 'As long as you're *sure* that you want to prioritize this over—'

'Please don't make me have the same argument twice, Charlie,' Helen replied firmly. 'I want this checked out ASAP. If there's nothing in it, if Naomi turns up safe and well, then that's on me. But I want to know for sure that she's not in any danger. She's so young, so inexperienced, and her mum's going out of her mind with worry...'

This swung it for Charlie, as Helen knew it would. As the

mother of two daughters, Charlie couldn't resist this blatant tug on her heartstrings.

'No problem. What sort of resources do you want to throw at this?'

'Just you and one other. That'll do until we know more. So pick anyone, someone you think we can spare from the main investigation and let me know as soon as you find anything.'

Nodding gratefully at her, Helen headed off, marching purposefully away to her office. Surprised, Charlie nevertheless knew from experience that there was no point fighting Helen when she'd made up her mind, so she turned her thoughts to the task in hand, running her eye over the panorama of colleagues in front of her. As she did so, a thought formed in her mind, a very pleasing thought.

'DC Jennings?'

The junior officer was busy texting, but looked up sharply now, as if caught out.

'Could I have a word? I've got a little job for you.'

Chapter 13

She paced back and forth relentlessly, her heavy chain clanking noisily, beating out the rhythm of her fury. Despite her captor's determination that Naomi should eat his vile concoction, Naomi had held out, fighting so viciously that in the end, he'd given up, departing with the full bowl in a fit of rage. For a moment, Naomi had felt a brief, euphoric flush of triumph, but then the door had slammed shut and she was cast back into the darkness once more, her stomach aching with hunger.

Part of Naomi wanted to slump to the floor, to dissolve into tears, but she refused to give him that satisfaction, so instead she marched up and down, swearing, ranting, ruing the day that she'd ever accepted that bastard's 'charity'. She still couldn't quite believe that he'd betrayed her trust so outrageously. She had put her faith in him, thought he was a white knight coming to rescue her, but instead he'd kidnapped her, imprisoned her. How Naomi longed to have a weapon in her hand, something she could bring crashing down on his head, to end this awful nightmare and propel her to freedom.

But there was no such salvation at hand. For all her pride at her defiance, Naomi knew that she was reliant on her tormentor – for food, water, medicine, anything that might make her stay here less grim. She noticed that he'd emptied, then replaced, the bucket that was used as the toilet down here, one tiny nod towards their comfort. That would be the extent of his 'care', however, as this morning's altercation had proven. Any *actual* help, encouragement or solidarity would have to come from her hostile companion.

Casting another glance through the gloom in her direction, Naomi was taken aback to find the teenage girl looking directly at her. This sight came as quite a shock; even through the half-light, Naomi could see that this girl was pretty, with long blonde hair and piercing blue eyes, but that recent events had taken their toll. Her face was gaunt, her features and her eyes sunken. She was part beauty, part wraith.

The girl continued to stare, then reaching behind her, produced her own porridge bowl. Naomi was surprised, and intrigued, to find that it was still half full. Carefully, deliberately, the girl pushed it across the floor towards Naomi, signalling that she should take it.

From nowhere, Naomi suddenly felt choked with emotion. She didn't know this person, she owed Naomi nothing, and yet here she was, risking her own skin to help a stranger. Naomi felt tears prick her eyes at this simple act of humanity, of generosity, in the darkness.

'Thank you, thank you,' she whispered, snatching it up.

Naomi was starving. She had to eat and, even though the grim contents repelled her, her will to survive now took over. She scooped a mound of porridge into her mouth, half choking herself in her desire to fill her stomach. Ravenous, she managed one more mouthful, forcing it down despite her overwhelming desire to retch, before sliding the remnants back across the floor towards the teenager. Her benefactor didn't take the bowl, however, leaving it where it lay, as she whispered, 'My name's Mia by the way.'

Another sucker punch, Naomi undone by this friendly voice in the dark. As a tear crept down her cheek, Naomi realized how crushingly lonely she felt, how much she craved companionship at the very worst moment of her life.

'I'm Naomi…' she stuttered in reply. 'Naomi Watson.'

Mia nodded, managing a brief smile. Having been so terse and aggressive earlier, now the teenager seemed harmless and kind, clearly pleased to have some company.

'I'm sorry about earlier,' Mia replied quietly. 'But I knew he'd be coming and he wouldn't want us talking. He'd think we were plotting against him…'

Naomi took this in, unnerved.

'But you're right, we *should* stick together,' Mia continued firmly.

'I'd like that,' Naomi replied, her voice catching.

'Me too.'

Another brief smile from the pale teenager.

'Where are you from?' Naomi asked keeping her tone bright.

For a moment, a cloud seemed to pass over Mia's expression, but then she rallied, replying, 'Woolston. You?'

'Same,' Naomi replied quickly, breaking into a smile. 'I don't remember you from school. I was at Weston…'

'St Patrick's,' Mia wheezed in response. 'Maybe that's why we got off on the wrong foot.'

Naomi let out a brief laugh. The schools were bitter local rivals with frequent end-of-term fights. She had witnessed a few over the years, standing in the B&Q car park that lay between the two institutions. Was it possible she'd rubbed shoulders with Mia before now?

'Guess so,' Naomi agreed, smiling. 'You like it there?'

'Not really. Didn't bother turning up much beyond Year 7. Teachers hated me and I felt the same, so—'

Mia was about to say more, but now she broke into another coughing fit, rich, bloody and harsh, before eventually managing to master herself.

'I'm sorry, I'm sorry,' she gasped, drawing air greedily back into her lungs. 'It's so damp down here, my lungs can't take it.'

Mia sucked in more oxygen, hitting herself harshly on her chest, trying to dislodge the mucus that was strangling her from the inside.

'If I...' she continued angrily, breathlessly, 'if I could just get out of here, get a break from this place... It's been so long since I had any fresh air, any sunlight, anything that might help me get rid of this bloody infection...'

Naomi felt a surge of sympathy for Mia, but also a pulse of anxiety.

'What do you mean?' she asked cautiously, her voice shaking a little. 'How long have you been down here?'

And now time seemed to stand still, a desolate Mia taking an age before she eventually looked up at Naomi, replying bleakly, 'I can't remember.'

Chapter 14

'Her name's Naomi Watson and she's been missing since last night...'

The young volunteer looked at the photo of Naomi carefully, then shook her head.

'I don't recognize her, I'm afraid, but I wasn't on duty last night. You're best off asking the hostel manager, Tara. You'll find her doing the rounds in the accommodation block.'

The woman gestured towards the back of the building. Thanking her, Charlie carried on her way, walking down a narrow corridor, before pushing into the main body of the shelter. This was the council's flagship centre, opened four years ago as the solution to the city's homelessness problems. But the Covid pandemic and subsequent economic downturn had put paid to their best-laid plans and the Lime Street centre now appeared woefully inadequate to deal with an ever-worsening situation.

The accommodation block opened up in front of Charlie, fifty solitary beds that provided warmth, comfort and safety, but nothing in the way of privacy or dignity. Everything was communal here, your troubles included. This was now brought home to Charlie as a teenage mum-to-be brushed past her without seeming to clock the presence of another human being, her hollow eyes signifiers of addiction, perhaps, or some deep-seated psychiatric problem. Saddened, Charlie pressed on, locating the only member of staff in the vicinity and hurrying towards her. Tara Bridges, the centre's manager, turned towards Charlie as she approached.

'Can I help you?' she asked brightly, clocking that Charlie was here on official business.

Offering her warrant card for inspection, Charlie replied, 'We've got a general alert out for a fifteen-year-old girl, who was reported missing by her mother this morning.'

Charlie offered Tara the photo, who took it, studying the girl's features.

'Hasn't been seen since last night and obviously we're very worried about her. I was wondering if maybe she turned up here? Or at one of your other hostels?'

It was said more in hope than expectation, but Tara Bridges' brow now furrowed, as recognition slowly took hold.

'Yes, she was here last night,' she replied promptly.

'You're sure it was her?'

'A hundred per cent. The dyed blue hair is pretty hard to miss, plus she was wearing this same necklace, the one that spells out her name. She's obviously called Naomi, though I didn't get her surname . . .'

'Naomi Watson,' Charlie responded, excited. 'That's our girl.'

'Right . . .' the manager replied thoughtfully, her eyes glued to the photo.

'So she stayed the night, then?' Charlie's tone was bright, but Bridges' face swiftly clouded over.

'Unfortunately not. We were full, we could barely move in here for clients. I . . . I told her to try the other hostels, but she said she already had.'

'So you turned her away?' Charlie asked, realizing too late how accusatory she sounded.

'I didn't want to,' Bridges replied defensively. 'But I had no choice. If we exceed capacity here things can become volatile very quickly...'

'Of course, I totally understand,' Charlie said, backtracking. 'I know what you're up against. But just to be clear, the two of you spoke?'

'For a few minutes, yes. It was by the front entrance and we shared a few words, then she went on her way.'

'And how did she seem?'

'Well, she was upset of course. A little scared. But she wasn't high or drunk or anything like that and seemed like a sensible girl.'

'Was anyone with her?'

'No, she was all alone, which is why she was so agitated. She was really disappointed not to find a place here and the weather was closing in...'

Bridges sounded genuinely tortured by this thought, by this line of questioning, but Charlie had to persist now that she had a sliver of a lead.

'So you've no idea where she went?'

'I'm afraid not. I was just glad she decided not to hang around here.'

'What do you mean?'

And now Bridges paused once more, looking troubled and uncomfortable.

'It's well known that... that pimps and paedophiles congregate outside our hostel around closing time. We shut up shop around nine o'clock – no one's allowed in or out after that – and we always have to turn some people away, so...'

She didn't need to spell it out. With each passing second, Charlie felt more uneasy, more sickened by what she was hearing. Had the world really become so cruel, so predatory?

'And this happens every night?'

More or less. It's got so predictable that we even have nick-names for some of the worst offenders.'

'Jesus…'

'I know it sounds awful, but actually it's quite helpful. We can warn the young people we turn away to stay clear of specific characters. That, at least, we've got a handle on. It's not those losers that concern me…'

She looked Charlie straight in the eye, dropping her voice as she concluded:

'It's the ones we *don't* know about that worry me.'

Chapter 15

Helen Grace scanned the busy scene, eagerly seeking out her quarry. The canteen at Southampton Central was heaving and at first she struggled to spot her man amidst the sea of navy-blue uniforms, but eventually she made out the familiar face of PC Dave Reynolds, chatting animatedly with colleagues.

Pushing through the throng, Helen soon found herself next to his table. Almost immediately, the experienced officer broke off his conversation, rising to greet her, whilst gesturing to his junior colleague to do likewise.

'It's all right guys, no need for any formalities…'

But Reynolds remained standing, smiling as he turned to face her. He was a genial, popular officer with an engaging manner, always ready to crack a joke or share your woes.

'DI Grace, can I introduce you to my probationer, PC Beth Beamer. She joined us six weeks ago and is a very welcome addition to the ranks.'

Turning away from the experienced PC, Helen took in the shy-looking young woman, all eagerness and freckles, who nodded earnestly at her. It took Helen right back to when *she* first wore the uniform, remembering the sense of pride and purpose it afforded her. Part of her longed to be back then, when life was less demanding, but there was no time for reminiscing.

'Sorry to intrude on your break, PC Reynolds, but we've got an urgent search on for this vulnerable teenager.'

She handed him a copy of Naomi Watson's photo.

'We believe she was in the Hoglands Park area of the city last night, around the time you and PC Beamer were walking the beat. I was wondering if you caught sight of her at any point? She's quite distinctive with her dyed blue hair and pink DM boots...'

Reynolds scrutinized the photo intently.

'Sorry, no, I'd have remembered if we'd seen someone like that. I'm afraid it was just the usual round of tearaways and users last night,' he replied gravely. 'That said, myself and PC Beamer are due out again in ten minutes. So we'll make it a priority to have a poke around Hoglands and its surroundings. Is it all right if I keep this photo to circulate to the team?'

'Of course,' Helen replied gratefully. 'The more eyes we have on the streets the better. I've circulated a general alert, but a personal prompt from you could really make a difference.'

'Absolutely,' Reynolds reassured her, draining his coffee and nodding at Beamer urgently to do likewise. 'We'll get right on it. Odds on, we'll have her home safe and sound before the day's out.'

The whole table seemed to react, half a dozen officers rising to join the search. Thanking them warmly, Helen headed on her way, keen to get back to the incident room. She was grateful for the support and enthusiasm of the officers on the street, but in truth her interview with Reynolds and Beamer had only left her more worried. Beat officers such as Reynolds were the lifeblood of law and order in the city. They knew the faces on the street, the places to go and those to avoid, often picking up on issues and potential threats long before CID ever learned of them. They had their finger on the pulse, not only of criminal matters, but problems regarding teenage truancy, addiction, prostitution and more. If anyone would have spotted a lonely teenager wandering lost and scared through the city it would have been them, but they had obviously seen nothing.

It was as if Naomi had simply vanished into thin air.

Chapter 16

He walked alone through the underpass, cursing his fate. What had he done to deserve this?

Exiled to a run-down part of town, wasting time chasing a hapless teen runaway, who even now was probably shacked up with a friend, watching Netflix and smoking dope, utterly unaware of the fuss she was causing. DC Paul Jennings kicked out savagely at an empty coke can, sending it cannoning off the wall, before it landed next to a stray dog, who sniffed at it with mild interest before turning his attention to the police officer. Did he want a treat? A friendly pat on the head? Either way, he'd get neither. Jennings was *not* in a friendly mood.

Was this his fault? Had he irritated DS Brooks in some way? Is that why she'd picked him out to pursue this fruitless case? He didn't think he'd done anything wrong – offering to stay late in her stead last night, helping to organize the other DCs this morning – but there couldn't be any other explanation for it. This was a hospital pass, a lose-lose situation. Pulled off the shooting investigation, he'd been tasked with making progress in a case that was obviously hopeless. For reasons that were beyond him, DI Grace was clearly worried about this girl, hence the foolish deployment of manpower that was needed elsewhere. She would be expecting results, progress, but what chance was there of that?

There was no evidence that any crime had been committed, that this girl was on the streets and in danger, but even if she was, finding her would be like looking for a needle in a haystack. There were numerous parks, back alleys, industrial estates and abandoned warehouses where the dispossessed sought shelter. There was no way he could cover all those himself, yet that was his task, hence his bitter mood. All he had to look forward to was a day's hard walking with only the promise of an empty-handed return to Southampton Central. How the others must be laughing at him back at base, reveling in his demotion to duties fit only for uniform.

Seething, DC Jennings strode on. He had checked out Hoglands Park and the surrounding streets, finding no one there who'd even caught sight of Naomi Watson. Irked, he'd widened his search, stalking the roads that led away from Hoglands to the east of the city. Jennings knew that these dark lanes were a haven for dropouts, druggies and the homeless, and sure enough this grimy, rain-spattered underpass had more than its fair share. Jennings eyed them as he walked past, dismissing them as spaced out, dangerous or just plain odd. He'd never had much time for the dregs of society and hurried on quickly, scanning this way and that for any sign of the mythical Naomi, hoping that he would soon be shot of this place. Something about it sapped his spirit, made him uneasy, so he was keen to be away.

As he neared the mid-point of the tunnel, however, he paused. Scrunched up against the wall, her lower half hidden in a dirty sleeping bag, was a teenage girl. She was wearing a torn puffa and faded Southampton FC beanie, her arm lying casually on a bedraggled Border collie, which was clearly heavily pregnant. Jennings stared down at the mum-to-be with some-thing approaching sympathy; he often had more time for dogs than humans if he was honest, but as he moved his gaze on, he realized the teenager was looking directly at him. Surprised, he scrutinized her, clocking immediately that this wasn't the girl they were looking for, but of all the inhabitants of this forsaken place, she at least looked sane.

'Can I help you?' she asked, a hint of a challenge in her voice.

Jennings wasn't sure whether this was pushback or an invitation, so he responded quickly, flipping open his warrant card, keen to take charge of the conversation.

'You seen this girl?'

He offered her a photo of Naomi Watson.

'We think she's missing, might have passed through here.'

The girl took the photo from him, studying it as Jennings rocked back and forth on his heels, stealing a glance at his watch.

'Yeah, maybe.'

Jennings turned back to her, surprised by the runaway's response.

'Seriously?' he asked, surprised.

'It's hard to tell for sure,' she replied uncertainly. 'I think I saw her here last night, maybe around nine o'clock. I only clocked her from the side, so I can't be sure, but I remember noticing her hair ...'

'Where was she? What was she doing?'

Looking up, the pale teenager pointed to the opposite side of the underpass.

'She was dossing down over there, I think. There's a little doorway people sometimes claim if there's nowhere else good. Then again, she wasn't there when I woke up this morning, so maybe I imagined the whole thing ...'

Jennings stared at the empty doorway, annoyed, as his 'lead' slowly went up in smoke.

'No idea where she went? Which direction she headed off in?'

But the teenager was already shaking her head.

'Sorry, fella, best I can do...'

'Well, thanks for nothing,' Jennings muttered under his breath, turning and heading off without a word.

'Hey, don't I get anything? A bit of cash? A smoke? Play fair...'

But Jennings just raised his middle finger in the air and carried on, shaking his head at her cheek. Even if she had broken the case, he wouldn't have given her a penny. Marching on, he headed towards the far end of the underpass, keen to be back in the milky sunlight of this cold November morning. This place gave him the creeps, as did the pondlife that lurked in its shadows. Perhaps he could inspect a few more streets, then call it a day, suggesting that he'd covered most of this downtown area? Would he then be allowed back onto the shooting investigation to do some proper policework? He sincerely hoped so.

Emerging into the light, Jennings paused, pulling out a pack of Camel Lights and lighting one up in full of view of his underpass companion, who could be heard swearing at him. Smiling, Jennings took a long drag on his cigarette then, tipping his head back, blew out a column of smoke, watching it drift away into the opaque sky. But as he did so, he spotted something.

A traffic camera on the wall above him, staring directly down at him.

Chapter 17

'That's *her*. No question about it.'

Helen was pointing at the monitor, her voice tight with excitement. The screen was filled with a grab from the traffic cam, the timecode showing a young female entering the underpass last night.

'Obviously it's not perfect resolution, but you can still make out her hair colour and her bright Doc Marten boots. Do we all agree it's her?'

Helen turned to face the rest of her team, who were gathered round her in the incident room. Almost everyone present nodded in agreement, even Jennings, though his offering was more of a shrug. Helen hadn't held out much hope for his solo mission through Southampton's mean streets, but against the odds he'd come up with the goods.

'Good. So we're agreed that Naomi Watson entered this underpass just before 9 p.m. last night,' Helen continued crisply. 'But she clearly isn't there anymore and, as DC Jennings' enquiries have confirmed, she wasn't there when the other rough sleepers using the underpass woke up this morning. So she vanished at some point during the night. The most logical explanation is that she got cold, tired or thought better of her location, but…'

Helen fast-forwarded the footage. As the minutes, then hours ticked by, many cars and the occasional pedestrian exited the underpass, but there was no sign of Naomi leaving. Helen said nothing, letting the footage play out, pausing it only when DC Jennings stopped to look up at the camera.

'Fame at last,' DC Malik joked, staring at the frozen image.

'Is that an unauthorized fag break?' DC Reid overlapped, earning a friendly punch from Jennings.

'The point is,' Helen said, talking over them, 'that Naomi doesn't exit on foot from this side of the tunnel…'

'And we've checked the camera at the other end of the underpass,' Charlie piped up, lending her support to Helen. 'No sign of her leaving that way either.'

'Now the service hatches are locked, out of action, have been for years,' Helen continued, taking up the baton. 'Which means…'

'That she drove out,' DC Wilson offered, before correcting himself. 'Or was driven out.'

'Exactly,' Helen said meaningfully, letting this thought land before continuing. 'Clearly, scores of vehicles pass through this underpass every day, but the traffic is lighter during the night and we're only interested in vehicles that took longer than usual to exit the underpass. There's no roadworks there, no temporary lights, so if you're obeying the 30mph speed limit it should take you less than thirty seconds to pass through the tunnel. A small number of vehicles took considerably longer than that, however. DC McAndrew?'

The experienced officer now stepped forward. Crossing to the whiteboard, she began to scribble the details of several registration numbers on the board.

'There are five vehicles that spent two minutes or more in the underpass, before emerging from the tunnel. Three cars and two vans. Naomi could've been in any one of these, so we'll need to check them all out, but there is one that's of particular interest. A Renault Movano van, registration number OT16 VXL.'

Helen scrolled the traffic cam footage forward, freezing the image on the Renault van.

'Could be any number of reasons why these vehicles stopped for longer than necessary. Could be perfectly innocent, but might not be, given that dealers and sex workers frequent this underpass. As DC McAndrew says, we'll need to investigate each individual vehicle, check out the driver's story, but what interests me about this Renault Movano is that it shouldn't be on the road, in fact it shouldn't even *exist* anymore.'

Confused looks from some of the younger officers, so Helen pressed on.

'This van was seized as part of a drugs raid six months ago. It's working parts were shot, its chassis too corroded to think of selling it, so two months ago it was sent to the council pound for destruction. It should have been flat as a pancake and on its way to China weeks ago, but here it is, back on the roads...'

Now the team understood, their expression changing from confusion to excitement.

'I'm heading there right now to find out what happened. DS Brooks and DCs Jennings and Wilson will check out the other vehicles, whilst DC McAndrew holds the fort here.'

Helen clocked DC Jennings' look of exasperation, but carried on regardless. 'As of now, I am officially upgrading the Naomi Watson case from a missing persons to a potential abduction enquiry. I will action that now, deploying resources accordingly. I know we're spread thin, what with last night's shooting *and* Naomi's disappearance, so we'll have to be at our most dynamic and productive today, understood?'

She stared at them, expecting the team to jump to it, but they seemed uncertain, DCs Jennings and Reid looking particularly hesitant.

'*Now, please,*' Helen repeated more loudly, making several members of the team jump. 'We've two gunmen at large and a vulnerable girl whose life may be in imminent danger, so let's get to it...'

Thankfully, the unit now got the message, hurrying away to their desks. Shaking her head, Helen snatched up her jacket and marched to the door. Others might feel content to dawdle, but she was painfully aware of the danger Naomi was in, having faced similar dangers herself in days gone by. Had Naomi been abducted? Assaulted? Murdered? Helen had no idea, but she was determined to find the missing girl before it was too late.

Chapter 18

Naomi's eyes were glued to the cockroach as it scuttled across the floor. Mia's breakfast bowl lay on the floor between them and the pest clearly had designs on it. He wasn't the only insect in the place, but he was certainly the boldest. Reaching down, Naomi plucked the bowl off the floor, whisking it out of his reach. It was a tiny victory, but a victory nevertheless.

Looking down at the contents of the bowl, however, it was hard to tell exactly what her prize was. Their breakfast had been a foul mush to begin with, but the half-eaten remnants were even more unappetizing now – totally congealed and solid, with a tough crust forming on top. How anyone could eat this, insect or not, was beyond comprehension.

'You should finish it.'

Naomi looked up to find Mia staring directly at her. Her new friend was sitting with her back against the wall, her chin resting on her knees.

'You've got to keep your strength up,' she croaked.

'I'm not sure I can,' Naomi replied, staring at the unappetizing fare.

'You *have* to. You're strong, you're healthy, you can fight this thing. There must be people out looking for you, right? If you can hold on, maybe they'll find you, get you out of here...'

'Find *us*,' Naomi corrected her. 'We can both get out of here. We just have to be patient.'

Naomi was trying hard to sound upbeat, optimistic, but it made no impression on Mia.

'I'm not kidding myself,' she replied soberly, wheezing after another harsh bout of coughing. 'I'm too far gone. But you can survive, you *must* survive. I want someone to know what happened to me…'

The teenager's voice shook, prompting an instant response from Naomi.

'Don't say that, Mia. You're not going anywhere, you're going to be fine.'

'Do I *look* fine?'

Mia's resignation was crushing but, looking at her, Naomi couldn't deny she had a point. The teenager was skeletal and so pale that her gaunt features seemed to glow in the darkness. If there was a spark of life within her, it was hard to see.

'There you go then,' Mia concluded brusquely, wiping her nose with her sleeve, before coughing violently once more. 'I don't want your sympathy or your pity, Naomi. I just want to you to fight. To *survive*.'

Naomi said nothing at first, the concept that one of them might die down here too awful to comprehend. But what Mia had said made total sense.

'What's… what's wrong with you?' Naomi asked tentatively. 'I can see you're ill, but…'

Naomi knew the words were coming out wrong, that they were ham-fisted and clumsy, but she had to ask. Mia's coughing was so brutal, so violent, that Naomi had imagined all sorts of dire scenarios. Now she wanted to know what she was facing. What *they* were facing.

'Bronchitis,' Mia answered, gasping gently, trying to ward off another coughing fit. 'I've had it on and off for the last two years, but never as bad as this.'

'Jesus, I'm sorry.'

'It's not your fault, is it?' Mia countered ruefully. 'I've been on the streets for over two years, on smack for eighteen months. It's not a great combination, is it?'

Naomi offered a half-smile, but privately was shocked. She'd witnessed drug-taking many times, of course, but this girl seemed so young, so innocent, only sixteen years old at the most. It beggared belief that she'd been hooked on hard drugs for over a year.

'Isn't there anything you can do about it?' Naomi asked, increasingly desperate. 'Anything that could make you feel better?'

'Of course, but do you think he's interested?' Mia responded, her tone laced with anger. 'I've begged him for medicine, for decent food, for some bloody caffeine at the very least, but he's only interested in what *he* wants.'

Naomi was staring at her, horrified, so Mia now softened her tone.

'Look, I've tried to fight it, but I've nothing left. I've only got days, Naomi, so please, don't give up. I need you to live. I need to you to tell my dad, my mum that I love them, in spite of everything I've done, I *really* love them...'

Dropping her face to her hands, Mia began to cry, her chest heaving wildly in between harsh coughs and bitter tears. Angry, desperate, more saddened than she could say, Naomi looked down at the bowl's contents, then furiously spooned the sloppy muck into her mouth, forcing the remainder down, before tossing the metal bowl onto the floor with a clank. Immediately, the cockroach was on the move again, scuttling towards it.

This time Naomi didn't hesitate, balling up her fist and angrily crushing the pest.

Chapter 19

The folding metal shrieked in anguish as the two iron plates embraced each other, crushing the aged Ford Fiesta. It was an awesome sight, a solid, robust object that had once been someone's pride and joy flattened in a matter of seconds. But Helen was not here for sightseeing, she had a job to do.

'I'm simply asking how it could have happened,' she continued, returning her attention to her companion, as she marched past the flattened car. 'That Renault Movano was clearly scheduled for destruction *two months ago*, so what on earth is it doing on the roads?'

The site manager, a heavy-set, unshaven man in coveralls and a hi-vis jacket was struggling to keep up with Helen, his responses breathless and scared.

'Are you sure it's the same vehicle?' he enquired.

'Same reg plates, same colour, even the same alloys. So, yes, it's the same vehicle.'

'Well, I *can't* explain it. It doesn't make any sense.'

'Try again, Mr Chapman,' Helen replied dismissively, increasing her stride. 'I can shut this place down if I don't like the answers I get.'

'OK, OK,' he replied, wheezing, 'no need to fly off the handle.'

'Then talk.'

The site manager ground to a halt, utterly out of breath, holding up his hand for Helen to stop. Slowing, she turned to him, eyeballing him directly, giving him no room for manoeuvre.

'Look, from time to time, vehicles *do* go missing. They're on the schedule, then suddenly they're not. I should say this happens once in a blue moon and most of the lads here are extremely reliable, but I do get sent a lot of ex-offenders. I've been working with the probation service for a while now, it's a good source of cheap labour, and in general the boys I get want to make a go of it. But every now and again you get a bad apple and it's not possible for me to keep my eyes on them every second of every day. We're massively short-staffed, currently it's just me and the wife managing the place, so ...'

He looked at her entreatingly, perhaps soliciting pity, but Helen had none to give.

'So some site employees steal the vehicles, sell them on?'

'I'm guessing, but honestly it's incredibly rare, two or three times a year max. We try hard to run a tight ship here.'

'Not tight enough,' Helen replied coolly. 'All right, as you've been honest with me, I'm going to let you keep the site open for now.'

Relief flooded the man's face, but Helen was quick to qualify her generosity.

'But you are on probation for six months. Any more vehicles go walkies, I'll be straight round to the council and you can start planning your retirement, OK?'

He nodded dumbly, taken aback by her vehemence.

'Also, I want a full list of all your site employees, going back eighteen months. Names, addresses, telephone numbers, the works.'

'Sure ... but it'll take me a day or so to get that together, we've got a full schedule today.'

'I'll expect it via email within the next two hours,' Helen contradicted him, handing him her card. 'If I don't, I'll be straight back here. So I'd advise you to comply, Mr Chapman – this is me playing nice.'

Helen stared hard at the shrinking manager, then turned and walked away. John Chapman watched her go, open-mouthed. He had never met a woman – no, scratch that, he'd never met *anyone* quite like Detective Inspector Helen Grace.

Chapter 20

She was a curious figure – statuesque, powerful, clad in biking leathers. She didn't belong in this hole, amongst the discarded vehicles and discarded people. This was a dumping ground for society's refuse, a place where things came to rot and die, her surprising, energetic presence here providing a rare spark of life.

For all that, the woman's sudden appearance troubled Ryan Marwood deeply. It had been obvious from the start that she was police, despite her attire. Even if she hadn't flashed her warrant card at his terrified boss, you couldn't mistake her sense of purpose, her authority. She was a copper, probably a senior one. But why was she here? What was she after?

Ryan watched the departing officer mount her motorbike, then turned away from the window, crossing quickly to his locker. Tugging off his hi-vis jacket and tossing it inside, he pondered his next move, suddenly consumed with unease. He could ask Chapman straight out why she'd singled out this dump for special attention; the bumbling half-wit was too hapless to be able to hide anything. But could he do so without exciting his suspicion? This clearly wasn't an idle enquiry; the experienced officer had had an express purpose for visiting today and had discharged her duty urgently and effectively, the whole interview lasting less than ten minutes. Even now, Ryan could see a sweaty

Chapman pacing the portacabin office, hectoring his wife, who sat in front of her computer, looking stressed and scared. No, perhaps the best course of action was to sit tight, see what he could glean from the other lads over the next day or so, what titbits of information Chapman let slip. There was no point panicking, not yet at least.

Grabbing his rucksack, Ryan was about to head off when a voice rang out close by.

'In a hurry, mate?'

Startled, he froze, turning to discover a burly frame filling the doorway. To his relief, it was just Eze, smiling warmly at him.

'Shift's over, buddy,' he replied swiftly. 'No point hanging around...'

Slinging the rucksack over his shoulder, Ryan headed towards his co-worker.

'Same,' Eze replied, tugging on his jacket. 'Jack and me were going to have a couple at the Sailor's Boy, if you fancy it?'

For a moment, Ryan appeared to consider the invitation, then pulled a face.

'I'd love to, but guess what? I've got an AA meeting tonight...'

Eze laughed, long and loud.

'You still doing that shit?'

'No choice,' Ryan moaned theatrically. 'If I don't, I'm straight back inside.'

'Man, oh man...' his companion replied sympathetically, stepping aside to make way for him. 'Another time, then...'

'For sure.'

Clapping Eze on the shoulder, Ryan went on his way, confident that his lie had been swallowed. Even so, he made sure to cast a swift look over his shoulder as he left the site, content to see that his co-worker had disappeared from view. Breathing a sigh of relief, Ryan upped his speed, half walking, half jogging as he put some distance between himself and their prying eyes. Only when he was confident that he was no longer in sight did he suddenly dart to the left, finding a tear in the chain-link fence and pushing through it.

Now Ryan was in the scrub, still visible from the site if anyone happened to be on a high station, so he broke into a run, covering the ground quickly, before pushing into the dense woodland that flanked the site. Now the going became slower, the foliage thick and heavy, but he knew this path like the back of his hand, and within five minutes he'd emerged into a small copse on the other side of the wood. Here, half hidden by the dense bushes, was his prize. His beloved Renault Movano.

Normally, Ryan would have leapt straight in, roaring off, his anticipation high, his adrenaline pumping. But following this afternoon's site visit by the police, caution was required. Kneeling down by the registration plate, Ryan pulled a screwdriver from his backpack, deftly removing the screws. Then, tugging the new plates from his bag, he teased off the old ones and replaced them. Satisfied, he took in his work – OT16 VXL was now OP15 NMD – before moving swiftly round the vehicle to replace the rear plate. The whole enterprise had taken less than two minutes, but would save him years in prison. Rising, Ryan tossed the old plates into the bushes and hurried round to the cab. Maybe he was being paranoid, overcautious, but when the stakes were so high, there was no question of being careless.

Smiling to himself, Ryan Marwood fired up the engine and roared off into the night.

Chapter 21

'What a complete and utter waste of time that was...'

DC Paul Jennings marched across the incident room, angrily tossing his jacket onto his chair, turning to face his colleagues. A couple looked away, unwilling to get involved, but DC Reid turned to him, always a willing audience.

'The old boy I spoke to pulled over in the underpass to make a phone call. Big fucking deal!'

Exasperated, Jennings tossed his wallet and phone onto his desk, the latter landing with a heavy thunk.

'Took me half an hour to get there,' he continued, aggrieved. 'Best part of twenty minutes for him to shuffle to the front door and then another half-hour to get out of there, whilst he banged on about his dead wife, then the drive back. Two hours wasted. Two hours that could have been spent doing proper policework.'

'True enough,' DC Reid replied, nodding, as DC Edwards joined them.

'Same for me,' Edwards added. 'Guy I spoke to worked for the council. He was in the tunnel for ten minutes last night, checking the overflow drains. Showed me his itinerary, his inspection report, everything was totally kosher. Smashing bloke too.'

'Exactly. But because of Grace, you've wasted his time, your time, and for what? A wild goose chase for a kid who'll turn up in a day or two embarrassed and apologetic, wondering what all the fuss was about. All this whilst there's a gunman running around out there who wouldn't think twice before pulling the trigger on someone else. Honestly, the whole thing is a bloody farce…'

Jennings looked at Reid and Edwards, expecting both approval and confirmation, but suddenly his colleagues looked sheepish. And before he had even turned around, Jennings realized why.

'Is there a problem, DC Jennings?'

He turned to face DI Grace, who had slipped back into the interview room, without betraying any embarrassment or unease.

'The lads and I were just discussing operational priorities,' he replied coolly.

'And what was the collective conclusion?' Grace replied, eyeing up Reid and Edwards, both of whom avoided her gaze.

Jennings paused, considering his options. Should he back down, making weak excuses or go on the offensive? Irked, he opted for the latter.

'Well, we were just saying…' he replied, casting his eye around the incident room, 'that we feel that we should be out hunting *real* criminals, pursuing *real* cases, rather than prioritizing teen runaways.'

The room had suddenly gone quiet, his colleagues surprised by his boldness. But fortune favoured the brave, Jennings had always believed that, and he felt too strongly about it to back down now.

'A teenage girl not worthy of your interest, DC Jennings?'

'I didn't say that.'

'That's what it sounded like to me.'

'Look, as yet there's no evidence of any crime having been

committed,' Jennings insisted, but his intervention was short-lived, his superior talking over him.

'On the contrary, there is strong evidence that Naomi Watson has been abducted, probably by a stranger, and is potentially in grave danger.'

Jennings puffed out his cheeks, but Grace was not deterred.

'I can see why you might prefer to focus on the *male* victim of last night's shooting, why you might want to prioritize a case that's more high profile, more glamorous, but let me be very clear. In my opinion, there is a genuine and immediate threat to Naomi Watson's life and I expect *every* member of my team to pull out all the stops to find her. No exceptions, no free passes, everyone plays their part.'

She was glaring at him, but Jennings refused to break eye contact. Though she clearly held the whip hand in this confrontation because of her seniority, he wouldn't give her the satisfaction of backing down.

'To which end, I'd like you to go back over all local missing persons cases over the last six months to see if there were any other cases that might have a bearing on Naomi's disappearance.'

Jennings could hardly believe it. Having distracted him from his duties, was she now intent on humiliating him too?

'Similar circumstances, similar MO, similar victim profile, anything that might throw light on her abduction. Quick as you can, please.'

Having delivered this punishment, Grace pivoted, marching swiftly across the room to her office. Seething, Jennings turned to look at Reid and Edwards, who were shaking their heads, similarly confounded by Grace's priorities and leadership. This was some consolation, the sense that he was not alone in his frustration and disquiet, and Jennings was momentarily buoyed by this show of solidarity. Grace was his boss and obviously he had no choice but to comply with her orders, but for how long? The consensus amongst the team was growing, their sense of disillusionment plain as day.

Helen Grace was losing it.

Chapter 22

Charlie hurried through the lobby of Southampton Central, buzzing herself through the staff entrance and heading fast for the lift bank. As she approached, the doors slid open and she punched the button for the seventh floor, keen to be off. She'd had a frustrating afternoon.

As the doors closed and the lift began to rise, Charlie leaned against the wall, grateful for its support. She felt totally washed out, her mood not improved by her interview with Rachel Coombes, a young woman who'd briefly parked in the underpass last night to vomit, courtesy of her crippling morning sickness. Charlie had felt real sympathy for the young professional, remembering how stricken she'd been during her first pregnancy, but there was no point lingering to offer solidarity. The young mum-to-be clearly had no salient information to give Charlie – Coombes was above suspicion and hadn't seen anything untoward that night – so making her excuses, Charlie had headed on her way, irritated to have nothing to show for an afternoon's work.

The lift slowed to a halt and as the doors released, Charlie was swiftly on the move again, keen to make some kind of positive contribution before the day was done. She was eating up the yards towards the incident room, making her way fast down the corridor, but as she approached her destination, she clocked PC Beth Beamer hovering nearby. The probationer looked nervous, as if uncertain whether to breach the sanctuary of the station's CID. Having been there herself in years gone by, Charlie was quick to put her out of her misery.

'Can I help you, PC Beamer?'

Charlie smiled warmly at the young officer, but it was not reciprocated. Beamer looked pained.

'Is something wrong? Are you OK?'

'Yes, I'm fine,' Beamer replied unconvincingly. 'I just ... thought I ought to have a word with someone about the missing teenager.'

'Naomi Watson?'

Beamer nodded, but still looked stricken.

'Do you have any leads? A sighting perhaps or ...?'

'Sort of.'

'Well, spit it out then. Every second counts in a case like this.'

'Exactly,' the probationer responded with enthusiasm, suddenly finding her voice. 'That's why I thought I *had* to come to you.'

Now Charlie paused, intrigued by the young woman's passion, but also her evident discomfort. Drawing her aside, Charlie continued in a quieter voice, 'What's up, Beth?'

The PC darted a quick look down the corridor, then taking a step closer, replied, 'Well, it's just that I think ... I think PC Reynolds made a mistake when he was talking to DI Grace earlier. I think we *did* see Naomi Watson last night.'

'Right,' Charlie replied, wrong-footed. 'When you say you *think* you saw her ...?'

'Well, it wasn't me so much, as him. We were passing through the Lordship Road underpass, the one where it's thought she bedded down. I was talking to a guy I suspected was selling drugs – Brent Mason. Maybe you know him?'

'Oh, I know Brent,' Charlie replied archly. 'Been dealing since he could crawl.'

'That's him, he's a regular down there. Anyway, whilst I was questioning him,' Beamer continued urgently, 'PC Reynolds was checking up on a young girl who'd found herself a bit of shelter in a doorway halfway along the tunnel...'

'And was it her?' Charlie insisted, intrigued and confused in equal measure.

'Yes, I'm 95 per cent sure that it was. I didn't see her face clearly, but the description of what she was wearing certainly matched.'

Charlie said nothing, trying to process this curious development, before eventually replying, 'Have you spoken to PC Reynolds about this?'

'Not yet,' Beamer replied, dropping her gaze.

'And do you have any evidence to back up your suggestion, anything that might corroborate your version of events?'

To Charlie's surprise, Beamer was already nodding.

'Well, obviously when I confronted the dealer, I turned my bodycam on, in case I turned anything up or in case Mason became violent...'

'Standard procedure,' Charlie replied reassuringly.

'And, well, you can see for yourself from the footage...'

She offered her phone to Charlie, on which she'd lined up a video clip. Hitting play, Charlie watched with growing unease. She could see Brent Mason in the foreground, protesting as he was forced to turn out his pockets, but over his right shoulder, in the middle distance, Charlie could clearly see PC Reynolds crouched down on his haunches, talking to a young woman who was huddling in a little nook to the side of the dirty underpass. Scrutinizing the footage, Charlie placed her fingers on the screen, zooming in further. And now she paused, troubled and confused. The young woman's face wasn't visible, but the camera effortlessly picked up her striking blue hair, her ripped jeans and her bright pink Doc Marten boots. Looking up at PC Beamer, Charlie finally understood her discomfort. PC Dave Reynolds had clearly spoken with Naomi Watson last night, just hours before she went missing. The question now was why the experienced community officer hadn't offered up this information when asked about it directly by Helen.

Was it a mistake, a simple oversight? Or something more sinister?

Chapter 23

'So how was your day, son? Nose to the grindstone?'

PC Dave Reynolds leaned back in his chair, pushing his plate away and turning to Archie.

'Pretty much,' the sixteen-year-old replied, shrugging. 'It's basically just revision now.'

'So when's your first exam?'

'English lit, next week. *Macbeth, Jekyll and Hyde, An Inspector Calls.* There's loads to do ... but I think I'm getting through it.'

'You see, Jackie?' Reynolds replied, turning to his lithe, polished wife. 'What a conscientious boy we've raised. Like I always said, there's no substitute for hard work.'

Smiling, the thirty-two-year-old brunette squeezed her son's hand, her eyes sparkling.

'He's a good boy,' Jackie Reynolds agreed. 'We'll have to think what we're going to do after you've finished. You deserve a special treat, eh Archie?'

The teenager shrugged, blushing.

'Let's see how we go,' her husband replied cautiously. 'Plenty of bridges to cross first, eh? Now, have we got any pudding tonight or are we done?'

Jackie Reynolds' smile faltered momentarily, before she rose, picking up her plate and reaching over to take her husband's.

'Not tonight. I've literally been rushed off my feet all day. But there's ice cream in the freezer if you're still hungry ...'

Reynolds raised an eyebrow conspiratorially at his son, as he replied, 'Busy, busy, busy, eh? No, you're all right. I've got stuff to do anyway.'

He rose, taking a last swig of water.

'Any chance you could do the dishes first? I said I'd call Mum at nine and it's already ten past.'

'She can wait. What else has she got going on?'

'She gets worried if I'm late. And I'm sure Archie would give you a hand?'

'Of course,' the teenager said quickly, rising and picking up his own plate and glass.

'I've got to take the dog out,' Reynolds replied, more firmly. 'Poor thing's probably been stuck in here all day. Unless you've walked her?'

'Like I said, I haven't had the time.'

'She's a whippet, Jackie, she needs exercise. Come on, Willow ...'

Across the room, the dog's ears pricked up.

'I don't understand why you're being so pig-headed about this,' Jackie insisted, her voice shaking slightly. 'It'll only take you a few—'

Dave Reynolds snapped his fingers loudly, cutting off her protest and simultaneously summoning the dog.

'There, that's better, isn't it?' Reynolds said, bending down to stroke the dog affectionately. 'Enough talking, let's start walking, eh girl?'

As he spoke, he looked up at his wife. Jackie lowered her eyes, ducking his piercing gaze, keen to avoid further confrontation. Next to her, Archie hesitated, uncertain what to do, but now his father broke into a broad grin.

'Come on then. Let's give you a good run out.'

Crossing to the back door, Dave Reynolds picked up the lead and ushered the dog outside, shutting the door firmly behind him. Silence filled the room, a tense, pregnant silence, then breaking away, Jackie Reynolds crossed to the sink, roughly pulling on a pair of rubber gloves. Turning on the tap, she began scrubbing at the pots, but as she did so, her shoulders started to shake. From his vantage point at the table, Archie Reynolds watched his mother, his heart sinking further with each heave of her body, before picking up a tea towel and quietly crossing the room to join her.

Chapter 24

They lay in silence, each locked in their own torment. Mia's distress had gradually morphed into her worst coughing fit yet, during which she'd almost passed out due to lack of oxygen. In the end, the teenager just about managed to master herself and thereafter had lain flat on her back, her chest rising and falling erratically. She was in a bad way, struggling now to get sufficient air into her lungs, her breathless panting the soundtrack to their incarceration.

It was a sound that broke Naomi's heart. Her new friend was so young, so ill, and there was nothing Naomi could say or do to help. They were trapped in this hole without hope of salvation, slowly fading away in the inky darkness. Yes, Mia was in a much worse position than her, but who was to say that she wouldn't follow in time? Already the damp seemed to be settling on Naomi's hair, creeping into her airways. Was it this place, this dank cell that was the problem, as much as Mia's past experiences?

Naomi was so wrapped up in her thoughts that at first she didn't notice Mia move. Now, however, she became aware that her friend was rising to her feet, moving back to her corner. Instinctively, Naomi clambered upright too and now she heard it. A noise above. A door slamming. The sound of footsteps.

Naomi pressed herself against the brickwork, wishing she could disappear into it. She heard the sound of objects being tossed around outside, then suddenly the wall sprang open once more, light flooding in. Naomi turned away sharply, shielding herself from the onslaught and, when she turned back moments later, their captor was already stationed on the other side of the room, looming over the cowering Mia.

'Please, no...'

But Mia's abductor paid no heed, unchaining the teenager and grabbing her by the wrist.

'I'm begging you...'

Ignoring her pleas, their captor yanked Mia hard and she half fell, half stumbled towards the door. Naomi watched on aghast at her friend's terror, a fierce anger growing inside her.

'Leave her alone, you piece of shit.'

Advancing towards the pair, Naomi lashed out, kicking viciously at her attacker. She caught him square in the shin, pleased to hear him cry out in pain. A second later, she had reason to regret her rashness, the back of his hand connecting hard with her cheek, knocking her clean off her feet. She crashed to the cold floor, hitting her head sharply, yet somehow managed to bounce up onto her knees, scrabbling quickly to her feet.

'No way. You're *not* taking her.'

But Naomi was too late, too slow. They were already out of the cell and as she lunged toward them, the doors swung shut, plunging her back into darkness.

'Come back here, you...'

Naomi couldn't find the words, fear and desperation overwhelming her. What the hell was happening? What fate awaited Mia on the other side of the wall? Pacing back and forth, her anxiety rising with each passing second, Naomi became aware of a dull ache in her mouth and, pressing her fingers to her lips, was surprised to find blood trickling down her chin. Ferreting inside her mouth, she discovered that one of her teeth was missing and that her lip was swelling up. She touched her wound, then instantly recoiled, a searing pain shooting up to her brain and back again, making her feel lightheaded and bringing tears to her eyes.

She wiped them away roughly, determined not to be cowed. Moving back towards the hinged wall, Naomi advanced as far as she could before the chain bit, then rotating her ankle for maximum leverage, she raised her back foot off the ground and leaned forward, getting as close to the door joint as she could. Balancing precariously on one leg, she listened intently, praying that she might hear the pair returning. But there was no sound of movement at all outside and for a brief, terrifying moment, Naomi thought the pair had left the building. But then she heard it, the sound of Mia's shrill voice. Naomi couldn't make out the words, but she seemed to be pleading, before a loud slap silenced her. Once more, fury flared in Naomi. What made this piece of shit think he had the right to treat young girls like this?

Naomi strained to hear and this time she picked up sounds that struck fear into her soul. There were other voices, male voices, in the room just beyond. Where had *they* appeared from? Naomi hadn't heard anyone arrive. Were they already there when their captor threw the doors open? Part of Naomi wanted to retreat, to return to the sanctuary of her corner, but her feet seemed frozen to the floor. Outside, the voices were getting louder, as was Mia's, who'd started begging again. Agonized, Naomi held her breath, praying that their abductor would take pity on her, hoping against hope that Mia's heartfelt pleas would be heeded.

But they were not.

Chapter 25

'It's definitely her, isn't it?'

Helen looked up anxiously at Charlie, who nodded solemnly.

'Certainly matches the description. We know those pink boots were Naomi's pride and joy and the blue hair a recent act of rebellion. It would be a mighty coincidence if it *wasn't* her, right?'

Helen digested this, but said nothing. She and Charlie were closeted away in her private office, examining PC Beamer's bodycam footage. Helen hadn't liked what she'd seen on first viewing and she liked it even less now.

'I mean, Reynolds clearly *did* speak to her,' Helen eventually continued falteringly. 'And, yes, it could have been an oversight, but if so, it was a pretty massive one. I asked him directly if he'd seen her and he said no...'

Helen looked up at her deputy once more, as if seeking answers.

'And PC Beamer was there too?' Charlie replied. 'In the canteen, I mean...'

'Yes, she was standing right next to him.'

'And she didn't say anything?'

'No, but there could be any number of reasons for that, not least the fact that she is a lowly probationer and he is a very experienced officer who's well liked and respected by, well, by pretty much everyone in the building.'

Helen sighed heavily, deeply troubled by this strange development.

'Look,' she eventually continued, gathering herself. 'I'll talk to Reynolds first thing tomorrow, see if we can sort this out. In the meantime, I want the team to widen the perimeters of investigation.'

Helen clocked Charlie's look of surprise, but chose to ignore it.

'Surprisingly, DC Jennings has managed to pull something out the bag. I asked him to go back over recent miss pers cases to see if the circumstances of Naomi's disappearance chimed with any recent cases. And he came up with these...'

Helen crossed to her desk, pulling three photos from the file and laying them out.

'Laura White, Shanice Lloyd and Mia Davies.'

Charlie took in their innocent, happy faces, feeling a sudden pang of sadness.

'All female, all aged between fourteen and sixteen, and all living rough when they went missing.'

'Why do you think their disappearances are connected? Are they from the same part of town, same school, anything like that?' Charlie queried.

'Nothing specific. Naomi and Mia are from opposite ends of Woolston, but that's not what interests me,' Helen replied briskly, a hint of annoyance in her tone. 'They're all young teens, similar build, similar backgrounds, all of whom were living rough, all of whom have gone missing in the last year. It's possible that their disappearances *are* connected, that some guy, some predator, is driving around at night in his Movano van, spiriting them away.'

'Of course, it's *possible*,' Charlie responded evenly. 'And I know they're someone's daughter, someone's sister and they all need to be accounted for, but I'm not sure I see a clear link to Naomi yet.'

'Well, I do,' came the terse reply.

Charlie stared at Helen, surprised by her tone. Choosing her words carefully, she replied, 'Helen, do you not think you're perhaps letting yourself get carried away with this thing?'

'This "thing"?'

'You know what I mean. Just because you don't have much time for the Chief Super or for DC Jennings, it doesn't necessarily mean they're wrong. You don't have to escalate this just to make a point.'

'You think that's why I'm doing this?'

'I'm just saying that the team are unsettled. They're worried that we're spending too much time on the Naomi Watson case as it is.'

'And that's supposed to stop me, is it? Divert me from what I think is the right course of action?' Helen shot back. 'Charlie, it's my job, it's your job, to be a leader to those officers out there, *not* their friend.'

'Please don't patronize me, Helen.'

'I mean it,' her boss continued, undeterred. 'You can't be swayed by their feelings, their attitude, you have to do what you feel is best and hang the consequences.'

'But how on earth would we justify it to them? Or to Holmes for that matter? Deploying more resources? More manpower? On the basis of what *actual* evidence are we linking these other cases to Naomi?'

She gestured to the photos on Helen's desk, pleading with her to see sense, but her superior was having none of it.

'Say what you like, but I'm *sure* I'm onto something. And I intend to pursue it, with or without your help.'

Helen stared fiercely at her old friend, challenging her to push back. Gesturing at the photos, Charlie appeared about to do just that, when a sudden knock on the door interrupted her, forcing them both to turn in that direction. Seconds later, an awkward DC Japhet Wilson entered, clearly aware that he was disturbing a heated discussion.

'Sorry to interrupt, guv,' he said politely. 'But I've got something you ought to see.'

Smiling awkwardly at Charlie, he crossed the room, handing Helen a mug shot and rap sheet.

'I've been going through the list of employees at the car pound and this guy jumped out at me straightaway. Ryan Marwood. I didn't even know he'd been released, let alone that he'd be working at a place like that. There's minimal supervision there, despite what Chapman says. The ex-cons pretty much do what they like, so I was wondering if maybe *he'd* taken the van?'

Helen stared down at the sheet, stunned into silence. Ryan Marwood was infamous locally, a dangerous and persistent predator, with a beguiling, baby face. Preying on the trust of vulnerable women and girls, he'd posed as a St John Ambulance paramedic, dressing in the uniform, carrying the requisite ID, using the institution's good name in order to persuade his victims to accept his help, before violently sexually assaulting them. He'd targeted drunk teens on the streets late at night, drugged up young women at events and festivals, even homeless girls trying to find a bed for the night at one of the charity's drop-in centres. His crimes were sickening in their ingenuity, their cunning and their depravity, yet here he was, active in the community again, and nobody at the probation service had thought to tell them? It beggared belief.

'Well, you know what to do, DC Wilson. Find out where

he's living, alert the team and as soon as we're ready, let's bring him in.'

Nodding, DC Wilson hurried away. Turning to Charlie, Helen was pleased to see that all sense of hostility, of antagonism, had evaporated. She too had already forgotten their argument, her disquiet replaced by that familiar pulse of adrenaline.

Finally, they had a name.

Day Three

Chapter 26

Her face was pressed to the floor, her mouth open, trying to suck in oxygen. Naomi *craved* air to make her feel alive again – fresh, pure air – but the thin trickle that snuck apologetically into their cell was sickeningly insufficient, leaving her feeling helpless and suffocated. But her anguish, her suffering, was nothing compared to that of the poor girl lying next to her.

Mia hadn't said a word since her return. The doors had been flung open and the broken teenager tossed unceremoniously onto the floor by her attacker, before their captor snapped on her chain once more, departing as abruptly as he'd arrived. Naomi had been expecting tears and torment, readying herself to provide whatever solace she could, despite being hopelessly out of her depth. But her friend made no sound, save for the staccato hacking of her tortured cough, neither crying, nor moaning, just lying stock-still.

'Mia? Are you OK? Mia, please talk to me...'

Her heartfelt enquiries had elicited no response. It was as if the teenager was made of stone, petrified by her experiences. She didn't move, she didn't moan, she simply lay there motionless. As the minutes crept by, as the gloom seemed to deepen, Naomi's anguish grew. What had happened to her? And would she ever recover?

Stricken, scared, Naomi had reached out to Mia, her fingers seeking out the injured girl's hand. At first, Mia had flinched violently, making a startled Naomi jump, but then, realizing she was safe, Mia had grasped Naomi's outstretched hand, clinging to her as if her life depended on it. And so they had stayed all night, locked in shared misery, keeping each other warm, keeping each other sane.

Slowly the night had crept by, a dull light starting to penetrate their tiny cell. Maintaining her grip on Mia's hand, Naomi had instinctively slithered towards the light, like a flower opening up in the morning, desperate for some sustenance, some hope. This was the rhythm of her life now, insufficient but necessary, the sunlight reminding her that out there, life went on, that people were perhaps looking for her, that she might yet be rescued.

Closing her eyes, Naomi felt a cool breeze sweep over her, a sudden rush of air that was as refreshing as it was enlivening. For a moment, she afforded herself a smile, a moment's release, but then she realized what had caused this unexpected draft. The door to the basement had opened and their captor was approaching. Mia must have heard it too for she instantly relinquished her grip on Naomi's hand, hurrying back to her corner. Naomi did likewise, only just making it back to the cold comfort of her water pipe, before the wall parted and their abductor appeared.

For a moment, Naomi held her breath, but Mia's attacker barely looked at her, hurrying across the room to her companion. Grabbing her long ponytail, he held Mia's face up for inspection, checking for a spark of life in her eyes, before dropping her to the ground once more. Then, placing a bowl of porridge and a bottle of water on the floor, he turned to face Naomi. Instantly, she pressed her back to the wall, pulling her knees up to her chest. Her abductor watched on, amused rather than angered, then walked over to Naomi, placing her breakfast on the floor. Naomi didn't move a muscle, staring at him angrily, ready and willing to defend herself. Her fury, her tension, seemed to entertain him, however, for he now crouched down on his haunches, so that the pair of them were at eye level. Still she stared at him, her pupils wide, her heart pounding, which only seemed to encourage him further. Leaning forward, he gestured at the congealed porridge, whispering coarsely, 'Don't be shy. You need to keep your strength up...'

His eyes locked onto hers, as he concluded:

'It's your turn next.'

Chapter 27

A dozen pairs of eyes looked up at her, narrow and scared. The motley collection of waifs, strays and the terminally homeless had gathered together for security and stared at Charlie with suspicion and hostility, sensing that she was here on official business.

'It's all right, guys, I'm not here to cause you any grief, I just want to ask a few questions.'

But the mere sight of her warrant card made them shrink away. Charlie persisted, explaining the purpose of her visit and offering her hostile audience recent pictures of Mia Davies, Shanice Lloyd and Laura White, but she could tell they were in no mood to help. They had clearly suffered at the hands of the authorities before and didn't believe her story, convinced that as soon the girls were located, they would be dragged off in cuffs.

Relenting, Charlie headed on her way. At Helen's suggestion, she'd headed to the allotments on the south side of Portswood. The city's biggest homeless encampment was to be found here, dozens of unfortunates sleeping in the shadowy pathways that fringed the carefully tended plots. Charlie stalked them now, running an eye over the comatose users and shivering teens who turned away from her as she passed. Charlie was stunned by the sheer number of bodies and deeply saddened by their plight, at least a couple of the teenage girls displaying prominent baby bumps. Was it possible they would give birth out here? It was a fate too awful to contemplate, but tempted though she was to intervene, Charlie kept on walking. She was here to do a job and couldn't let her soft heart distract her.

Across town, the team were preparing to pull Ryan Marwood in, but Charlie had a different, though no less important role this morning. If there *was* a predator haunting the streets of Southampton, abducting girls at will, then surely they would find evidence of his crime spree here? Charlie still wasn't convinced that Helen was onto something, that such egregious crimes could have gone undetected, but walking these lonely walkways, Charlie couldn't deny that it was possible. The inhabitants of this forgotten part of town were so vulnerable, so isolated, that it would be easy for them to disappear. Who would report their disappearance? Who here would contact the police? Who would even know they'd gone? Trudging solemnly past the stained sleeping bags and discarded cider bottles, Charlie started to wonder if that was the whole point, their perpetrator deliberately targeting teenagers who would never be missed. It was a horrifying thought.

Turning the corner, Charlie kept close to the fence. She was approaching a more built-up area, tired-looking Edwardian houses coming into view, overlooking the allotment. Charlie's heart sank – there would be fewer homeless here because of the actions of the local residents, less chance of Charlie finding anyone to talk to. Disconsolate, she was on the point of giving up when she saw a pair of feet protruding from a gateway to the allotments. Summoning her resolve, Charlie bent her footsteps in that direction, soon finding herself in front of a gaunt teenager, whose tightly plaited pigtails sat in stark contrast to her pallid skin and hollow eyes.

'Hey there, how are you doing this morning?'

The young girl scowled at her, but there was fear, not anger, in her eyes.

'You've nothing to worry about,' Charlie continued. 'I'm not here to cause you any problems. I actually wanted to ask for your help.'

A moment's confusion, then the girl's face set once more.

'Well, you don't get something for nothing, do you? Got any fags?'

Charlie shook her head sadly; not being a smoker was often a bind in her line of work.

'Cash then?'

'I can't give you money,' Charlie responded gently, picking out the track marks on the girl's scrawny arms. 'But I've got chocolate, if you'd like some.'

She pulled a Twix from her bag, offering it to the young girl. Her companion hesitated, caught between disappointment and hunger, then snatched it from Charlie's grasp. The latter watched patiently, with sorrow, as the girl devoured the two chocolate fingers, forcing them down her throat as fast as she could.

'I'm looking for some girls,' Charlie said, pulling out her clutch of photos. 'Three girls who've been missing for some time now. Their parents are very worried about them and so are we.'

The young addict leaned forward, taking in the photos.

'This is Laura White.'

The girl studied the girl's pretty face, then shook her head.

'Shanice Lloyd.'

A short pause, then another "no".

'And this is Mia Davies.'

Instantly, Charlie saw it. A flash of recognition.

'Do you know her?'

The pale teenager stared hard at the photo, troubled.

'I can't stress enough that Mia's not in any trouble,' Charlie insisted earnestly. 'We just need to know if anyone's seen her, spoken to her recently...'

'I knew her a bit,' the girl finally conceded. 'In fact, this used to be her spot.'

Charlie felt a shiver of alarm, but kept her tone even as she asked, 'When?'

'Three months or so back, hard to say for sure. I used to see her around, we had the odd chat. Then one day she was gone.'

'You didn't see her leave?'

'No, one minute she was here, the next she wasn't. It was strange really, because she left most of her stuff here. This is her sleeping bag,' she continued, gesturing at the stained fabric. 'And I've got her belt too. Doesn't fit me, but I can still make use of it.'

Charlie didn't need to ask how, her eyes flitting to the tourniquet bruising on her arms.

'And you're absolutely *sure* it was her?' Charlie asked, holding the photo closer.

'Course, I'm not blind. Mia was here for over a year, before she took off...'

Charlie digested this, concerned.

'Has something happened to her?' the teenager asked, her voice shaking.

'That's what we're trying to find out,' Charlie said kindly. 'And you've been very helpful, thank you. I'd better go now, but... but you look after yourself, OK?'

Shrugging, the girl turned away, clearly not comfortable dwelling on what might lie in store. Saddened, Charlie moved away, her mind turning on this latest development, but she'd hardly taken a couple of steps, when another voice rang out.

'Well, well, well, an actual living, breathing police officer. Who'd have thought it?'

Surprise, Charlie pivoted to find a pensioner standing on the doorstep, staring at her with a pinched, cynical expression.

'I'm sorry?'

'I've been calling the local nick for *months* trying to get someone down here. Didn't expect CID if I'm honest, but I'll take what I can get. You've got some clout, correct?'

'Sorry, what's this regarding?' Charlie queried.

'What do you think it's about?' the pensioner retorted, visibly frustrated. 'This lot. The junkies, the pushers, the whores. Every night they're down here, plying their trade, leaving their ... their detritus everywhere.'

'I'm sorry to hear that.'

'So you should be. I've got grandkids who come round. Do you think I want them having to step over dirty needles, discarded johnnies?'

'I'm sure you don't,' Charlie replied evenly, taken aback by his vehemence. 'So this is a regular thing?'

'Are you deaf? I've told you it's like Piccadilly Circus down here most nights, people coming and going, parking up at the top of lane, blocking access to my property. They haven't even got any shame, bold as brass they are. At first, I used to go right up to them, tell 'em what I thought, but then one of them got a bit heavy, so I thought better of it. But I still let them know I'm here.'

'You watch them?'

'I don't have any choice, it's on my bloody doorstep. I warn them off as best I can, not that it does any bloody good. Which is why we need your lot to get involved.'

'I see,' Charlie replied, her mind, turning. 'Would you recognize any of these people? The men that come around here, I mean ...'

'Not really, it's always after dark, and it's hard to make out their faces. But I make sure to take a note of their vehicles. That's what I wanted to talk to you about.'

'You take down the registration details of the punters?' Charlie asked, suddenly interested.

'Yes,' the pensioner replied proudly, straightening up and standing tall. 'Every single one.'

Chapter 28

Helen had hardly pressed the bell, when the door was flung open. It was almost as if Sheila Watson had been expecting her, lying in wait in the hallway. The middle-aged mother looked like she hadn't slept a wink, drawn and pale, determined to stay awake in case of any developments, some positive news about her missing daughter. But Helen had none to give her today. Shepherding the desperate mum inside, she was quick to get to the point.

'I'm really sorry to have to tell you this, Sheila,' Helen said briskly, 'but our working theory is that Naomi has been abducted.'

Sheila stared at Helen blankly, fiddling feverishly with the buttons on her cardigan.

'We believe she spent the night of the ninth of November sheltering in an underpass a mile east of Hoglands Park...'

Sheila shuddered at the thought of her baby girl ending up in such a revolting place, but Helen knew there was worse to come.

'...and that at some point during that night she was picked up and driven off by a motorist passing through the tunnel. We don't yet know if she went willingly, if she knew whoever picked her up...'

'She wouldn't know anyone who could pick her up,' Sheila

responded, alarmed. 'Her dad's in the States, my sister's in Wales and none of her friends drive. She's fifteen, for pity's sake…'

'Exactly, so we have to assume she was driven out of the tunnel by a stranger.'

'Could they not have been *helping* her?' Sheila insisted. 'A good Samaritan? A charity worker of some kind?'

'Of course, that's perfectly possible,' Helen replied calmly, trying to reassure her. 'But I am concerned by the fact that Naomi's phone has not been switched on since last night. If she'd been taken to a hostel or place of sanctuary, I would have thought she would have charged it up, perhaps used it to contact you…'

'She practically lived on that thing, it was impossible to get her off it,' Shelia confirmed, visibly worried now.

'Maybe she lost it, or had it stolen from her in the underpass,' Helen continued. 'But we also have to face the possibility that it's been taken from her, deliberately discarded, that someone doesn't want us to know where she is…'

Immediately, Helen regretted her candor, tears filling the desperate mother's eyes.

'But who would do such a thing? Where would they have taken her?'

'We don't know,' Helen replied, leaning forward. 'But trust me, Sheila, we are working night and day to find out where she is, so we can bring her home safe.'

Sheila nodded, but said nothing, staring down at her hands, as she toyed desperately with an eternity ring that clung fast to her ring finger.

'This is my doing,' she breathed through tears.

'Absolutely not,' Helen chided.

'I drove her away, with my nagging, the endless arguments…'

'No, no, you were trying to help her, to ensure she made the right choices.'

'And what good did it do? Any of it? I'm her *mother*, it was my job to protect her...'

She stared up at Helen, tear-stained and fearful, as if the true horror of Naomi's predicament was only now hitting home.

'If anything happens to her, if she's hurt, then it'll be my fault...

'No.'

The word shot out faster than Helen had intended, but she was quick to soften her response, grasping Sheila's hands in hers.

'Listen to me, Sheila, you have absolutely nothing to reproach yourself for. None of this is your fault.'

The stricken mother shook her head vigorously, her guilt total, but Helen persisted. 'You have never been anything less than a committed, loving mother. You've made endless sacrifices to bring Naomi up right, to nurture her, to guide her, and you've done a great job.'

Another dismissive shake of the head.

'Trust me, I would have given anything to have *a tenth* of the love and affection you've showered on Naomi. You're an incredible mum and she's a very lucky girl. And when we've found her, when we bring her back to you, I'm sure she'll say as much herself.'

Helen knew she was going too far, but she couldn't help it. Sheila's fear, her distress was so overwhelming, her guilt so misplaced, that Helen felt she *had* to buoy her up, even at the risk of giving her false hope. Moreover, Helen actually meant what she said, ashamed to admit that she was actually a little jealous of the tender care Naomi had received. To her relief, Sheila now stemmed her tears, wiping them away, looking up at Helen entreatingly.

'Do you really mean that?'

'With all my heart.'

*

Taking her leave of the Watson home, Helen walked back to her bike, deep in thought. She was out of her comfort zone here, humbled by the vehemence of a mother's love. Her own childhood had been so barren, so traumatic, that Helen had never felt its full force before. But she felt it now and it rocked her to the core, leaving her deeply moved, but also profoundly shaken. Naomi was Sheila's whole world, her reason for living, the cornerstone of her heart, the focus of her hopes and dreams. In one way this was very affecting, but it also made the current situation even worse. If anything happened to Naomi, Sheila would never forgive herself. And neither would Helen. Marching back to her bike, wiping tears from her own eyes, Helen knew she had to find the missing teen – and *fast*.

Chapter 29

'I just want the truth, Ryan. Is that too much to ask?'

Lorraine Marwood stared at her son, tearful but resolute.

'Where you were last night? *And* the night before that?'

'I was here, in this house, in my room, wishing I was dead.'

'No, no,' Lorraine countered forcefully. 'I checked your bedroom on both nights and there was no sign of you.'

'I must have been in the loo or watching TV.'

'I checked every room in house, Ryan, *twice*.'

'Then I was probably in the garden, having a fag.'

'I checked there too. Just like I checked your windowsill this morning. And what did I find? Muddy footprints. You've been sneaking out, I bloody *know* you have.'

For a moment, Ryan was silenced, shocked by his mum's outburst. His mother never swore, even though she'd had plenty of cause to over the years.

'It's not what you think...' he conceded weakly.

'It's *exactly* what I think,' Lorraine fired back. 'It's exactly what I feared would happen.'

'No, no. You're getting yourself worked up over nothing—'

'I gave you a way back, Ryan,' his mother interrupted, devastated. 'In spite of all the damage you've done, all the misery you've inflicted on those poor girls. I gave you a roof over your head, food, money, *love*. And I asked one thing in return. That you did as your probation officer told you, obeyed your curfew and tried to be a decent human being.'

'Mum, please...'

'I've tried with you, Ryan. God knows I have. But none of it makes any difference, does it? Because you're sick in the head...'

'Don't say that, Mum.'

'...sick in the heart, sick in the soul. Sick, sick, sick.'

She vomited out the final words, staring at her son with sad, tired eyes. Ryan knew he had to offer her something, to try and talk her round. But what could he possibly say?

'Look, Mum, I'm sorry, OK? I know I haven't done as you – as *they* asked – but if you'll give me a chance to expl—'

'No!' Lorraine countered. 'I've given you more than enough chances already. I'm not interested in your "explanations", your lies. I've reached the end of my tether, son.'

And now she saw his expression change, fear infecting his guilt.

'What do you mean?' he demanded.

'I'm going to have to tell the authorities.'

'You can't! They'll throw me back inside.'

'I don't have a choice. I gave my word – so did you. But you broke your promise. I *have* to call your probation officer.'

Determined, Lorraine marched over to her handbag, tugging out her mobile. But as she raised it to her ear, Ryan was upon her, grabbing her wrist.

'Please, Mum. I'll do whatever you ask... just don't call them.'

Lorraine wrenched her arm free, stepping away from him, fearful but resolute.

'No, Ryan, you can't talk your way out of this one. I'm your mother, I *know* you.'

'Go on then, do it,' Ryan challenged her angrily. 'If you want to kill your only child, call them.'

And now Lorraine paused. In spite of everything, Ryan still had the power to affect her.

'If you want to send me back to that hellhole, if you want rid of me, then call that bitch, grass me up.'

Lorraine hesitated, her fingers hovering over the keypad.

'I just hope you'll be able to live with yourself.'

He was glaring at her now, fury writ large in his expression. But there was something else there that unnerved Lorraine – horror.

'Do you remember what they did to me when I was in prison?'

Lorraine dropped her gaze, upset, not wanting to remember.

'With the broom handles? The iron bars? The razor blades? Can you picture what I looked like when you visited me in that prison infirmary?'

Lorraine shook her head violently, pushing the thought away. It was an image of her child that still haunted her.

'That's what you'll be sending me back to. And they won't hold back this time. They'll finish the job. They'll finish *me*. So think, Mum. Think *hard*. Because my future, my life, is in your hands.'

Still Ryan held her wrist, beseeching her to show him mercy. But when Lorraine finally looked up at him, there was resigned determination in her expression.

'I'm sorry, Ryan, but you've left me with no choice. I couldn't live with myself if I didn't do the right thing.'

'Then I hope you burn in Hell,' Ryan exploded, spitting viciously at her before storming from the room.

For a moment, Lorraine stood motionless, devastated. Then angrily, she wiped the offending mucus from her face and marched over to the living room window, stabbing her mobile phone violently.

But as the call connected, she paused. Two smartly dressed men were walking up the garden path, their warrant cards already visible in their hands, stopping Lorraine in the tracks. What the hell were they doing here? Did they somehow know already?

Chapter 30

'So our top priority now is to find the Renault Movano, registration OT16 VXL.'

Charlie was addressing the team, who were crowded around her in the incident room.

'Thanks to the testimony of an eyewitness I spoke to this morning, we can now link this van to the sites of *two* possible abductions...'

As she spoke, Charlie clocked surprised reactions on several faces, but she pressed on:

'...at the Lordship Road underpass *and* at the Portswood allotments. We are therefore now formally adding Mia Davies as a possible victim, so I'll need someone to contact her family, see what we can find out about her movements, her family history?'

Eyes dropped, no one present relishing the idea of acting as a glorified family liaison officer. Predictably it was DC Malik, solid, reliable DC Malik, who finally stepped forward.

'Thank you, DC Malik, much appreciated. I shouldn't have to remind the rest of you that it's often the unglamorous tasks that hold the key to bringing an investigation such as this to a successful conclusion. I'm glad one of you seems to have heeded this lesson. DC Malik will take point on Mia Davies then...'

Charlie pinned a photo of the smiling blonde teen to the board, before turning her attention back to the team.

'As for the rest of you, I want you to focus on Ryan Marwood. He's currently on his way back to the station – DI Grace and I will question him shortly. In the meantime, we need chapter and verse on his recent movements, his known associates, his digital footprint. DC Reid, perhaps you can make contact with his mother, Lorraine? She was quite agitated when our officers showed up to bring Ryan in, so we might glean something from her if you can get her on side.'

'Sure thing,' DC Reid responded, looking less than thrilled.

'Let's also get down to the council pound. Talk to Marwood's co-workers, see if they've witnessed anything suspicious, if Marwood let slip anything that might be pertinent to our en-quiries and, DC Edwards, I want you to liaise with traffic and uniform. Odds on, it was Marwood who took that van from his workplace, using it to cruise the streets looking for vulnerable girls. Where did it go after it left the underpass that night? Has it been spotted anywhere since? Picked up any parking fines or speeding tickets? Let's have uniformed officers searching car parks, lock-ups, back streets near the Marwood home, ditto the woodland and industrial estates near where he works. Locate that van and I think we'll have Marwood bang to rights, prob-ably on forensic evidence alone.'

'Straightaway, boss.'

'That's the spirit. Same goes for the rest of you…'

Charlie hesitated now as she saw the main door open behind them. She'd been expecting Helen and was surprised, and disconcerted, to see that it was Chief Superintendent Rebecca Holmes. It was unusual for top brass to penetrate this private space, and it usually only meant one thing – trouble. Swallowing down her unease, however, Charlie pressed on, trying to sound confident and purposeful.

'This is an urgent, developing situation, so I need maximum energy and total focus. Lives hang in the balance, so no distractions, no excuses please, we need *results*.'

'Well said, DS Brooks,' Holmes said as she approached, smiling approvingly. 'A very rousing speech, which I'm sure this fine team of officers will respond to.'

Holmes ran an eye over them, as if daring any of them to dissent.

'So what's the latest?' the station chief continued, returning her gaze to Charlie. 'Are we making progress?'

'Yes, we have several important new leads,' Charlie responded briskly. 'We have a Renault Movano van which we think our prime suspect Ryan Marwood used to abduct Naomi Watson. We also believe we can link the same van to the possible abduction of another suspect—'

'I meant with the shooting in Freemantle?' Holmes interrupted curtly, her good humour evaporating.

'Yes, we're making progress on that too,' Charlie blustered, wrong-footed. 'But it's still early days and we're very much in the information gathering phase – talking to witnesses, chasing down the ballistics results...'

'And who's taking the lead on it?' Holmes persisted, unimpressed.

'Well, DI Grace, of course, but—'

'So where is she?'

'I'm not entirely sure,' Charlie responded uncertainly, her eye drifting to the open doorway. 'But I've no doubt she'll be back soon and then—'

'So in the meantime, you are the senior officer in charge?'

'That's right.'

'Yet you appear to have deployed pretty much the whole team to work a putative missing person's case. How many officers are currently working the Freemantle shooting, DS Brooks?'

Charlie hesitated, well aware that the whole team was watching her, intrigued, amused even, by the unfolding spectacle. Were they expecting her to backtrack? To throw Helen under a bus? If so, they were sorely mistaken, Charlie increasingly convinced that Helen's suspicions about an active predator might be right.

'Just... just a couple of officers at the moment. DI Grace felt that the unfolding Naomi Watson situation was more urgent and that a short, sharp burst of activity, deploying maximum resources, was necessary and most likely to result in a successful—'

'But I expressly told DI Grace to prioritize the shooting investigation.'

All sense of bonhomie was now long gone, Holmes' fury clear for all to see.

'Of course, ma'am, and we all understand the importance of that investigation. It's just that DI Grace, well both of us, think we're really onto something here, so—'

'I'll leave it to DI Grace to explain why she deliberately disobeyed a direct order,' Holmes continued, almost as if she hadn't heard Charlie's interjection. 'But let me make one thing plain. The Freemantle shooting is your, *our*, top priority and I expect resources and manpower to be deployed accordingly.'

There was little Charlie could do but nod, provoking a smirk from DC Jennings.

'I'm glad we understand each other. I expect to hear news of progress shortly.'

Another nod from Charlie, as Holmes pivoted and walked

away. But as she reached the door, she paused, turning back to fix Charlie with a stare.

'And you can tell DI Grace that I want to see her in my office as *soon* as she's back.'

With that, she departed, slamming the door loudly behind her.

Chapter 31

Grasping the door handle, Helen took a breath, then pushed inside.

Immediately, several surprised faces looked up. It was unusual for CID officers to frequent the men's locker rooms and rarer still for those officers to be female. Helen's unexpected arrival provoked much scrambling, as officers hauled up their trousers and pulled on shirts, partly to save themselves from embarrassment, but also to show due respect to a senior officer.

'As you were,' Helen said, suppressing a smile as she made her way past the startled constables. 'There's nothing here that I could possibly wish to see.'

There was laughter from the assembled officers, followed by a brief cry of 'too right', as the throng returned to their conversations, readying themselves for another challenging day. Pressing on, Helen made her way through the cloistered space towards the rear of the room, where she spotted PC Dave Reynolds getting changed into his uniform. Though relatively short for a police constable, the experienced officer nevertheless cut a lean, athletic figure, well toned after numerous charity runs in aid of less fortunate colleagues. He appeared totally unfazed by Helen's sudden appearance this morning, tugging on his shirt as he turned to his superior officer with a broad, friendly smile.

'Morning, ma'am. To what do I owe this unexpected pleasure?' he asked, buttoning up his shirt.

'I just wanted another quick word with you about our missing teen, Naomi Watson.'

'Of course. Happy to help. Though I'm afraid none of the guys on the beat have seen hide nor hair of her yet.'

'That's what I wanted to raise with you,' Helen continued, her tone serious now. 'I had a quick chat with your probationer yesterday ... and she seems pretty convinced that you *did* encounter Naomi Watson on the night she went missing. Would have been about 9 p.m., just before you clocked off? PC Beamer was patting down a dealer, but her bodycam shows you talking to a young homeless woman who matches Naomi's description.'

Slowly, a frown spread across Reynolds' face. But whether this was caused by anger at Beamer for telling tales or confusion at Helen's assertion was unclear.

'Right ... and this would have been Thursday night?' Reynolds said hesitantly, scrolling back to that day.

'That's correct. I've seen the footage and it appears you chatted to Naomi for a minute or two, presumably checking whether she was OK, whether there was anywhere she could go?'

'Well, I guess it's *possible*,' Reynolds conceded amiably. 'You know what the city is like at the moment and that part of town in particular. You're falling over the homeless down there.'

'But it doesn't ring any bells? You can't remember what you spoke to her about?'

Reynolds was already shaking his head gravely, looking annoyed with himself.

'To be honest, I'm struggling to place her at all. I'm not being funny, but you meet so many of these folk and they've all got the same tale of woe.'

'It's just that Naomi's quite striking,' Helen persisted. 'The colour of her hair, the way she dresses, I'd have thought she'd make an impression. And it *was* only two days ago...'

'Honestly, ma'am, I wish I could help, especially if you think the poor girl's in danger,' Reynolds replied, crestfallen. 'And if I've made a mistake, I'll hold my hands up to that. But to be truthful, all these faces blur into one another after a while.'

'Unlike you though, Dave,' Helen countered. 'You're known as having the sharpest eyes and ears on the street. A guy who really knows his patch, who's adept at spotting new faces amongst the throng. I would have thought your chat with Naomi would have registered a little more?'

And now Reynolds' expression changed slightly, something in Helen's dogged persistence, her keen, accusatory tone, clearly irking him.

'Well, look, if anything comes to me, then obviously I'll let you know straightaway,' he responded, retrieving his jacket from his locker and slipping it on. 'In the meantime, the best thing I – and all the lads here – can do is get out on the street, see if we can track Naomi down, get her home safe.'

'Sure thing, don't let me stand in your way,' Helen replied cheerfully, making no attempt to get out of his way.

For a moment, Reynolds looked surprised, even confounded, as if some silent challenge had been thrown down. Then, turning away from her, he pushed his locker door shut. As he did so, however, Helen clocked something. A raised, red mark on his right hand that looked very much like a bite.

'Done yourself a mischief, PC Reynolds?'

Surprised, Reynolds followed her gaze to his injury.

'Looks nasty. Fresh, is it?' Helen persisted.

A moment's hesitation, then Reynolds scowled.

'Bloody dog bite. Some idiot let their boxer have a go at my

Willow. I had to pull the wretched thing off, got a nasty bite for my pains.'

'I'm sorry to hear that. I trust you reported the owner and the dog to front desk when you got in this morning?'

'What would be the point?' Reynolds replied quickly. 'Didn't get the guy's name and we'd hardly have the resources to follow it up, would we?'

'Even so,' Helen replied evenly. 'We can't expect the public to do the right thing if we don't lead by example, can we?'

'Spot on,' Reynolds replied, conceding the point with a little bow. 'I'll be sure to make a report on my way out this morning. Now will that be all or ...?'

Smiling, Helen stepped aside, letting the PC pass. But as he walked away, Helen's smile faded. The experienced police constable had been polite, deferential and seemingly surprised by her accusations, yet somehow his responses hadn't rung true, a tension, a hostility seeming to lurk beneath his bland responses. Helen had come here this morning hoping to be proved wrong, to quell that nagging feeling in her gut, yet she had achieved the exact opposite. Try as she might, Helen couldn't shake the feeling that there was something *off* about PC Dave Reynolds.

Chapter 32

'Help! Please, someone, help us...'

Naomi's cries bounced off the wall, mocking her, but she persisted nevertheless. Going out of her mind with worry, terrified by her captor's threats, she had to *try*.

'We're trapped down here. If you can hear us, please, we need your help...'

Naomi was shattered after fifteen minutes of solid screaming, sweat trickling down her dirty face, her throat parched and sore. But she knew she couldn't relent. She couldn't stay down here, waiting for that loathsome creep to return. She *had* to get away.

'My name's Naomi Watson. I've... I've been abducted, we're being held down here against our will...'

The words stuck in her throat, so alien, so sickening.

'We're desperate, please help us!'

Finally she ran out of steam, exhausted. For a moment, the gloomy space was filled with an awful, desperate silence, then suddenly she heard Mia croak:

'You mustn't give up.'

In normal circumstances, this pained wheeze would hardly have been audible, but in this close space it filled the room, startling Naomi out of her lethargy. It was clearly painful for Mia to speak, but she seemed determined to try, continuing:

'You can survive this, you can beat this piece of shit...'

Mia petered out, the effort of talking clearly too much for her. Desperately concerned, Naomi hurried across the room, kneeling down next to her.

'Are you OK, Mia? Is there anything I can do for you?' Naomi asked urgently.

Mia stared at her, but said nothing.

'Please...' Naomi continued, feeling suddenly panicky. 'Whatever I can do to help, I'll do it. Are you cold? You look like you're shivering. You can have my jumper if you like...'

She was already tugging it off, determined to help, but a slight shake of the head from Mia stopped her in her tracks.

'There's nothing you can do,' her friend whispered weakly. 'Only *he* has the power to stop this. He's in charge here.'

Naomi stared at her friend, wishing with all her heart that she could breathe strength, breathe life into her, but she knew it was hopeless. The damage done to this innocent girl was far beyond anything she could repair.

'What... what did he do to you out there?'

The words tumbled from Naomi unsolicited, fear and anxiety forcing them out. For a moment, Mia didn't respond, her deadened gaze holding Naomi's, before she dropped her eyes, shivering violently.

'Do you *really* want to know?'

What could Naomi say to that? Part of her *had* to know. But another part wanted to bury her head in the sand and pretend that none of this was actually happening.

'Not if you don't want to tell me,' Naomi replied quickly, painfully aware of how difficult this must be for her.

'It's better you know.'

She didn't need to explain why, Naomi clamping her eyes shut in horror as the fear of future tortures consumed her.

134

'First...' Mia began hesitantly, her voice shaking. 'First, he makes me take my clothes off. In front of all of them...'

'There are other men there? In the room with you?'

A brief shake of the head.

'No, they're on his computer, a Zoom call or something, there must be a dozen of them...'

Naomi stared at Mia, aghast.

'Some have their cameras off, so you can't see who they are. But others have theirs on, so you can see their fat, sweaty faces...'

Anger flared in Mia's voice now, a righteous, bitter anger.

'Those ones are the worst, they're the ones who really enjoy themselves. Telling that creep what to do, how to do it...'

'Oh Mia, I'm so sorry,' Naomi gasped, breathless, sickened.

'There's this bald Scottish guy. He's the one in charge. He's the worst. His... his voice is so cold, it goes right through me...'

Naomi was crying now, unable to process this horror, unable to offer even a token of comfort or solace.

'And there's this greasy, fat red-headed guy. I call him the Ginger Pig. He's disgusting...'

It was beyond awful. Not just what Mia had had to endure, but that she actually had nicknames for her abusers.

'They never speak to me. Just him. Telling him what to do, like he's their puppet...'

Instinctively Mia was curling herself up into a ball, as if to protect herself from further harm. But the damage had clearly already been done.

'Oh, Mia, I'm so sorry. I can't imagine what you've been through...'

'I've never fought him, never resisted,' Mia cried bitterly. 'I thought... I thought if I did what he said, then maybe he'd get bored or take pity on me, let me go. But there's no pity in him, none. He'll never stop...'

Naomi held her tight, wanting to find the right words to comfort her. But what on earth could she say?

'Which is why you must stay strong, Naomi, why you must fight him. You can survive this, but it's too late for me...'

She paused, gulping down a heartfelt sob, as she concluded: '...I'm never getting out of here.'

Chapter 33

She closed the door firmly, then turned to face her colleague. DC Japhet Wilson was trying his best to look intrigued and eager, but he couldn't entirely conceal his anxiety at having been summoned to a private interview in Helen's private office.

'Sorry for the cloak and dagger,' Helen said, dropping the blind. 'But this is delicate, so discretion is required.'

Wilson nodded mutely, clearly fearing that he was about to reprimanded.

'Don't worry, it's nothing *you've* done,' Helen continued quickly, to his evident relief. 'It's to do with the Naomi Watson case. I need you to do some digging for me, background stuff, about a member of our own force.'

'Right...' Wilson responded cautiously.

'PC Dave Reynolds. Do you know him?'

'Not personally, but I obviously know who he is. He's the one who does all those charity runs, right? The guy who's always in the papers?' Wilson continued, barely able to conceal his discomfort at this new, surprising line of enquiry.

'That's right, everyone's favourite copper.'

Wilson looked puzzled by Helen's sarcastic tone, so she carried on:

'Couple of years back he managed to foil an armed robbery

in which a colleague of his was seriously injured, a colleague who later had to retire from service. Reynolds has been raising money for the Police Benevolent Fund ever since and, hats off to him, he's raised a lot of cash for former officers, but he doesn't half let you know about it. He's got his own YouTube channel promoting his charity work, a dedicated JustGiving page, you name it. Most of the CID officers round here used to call him Saint Dave, though never to his face of course.'

Wilson nodded, but still seemed wary.

'Anyway, I want a background check done on him. Any disciplinary issues, any accusations, any dirt, any rumours, anything that might suggest he's not the angel he's cracked up to be.'

'And this is because ...?' Wilson asked, fishing for reassurance.

'Because I asked you to,' Helen replied briskly. 'Quick as you can, quiet as you can, and you report back directly to me. Clear?'

'Crystal.'

'Good. Whilst you're at it, I want the team to put out feelers for Brent Mason. He's the dealer that PC Beamer patted down a couple of nights ago in the Lordship Road underpass. He's a possible witness in the Naomi Watson case, so the sooner we can bring him in, the better. Can you ask uniform to find him, bring him in?'

'Sure thing, boss.'

'Great, well that's all. Hop to it.'

Wilson turned to leave, even as there was a gentle knocking on Helen's door.

'Oh and Japhet, careless talk costs lives, so ...'

Her colleague looked back at her, nodding seriously.

'I'm glad we understand each other.'

Smiling, Wilson opened the door to reveal Charlie standing in the doorway. Stepping aside, he let his superior enter, before he slipped out.

'Everything OK?' Charlie enquired, as Wilson hurried away.

'Just asking DC Wilson to do a little research for me.'

'About?'

'About our friend Dave Reynolds,' Helen replied quickly, before changing the subject. 'In the meantime, is Marwood ready?'

'Waiting for us in the interview suite.'

'Then let's get on with it.'

Helen rose to leave, but Charlie stepped forward, arresting her progress.

'Before we do, I should let you know that the Chief Super was in here this morning. She was pretty pissed off about the amount of time and resources being expended on the Naomi Watson case, demanding that we all switch tack to the Freemantle shooting. Oh, and she wants to see you in her office ASAP. Do you want to deal with that before we—'

'No,' Helen interrupted firmly. 'Work first, chit-chat later.'

Picking up her file, Helen marched to the door.

'Let's see what Ryan Marwood's got to say for himself.'

Chapter 34

'You've got no right to do this. This is harassment ...'

Ryan Marwood launched the words at Helen, as if she alone was responsible for his predicament.

'I've done nothing wrong, but you still turn up at my house, dragging me out the door in front of the whole street ...'

'I'm sorry to hear that, Ryan. It wasn't our intention to embarrass you in any way. My officers were just discharging their duti—'

'Bullshit, you knew *exactly* what you were doing,' Marwood retorted, incandescent with rage. 'And it's bang out of order.'

Helen said nothing, pleased at Marwood's anger. Some suspects took a while to warm up, others refused to say a word. But Marwood had started talking the minute she'd entered the room, his fury growing with each passing minute. This suited Helen fine – the more riled their suspect was, the better.

'Why is it you think you're here, Ryan?' Charlie asked innocently, stepping into the fray.

'Because you need someone to fit up, a bloody scapegoat. I've been a good boy, done everything the probation service have asked of me, but as soon as you've got a problem, you come at me.'

'Why would we do that?' Charlie persisted.

'Because my face fits. Because I'm a bad seed, right?'

'Your words, Ryan. Not ours.'

'Well, it's a load of crap. I'm not involved and you can't prove it.'

'We haven't even told you what we want to talk about yet,' Helen interjected, laughing.

'Don't need to. I can guess what it's about…'

'Care to enlighten us?'

Marwood was about to respond, then thought better of it, sitting back in his chair.

'Let me help you,' Helen continued. 'Two days ago, fifteen-year-old Naomi Watson went missing. She was last seen in the southern part of the city, in the Lordship Road underpass.'

Helen slid a photo of Naomi across the table towards Marwood, but he refused to look at it.

'We believe she was driven out of that underpass in a Renault Movano van, registration number OT16 VXL. Ring any bells?'

'Don't drive a van,' Marwood replied grudgingly. 'Don't even have a car…'

'Thing is, this van was supposed to have been destroyed two months ago, at the council pound where you work.'

'Nothing to do with me,' the suspect replied, shrugging.

'Once more with feeling, Ryan. And this time look at me when you're lying.'

Marwood refused to oblige, keeping his gaze glued to the floor.

'When did you steal it?'

'Don't know what you're talking about.'

'And did you steal it with the express purpose of using it to abduct young girls? Or was there another reason you needed it?'

'Ah, this is nuts,' Marwood responded angrily, finally looking up. 'Why would I steal something when I'm on probation? When I could get thrown back inside in a heartbeat?'

'The same reason that you targeted those poor girls, that you forced yourself on young women who were too intoxicated or scared to resist. Because you can't stop yourself. Because you can't control your desire to subjugate and degrade young women.'

'That was the old me. It's not who I am *now*.'

'So if I was to talk to your probation officer, your co-workers, your mum, they'd confirm that you're a changed man, would they?' Helen persisted. 'A little angel?'

'No need to take the piss, all right?' Marwood responded, visibly annoyed. 'I've done my time, done my therapy, I've dealt with my issues.'

'Well, forgive me if I don't believe you,' Helen retorted angrily. 'But I still remember what you did to those girls. How you preyed on their trust, won their confidence with your smart uniform and your comforting words, convinced them that you were there to *help*. I interviewed half of them and let me tell you, their testimonies are *burned* in my memory. The things you said to them, the depraved way you treated them, how you tried to shame them into keeping silent afterwards. Yes, you may have sat through your therapy sessions, said all the right things, but I don't think you've changed one bit. You're still the old Ryan. Still a serious, active danger to women and girls...'

Marwood shook his head violently, but refused to engage, glaring fiercely at Helen.

'I'm showing the suspect a picture of Mia Davies,' Helen continued, unabashed. 'We believe she may also have been abducted by the same perpetrator. Would you look at the photo and tell me if you recognize her, Ryan?'

Reluctantly, the suspect lowered his eyes to take in first Mia's photo, then Naomi's.

'Don't recognize her. Nor the other one neither.'

'They have names, Ryan. Mia Davies and Naomi Watson. They are people's daughters, people's friends. And they belong at home, safe and sound. This is your opportunity to help them, to help yourself. Tell us where they are, tell us where the van is, maybe we can still make this right.'

'I don't know anything about them, I don't know anything about any van…'

Unimpressed, Helen sat back in her head, shaking her head dismissively.

'Shake your head all you want,' Marwood continued angrily. 'But you don't know what's inside me, who I am.'

'Maybe not, but your mother does, right?' Charlie interjected, cutting off his protest. 'Your poor mum, who's stuck with you through thick and thin, who's tried to do right by you…'

Marwood's anger seemed to evaporate almost immediately, replaced by blushing shame.

'She knows you better than anyone and *she* thinks you're responsible for these girls' disappearance.'

The effect on Marwood was instant, the suspect darting a charged look at Charlie, fearful and concerned.

'She told us how you've been breaking curfew, returning after sun up, refusing to say where you've been. How you've been pulling the wool over the eyes of the probation service, your counsellor, even your own mother, all in a desperate attempt to conceal your criminality.'

'She never said that.'

'She said that *and* more. And guess what? We believe her. Which is why we're not going anywhere – why *you're* not going anywhere – until you tell us where those girls are.'

Marwood glared at Charlie, stung by the ferocity of her

attack. He seemed shocked by this sudden cranking up of the pressure and Helen was quick to take advantage.

'This is the end of the road, Ryan. She's given you up. At long last, your poor mother has finally seen sense. She says you're too far gone, that...'

Helen paused, making a show of consulting her notes.

'...that you're sick in the head.'

Helen was pleased to see Marwood flinch, her words striking home.

'That you've deliberately flouted the terms of your licence in order to target, stalk and abduct vulnerable girls. Which is why I'll ask you again if you recognize Naomi Watson?'

'I've said no, all right? How many more times?'

'So where were you on the night of the ninth of November? Between the hours of 9 p.m. and midnight?'

'I was at home.'

'Except you weren't, Ryan. Your mother has confirmed that she is prepared to testify *under oath* that you weren't at the home that night.'

'OK, so maybe I did nip out for a bit – no big deal.'

'On the contrary, it's a *very* big deal. What were up to?'

'I don't know, driving around, whatever.'

'So you *do* have a vehicle?' Charlie interjected quickly.

'No, I mean walking. I was probably just walking...'

'Do you have any idea how unconvincing this all sounds?' Helen goaded, her tone withering.

'Look, I'm telling you the truth,' he blurted out.

'Bullshit. You've been lying to us since the moment you set foot in this room. Why? Because you're guilty, guilty of abducting Mia Davies, of abducting Naomi Watson, to satiate your own twisted desires. So why don't you stop treating us like mugs, eh? Tell us where are they, Ryan. Tell us where you've taken those poor girls.'

Silence in the room. Marwood continued to stare at the floor, fidgeting unhappily. Helen was watching him intently, hoping to see a sign of submission, that her words had finally cut through. But when Marwood finally looked up, she saw only a dull, dead-eyed defiance.

'Like I said, I never touched those girls and you can't prove that I did. So why don't you just cut the crap and let me go, eh?'

Chapter 35

'We're going to get out of here, Mia. We're going to be OK.'

Did any part of her believe this was true? Naomi wasn't sure, but she felt compelled to say it, so complete, so consuming was her friend's despair.

'This is not the end for you, for us ...'

Mia looked up at her, her eyes wan and sad. But was there a spark of something there? A need to hope despite all the horrors and privations she'd endured?

'I know it seems hopeless, but remember they are out there looking for us right now. Whole teams of folk searching. And how many places can there be like this? They *will* find us.'

Naomi was talking without thinking, expressing any hopeful thought she could muster. And now to her surprise and pleasure, she saw Mia respond.

'Do you really think so?' she whispered.

'Totally. You've never met my mum, you don't know what she's like, but let me tell you she will be going *nuts* right now, kicking the cops' arses, hammering down their door. She won't let up until she's got them all out looking for me.'

Naomi dearly wished this was true. And there was no question her mum would be going out of her mind with worry. But would she really have the courage, the strength to make anyone listen? She'd always been such a meek character. Would she rise to the occasion in this dire emergency? Even if she did, would anyone be interested in another teen runaway?

'She sounds great,' Mia offered, sadness punching through her admiration.

'Yeah, she's a right hard ass. She'll be front and centre in the search, but she won't be doing it alone. No, she'll have search teams, sniffer dogs, helicopters, the works, sweeping the whole city.'

'But how will they even know where to start?'

'Because I told her where I was bedding down,' Naomi lied. 'And I don't think I moved far from there, with him I mean...'

Naomi pushed that thought away, didn't want to think back to that crazy, fateful moment when she'd accepted his offer of a lift.

'So when you think about it, they haven't got a very wide area to cover. I'm betting if we listen closely, we might even be able to hear them, getting closer...'

And, now for the first time, Mia smiled, her teeth catching the sliver of light that crept underneath the door, glowing like a beacon. Mia genuinely seemed to be listening, enchanted by the idea of ranks of boots marching remorselessly towards their hiding place, the slow, dull murmur of a helicopter as it zeroed in on them.

'Do you honestly think that? That they're doing all that for *us*?'

She seemed shocked at this notion, the idea that anyone would care enough to search for her, for them. Naomi felt a rush of emotion, a sense of deep sadness at Mia's total lack of self-worth, but pushed these feelings away, determined to keep their spirits high.

'You better believe it. I guess there might be a reward of some kind too. Cash, or perhaps a medal of some kind for the person who finds us first. Not sure what they'll give to a dog if he wins the race. Sausages, maybe? A bacon sandwich?'

Mia smiled at this notion, letting out a little laugh, which hit Naomi like a shot of adrenaline. From nowhere she felt a surge of determination, resolve and purpose. So now she didn't hold back, letting her imagination run riot as she continued to spin her inspired, detailed narrative of industrious endeavour and imminent salvation. She didn't believe it, didn't know where this stuff was coming from, but as her heart thrilled to see Mia's broad, believing smile, she knew that both girls needed these lies today.

Chapter 36

'Have we done the right thing?'

Helen's question was terse, her tone solemn, as she paced the interview suite in front of Charlie, their prime suspect long since departed.

'We don't have enough to hold Marwood. We *had* to let him go,' Charlie responded evenly.

'Do you think we pulled him in too early?' Helen insisted. 'Should we have put him under surveillance first?'

'Maybe, but the evidence was there to bring him in – a strong, credible link to the abduction vehicle. And, besides, his mother was calling 999 when our officers arrived. We *had* to act.'

Helen nodded distractedly, Charlie's words providing little comfort. Marwood was clearly holding out on them, desperate to conceal the full extent of his offending, and it stuck in Helen's craw to let him walk out of the station a free man.

'We could have held him though,' Helen persisted, unable to stop picking at the sore. 'We could have made him spend a night in the cells, sweated him again in the morning...'

'He's not going to tell us anything,' Charlie replied calmly. 'He's never going to admit anything incriminating because he's terrified of going back inside. The best thing we can do now is let him think that he's won, that we can't touch him. If we're lucky, he'll get overconfident, maybe he'll lead us straight to the van, or better still, the girls.'

'Even so, it's massively risky, especially for Naomi and Mia. If he goes to ground now, or somehow manages to steal away...'

'He won't, he can't. Our people are all over him.'

'Sure, but you know what this guy's like,' Helen persisted, uneasy. 'If he can slip the noose now, he will, and then what hope have we got of finding our girls?'

'Look, would it help if I took personal charge of the surveillance? Would that reassure you?'

To Charlie's surprise, Helen broke into a broad smile.

'Sometimes I think you can read my mind,' she replied, smiling gratefully.

'OK, I'll do it. So try not to worry. Marwood's too reckless, too impulsive to keep up an innocent front for long. If we keep a close eye on him, he *will* lead us to those girls.'

Relieved, Helen nodded, stoically, hopefully. She was about to say more, to express her gratitude for her friend's loyalty and support, when a sudden knocking made her look up. Grimacing apologetically, DC Japhet Wilson entered.

'Got a minute, boss?'

Immediately, Helen was intrigued, her colleague's tone anxious and tense.

'What have you got for us, Japhet?'

'Well, I...' he responded hesitantly. 'I did a bit of digging on PC Reynolds, like you asked, and I was, well I was a bit surprised by the results.'

He handed Helen photocopied documents from Reynolds' official personnel file.

'It seems that three official complaints have been made against him during the last ten years or so. All by young women who said he propositioned them, then sexually assaulted them whilst on duty.'

Helen stared at the sheet of paper in shock, barely crediting what she was reading.

'All the complainants withdrew their allegations before he even got close to being charged, hence why's he still working, why none of us had any idea about this. Obviously he's not been convicted of anything, but I have to say, guv, it doesn't look great.'

Helen looked up at Wilson, lost for words. Too right it didn't look great. What the hell was this creep still doing in uniform?

Chapter 37

'Absolutely not.'

Chief Superintendent Rebecca Holmes was defiant, staring at Helen with incredulity, but Helen was too enraged, too shell-shocked, to back down.

'Look at his file, look at those complaints,' Helen insisted, jabbing her finger angrily at the files now spread open on her superior's desk. 'Three different victims, three different occasions, but what do they all have in common? They're all teenage girls, one of them only fifteen years of age. The man is *clearly* a danger to women.'

'That's your considered opinion is it, DI Grace? Having sifted all the evidence, having spoken to the complainants?'

'It's too much of a coincidence,' Helen retorted, ignoring Holmes' jibe. 'Especially when taken in conjunction with his connection to the Naomi Watson case.'

'A connection which is unproven and, to my mind, unfounded. As seemingly were these allegations, otherwise he would have been charged.'

'Oh come off it, you don't really believe that, do you? The complainants all withdrew their allegations. What does that tell you? That they were pressured into doing so or didn't feel they'd be given sufficient support to proceed with a case against a serving police officer.'

'Once again, DI Grace, this is all conjecture and supposition. And so I can only repeat myself. I'm not going to suspend a popular and well-regarded police constable on your say-so. These are historical issues that were dealt with at the time. I see no value in dredging them up again now. Unless of course you have some kind of personal animus against PC Reynolds?'

'Of course not.'

'Then may I respectfully suggest that you are letting yourself be influenced by outside pressures, by the media agenda, by those who wish to slander and denigrate this police force and others like it up and down the country.'

'Don't be ridiculous,' Helen shot back. 'This isn't some confected story, some media witch hunt. This is about a pattern of behaviour, a very worrying pattern of behaviour, that to my mind warrants instant suspension. It beggars belief that you could put your trust in a man when there's such a huge question mark over his credibility, his trustworthiness.'

'Yet no crime has been committed.'

'No crime has been *proven*.'

'And you know as well as I do that the policing union would have us for breakfast if we even hinted at any kind of suspension when his record shows he's done nothing wrong.'

'That's not my problem, nor should it be your first concern. Put these crimes in context. This is a man who spoke to Naomi Watson on the night she disappeared, then lied to my face when I challenged him about it.'

'He would tell a very different story, I'm sure, and I expect his union rep would take a dim view of a senior CID officer invading the male changing rooms to interrogate and accuse a serving police officer when he was readying himself for duty.'

'The circumstances are immaterial—' Helen countered, but was quickly cut off by her superior.

'On the contrary, the circumstances are *everything*. If I was ever to sanction suspending a police officer under my command, I would expect the accused to be interviewed in the proper manner, with the standard safeguards in place, and I would expect the charges to be proven beyond reasonable doubt.'

'Jesus Christ, do you want him boxed and gift-wrapped too?'

Holmes' reaction was instant and surprising, the station chief rising and marching round her desk to confront Helen directly.

'I would strongly advise you to moderate your tone, DI Grace,' she rasped, her anger clear, despite her measured words. 'To get a hold of yourself. Be clear on this – I have no interest in PC Reynolds, or any reason to spare him from justified scrutiny. What I *do* have an interest in is sparing this force from the sort of public evisceration the Met endured after Wayne Couzens and David Carrick. Those officers, those criminals, set that force back decades in terms of relations with the community, with women, with the media. I will not invite that kind of opprobrium down on this organization, I will not subject the hundreds of hard-working officers under my command to that ordeal, unless there is *clear evidence of wrong-doing*. And that is not the case in regards to PC Reynolds. All you have is a scattering of unsubstantiated allegations against an officer of many years' good service who by all accounts is the beating heart of Southampton Central.'

'Being a good bloke gets you a free pass now, does it?'

For a minute, Helen thought Holmes was going to explode, but at the last minute the station chief reined in her fury.

'I know that your... your zeal comes from a good place, Helen,' Holmes said carefully, measuring every word. 'So I'm going to overlook your conduct today. But I will not condone or support an unjustified vendetta against an innocent man. A man with an unblemished record, whose spent his life helping those less fortunate than himself. Forget Reynolds. Focus on the main prize, on Marwood. Keep an eye on him, whilst remembering to attend to your *other* duties. I have seen nothing in the way of progress on the Freemantle shooting, despite clear instructions that you were to make that investigation a priority. So, please, return to your duties, do your job, be the officer we all know you can be. Is that clear?'

Helen would gladly have slapped her superior, Holmes' patronizing tone unbearable, her self-interest so palpable. Clearly her main concern was to avoid a major scandal early in her tenure, to ensure *her* reputation did not suffer. It was monstrous, wilfully blind, and Helen was tempted to tell her so, but instead she nodded curtly, as she knew she had to.

'Absolutely, ma'am.'

'Good. I'm glad we understand each other.'

Helen turned and made fast for the door, only for Holmes' voice to ring out once more.

'Oh, and DI Grace…?'

Helen turned back to her boss.

'When I ask to see you urgently, I expect you in my office immediately. I will not be ignored, not by you or anyone else in this building.'

Her eyes locked onto Helen's challenging, piercing gaze, as she added:

'Respect the chain of command.'

Chapter 38

He had searched everywhere. The canteen, the common room, even the ladies' locker room, but still his quarry eluded him. But as Dave Reynolds was about to give up, frustrated and enraged, he spotted her, fiddling with her bike chain in the station car park.

Hurrying out of the main doors, he marched across the tarmac towards Beamer. The young probationer had just unlocked her bike and was stowing her chain when she heard his approach, looking up sharply at her colleague with an anxious, uneasy expression.

'Yes, you might well look worried,' Reynolds hissed at her. 'Being the station grass and all ...'

Beth Beamer stared at him, cornered and helpless, unable to formulate a response.

'You're not even going to bother to deny it?' her irate colleague demanded. 'It was a mistake. DI Grace misinterpreted what I said.'

'Listen, Dave, I—'

'Don't you fucking call me, Dave. You're not my mate. You're a worm, a snitch, a parasite ...'

He was gratified to see tears threatening. She deserved this and more.

'Look, I'm sorry,' the probationer blustered, unable to meet his eye. 'I didn't mean to get you into trouble or cause any problems between us, really I didn't.'

She was staring at him beseechingly, but it cut no ice. 'I was just trying to help the missing girl. I thought maybe it had slipped your mind...'

'Jesus, how stupid do you think I am? You were trying to drop me in it. To make me look negligent, incompetent...'

'I wasn't, I swear!' Beamer protested.

'Then why did you go straight to Grace?'

As expected, this silenced her, so he was quick to double down.

'If you *really* thought it had slipped my mind, if you *really* thought reminding me might help Naomi Watson...'

'That's all it was, please believe me...'

'If that *was* the case, why didn't you come to me first? Why go to Grace telling tales?'

'I don't know, I... I wasn't sure what to do for the best. And I happened to see DS Brooks in the corridor...'

'Sure you did.'

'Honest to God, it's true. So I told her. I thought I was being helpful. And now all *this*...'

She looked distraught, which was something. Even so, there could be no room for mercy.

'PC Beamer, you are a very young, very inexperienced officer. You have been entrusted to my care so that you can learn the ropes. Your job is to keep your mouth shut and do as you're told, whilst you find your feet here. Is that clear?'

Beamer nodded, seemingly unable to speak.

'You are very green, you are very clumsy. And you've got a long road ahead of you if you're ever to make the grade here. Maybe your inexperience is the root cause of this *gross* error of judgement, but you better make sure it's your last. People don't get second chances round here.'

Beamer blinked, then nodded, too intimidated to offer any resistance.

'Rule Number One – respect your superiors. Got it?'

'Of course, yes.'

'Good. Now piss off home.'

The startled probationer was only too happy to oblige, scrambling onto her bike and hastening away. Dave Reynolds watched her all the way down the road, his blood boiling, then he turned away, stalking back towards the station. But no sooner had he set foot in the lobby than the custody sergeant called out to him.

'DI Grace was after a word with you,' he offered cheerily. 'It's about that missing fifteen-year-old.'

Chapter 39

'It's a simple question, PC Reynolds. Perhaps you'd do me the courtesy of answering it?'

Helen leaned forwards, reducing the space between them. Almost instinctively, Dave Reynolds reclined in his seat, as if keen to keep a safe distance between them. His eyes flitted from Grace to DC Wilson, then back to her again, before he eventually replied:

'Look, I've always said that I'm keen to help, but I honestly don't remember the details of what we talked about.'

'Come now, Dave, it was *two days ago*,' Helen countered, gently chiding him. 'Surely you can't have forgotten everything? You're in the underpass, you see this girl, young, homeless, vulnerable, so you approach her. Are you wanting to see if she's in trouble? If she's conscious? If she's on drugs? What's your primary concern?'

'To check that she's OK, I suppose. If a beat officer sees someone dossing down outdoors, we chat to them, see what their situation is.'

'And what was hers?'

'I don't recall specifically, but maybe ... she'd run away from home. Or been kicked out ...'

Helen said nothing, darting a look at DC Wilson, who was studiously taking notes.

'Look, why is he taking notes?' Reynolds interjected angrily. 'I thought this was just a chat.'

'It is. If this was a formal interview, you'd know about it. This is just an information-gathering exercise.'

'In an interview suite?'

'I thought it was best to conduct it here. More discreet, more private.'

Reynolds didn't respond, but looked deeply disgruntled.

'Sorry, so just to clarify,' DC Wilson piped up, checking his notes. 'She said she'd run away from home and then what?'

'How many times?' Reynolds fired back. 'I probably I asked her if she had somewhere to go, she said no, and I made a mental note to check back in on her the following day.'

'So you *do* remember what you talked about?'

'It's what I say to *all* of them. Look, I don't mean to talk out of turn, but I've already apologized for my oversight, I've reassured you that I don't have any specific information relating to Naomi Watson, so honestly I don't see what purpose is served by us sitting here talking in circles. I've said all I have to say and as my shift is long since finished, I really would like to—'

'It wasn't just Naomi I wanted to talk to you about.'

Helen's tone was firm and it had the desired effect, silencing Reynolds instantly. Opening her file, she continued:

'I'd also like to ask you about some accusations that were made against you in 2021, 2018 and 2016. Allegations of sexual misconduct...'

Reynolds didn't blink, but Helen clocked the colour slowly draining from his face.

'They were made by young women, whose ages ranged from fourteen to seventeen years old, who allege that you sexually assaulted them whilst on duty, gaining their trust and th—'

'What the hell is this?' Reynolds demanded loudly. 'Those

allegations were fully investigated and revealed to be total fabrications. Outright lies.'

'All of them? They were *all* lying?'

'Hundred per cent and it's outrageous that you'd suggest otherwise.'

'But why would three young women, who were totally unknown to you, unknown to each other, separately allege that you'd attacked them?'

'You'd have to ask them that.'

'Maybe I will.'

Helen was pleased to see a reaction, so she pressed on.

'But I'd like to hear your explanation first.'

'Look, they were pissed, drugged up, whatever. Young girls who should have been at home, studying, but instead were out on the town late at night. Maybe they were from broken homes, maybe their parents didn't love them, maybe they thought they might get a pay-off. I don't know why they made up those allegations, it's beyond comprehension. I never did anything to them, other than try to get them home safely.'

'Yet their testimonies are striking similar,' Helen continued, keeping up the pressure. 'They all alleged that you won their trust, said you'd take them somewhere safe, then assaulted them somewhere out of sight – in a derelict building, in the back of a police van.'

'No, no, no. I never touched them. They are fantasists, liars, junkies. Yet apparently you'd believe their word over mine?'

It was a challenge, but one Helen wasn't minded to respond to.

'Well thanks for clearing that up, PC Reynolds,' she responded genially, sitting back in her chair. 'Just for the record, so I'm clear, there's no connection between these past allegations and Naomi

Watson's recent disappearance? Nothing you'd like to add to your account or tell me ab—'

'I've said all I'm going to say. If you are going to slander me, harass me, then I want my police rep *and* a lawyer present.'

'As is your right,' Helen intoned, nodding solemnly. 'Well that's all for now, we're done here.'

Helen rose, but Reynolds made no move to leave, glaring at her with contempt.

'DI Grace, before you go, let me just say this,' the constable replied, eyeballing DC Wilson until he lowered his pen. 'I have worked at this station for a very long time. I am a well-respected, well-liked member of this police community, with several decorations on my record and a history of sticking up for my fellow officers. No one in this place has a bad word to say about me, never has done. You might do well to remember that. I would hate for you to embarrass me, or indeed embarrass yourself, by spreading these wild theories any further. I don't mean to teach an old dog new tricks, but a word of advice from an experienced, comrade-in-arms. *Let this go.*'

Chapter 40

Charlie had been expecting insubordination, a barrage of complaints and recriminations, but she hadn't expected it to surface so quickly. She and DC Jennings had barely been on stakeout for five minutes before her colleague launched his attack.

'This is bloody criminal. No other word for it.'

'Are you referring to the suspect's behaviour?' Charlie replied, running her eye over Ryan Marwood's residence, which looked gloomy and lifeless. 'Or you and I being paired together again? If it's the latter, believe you me, it wasn't *my* choice ...'

'You know what I'm talking about,' Jennings replied irritably. 'We've got two officers out front, two round the back, four more covering the ends of the street. That's eight officers. Eight officers babysitting a guy who *may* have stolen a van, who *may* have bumped into a teen runaway. The whole thing is a complete waste of time and resources.'

'Remember the basics tenets of policing, DC Jennings,' Charlie responded, just about controlling her irritation. 'Motive, means and opportunity. Marwood could easily have taken that van. He could just as easily have been in the underpass that night. And as for motive, well the guy is a convicted rapist with a history of targeting vulnerable girls. So forgive me if I don't jump on your bandwagon just yet.'

'Fair play, the guy's a slime ball,' Jennings huffed, clearly intent on a fight. 'But the whole thing is ifs, buts and maybes. There is no solid evidence connecting Marwood to anything, yet the boss has got half the team camped outside this sad little semi. If it was Pablo Escobar in there, you couldn't have any more eyes on him.'

Charlie let her eyes drift back to the house, her gaze scanning the windows. But the curtains remained closed, mother and son hiding away from the world, prisoners in their own home.

'Well if a job's worth doing...' Charlie replied evenly.

Jennings puffed out his cheeks, annoyed that she wouldn't rise to the bait.

'Seriously, Jennings,' Charlie continued, trying her best to be reasonable, 'we cannot let this guy out of our sight. Whatever you may think, he remains our strongest lead and now that he's rattled, now that he knows the heat's on, we've *got* to keep a close eye on him. I promised the boss I wouldn't let him off the hook and it's a promise I intend to keep, with or without your help.'

'More fool you then.'

'I beg your pardon?'

This time anger *had* crept into her tone. Jennings' total lack of respect for her, for Helen, was hard to stomach.

'Look, I know you two are mates from way back, but you must see that she's got this all wrong.'

'Got *what* wrong?'

'*This*, her priorities, her focus. Blowing all her credit, all her resources on a glorified missing person's case. Honestly, I hope Marwood *is* guilty of something, that he *does* walk out the front door and lead us straight to his "evil lair". Then we can nick him and get back to work. But I wouldn't bet the house on it, believe you me.'

'And when did *you* become such an expert?'

This time Jennings couldn't miss her tone, harsh and withering.

'All right, all right, keep your hair on. I'm just saying that if Grace is wrong, if this blows up in her face, then we're all going to suffer. The unit's reputation is on the—'

'I asked you a question, DC Jennings.'

She turned to him, her eyes blazing.

'Is it your *five years* dogged policework in CID or just natural talent that makes you a world authority on running major investigations?'

'Easy now, I've done my time. I've earned the right to comment…'

'You've done what you're told, nothing more,' Charlie spat back, furious. 'So let me make one thing very clear. When you've achieved *half* of what DI Grace has in her career, then maybe, just maybe, you'll have the right to comment. But until then, keep it zipped.'

Stunned, Jennings held Charlie's intense gaze for a minute, then looked away, staring hard out the windscreen at the Marwood house. Charlie wanted to say more, wanted to tear a strip off this arrogant upstart, but recovered her professionalism in the nick of time, buttoning her lip. So instead the pair sat in silence, watching the suspect's house, a heavy, uncomfortable atmosphere filling the car.

Chapter 41

Even caged animals have moments of happiness. Crazy to say it, but Naomi felt strangely elated, buoyed up by her tissue of lies. She'd spoken for well over half an hour, taking great pleasure in detailing the concerted efforts underway in the hunt for the missing girls. It had raised her spirits immeasurably, even though most of it was fantasy, and she could see it had had the same effect on Mia, who had shrugged off her despair, for the time being at least. It was amazing what a little hope can do, and Naomi resolved to return to her theme again soon. Having seen Mia's magical smile once, she didn't want to let it go.

'Thank you, Naomi.'

She turned to Mia, surprised. Usually taciturn, her friend seemed positively talkative now.

'For what?'

'For being you. For being happy. For being here.'

'Well, I would rather I wasn't, but you know...'

Shrugging casually, she smiled at Mia, earning a sheepish grin in return.

'I mean it. I think I was on the point of going properly mad, you know. Stuck in this awful place by myself. It's so nice to be able to share things, to comfort each other. It's been so long since I had someone to talk to down here.'

Instantly, Naomi felt her stomach tighten. Mia was still smiling at her, but Naomi's blood had suddenly run cold, her friend's happiness suddenly sickeningly inappropriate.

'You mean ... there were *others* here before me?'

Mia's grin slowly faded, shocked and distressed by the effect of her words.

'Sure,' Mia blustered. 'Though I only met one. And she'd already been here a while when I arrived.'

Naomi stared at her, unable to speak.

'Her name was Shanice. She was OK, you know ... though not as nice as you.'

Mia smiled gamely at Naomi, but the joy had evaporated from the room.

'How long ... how long had she been down here?' Naomi eventually breathed.

'A while, I think. Certainly a couple of months or so. You can probably work it out if you want. I haven't tried to, but ...'

Naomi was staring at Mia as if she was mad. Clocking this, her fellow captive nodded grimly at the hinged doors that imprisoned them.

'Over there.'

Naomi turned, but saw nothing other than the sealed wall.

'Look closer.'

Naomi moved over to the secret doors and now she spotted something. The right-hand door was covered in markings; neat, ordered rows of shapes scratched into the plaster. Naomi ran her fingers over them, taking in the strange sequence of lines and crosses.

'It was her way of marking the days,' Mia whispered, suddenly sombre. 'A kind of diary.'

Instantly, Naomi felt sickened. There were *dozens* of marks.

'She made one for each day, just before she went to sleep. It became a kind of ritual, part of her routine.'

It was awful, the notion that you could have a routine in a place like this.

'But what did... what do they mean?' Naomi blustered.

'Naomi, don't, please. You don't need to—'

'I want to know, Mia. Tell me what they mean.'

'It won't do you any good.'

'Tell me.'

Her companion flinched, retreating slightly as if scared. In other circumstances, Naomi would have felt guilty, shouting at someone so fragile, but not today, not now.

'There are three kinds of symbols: lines, crosses and crosses with circles round them,' Mia conceded despondently.

'And? What does they mean?'

Mia sighed heavily; a deep, painful sigh.

'A straight line was an OK day, a day where he didn't hurt her, when she had food and water, when she wasn't too cold. A cross meant a bad day.'

Mia blinked, her own distress surfacing once more.

'And... a cross with a circle round it meant a really bad day.'

Mia's voice was shaking, memories of her own agonies resurfacing. She clearly wanted this conversation to end, to return to blissful lies, but Naomi couldn't let it go.

'And what... what happened to her? Where is she now?'

Mia stared directly at Naomi, her eyes sparkling fiercely with desperation and despair, then slowly she shook her head and turned away.

Chapter 42

She kept her eyes glued to him, never allowing him to disappear; determinedly, patiently, dogging his heels. Helen knew she was taking a massive risk, following Dave Reynolds as he left the family home to walk through nearby woodland, but she felt compelled to do so, convinced that he would somehow give himself away. Nevertheless, she shuddered at the thought of what she would do if Reynolds spotted her, or worse, confronted her. There was no way she could excuse her presence here, this remote wood was miles from her flat, and even further from Southampton Central. No, if detected, there would be nothing for it but to come clean. Helen was here after hours for one reason and one reason alone. To expose Dave Reynolds as a liar, a rapist, a serial offender who posed a profound threat to women.

Yet there seemed little that was dangerous or intimidating about the middle-aged officer tonight. He'd emerged from his impressive detached house in Bitterne Park, clad in jeans, muck boots and a faded North Face puffa, his loyal whippet gazing up at him lovingly as it trotted by his side. And this unreserved affection seemed to be returned by everyone Reynolds encountered on his evening stroll. On several occasions, the diminutive officer paused to talk to fellow dog walkers, to joggers, to friends, all of whom seemed delighted to see him. Young or old, female or male, they went out of their way to pass the time of day with him, smiling, often guffawing at his impromptu remarks. They all seemed delighted by these chance meetings, as did Reynolds, who wore a happy, relaxed smile. Indeed, the only participant who seemed frustrated by these regular stops was the dog, who was clearly keen to get on with the serious business of chasing squirrels.

Helen kept pace with the off-duty police constable, matching him stride for stride, disappearing into the shadows whenever he paused to chat to another well-wisher. From her discreet vantage point, she watched him, drinking in his gestures, his body language, the timbre of his voice. There was no doubt he was a likeable figure, with a handsome face and a ready wit, as evidenced by the laughter he often provoked. Clearly, he was a genuinely popular figure, both within the Force and in civilian life. Was it possible that all his admirers were wrong? That they'd all had the wool pulled over their eyes?

Reynolds was moving away from his latest conversation and Helen kept with him, her mind a jumble of conflicting thoughts. She'd been warned off Reynolds in no uncertain terms by Holmes, yet she was damned if she was going to let it go. No smoke without fire was hardly a healthy precept for responsible policing, but there was something in his accusers' testimonies that rang true for Helen. It was the arrogance with which they'd allegedly been treated, the casual disregard for their feelings, their well-being, their very existence that struck home, leaving a bitter taste in Helen's mouth. Part of her knew she was clutching at straws, but part of her felt convinced that if she watched Reynolds for long enough, he would eventually reveal his true self.

That's why she was here tonight, hoping against hope that he might lead her to some remote location, some forgotten building, or perhaps even ditch the dog and sneak back into the city centre. At the very least, she hoped the family man would reveal his inner darkness, his disinterest in his wife and teenage son who he'd left at home, by chatting to, sizing up, then following a young female that he chanced upon in the woods. God knows there were enough of them about, either dutifully walking family pets or sneaking off to meet boys and smoke dope. Helen had spotted a couple tonight, but Reynolds appeared barely to notice them, with eyes only for old friends. It made Helen's blood boil, she was absolutely convinced he was dangerous, that he'd reveal himself instantly when he thought he wasn't being watched. But there was no evidence of wrongdoing on show tonight; in fact, there was nothing out of the ordinary at all.

Snapping out of her thoughts, Helen realized that Reynolds had suddenly stopped. Now he was turning, as if preparing to look in her direction. Darting forwards, she flattened herself against a nearby tree, her heart thumping. Now she heard rustling leaves, Reynolds on the move ... but to Helen's huge relief, she realized his footsteps were getting fainter as he continued on his way. Unnerved, panicking, Helen breathed out, long and low, trying to still the thumping in her chest. What should she do now? Take heed of this warning and retreat? Or press on regardless? She knew what she *should* do, what the sensible course of action was, but Helen had never taken the easy path. So, emerging from her hiding place, she crept carefully forwards, keeping a wary eye on her quarry. But with each step a little voice in her head warned her of her folly. What if she was discovered? What if she was exposed? And what if she'd got it all wrong?

What if Dave Reynolds was an innocent man?

Chapter 43

When would this purgatory finally be over?

Charlie had spent nearly two hours in Jennings' company and the novelty had well and truly worn off. First his grumbling, then their spat, then the heavy silence, then this: a subtle-as-a-sledgehammer dumb show of disgruntlement. The sighing, the endless tapping of his feet, the constant checking of his watch. It would have been amusing if it wasn't so annoying. For a grown man, an experienced police officer, it was both staggeringly infantile and completely inappropriate.

'Look, I get the message, OK?' Charlie eventually responded, her annoyance boiling over. 'You're pissed off with the boss, you're pissed off with me, you'd rather be busting heads in Freemantle, but we are where we are, so can we drop the histrionics and just do our job?'

'So I'm not allowed to have an opinion, am I?'

Dear God, was he going to start up again?

'Of course you are. But is it possible you might be a little less emotionally incontinent? Honestly, you're worse than my kids...'

This seemed to have the desired effect, her junior colleague calling time on his pantomime of disaffection. Settling back in her seat, Charlie smiled, privately congratulating herself on this small victory for common sense. But as she relaxed back into the well-worn fabric, she noticed something that immediately dispelled her good humour. Lorraine Marwood had suddenly emerged from her house, hurrying out the front door and scanning the street wildly. Her gaze seemed to sweep over them, but she registered no surprise or concern. Indeed, she didn't even seem to notice their presence, desperately searching for something, or someone. Now she was turning back to the house, retrieving her mobile from her pocket and punching the keys furiously. Seconds later, the front door closed with a bang.

Charlie was out of the car before the sound had died away, hurrying towards the suspect's house. She heard Jennings' door open, heard her colleague call after her, but she ignored him, hurrying up to the front door and pounding on it. She knew what she was doing was rash, ill-considered even, but she was suddenly filled with a terrible sense of foreboding.

The door flew open to reveal Lorraine Marwood. Charlie noted the two stages of her reaction: first hope, then disappointment.

'Hello, Mrs Marwood. I'm DS Brooks,' she said quickly, presenting her warrant card for inspection. 'Is Ryan home?'

Instantly, Charlie knew she was right to be worried. The blood drained from Lorraine Marwood's face and her lie was swift and unconvincing.

'He's asleep. He's ... he's completely exhausted after this morning. Can you come back—'

But Charlie was already pushing past her.

'Ryan? Ryan, are you there? If so, please show yourself immediately.'

'What on earth do you think you're doing? You can't just barge in here.'

But Charlie held up a finger, silencing her. Taking a few paces forwards, she darted a glance into the living room, then the kitchen, before turning her attention to the stairs, driving up them two at a time.

'Ryan? It's DS Brooks. Please show yourself.'

She knocked on his bedroom door, then pushed it open. Stepping inside, she saw that the light was still on, the computer playing a movie, but there was no sign of Marwood.

'Shit.'

Retreating, she checked the family bathroom, the master bedroom and finally the guest suite. But all were deserted, as she'd known they would be. Returning to the landing, she collided with a flustered Lorraine Marwood.

'Where is he, Lorraine?' Charlie demanded tersely.

'I don't know,' the tearful mother protested, giving up all pretence at resistance.

'Where's he gone?' she persisted, advancing on the middle-aged woman.

'I've no idea, please believe me...'

But Charlie shook her head, determined not to cut her any slack.

'It's the truth, I swear,' Lorraine persisted, anguished. 'I went into the kitchen to get a cup of tea and I noticed that the back door was ajar. I called up to Ryan and when he didn't answer, I went upstairs...'

Charlie didn't linger to hear the rest, tearing past the shocked mother, and out through the kitchen into the garden. Haring down the path, she made straight for the far fence, which backed onto a rear access alleyway, bordering thick woodland. If Marwood had managed to spirit himself across the alleyway, he would be free and clear by now, but how was that possible? There'd been no contact from the surveillance officers stationed at the top of the alley and the padlock was clearly still in place on the rear gate. How then?

Charlie could hear DC Jennings thundering down the garden path towards her, but she paid him no heed, desperately scanning the fence for an answer to the mystery. And now, to her horror, she found it. In the far left-hand corner of the garden, a bulky bag of compost had been cast aside, revealing a deep hole abutting the back fence. Dropping to her knees, Charlie fired her torch into the darkness. It was makeshift, it was narrow, but there was no question that the tunnel was big enough for Marwood to squeeze himself through, bringing him out in the thick grass of the alleyway beyond. Had he used that cover to crawl away, eluding the attention of the officers parked at the head of the alleyway?

Anguished, Charlie radioed the team urgently, but they merely confirmed her worst fears – they had neither heard nor seen anything. Furious, Charlie stared down into the abyss. Was this Marwood's favoured escape route? The way he'd repeatedly managed to escape the surveillance of his mother, the probation service and now them too?

The sound of Jennings' arrival made Charlie turn, junior officer skidding to a halt beside her.

'Where's the fire?' he demanded. 'What the hell's happening?'

'Marwood's done a bunk,' Charlie shot back fiercely. 'We've lost the suspect. That's what's happening...'

Jennings looked aghast, but Charlie was swift to follow up.

'Now are you going to tell DI Grace? Or am I?'

Day Four

Chapter 44

He hammered on the door, the sound echoing around the quiet suburban street. Passers-by on their way to work turned their heads to see what was happening, even as neighbours started to appear in their front yards, curious to see what all the fuss was about. PC Beth Beamer looked on anxiously, suspecting that her colleague was overdoing it, but he didn't seem to care. PC Dave Reynolds had made it clear on the walk over that Ryan Marwood had brought this all on himself – let the world see his shame.

Thankfully, Reynolds relented now, as the door swung open to reveal the angry owner.

'What on earth do you think you're doing?' a tired Lorraine Marwood demanded, tugging her dressing gown tightly around her. 'It's eight in the morning.'

'Spare us the outrage, Mrs Marwood,' Reynolds replied tersely, showing her his warrant card. 'I think you know why we're here.'

'Your lot were all over this place last night. Ryan wasn't here then, and he's not here now.'

'Why don't you let us be the judge of that, eh?'

'This is harassment, pure and simple. Why can't you lot just leave me alone?'

Beth Beamer could see her colleague was about to put the middle-aged woman in her place, so she quickly stepped in:

'We honestly don't mean to trouble you, but your house is on our beat and there *is* a warrant out for Ryan, so I hope you'll understand that we're obliged to take a look for ourselves. Five minutes and we'll be out of your hair, I promise.'

The ashen mum looked surprised, as if she'd never encountered politeness or humanity from a police officer before, Beth's diplomacy striking home.

'Well, you'd better come in then,' she said, stepping aside. 'But don't touch anything.'

Stepping aside, she let them into the house. Beth was immediately struck by the sepulchral quiet, the oddly lifeless atmosphere.

'Up or down?' Reynolds demanded, keen to crack on.

'Down, please,' Beth replied quickly, her feet sore after a solid week pounding the beat.

Nodding, Reynolds raced up the stairs, calling out the suspect's name as he went. Beth turned away, hurrying into the kitchen, anxious to be alone. This morning had been *awful*. She hadn't slept a wink last night, following her argument with Reynolds, fearing she'd done the wrong thing, yet convinced she'd been right to point out his error. Perhaps she'd played it wrong, perhaps she should have gone to her beat colleague first, but he didn't seem terribly interested in her opinion generally and she had the distinct impression he would have swept it under the carpet. Arriving knackered and apprehensive this morning, she'd greeted her colleague in as hearty and positive a manner as she could muster, but it had not been reciprocated. They were stuck together, beat buddies, but any sense of solidarity between them had been destroyed now and they walked the beat in heavy, toxic silence, Beth *hating* every tense minute of it. At least now they were at the Marwood residence, they had something to do, a task which allowed her to have a brief moment to herself.

But Beth suspected it wouldn't distract them for long. She had already left the kitchen empty-handed and there was clearly nobody hiding in the front room. Which just left the poky downstairs bathroom, which was empty too. Turning away, Beth clocked Dave Reynolds thundering down the stairs.

'No sign of him, we'd best crack on. You OK to call it in?'

He didn't wait for an answer, hurrying out the front door.

'Well, he's a charmer, isn't he?' Lorraine Marwood commented darkly.

Smiling awkwardly, Beth made her excuses and left, radioing Southampton Central as she walked down the garden path. Clicking off, she turned to look back at the house. Marwood had slipped the net last night and since then nothing. No sightings, no witnesses, no chance encounters, no sign of him anywhere in the city.

Where was he?

Chapter 45

It was strangely fitting that he should have ended up here, hiding out amongst the city's homeless. In years gone by, Ryan Marwood had spent much of his time amidst these lost souls, his St John Ambulance uniform earning him the goodwill and acceptance of everyone he encountered. He'd always had a kind word for them, occasionally doling out chocolate bars and cigarettes, but in reality he'd felt nothing for them. They were simply the backdrop to his search for vulnerable young girls – new faces on the street who'd respond to his baby face, his winning manner, following him obediently to his van in the hope of better things. The terminally dispossessed, with their grimy faces and their gnarled hands forever petting one-eyed dogs, repelled him. He couldn't endure their awful odour, their listless, lifeless eyes, but he'd concealed his distaste, preferring to present himself as a friend of those in need, a kind-hearted charity worker, in order to earn their trust. In that way, he had eventually become almost invisible to them, an ever-present fixture in their company, able to come and go without scrutiny or censure.

Last night had been a very different experience, however. Having escaped the family home, Ryan had made his way across town on foot, keeping to the back roads, hugging the shadows, praying he would not be spotted. His progress was swift and determined, interrupted only once by the sudden and unwelcome appearance of a patrol car as he neared Itchen Bridge. He had no idea if his disappearance had already been detected, if they were even now sweeping the city for him, so he took no chances, darting off the main road and running for the shelter of the murky underpass beneath. It was only once his heart had stopped thundering, once he'd caught his breath, that he'd taken in his surroundings. A dozen pairs of eyes stared back at him from within the cardboard settlement beneath the bridge, their suspicion and alarm palpable. The silence, the piercing quality of their gaze, let Ryan Marwood know that he wasn't welcome here, that intruders were to be repelled rather than accommodated, but he did his best to reassure the motley crew of unfortunates, holding up his hands in surrender to show that he meant them no harm, whilst scuttling away to the far corner of the bridge, finding a small, dry space amongst the discarded rubbish to bed down. It was disgusting, it was fetid, a far cry from his crisp clean sheets at home, but if he could hide out here unmolested for the night, he knew this counted as a small victory.

The night had passed slowly, the agitation of his mind echoed by the fevered scurrying in the darkness around him, foxes, rats and more searching for scraps. He'd tried to block them out, but he was on edge, his whole body tensed for flight, and sleep when it did come was punctured by terrible nightmares – vivid dreams that thrust him back into his prison hell, to that endless repetitive cycle of torture and violence, his fellow inmates gorging themselves on his fear. He'd woken at first light, unsettled, and was soon on his way, the same dozen pairs of eyes watching him every step of the way. Had they stayed awake all night? It didn't seem possible, yet Ryan's paranoia argued strongly that he had been under surveillance since his arrival. Indeed, to him it felt as if the eyes of the whole city were on him now.

Moving on, he stuck to quiet out-of-the-way streets, clinging to the wall as he hurried eastwards. His plan was simple – to make it to the Western Docks and then see if he could find his way onto one of the cargo trucks heading to London. He had some money on him, enough to bribe his way out of the city, but if all else failed, he would have to try and stow away, sneaking on board one of the vehicles whose drivers thought that they'd made it to the UK without any unsolicited human cargo. If he could do that, then he still might make it away.

He clocked the road signs for the docks and picked up his pace once more. Even at this early hour, when there were few people about, Ryan still scented danger. Every passer-by seemed to be scrutinizing him, the slow purr of every vehicle seemed to presage the arrival of another patrol car, his shame, his depravity visible to anyone who turned in his direction. If just one person stopped to look at him properly, to take in his sallow features, his downcast gaze, then he would be exposed and captured, he felt sure of it, hence his furious pace.

It was time to get out of Southampton for good.

Chapter 46

Where *was* he? Had something happened to their captor? Or had he simply decided to cut his losses, abandoning them both for good?

Pressing her face to the concrete, Naomi tried to peer under the tiny gap at the bottom of the cell doors, but she could see nothing through the dull glow of sunlight, nor when she strained to hear, could she detect any movement above. There was just silence – a heavy, crushing silence.

None of this made any sense. So far her abductor had been punctual, turning up in the morning to give them their breakfast and empty their bucket, repeating the same routine every evening. He seemed totally in control – unhurried and calm or gleeful and malevolent, as the mood took him. There seemed no imminent danger, no tension in the air, no sense of any outside forces closing in on him. He was serene, powerful, the all-conquering god of their dark universe.

So where was he this morning? Naomi was able to mark the passing of time now, waking the moment the first glimpse of sunlight crept underneath the door and remaining awake long after dark. She knew now that an hour or two after she woke, their captor would appear, to chill their souls, but also offer some relief from the gnawing hunger that gripped them both from morning until night. Today, however, there was no sign of him.

Initially, she'd reasoned that he must simply have got delayed – traffic or some other minor inconvenience. But as the minutes, then hours passed, Naomi changed the narrative, imagining some more intractable issue – police attention, a problem at work, suspicions from a family member – that he would nevertheless circumvent with time and effort. Naomi was still clinging to this explanation, but as the strength of the sunlight increased, as dawn became morning, she was steadily assailed by doubts. What could have happened to him today of all days? Why, when they needed him most, had he suddenly vanished?

Straightening up, Naomi turned to peer through the gentle gloom, picking out Mia's prone form. She was worse than ever this morning. The night had brought her no respite, her agonized cough wracking her emaciated frame, even as her head pounded fit to burst, her friend gripped by a raging fever. Naomi had spent half the night blowing on her new friend's face, trying to stem the streaks of sweat that crept down her grimy features, to quell her agony, but the air down here was so close that her efforts were doomed. Still she refused to leave her side, however, Mia seeming to take some comfort from clutching Naomi's hand, squeezing it hard to alleviate her own suffering by visiting it on her nursemaid. Naomi's bruised fingers throbbed this morning, but it had been worth it, if only to let her ailing friend know that she was not alone.

Eventually, just before dawn, sleep had finally claimed Mia, Naomi watching on as her eyes drooped. At first, Naomi had continued to hold her hand, fearful of waking her if she moved, but eventually she'd untangled her fingers and moved away, exhausted beyond measure. Sleep had claimed her briefly then, but Naomi awoke soon after, disoriented and confused, as light penetrated their sanctum, unwelcome and unwanted. Since then, she'd been creeping back and forth to the margins of their cage, hoping to welcome his presence, his curt greeting, their cloying breakfast, but even these 'delights' were denied her today.

Suddenly, a noise behind made her turn. A familiar, distressing sound, as Mia wheezed back into consciousness, her body starting violently, before she broke into a bitter, relentless coughing fit. Each desperate hack, each agonized gasp, cut right through Naomi, rattling her nerves and aggravating her fear. Nevertheless, she was quick to slide across the floor to her fallen friend, gripping her outstretched hand, whilst stroking her fevered forehead. All the while, however, her anxiety continued to mount. What would happen if he didn't return? How could she help Mia? She wanted to give her some water, to pour some cooling balm on her face, but their supplies had long since run out, leaving them helpless and desperate. Naomi clutched Mia's hand tightly, fighting back tears, but she couldn't stem the rising panic slowly taking hold of her.

Where the hell was he?

Chapter 47

She bided her time, waiting for the right moment to pounce. Helen had carefully tailed her target from the family home to the gym, then to the post office, at each turn weighing up the value of revealing her hand by descending upon her, warrant card in hand. But on each occasion, she'd held off, knowing that it'd be better to swoop when she was closer to home.

Lowering her speed, Helen watched intently as the shiny BMW X5 pulled off the road, parking up on the neat drive. As the sound of her engine died away, Helen brought her Kawasaki to an abrupt halt, sliding off it in one fluid movement. Now she was on the march, cresting the drive, just as Jackie Reynolds climbed out of the family car, clutching a large gym bag. Sensing Helen's presence, she turned quickly to face the intruder, startled.

'Can I help you?' she demanded, her voice brisk but shrill.

In response, Helen flipped open her warrant card.

'Are you aware that your rear right brake light isn't working?'

For a moment, Jackie looked totally dumbfounded, as if Helen's words didn't make sense, but then she recovered herself.

'No, I wasn't. We only had them replaced recently and I'm sure they were working at the weekend...'

'Well, they're not now,' Helen replied gravely. 'As you know, that's against the law, so I'm afraid I'm going to have to write you a fixed charge penalty notice.'

Once more, Jackie stared at Helen, as if she was speaking some kind of alien language, the startled wife and mother perplexed to have been put on the spot like this. Clutching her shopping to her chest, she eventually found her voice, protesting:

'Look, I don't suppose there's any way we could let this go, is there? First offence and all that. I promise I'll get it fixed this afternoon.'

'I can't make any exceptions, I'm afraid. Rules are rules. So, would you like me to write up the ticket here or...?'

Immediately, Jackie Reynolds' gaze flitted over Helen's shoulder, clocking the neighbours across the road who appeared to be taking an unhealthy interest in their conversation. Flustered, embarrassed, Jackie's response was swift and decisive:

'Why don't we step inside?'

Placing her helmet gently on the kitchen island, Helen cast her eye over the Reynolds' well-appointed interior. The facade of the house was nothing special, all the houses in this neighborhood looking alike, but real effort had gone into the fixtures and fittings. The surfaces were granite, the colour scheme bold and modern, the expansive sofas plush and inviting. A huge plasma screen graced the far wall, Helen counting at least six surrounding speakers, and there were signs of affluence everywhere, be it in the prominently displayed wine fridge in the kitchen or the fresh flowers that seemed to grace every surface. Jackie Reynolds herself was equally well turned out, a powerful, statuesque women clad in immaculate gym gear, yet Helen couldn't help but clock a weary anxiety in her hostess's handsome, honed features, as she rootled nervously for something in her handbag.

'Someone's birthday, is it?' Helen offered genially, her eye falling on the brightly coloured envelopes propped up on the kitchen island, unopened.

Jackie looked up from her bag, following Helen's gaze.

'Yes, my husband. Normally we would have opened them together this morning, but he had to shoot off early. You probably know him. Dave Reynolds? He's based out of Southampton Central...'

'Sure, I know Dave,' Helen said, smiling warmly. 'Everybody does. What was the emergency this morning?'

'Oh, I don't know,' Jackie replied, resuming her rummaging. 'I never really ask him about this work. Don't want to know, if I'm honest, the stuff he has to deal with...'

Jackie smiled at Helen, but still appeared stressed and ill at ease. Pulling out a compact and a packet of mints, she finally located her purse.

'So how much do I owe y—'

'Must be hard being married to a copper,' Helen said, moving away from the counter and crossing the large, open-plan living room. 'Unpredictable hours, lots of night work. Must be difficult to live a normal, family life I suppose.'

'We've got used to it over the years. If he's here, he's here. We can't rely on it, so we just crack on as best we can. You married?'

'Not yet,' Helen replied, suppressing a smile. 'So Dave's never been tempted by a more nine-to-five job? I know he's been put forward for promotion on several occasions.'

'He won't have it,' Jackie replied ruefully, shaking her head. 'Says he likes to be out on the street, where he can make a difference.'

Digesting this, Helen crossed to the mantelpiece, taking in the framed photos, many of a young boy-now-teen with curly blond hair and a winning smile.

'This your son?'

'Archie,' Jackie replied uncertainly, as if unnerved by Helen's pleasant tone, by their extended conversation. 'He's doing his GCSEs at the moment.'

'Poor kid. Is he going to follow in his father's footsteps, do you think? Join the Force?'

Helen had turned to face Jackie Reynolds and she clocked it instantly, the middle-aged mum blinking in surprise as if the question was preposterous, even unwanted.

'No, Archie... Archie's got different interests to his dad. I'm not sure the police is for him.'

'More like you, is he?'

'Something like that.'

There was a hint of impatience, even irritation in her voice now. Jackie was clearly unnerved by the strange turn of events this morning and keen to wrap this conversation up as soon as possible, as if fearful of detection. Whether this was natural timidity or simply fear of Reynolds, Helen couldn't be certain.

'Still, it certainly hasn't done Dave any harm. You've got a lovely home here, not to mention that spanking new BMW. He must be doing all right for himself. Unless you're the breadwinner, of course?'

'Oh no, nothing like that. I've got enough to do keeping house and home together, but speaking of cash, how much do you need? For the fine, I mean.'

Tugging her pad from her pocket, Helen flipped to the correct sheet, filling in the details as she replied:

'Well, it's a standard £80 fine, but obviously you only pay half if you settle it within fourteen days.'

She tore off the ticket, handing it to Jackie.

'The details of how to pay are on the back, just there...'

Helen indicated details of the payment website, but her companion seemed little interested in the text.

'I was wondering if I could pay now?' she offered tentatively, holding up her purse.

'Well, we're not really allowed to accept cash.'

'Sure, but you can be trusted, right? You're not going to run off with it. Honestly, it would be much easier for me if I could just pay this now. I've got a ton of things to do today…'

Jackie seemed oddly insistent, determined even, but Helen could see the anxiety that lay beneath this desire to draw a discreet veil over her infraction. Something was worrying her.

'I suppose I *could* make an exception,' Helen replied carefully. 'No need for anyone else to be involved.'

'Exactly,' Jackie agreed gratefully. 'Honestly, I'd never hear the end of it from Dave. He thinks I'm a liability on the roads as it is…'

Smiling, Helen handed her the ticket.

'Then we'll keep this between ourselves, eh?'

'That would be perfect, thank you.'

Relieved, Jackie Reynolds unzipped her purse, revealing a thick roll of £20 notes inside. Extracting two, she handed them over to Helen.

'Thanks again for your understanding…'

She was about to add Helen's name, before realizing she didn't know what it was.

'Sorry, I've forgotten your name. I did see it on your ID, but didn't really take it in…'

'Helen Grace,' she responded confidently. 'DI Helen Grace.'

'Well, very nice to meet you, Helen, and sorry again for the broken light.'

She was ushering her guest to the door, clearly keen to be rid of her. Helen was happy to be shepherded away – she'd got what she came for – but paused now on the threshold to take in the scene one last time. Her visit had been useful and instructive, setting Jackie Reynolds on edge, whilst posing several intriguing questions. How was Reynolds so well off on a copper's wage? What was the nature of Dave Reynolds' relationship with his only child?

And why did Jackie Reynolds seem so scared?

Chapter 48

The atmosphere was hushed and tense. Fighting off the tired-ness that threatened to overwhelm her, Charlie stared straight ahead, her eyes scanning the horizon, ignoring the truculent presence next to her. Perhaps it was foolish to insist that Jennings accompany her once again this morning, knowing how mistrustful he was of the whole enterprise, how little faith he had in her personally. Yet he had been part of the team that had lost their prime suspect and she was damned if she was going to reward her graceless colleague by liberating him to return to the Freemantle shooting. He was stuck with her now.

Jennings remained hunched in the passenger seat, his body angled away from her, his eyes glued to the street. He would insist he was just being diligent, searching for the fugitive, but Charlie knew he was sulking, determined to make their time together as uncomfortable as possible. Charlie tried to ignore him, as he was ultimately harming no one but himself, yet as the minutes crawled by without incident, Charlie felt her irritation growing. It was one thing to be stuck with a truculent col-league, it was another thing to be locked together in a fruitless endeavour.

They had been searching for Ryan Marwood since first light, one of four crews currently scouring the streets for the missing fugitive. At first, Charlie had been terrified that Marwood had fled the family home in order to offend once more, but the discovery late last night of his abandoned Renault Movano van in thick woodland near the city pound suggested to her that he was now intent on escape, putting as much distance between himself and his past offending as possible. This was an equally alarming prospect. If he made it beyond their jurisdiction, there was no telling how long it might take to bring Marwood to justice. The imperative now was to find him – and fast.

Frustrated, Charlie snatched up the radio, finally breaking the silence.

'DC Reid, come in, over?'

'Hearing you loud and clear, over,' came the disembodied reply.

'Any sign of movement at the Marwood home?' Charlie continued, more in hope than expectation.

'Nothing doing. Got people in the house, in the garden, out front. He won't be coming back here if he knows what's good for him, over.'

Signing off, Charlie swiftly contacted the other teams, who were positioned at the train station and ferry ports, but they too had nothing to report. What was Marwood up to? What was his plan? He was high and dry, with little in the way of resources or allies, even his own mother having now turned against him. Would he hunker down, try to disappear from view, until the manhunt eased? Or would he make a break for it today, *now*?

Charlie strongly suspected the latter. Southampton was an unforgiving city and he could certainly not count on a warm welcome amongst its growing homeless population or its criminal underbelly. In those communities, well-known offenders, those who might attract a heavy police presence, were shunned. Once word got out that the police were seeking him, with beat officers combing the streets, life would get even harder for Marwood, any sharp-eyed rogue worth his salt appreciating the potential for gain by betraying him to the authorities. No, if he was smart, Ryan Marwood would get out of town as fast as he could.

Travelling by conventional means would lay him open to arrest, so surely he would try to sneak away from the city, unseen and unheralded? He could hitch his way out along one of the main arteries, hence why they'd doubled traffic patrols on the major roads. He could jump aboard one of the many freight trains that passed through the city, which was why CID had been deployed to various sites along the line. Or he could use the ports, either to hop on board a ship bound for sunnier climes or to secrete himself on a cargo lorry heading to London. DC McAndrew was currently portside with a couple of colleagues, leaving Charlie and Jennings as the sole remaining members of the unit driving the lonely back streets that flanked the Western Docks.

Theory was one thing, however, reality something else entirely. It was already pushing eleven o'clock; they'd been driving the city streets for over four hours now and the only excitement they'd seen so far was a seagull stealing a hipster's breakfast burrito. Jennings had enjoyed that – he was not part of the woke generation, enjoying any misfortune that befell a bloke with a top knot – but the amusement value of this was long since exhausted, her colleague looking as grumpy and hopeless as Charlie.

'We'll give it another thirty minutes. If he hasn't shown himself by then, we'll head back to base, review our strategy.'

Jennings nodded slowly but said nothing, as if even that modest movement was too much trouble for him. Shaking her head, Charlie resumed her task, keeping a close eye on the pedestrians making their way to and from the docks. But the human traffic seemed utterly unremarkable – a vaping dockworker, a hooded low-life, a *Big Issue* seller, a couple of sex workers making their way home.

'There!'

The word exploded from Jennings' mouth, making Charlie jump. Slowing the car instantly, she turned to her colleague.

'What?'

'The guy in the dark trackies, the hoodie. I'm sure that's what Marwood was wearing last night.'

Bringing the car to a halt, Charlie stared at the retreating figure in the rearview. She had dismissed the figure as a druggie heading home after a wild night, but now, as she watched his progress, she noted how fast the hooded figure was travelling and how he kept darting furtive looks around him.

'Got to be worth a look…' she muttered, swinging the car round in one fluid move.

They glided along the street towards the retreating figure. He had a head start on them, but they soon made up the distance, shadowing his progress on the opposite side of the street. The figure paid them no heed, however, keeping his eyes to the floor, marching onward.

'Give the siren a blast, see what he does…'

Without hesitation, Jennings obliged, giving a short, sharp burst. The sound bounced off the dock's brick perimeter, startling everyone present. But no one looked up more sharply than the figure in the blue tracksuit, turning his face to the offending vehicle. Immediately, Charlie clocked his haunted expression, his anguished alarm, those familiar features.

It was Ryan Marwood.

Chapter 49

Helen marched towards her bike, keeping half an eye on the house behind her. Only once she was sure she was no longer in sight of the Reynolds home did she pull the brake light from her pocket, tossing it into a nearby bin. She had removed it whilst Jackie Reynolds visited the gym, but in the end this had proved an unnecessary precaution. Faced with a police badge and the prospect of public embarrassment, Jackie Reynolds had folded quickly, inviting Helen inside.

Satisfied with her morning's work, Helen climbed back onto her Kawasaki, ready to race back to Southampton Central. But as she did so, her radio squawked into life. Immediately, she recognized Charlie's breathless tones.

'Suspect spotted heading east on Millbrook Road West. Repeat, Ryan Marwood spotted on Millbrook Road West. Officers Brooks and Jennings in pursuit.'

Suddenly all thoughts of returning to base evaporated. Firing up the engine, Helen roared away down the quiet suburban street, determined to be in on the chase.

Racing through the city with the blues and twos blaring was an exhilarating experience, but nothing beat riding on two wheels, dancing in and out of the city's heavy traffic as if it wasn't there. Normally it would take ten minutes or more to get from Bitterne Park to the Western Docks, but Helen managed it in four, keeping her speed assertive and steady. Now that they had Marwood in their sights, there was no question of letting him escape again.

Swinging past an articulated lorry, Helen sped along Millbrook Road, heading swiftly in a westerly direction. She could already hear the sound of sirens up ahead, knew she was getting close and readied herself for action, her eyes sweeping the road, searching for their prize. A flash of blue in the middle distance as Charlie's pool car finally came into view and then she saw him, a shadowy figure in dark blue, sprinting along the pavement. She could instantly see what his plan was. Coming up fast on his left was a residential cul-de-sac, with bollards at the top to stop vans and trucks using it as a cut-through. If Marwood could make it there, he would at least force Charlie and Jennings to abandon their car, wiping out their advantage in a stroke.

There was no way Helen could allow that, so cutting across her lane, she mounted the central reservation. Instantly she was thrown forward in her seat, as rubber connected with concrete, but gripping the fuel tank with her knees, she managed to stay aboard her ride, the bike landing safely on the other side. Now the danger doubled as she was riding against the oncoming traffic, a huge truck blaring out its horn as it roared towards her. For a second, it seemed as though a savage impact was inevitable, but as Helen ripped back the throttle, the bike leapt forward, narrowly missing the oncoming truck before mounting the pavement beyond. Now Helen jammed on the brakes, the bike bucking to a violent stop just in front of the brightly painted bollards.

Killing the engine, Helen dismounted. She was at the mouth of the cul-de-sac and looking up, she noticed that a stunned Ryan Marwood had skidded to a halt not twenty yards from her, his escape plans now in tatters. Terrified, he turned on his heel, but as he did so, Charlie pulled her car off the road behind him, blocking the pavement, cutting off his retreat.

'Come on, Ryan, let's do this the easy way...'

Helen was already advancing down the street towards him, her helmet off, warrant card in hand. But the fugitive had no intention of complying, looking around desperately for any means of escape. His options were running out, however. Helen was bearing down on him from the front, Charlie and Jennings from the rear and, unless he wanted to run into the moving traffic, that left him with only one option. Realizing this, Marwood darted left into the Maltings Business Park, scurrying as fast as he could towards the clutch of industrial buildings that loomed over the Western Docks.

Dropping her helmet, Helen raced after him, confident that this was a fight Marwood couldn't win. He was young but in poor physical shape. Surely a lengthy pursuit would only end one way? As if reading her thoughts, Marwood suddenly changed direction, cutting sharp right, momentarily throwing Helen off course. She'd assumed he'd try to cut through the industrial estate, which connected to residential streets on the other side, but realizing that he wouldn't make it that far, the fugitive diverted towards the concrete husk of an office block close by, which was only partway through construction. Burly builders in hard hats and hi-vis jackets looked up bewildered as Marwood sprinted onto the site, careering towards the heart of the construction.

'Hey, no members of the public allowed—'

The startled foreman didn't get any further, the desperate Marwood cannoning into him, sending him sprawling backwards. Bouncing off him, the fugitive raced on, but the collision had cost him valuable seconds and Helen raced forwards, zeroing in for the kill. Marwood stumbled into the shell of the building with his pursuer now only seconds behind. Spying a rough concrete staircase ahead, he lurched towards it, Helen having to change direction sharply to keep pace with him. Marwood had reached the foot of the steps, which were surrounded by various bits of building detritus, but she was hot on his heels now. Lunging forward, Helen grasped at his hoodie, determined to bring him down. But just as she made contact with him, gripping the heavy cotton, Marwood span round, aiming something at her head. Helen only had a second to react, ducking swiftly as the metal pole whistled over her head. The scaffolding offcut fell from her attacker's grasp and Helen took full advantage, springing up and knocking Marwood backwards. As she did so, however, his elbow swung sharply down, catching Helen on the temple. The impact was crisp and clean, sending her tumbling back onto the floor. For a second, the world seemed to spin, Helen prone on her hands and knees, utterly at the mercy of her assailant. She half expected a second, decisive blow, but when she looked up, Helen saw that Marwood had chosen flight over fight, scuttling away up the half-finished staircase. Hauling herself back onto her feet, Helen took a moment to steady herself, then set off in pursuit.

It was reckless, dangerous, insane. The concrete steps, which formed an emergency stairwell that crisscrossed back and forth on the vertiginous left wall, were not yet completed. It reached all the way to the top of the building, but had no banisters, no rails, nothing to stop you plunging off the side. Already, worried builders were calling up after them, imploring both Marwood and Helen to come down, to realize the terrible danger they were in, but the fugitive paid no heed to their cries, nor did Helen, tearing up the steps after him. It seemed highly improbable that there was any other way off this concrete shell, but if there was one, Helen was sure Marwood would find it, hence her desperate pursuit.

As she scrambled up the rough, uneven stairs, Helen was surprised to see that her quarry had already opened up a significant lead over her. Alarmed, she redoubled her efforts, bounding up the steps two at a time. Slowly she was narrowing the gap between them, but they were climbing ever higher, the figures beneath them growing smaller all the time. Helen had a head for heights, but still the dizzying drop off the side of the rough-hewn steps made her stomach lurch. She had to balance speed with caution if she was to avoid paying her a heavy price for her impetuousness.

Up, up, up they raced. Helen was struggling to breathe, the unremitting upward sprint taking its toll on her body, whilst fear slowly assailed her brain. She could already foresee what lay ahead – a death-defying tussle on top of a thirty-storey building – and who could say she would prevail this time? Was this really how she wanted to die, the victim of a multiple rapist, who would surely kill her as soon as look at her? Yet what was the alternative? They needed Marwood in custody, they needed him to talk. If he *was* responsible for Naomi Watson's abduction, then only he could lead them to her.

The sunlight above was growing stronger, only a couple of flights of stairs separating them from the half-constructed roof. Still Helen kept up her pace, giving Marwood no quarter, no encouragement, and moments later they emerged onto the summit.

She was only seconds behind him now, but even as she reached out to grab him, Helen felt herself knocked backwards, a savage blast of wind ripping over her, as she finally broke cover. For a moment, Helen was unable to stop herself, staggering back towards the outer edge of the roof, but at the last minute she righted herself, throwing her weight forward in a desperate attempt to save her skin. To her surprise, Marwood was already on the move, edging along the thin, wooden planks that provided the only route across this terrifying abyss. It was a crazy stunt, the dusty concrete floor barely visible below, the scurrying workers now mere ants, but desperation drove him on.

'Please, Ryan. It's too dangerous...'

Her words drifted away in the wind, the fugitive intent on escape. But where could he go? There was no staircase on the other side of the building, no way down, so what was he hoping to do? Balance on the edge and hope Helen wasn't brave enough to follow? Negotiate from that desperate position? What could he possibly hope to gain?

Another heavy gust of wind swept over them, unbalancing Marwood, whose arms cartwheeled wildly.

'Ryan!' Helen screamed, taking a step onto the narrow plank.

Still Marwood waved his arms frantically, but regaining his balance, he stumbled on, finally reaching the other side of the building. Alighting onto the perilously narrow concrete lip, he turned to face her once more.

'Please, Ryan, this is the end of the road. There's nowhere to go.'

He looked around, hopelessly searching for some means of escape, but he knew she was telling the truth. He was trapped.

'Let's get you down safely and then we can talk.'

But already he was shaking his head. Marwood was white as a sheet, his body limp, his wild eyes wet with tears.

'I know you're hurting, I know you're in a bad place, but I can help you.'

Another savage shake of the head. Holding out her hand, Helen took a step onto the plank.

'Stay where you are!' the fugitive barked.

Immediately, Helen arrested her progress. But she kept her hand outstretched.

'I mean it, Ryan. I want to help you. So please do the right thing. Think of yourself, think of your mother, come back down with me now.'

'If I come back down, they'll send me back. I know they will.'

'Not if you co-operate,' Helen returned quickly. 'Not if you help us make things right.'

'You know the rules,' Marwood replied scornfully. 'I've violated my probation – they'll have no choice but to bang me up.'

'I'll talk to them, explain that these are exceptional circumstances.'

'And once I'm inside, they'll finish the job,' Marwood insisted, as if he hadn't heard Helen's reply at all. 'They'll finish the job, slowly and painfully...'

'Look, if you're worried about your safety, we can make special arrangements. If you do go back to prison, we can separate you from the others...'

'And go quietly mad in solitary? No, thanks.'

He glanced around him, peering over the edge of the building. Feeling a spike of alarm, Helen stepped forward.

'You're getting ahead of yourself, Ryan,' she continued, inching forwards. 'None of this needs to happen if you do the right thing now.'

But the ex-offender simply shook his head.

'No, I had my chance. And I messed it up. Tell my Mum I'm sorry.'

As he turned, Helen raced forwards. Careless of her own safety, she lunged towards him, her hand outstretched. But she was a second too late, Marwood hopping off the side of the building, leaving Helen clutching fresh air. She crashed onto the plank, gripping it fiercely to avoid sliding off, and she was still hanging onto it for dear life seconds later, when she heard the sickening sound of the impact below.

Chapter 50

Cradling her head, Naomi wiped the sweat from Mia's brow. Her cough was worse than ever now, her fever raging.

'Water, I need some water…'

The word tumbled from Mia's cracked lips. Immediately, Naomi felt her stomach tighten, glancing at the two empty bottles that lay beside them. Desperate, she picked up the nearest one and, squeezing it with all her might, shook it back and forth. A tiny droplet of vapour emerged from the mouth of the bottle, but it was too inconsequential to trouble gravity, drifting away into the ether before it could make contact with Mia's lips. This failure seemed to taunt the stricken teen, whose eyes now filled with tears.

'What shall we talk about?'

Naomi's voice was high-pitched and tight. She was all at sea, but knew that somehow she had to keep Mia distracted.

'I know,' she continued quickly. 'Why don't you tell me more about you? I've told you about my situation, my mum, the billion mistakes I've made. Why don't you tell me more about you?'

For a moment, Naomi thought her fellow captive had mis-understood the question, Mia looking confused and uncertain, but then a look of profound sadness gripped her. Naomi didn't want to upset her friend, but at least it was a reaction, signs of life.

'Not much to tell,' she eventually croaked.

'I'm sure there is,' Naomi encouraged. 'You've told me about your time on the streets. But what about before that? Did you have a mum? A dad? Siblings?'

Again, Mia looked downcast, but eventually she responded:

'Mum left when I was four, ran off with another guy. Dad ... Dad sort of fell apart after that. He did what he could ... but he was always drinking, trying to blot out his shame, his loneliness. I had to bring up myself and my little brother, had to get clothes and food. I used the food bank but I still needed money for the gas and electric. I did the best I could, a bit of thieving, bit of shoplifting. Council soon got on to us, wanted to take us into care, so me and Freddie ran away from home. Lived by our wits for a few weeks, but they caught up with us in the end. Still, they were fun times, just me and my kid brother, doing what we wanted, when we wanted ...'

'Tell me about him,' Naomi said quickly, desperate to find something positive to talk about.

And now that magical smile once more graced Mia's ravaged features.

'Freddie was the dead spit of me,' she breathed, beaming at the memory. 'But twice as naughty. When we were in care, I took endless hidings for him, but I didn't care. He was a great kid and he loved me, *really* loved me ...'

Tears sparkled in her red-rimmed eyes now, the memories bittersweet.

'We got tattoos done when I was twelve and he was ten. The social workers didn't like that, but we didn't care. Showed we were part of the same team, together forever. Of course that didn't last and they split us up. They should never have done that...'

Now in her emotion, Mia began to cough again, angrily, violently. Pulling her towards her, Naomi embraced her patient, keeping her fully vertical until the hacking stopped.

'So he's still out there? Freddie, I mean?'

'I guess so,' Mia whispered. 'I haven't seen him in years.'

'Then live for him,' Naomi insisted. 'Stay strong for him.'

Lowering Mia back to the ground, Naomi stared directly into her eyes, stroking her cheek.

'He's still out there, he still loves you, and once we get out, we'll find him. I swear on my life we will track him down and you will be together again. Maybe you can get some more tattoos done?'

Mia smiled happily, then closed her eyes once more, seeking peace. This time Naomi left her unmolested, happy that the coughing had subsided, that her breathing was regular. It had been a troubling few hours and though Mia's equilibrium had been restored, Naomi knew the respite would be brief. Mia's strength was waning, her resolve fading. Their captor's absence was inexplicable and if he didn't arrive soon, Naomi felt sure it would be too late.

'Please stay with me,' she whispered gently, her voice shaking as distress mastered her. 'Don't leave me down here by myself.'

She hadn't meant to say this, hadn't meant to lay this on Mia, but she couldn't help herself. Suddenly Naomi saw with awful clarity that if Mia died down here, if she *did* finally give up her desperate struggle to survive, then Naomi would be left without a friend in the world.

Chapter 51

She was like an island in the midst of a swirling storm, the still centre amidst the frenetic activity around her. Lorraine Marwood sat mute on the sofa, staring blankly at an untouched cup of tea. She had resisted all attempts to move her, to seek sanctuary with a friend or relative, instead cleaving close to the family home, as if abandoning it would somehow be tantamount to abandoning Ryan. Helen didn't pretend to understand her emotions – there were no photos of Ryan in the house, suggesting she felt some shame about his appalling crimes – and yet it was hard not to feel sorry for the woman who'd loved too much and been repaid with betrayal, misery and now death.

To her surprise, Lorraine Marwood now looked up, her eyes seeking out the detective inspector. There was deep sadness in her expression, aching grief too, but was there something else there too? An accusation? So far, Lorraine had only been given the bare details, that her son had resisted arrest, been involved in a chase and fallen to his death, with no concrete information about how it had happened or who was involved. So why did her gaze seek out Helen specifically? Was it to locate her son's killer and shame her? To lay the blame at her door for his untimely death?

Nodding curtly at her, Helen took her leave, stepping out

into the hallway. There was nothing Lorraine Marwood could do that would make Helen feel any worse. Ryan had been a deeply troubled individual, who had brought most of the misery he'd endured upon himself, but the death of any young man was always deeply upsetting, especially when played out in such a catastrophic and destructive way. Helen felt this all the more keenly as Ryan's terrible end had robbed her of the chance to question him, to get to the bottom of his recent offending, to find out if he was truly responsible for Naomi's disappearance. All the evidence pointed in that direction, but how could Helen know, how could she be sure, without looking him in the eye?

Climbing the stairs, Helen felt her frustration mounting. Part of her wanted to be wrong, wanted Naomi's real abductor to be still at large, so she could capture him, wringing the missing girl's location from him in fierce interrogation. But another part of her wanted Marwood confirmed as her captor, taking a dangerous offender off the streets and perhaps ultimately leading to Naomi's rescue, if they could track his recent move-ments. But in her heart of hearts, Helen feared an unsatisfactory middle ground, all the circumstantial evidence pointing towards Marwood's guilt, with no actual evidence of his crime, nor any clear lead to Naomi's whereabouts. In these circumstances, Marwood's death and the potential closing of the investigation would prove a pyrrhic victory.

Helen climbed higher, her mood descending with each step, but as she mounted the upstairs landing, a cry suddenly rang out.

'Here!'

Immediately, Helen was on the move, hurrying into Ryan's bedroom to find a suited forensics officer standing by the dead man's bed, a triumphant smile on his face. The room had already been turned upside down, the cramped space packed with bodies, but the anonymous figure by the bed now held out his hand.

'Found it hidden in his pillow,' he murmured, his tone respectful, despite his excitement.

Stepping forward, Helen's heart skipped a beat as she saw the yellow metal glinting up at her. Nestled in her colleague's hand was a gold necklace with a pendant attached that spelled out the name NAOMI. The same necklace Naomi Watson had been wearing the night that she was abducted.

Chapter 52

Helen marched swiftly away from the Marwood residence, ignoring the scattering of uniformed officers and the growing crowd of bystanders. Her emotions were in tumult, her mind a blur of conflicting thoughts, and she needed to get back to base to try and process the morning's shocking events. As she neared her Kawasaki, however, she saw someone making a beeline for her, intent on cutting her off before she could escape. Slowing her stride, she turned to see PC Dave Reynolds approaching.

'Just been manning the barricades,' he offered genially, nodding towards the police tape that was keeping the press and neighbours at bay. 'But I couldn't let you go without offering my congratulations.'

Helen starred at Reynolds, taken aback. He was either completely innocent or the most brazen liar she'd ever met.

'I know we've had our differences, but I appreciate you were only doing your job. And what a job you've done! So, no hard feelings, eh?'

He offered his hand to her, a warm act of generosity. Aware that other officers were watching, Helen had no choice but to respond with a cursory shake. To her surprise, however, Reynolds clung fast to her hand, refusing to let it go.

'Say what they like about you, DI Grace,' he continued, smiling broadly. 'You always get your man.'

His eyes were locked onto hers now, their naked hostility belying the warmth of his smile. It was instantly clear that all professions of goodwill were paper-thin, that he hated Helen as much now as he had done last night. This was a challenge, a way of letting Helen know that nothing was forgotten, nor forgiven, and it was not a challenge she was minded to duck. So instead of pulling her hand away, Helen increased the pressure herself, her long fingers seeking out Reynolds' recent bite injury and pressing down hard on it. She was pleased to see a jerk of pain, a flash of anger, before the PC suddenly tugged his hand free.

'The feeling's mutual, PC Reynolds,' Helen responded, smiling coldly. 'It's been an honour working with you.'

Aware that others were watching, Reynolds didn't respond, instead nodding politely and heading back to his duties. Helen watched him go, unnerved, more convinced than ever that there was something malign, something unseen, about PC Dave Reynolds. Turning, she walked back to her bike, deep in thought, changing course only at the very last moment to divert to DC Wilson, who was standing by the police tape, watching the circus unfold.

'DC Wilson, a word...?'

He hurried over to her. Tugging her purse from her jacket, Helen retrieved the two £20 notes Jackie Reynolds had given her, using her gloved fingers to extract them and drop them into an evidence bag.

'Get these to Meredith ASAP, will you? Ask her to look for traces of drugs, fingerprints of known felons, anything remotely criminal, OK?'

'And this is?' her colleague enquired, intrigued.

'Quick as you can please.'

Taking the hint, Wilson hurried off to the car. Helen loitered by her bike, lost in her own reflections. Was she right to pursue this line of enquiry? Was PC Reynolds really worthy of her special attention? Or had she lost her bearings completely?

Had her instincts been wrong all along?

Chapter 53

'I just wanted to offer my heartfelt congratulations to the team on the swift and decisive resolution to the case.'

Charlie stared at Chief Superintendent Rebecca Holmes, clamping down her rising anger. Clearly, she was alone in feeling this, as the rest of the unit were in party mood, and Holmes seemed determined to join in, appearing in the incident room as if by magic, bestowing smiles and handshakes on all and sundry.

'Obviously, there is work still to be done,' the station chief continued brightly. 'Finding Naomi Watson remains our top priority, as far as this case is concerned at least, and a forensic analysis of Ryan Marwood's movements over the past few days is required. But I'm confident that with careful, methodical detective work, we can find our girl and bring her home safe.'

Unbelievably, a couple of the team broke into a round of applause, one of them even whooping. Holmes took the acclaim graciously, before continuing:

'Anyway, I wanted to add my thanks to those of the police commissioner for your diligent work on this case. Although we'd obviously have preferred to have Marwood in custody, a dangerous predator has been removed from the streets, for which we can all be thankful.'

Charlie eyed Holmes carefully. Was that a tacit dig at Helen?

Despite the fact that she had risked her own life to try and bring him in? It was impossible to say, but her superior wasn't finished yet.

'Credit must also go to DC Jennings. Without his dogged determination and eagle-eyed vigilance, Ryan Marwood might have slipped the net. The women, the citizens of this city, owe him a real debt of gratitude.'

Another round of applause broke out, louder this time, accompanied by many pats on the back. Charlie was virtually choking on her fury now – Jennings had done little, and was the death of a suspect really a cause for celebration? – waiting for Holmes to bestow a few words of thanks on her. She had her best fake smile ready and was prepared to accept the praise with grace, but to her surprise and astonishment, Holmes now changed tack.

'Anyway, that's all I wanted to say. When DI Grace reappears, I'm sure she'll apportion individual tasks to you. Obviously Naomi Watson is a priority, especially given the attention her disappearance has provoked, but I'm hopeful now that we can make progress on the Freemantle shooting too, so that we can really show the breadth of our operation.'

Charlie was already on her way to the door. She knew her abrupt departure would be remarked upon, but she was not prepared to be humiliated in front of the team. She was a vital part of the leadership team, reliant on the unit's respect and loyalty in order to be able to do her job, and Holmes' calculated snub seemed designed to undermine her. Well, she wasn't going to sit quietly and take that kind of insult, she was too long in the tooth for that.

Pushing angrily out the door, Charlie emerged into the long corridor beyond, heading fast for the lift bank. She needed some fresh air, some time to think, to gather herself in order to avoid a very public, very damaging explosion of anger. Hammering the button, she paced back and forth, awaiting release, but as she did so, she heard footsteps approaching. Fearing the worst, she looked up sharply, her face set in angry hostility, but her expression softened when she saw PC Beth Beamer approaching.

'Sorry to disturb you, DS Brooks,' the young probationer said tentatively, instantly clocking her dark mood. 'But I thought you ought to know that I've just brought Brent Mason in. DI Grace said you were keen to have a word with him?'

Instantly, Charlie felt her mood lighten and she smiled as she replied, 'Let DI Grace know straightaway please. And tell her I'll join her in the interrogation suite.'

Charlie was already on the move, entering the lift and pressing the button for the first floor. Frustrated, angry, she now had an outlet for her simmering emotions: an unwitting, pliant victim waiting for her downstairs. And she intended to make the most of it.

Chapter 54

He stared at them, dead-eyed and hostile, defiance etched in his sullen features.

'If you've pulled me in about the Freemantle shooting, you're barking up the wrong tree. I don't know nothing about that.'

Brent Mason scratched at his stubble, staring assertively at the two women opposite him. Charlie could have laughed out loud, his 'attack is the best form of defence' strategy woefully misguided. Shooting a look at Helen, she turned back to Mason.

'But you do run with the Main Street crew, right? Dealing, picking up money, making drops...'

'Never, not once,' the dealer spat back, defiant.

'Brent, you had a very healthy quantity of cocaine on you when you were picked up earlier, all in neat little bags.'

'Not mine. I wouldn't touch that kind of shit.'

Mason was scowling at Charlie, openly defiant, so Helen stepped in now, keen to put him at his ease.

'The good news, Brent, is that you're not here to talk about that *or* about the Freemantle incident.'

Nodding slowly, Mason sat back slowly in his chair, relief mingling with suspicion. His eyes remained on Helen, so she continued.

'I understand that you ran into one of our officers three nights ago in the Lordship Road underpass. The same officer who felt your collar this morning, in fact,' Helen continued briskly. 'Ring any bells?'

'You'll have to remind me?'

'PC Beth Beamer spoke to you just after 9 p.m. on Thursday, the ninth of November. She suspected that you were in possession of Class C drugs, potentially with intent to supply, so she patted you down.'

Mason was about to protest, so Helen nipped in first.

'Brent, we've got the whole encounter on film, thanks to her bodycam. The conversation, your face, the date and time *and* the baggies she retrieved from your green North Face puffa, so please, can we cut the crap?'

Once again, the dealer looked taken aback, surprised by the level of detail in her accusation, but swiftly affected nonchalance, shrugging as if begrudgingly granting Helen a favour.

'What more is there to say then? If all this is about a bloody possession charge, you really haven't got enough to do,' he goaded.

'It's about who else was with you in the tunnel that night,' Charlie interjected. 'We're not interested in your dealing – unless we feel you're keeping things from us of course. Tell me, do you recognize this girl?'

She slid a photo of Naomi Watson across the table towards the dealer. Reluctantly, Brent Mason picked it up, studying it closely.

'What is she? Hooker? Junkie? Homeless?' he asked.

'The latter, but new to the scene.'

'Don't remember seeing her,' Mason continued, replacing the photo on the table. 'But there's always a fair few of them down there, so I'm not sure I'd be able to pick out any individuals.'

'And what about this guy?'

Helen handed him a recent photo of Ryan Marwood. Again, he appeared to scrutinize it closely but Helen could immediately tell from his dilating pupils that the dealer recognized him. Brent was probably already attempting to cobble together a lie to distance himself from this depraved, notorious figure, so Helen jumped in quickly.

'I can see you know him, but I don't need to know the full history. I just need you to tell me whether you saw him in the Lordship Road underpass on Thursday evening?'

There was a long pause, Brent looking from Helen to Charlie and back again, buying himself valuable seconds. He was obviously weighing up what answer they wanted, what response might get him off the hook.

'Yeah, he was there. Turned up around 9.15, I think.'

Helen felt the knot in her stomach relax. He was hardly an ideal witness, but at least they had *some* proof that Marwood was there that night.

'How can you be sure?'

'Because I spoke to him.'

Now it was Helen's turn to look surprised.

'You actually engaged with him, had a conversation?'

'Sure,' Mason replied cautiously. 'We... we do business together every once in a while.'

'Plain English, please, Brent,' Helen insisted. 'Do you mean you're his dealer?'

'Guess so,' he responded, sniffing loudly and looking up to the ceiling, as if that would help his confession fly away.

'How long's this been going on?'

'Six months, on and off?'

'Pretty much straight after he was released,' Charlie interjected, doing the maths.

'And what did he buy from you?' Helen continued, keeping the pressure on.

'All sorts, weed, uppers, downers. But recently, well, it's just been the hard stuff really.'

'Specifics?'

'Heroin.'

Now Mason's gaze was nailed to the floor, but Helen waved away his concerns.

'Brent, like I said, I'm not interested in how you pay your way in life, but I do want to clarify the circumstances of your encounter with Ryan Marwood that night. So please, tell me, in detail, exactly what happened.'

Relaxing back into his chair, the fidgeting dealer replied:

'Well, I guess I got there about just before 9 p.m. It's a good spot for me, easy to access, no cameras in the tunnel, customers like it. Anyhow, like I said, around 9.15 I see this van pull up. And Marwood's at the wheel.'

'Could this have been the van?' Charlie interrupted, slipping Mason a photo of the Renault Movano.

'Looks about right. It was definitely that colour, and that kind of shape, boxy you know ...'

'Did you see the van enter the tunnel?'

'Sure, I was looking that way when he drove up.'

'And what happened during your conversation with him?'

'The usual. Bit of banter, then he asked for the gear. He had the cash on him, so I nodded to a pal, who brought it over.'

'And then?' Helen queried, trying to conceal her anxiety.

'Then nothing. He took off and I hung around for the next punter.'

'He drove off.'

'Sure. He wanted to get stuck into the gear, I guess. He looked fucking twitchy.'

'You saw the van leave the tunnel?'

'Aye,' Mason replied quizzically, confused by the intensity and seriousness of Helen's tone.

'He didn't stop elsewhere in the tunnel? Talk to anyone? Pick anyone up?'

'No, he burned off. Left me with a mouth full of fumes.'

'And he didn't return later? He couldn't have driven back in without you noticing?'

Helen knew this was nigh on impossible, especially as there was no footage of Marwood doing so, but she had to be sure.

'No way. I was keeping a close eye on every vehicle that drove past. You've got to at the moment, with all the shit going on.'

Helen looked at Charlie, then turned back to the dealer, her expression grave.

'Honest to God, that's exactly what happened,' Mason protested, clearly weirded out by the mood shift in the room. 'He drove in, got the gear, drove out, end of story. Now did you want anything else from me or can I go?'

'Sure you can,' Helen confirmed, rising, before adding, 'First thing in the morning.'

'What?' the dealer shot back, aghast. 'I ain't spending a night in no custody cell.'

'Oh, I think you are, Brent,' Helen countered swiftly. 'You don't get picked up with that amount of cocaine on you and expect to waltz straight out of here...'

'No, no, that wasn't the deal. You said you didn't care how I made my dough...'

The dealer continued to protest, but Helen had already turned away, heading fast for the door, her mind whirring. Though Brent Mason had a relaxing evening in the cells to look forward to, for Helen and Charlie the night was just beginning. Though he had no way of knowing it, the small-time dealer had just cleared Ryan Marwood of any involvement in the abduction of Naomi Watson.

Chapter 55

PC Dave Reynolds looked up from the stack of presents, taking in his smartly dressed wife, who hovered in front of him, nervous and excited.

'Well, go on then, open them!' she implored him. 'We've been waiting all day for you to get home.'

'We?' Reynolds replied coolly.

'Well, Archie wanted to be here,' she added defensively. 'He waited in until five, but he's got football practice. I did tell you about it, would have reminded you this morning, but you shot off so early...'

'So it's my fault we can't all be together?'

'Oh, don't be like that, Dave, it's just the way things worked out. So, go on, open them.'

Relenting, Reynolds hung his jacket over the nearest chair, picking up the first present. Ripping the paper off, he discovered a brand-new Apple watch.

'Is that the one you wanted?' Jackie twittered. 'The right model and colour?'

'Spot on. Thank you.'

'It's my pleasure, treasure,' Jackie cooed. 'And the rest?'

Reynolds opened his haul methodically, discovering a new pair of running shoes, a book on share trading, a poker set, some black jeans and, finally, a new leather collar for the dog, complete with hi-vis edging.

'Thought Willow would look rather smart in that. Plus, it would keep her safe.'

'That's very thoughtful of you,' Reynolds replied softly. 'In fact, *all* this is very thoughtful of you ...'

'We aim to please.'

Jackie Reynolds did a little curtsey, giggling to herself as she did so.

'Now, I've got a couple of steaks in the fridge. Why don't I get cracking on them, we can open some wine, have a nice dinner together?'

She smiled at her husband, loving and warm, but received nothing in response.

'It's been ages since we had the place to ourselves,' Jackie continued gamely, a nervousness creeping into her tone now. 'Be nice to have a romantic night in ...'

'Well, that all sounds very pleasant,' Reynolds responded calmly. 'But before we get to that, is there anything else we need to discuss?'

'I don't think so,' Jackie responded uncertainly.

'Anything you want to tell me?'

'No, no. Like I said, I've just been waitin—'

'Like the fact that you had a visitor this morning.'

Instantly, Jackie's face fell. She'd been hoping to get away without confessing this to her husband, but now she had little choice.

'Neighbours been gossiping again, have they?' she responded tersely. 'Who was it? Janet? Peter?' she accused.

'It doesn't matter who told me. Who was it?'

'It was ... it was a police officer.'

Reynolds stared at her, hard and cold. Jackie was already

starting to panic, her chest rising and falling sharply, as if she was struggling to breathe.

'The brake light on the car wasn't working, so she pulled me over.'

'Where?'

'Here. On the drive. Said she had to give me a ticket.'

'Did you check that the light wasn't working?'

'Why would I?' Jackie wheezed, putting her hand to her chest.

'Never mind. Who was it?'

'Helen Grace, I think she said. She's based in Southampton Central, said she knew you.'

'What happened?'

'Nothing,' Jackie insisted, looking ever more alarmed. 'She said she had to write me a ticket, so we stepped inside and—'

'She came in *here*?' Reynolds demanded, furious.

Jackie looked at her husband, terrified now. She was beginning to hyperventilate, her asthma robbing her of energy, of breath.

'Let me get my inhaler and then I'll—'

'Answer the question first.'

Jackie stopped in her tracks, looking back at her husband beseechingly. But his face was set like granite.

'Yes, she ... she came in here,' she stuttered.

'And? What then?'

'She wrote it up, we chatted a bit. About policework, about you.'

'You stupid bitch.'

The words hit Jackie like a slap in the face. All tenderness, any sense of celebration had now evaporated, replaced by burning anger and bitter disappointment.

'Why the fuck did you open your big mouth?'

'I had no choice. She was in here, she was asking questions, what was I supposed to do?'

'You were supposed to say nothing, take the ticket and keep your trap shut. You must see that the whole thing was a bloody ruse, to get in here, to take a look at our house, our life. I bet she had a good look around, didn't she?'

'No, not really. I mean she stayed a bit longer than I expected, but I just thought she was being chatty.'

'Jesus Christ, Jackie, use your brain. She's a plain-clothes officer, bloody CID. What business does she have pulling you over for a traffic offence, writing you up a ticket, talking her way into our bloody home. Did none of that seem odd to you? Are you *really* that stupid?'

'I wasn't thinking straight,' Jackie protested tearfully. 'I was freaked out about getting a ticket. I thought she was just doing her job and that I should play nice.'

'Well, isn't that just you all over,' Reynolds sneered. 'Never were the sharpest tool in the box, were you?'

'Look, I'm sorry all right? I don't know what I've done wrong, but I'm sorry. Now please...'

She paused, breathless, unable to find the words, before rasping:

'...please can we just have a nice evening together?'

'You've already ruined the evening, so what would be the point?'

'Don't say that...'

She gasped, looking unsteady on her feet now, but managed to persevere.

'Please don't say that, Dave. We've got the whole night ahead of us... I've got... I've got plans...'

She couldn't continue, moving away now to pick up her inhaler from the mantelpiece. But Reynolds was too quick for her, nipping in first and snatching it up. Confused, she grasped for it, but once more she was frustrated. Though no taller than his wife, Reynolds' reach was longer and he held it out behind his back, a triumphant expression on his face.

'Dave, please ...'

But he continued to stare at her hatefully, keeping her at bay with an outstretched arm. Desperate, Jackie made a grab for the inhaler, but he batted her away.

'I need ... I ...'

She gripped the chair, suddenly unsteady on her feet. Her chest was tight enough to burst, her breathing laboured and her vision darkening. She felt as if the room was closing in on her.

'Dave, I ...'

She took another step forward, holding out her hand beseechingly. He watched, half angered, half amused, enjoying her desperation. Then slowly he brought his arm round, pressing it into her grateful palm.

'Thank you,' she breathed.

But she didn't get any further, Reynolds slamming his fist into her stomach. Immediately, Jackie doubled up, collapsing to the floor. But Reynolds made no attempt to tend to her, to help her up. Instead, he snatched up his jacket whilst whistling for the dog. As Willow trotted to his side, Reynolds looked down to his wife, his expression full of scorn and anger.

'Thanks for nothing, bitch.'

And then he was gone, slamming the back door shut behind him as Jackie tore the top off her inhaler, sucking on it greedily, even as she sobbed her heart out.

Chapter 56

'Help me, please! Somebody *please* help me...'

Naomi was screaming, breathless, tear-stained, dizzy with fear, as Mia lay unconscious on the ground, her damaged lungs slowly giving up the fight. Naomi had laboured to revive her friend, slapping Mia, stroking her, even resorting to spitting on her, rubbing the stringy saliva into her lips, her mouth, in a vain attempt to give her some hydration. But nothing had worked, her friend remaining supine and lifeless in her arms, so in the end she had abandoned her charge, shuffling away towards the hinged doors. If there was to be any hope of salvation now, it would have to come from outside. Mia needed medical attention, proper help – from their captor, a passer-by, anyone who could hear her desperate pleas.

'We're dying down here. Please, somebody...'

But her cries echoed back at her, taunting and hopeless. Naomi was burning up, her body shaking, in the midst of a full-on panic attack, but she refused to relent until she had no strength or breath left in her body.

'Pleeeeaaaaasssssseeeeee!' she cried, holding it for as long as possible, before she running out of steam.

Leaning her head on the wall, Naomi breathed heavily, her chest pumping furiously, her resolve weakening with each passing second. Trying to hold back the tears that threatened to engulf her, she closed her eyes and muttered a silent prayer.

And then she heard it. A noise up above. Footsteps getting louder, heading straight for their cell. Moments later, the door sprang open, a rush of cool air flooding in as their captor entered. Naomi clung to the brickwork, barely trusting herself to stay upright. She was exhausted, distraught, yet relieved beyond measure. They hadn't been abandoned. He'd come back.

'What the hell happened to her?'

Their tormentor was already crouched down next to Mia.

'She has an infection, a high fever,' Naomi croaked. 'Her lungs are shot. She needs to see a doctor; she needs to go to hospital.'

Ignoring her, he pulled a syringe from his jacket pocket. Rolling up Mia's dirty sleeve, he took his time, picking a clean spot for his incision, before gently pushing down the stopper. Removing the syringe, he watched her closely. Naomi did likewise from across the room, desperate for a miraculous recovery, any signs of life. A second passed, then another, each one feeling like an eternity. Then suddenly Mia gasped, sitting bolt upright, sucking air into her lungs wildly, before breaking into a coughing fit. Their captor held her upright, watching with evident concern, until the hacking eventually subsided. Then he laid her back down on the floor, where she lay, her chest rising and falling fitfully, desperately ill and wracked with pain, but alive.

'Thank God …' Naomi whispered, relief coursing through her. 'What *is* that stuff?'

But he ignored her, his attention exclusively focused on his charge. He was holding Mia, whispering to her, as if his ministrations alone were responsible for her recovery. Naomi shivered, not simply with pure relief, but also because the temperature in the close space had dropped markedly since his sudden arrival.

And now Naomi realized why. He had forgotten to close the door. The hinged wall lay open in front of her, tantalizing, inviting.

Looking back at their captor, she realized his attention was totally focused on Mia. She was still bound by the chains to the wall, but this was too good an opportunity to miss. Perhaps if she got rid of her shoes, her socks, she could somehow slip her feet out of her bonds. It seemed far-fetched, but Naomi was seized by a desire to escape, to flee this awful place.

She took a tentative step towards the opening, then another, then another. Still he didn't react, so now she peered out, glimpsing the messy room outside, the staircase in the far corner leading up and away. Easing her foot out of her shoe, she bent down silently tugging her dirty sock from her sweaty toes. Then, gripping the ring round her ankle, she wriggled her ankle, trying to get some purchase, some movement. If she could just get her foot out, she could run, run for her life...

'Want to get out of here, do you?'

Horrified, Naomi looked up to see that her kidnapper had risen and was now staring directly at her, a sardonic look on his face.

'Well, you're in luck, sweetheart,' he continued, grinning. 'I was going to use Mia tonight but she's no good to anyone, so I guess it's your turn.'

Suddenly Naomi was gripped with terror, the horror of what he was suggesting hitting home.

'Bit of fresh air would do you good.'

'No, please...'

Naomi was backing away fast, but he fell upon her faster, his fist driving into her stomach. Shocked, Naomi doubled up, gasping, and before she could react, before she could fight back, he was upon her, unlocking her bonds and snatching hold of her wrist.

'No, no, I don't want this.'

But it was as if he couldn't hear her, as if her feelings, her anguish, didn't exist. Straightening up, her captor shot her a look of vile excitement, then dragged her from the room.

Chapter 57

'What the hell has he done to you?'

Archie was crouching down by his mother, who lay curled up on floor, breathless and tearful from her ordeal.

'It's nothing, I'm OK,' Jackie protested, wheezing. 'Just didn't get to my inhaler in time.'

She took another long pull on it, drawing the all-important vapour into her lungs.

'Don't lie to me,' the teenager retorted. '*He* did this to you, didn't he?'

His eyes flitted to the opened presents, the birthday cards.

'What happened? What was the argument about?'

But his mother just shook her head, saving her breath, gathering herself.

'It's his bloody birthday, for God's sake. The one day of the year that he should be in good mood. And he does *this*?'

'It's OK, I'm fine,' Jackie replied, struggling up onto her feet. 'It was just a silly misunderstanding.'

'Where did he hit you?' Archie persisted.

'Please, love, can we just let this go?' she implored, reaching out to him.

'No, no, we can't just "let this go". We always "let this go". Which is why he always treats us like shit.'

Marching towards the counter, Archie swept the cards and presents onto the floor. They crashed to the ground, then there was silence. A heavy, loaded silence. Archie, sweating and angry, caught sight of himself in the mirror, then turned away, horrified to see his features contorted in rage. Jackie stared at him, tearful and bereft, then stepping round her son, she bent down to start picking up the cards.

'Leave them.'

But she paid him no heed, gathering the scattered cards together.

'I said, leave them!'

'And have the place looking a mess?' Jackie replied, her words jarring in their false brightness. 'I don't think so. It's a special day today, I've put loads of effort into getting everything ready, I won't have things ruined at the last minute.'

She turned to find her son staring at her as if she was mad.

'You're not seriously going to go through with this, are you? You're not going to carry on as though nothing's happened?'

'Nothing *has* happened.'

'He hit you, Mum. He left you in a heap on the ground.'

'You don't know what you're talking about, Archie. You weren't here.'

'I don't need to be. I know him, I know what he's capable of...'

He was about to expand further, reeling off his father's numerous crimes against the family, but Jackie stepped forwards purposefully now, laying a finger on his lips.

'Please, baby, not today. I know things are difficult, I know you're unhappy, but please can we not do this today.'

Her sad, tear-stained eyes locked onto his, beseeching, imploring.

'Please, for me, can we just pretend it never happened? That we've had a nice family day?'

It was outrageous, preposterous, a charade that would surely fool no one. But faced with his mother's desperation, her torment, what else could he do? So, swallowing down his bile and pasting a pained smile on his face, Archie nodded slowly, before taking his mother into his arms, clinging onto her for dear life.

Chapter 58

Sixteen stunned faces stared back at her, some looking confused and unnerved, others downright angry. Following her interview with Brent Mason, Helen had put a general call out to the Major Incident Team, pulling them all back to base. Now they were arrayed in front of her, silent and brooding, stunned by what they'd just heard.

'We have to get this right,' Helen continued, refusing to be intimidated or diverted. 'And given what we now know, I think we have to seriously question whether Ryan Marwood was involved in the abductions of Naomi Watson and Mia Davies.'

DC Jennings exhaled, long and loud, as a couple of his colleagues shook their heads dolefully, deeply unimpressed.

'Meredith Walker's team has now completed a thorough sweep of the Renault Movano that Marwood's been driving. There is no DNA trace at all of Naomi or Mia, or anyone else for that matter, apart from Ryan Marwood.'

'He could have cleaned it?' DC Reid offered.

'That thoroughly?' Helen replied, sceptical. 'To leave no trace *at all*?'

'Furthermore,' Charlie said, stepping into the fray, 'Jim Grieves' examination of Marwood's body revealed no signs of recent sexual activity. Now Marwood was not a guy who washed much, showering at best once a week, yet there was no trace of semen, or lubricant, or foreign pubic hairs on his body, nothing. Nor did he have any recent injuries, any foreign skin cells or DNA under his fingernails, anything suggestive of a struggle or recent sexual assault.'

'What he did have on his body, according to Jim,' Helen added, 'were plenty of fresh track marks and a very healthy concentration of heroin in his blood stream. All this, allied to the testimony from Brent Mason about their encounter in the underpass, leads me to speculate that Marwood's current affliction, his current obsession, was hard drugs. Maybe his time inside, the endless therapy sessions and group workshops, *had* helped him gain control over his darker urges, his sexual deviancy, but he still couldn't kick the drugs. We know he used them heavily during his time in prison to blot out the violence, the misery. He must have known that if he got caught buying or using drugs again, he'd be straight back inside. Perhaps that's why he used an unlicensed vehicle when he went out at night, a van that couldn't immediately be traced back to him. Perhaps that's also why he resisted arrest, why he ultimately took his own life rather than be caught.'

'So we're taking the word of junkies and dealers now, are we?' Jennings interrupted, exasperated. 'Brent Mason is a roach, nothing more, nothing less.'

'You've got to say,' DC McAndrew added cautiously, 'he's not exactly a model witness, guv?'

'Maybe so,' Helen countered, 'but he was extremely honest about everything else, admitting to regularly selling hard drugs in that underpass. Both DS Brooks and I believed his testimony, believed him when he said that Marwood was only there to score drugs.'

'So we're back to square one?' DC Malik asked nervously, looking downcast.

Helen understood her pain. The team were keen to celebrate a successful investigation, they'd had the station chief in earlier encouraging them to do just that. But they had to follow the evidence, wherever it might lead them.

'Not quite,' Helen replied forcefully. 'I'd like us to take a closer look at PC Dave Reynolds.'

'Oh, come off it,' DC Jennings protested angrily. 'You can't be serious?'

'Does it not strike you as odd that the only piece of evidence linking Ryan Marwood to Naomi Watson was found just hours after PC Reynolds was in his house?' Helen countered forcefully. 'Beth Beamer has confirmed that she searched the downstairs rooms, whilst Reynolds was alone upstairs in Ryan Marwood's bedroom. Earlier search teams found nothing, yet second time round, after Marwood's death, suddenly they chance upon a key piece of evidence?'

'Maybe they just did their job *properly* second time round,' Jennings retorted. 'Just as Reynolds was doing his when he turned up at the Marwood home. He was hunting down an escaped suspect, doing what *you* asked him to do, and for that we're going to damn him? Slander an innocent man, a brave and popular colleague ...'

'Think about it,' Charlie stepped in, her voice laced with frustration. 'Reynolds walks the streets of Southampton every day in his role as a beat officer. According to his HR record, he could have taken a desk job *years* ago, but he's insisted on remaining a lowly foot soldier. Pounding the streets in all weathers, slowly earning people's trust, becoming a known face, a fixture on the scene. Plenty of opportunity there to scope his victims, talk to them, check out whether they are isolated and vulnerable. Plus, if he returned to them later, they'd probably go off with him without a fuss, out of fear of arrest or because they trusted the uniform.'

It was a hideous idea, one which clearly troubled several members of the team.

'Well it's *possible* of course,' DC Reid replied, uncomfortable. 'But there's no actual evidence supporting *any* of this. It's all supposition and innuendo, based on a single lapse of memory. I think it's a massive gamble to go further with this, unless we're absolutely sure. Think of the damage it would do station morale, to any sense of camaraderie between us and the ranks. He's seriously popular round here – a mentor, a mate, the best of colleagues. Personally, I think the risk is just too great.'

'I don't agree,' Helen replied firmly, staring directly at Reid, before letting her gaze run over the rest of the team. 'If I'm wrong, I'll take full responsibility. But I'm not prepared to over-look potential criminal wrongdoing simply because we're scared of ruffling feathers. I want a full investigation into PC Dave Reynolds – his recent movements, his beat pattern, his digital footprint and communications, as well as a thorough trawl of medical, financial and HR records for both him *and* his family.'

Already loud mutterings could be heard, so Charlie stepped in.

'I will talk to you individually, apportioning specific tasks. In the meantime, DI Grace and I will take point on trying to contact those young women who have complained about PC Reynolds historically, to see what light they can shed on things. DC Wilson, whilst we're doing that, I'd like you to go over the statements given by the other drivers who dawdled in the Lordship Road underpass on the night of the ninth, to see if we can detect any inconsistencies.'

'This is desperate stuff,' DC Jennings complained, shaking his head. 'Really desperate.'

'I disagree,' Helen responded coolly. 'But if that's how you really feel, you're free to put in a transfer request at any time. That goes for any others present who have a problem with this unit's senior leadership team.'

Her eyes never left Jennings as she spoke, her gaze boring into him. Caught off guard, he now backtracked quickly.

'I'm not going anywhere – I've worked too hard to get here. But I'm saying openly, for all to hear, that I think this is a huge mistake.'

His eyes were locked onto Helen's. Taking confidence from the small gaggle of officers who now gathered around him, offering their support, Jennings added:

'One you'll come to regret.'

Chapter 59

'Please don't do this...'

Naomi could barely speak, her anguish consumed by wracking sobs. But her captor paid no heed, gripping her by the neck with one hand, as he manipulated a laptop with the other.

It couldn't be true, it couldn't be happening, yet this nightmare was real. Naomi was standing in the storeroom just beyond her cell, caught in the powerful beams of two arc lamps. In front of her, next to the workbench on which the laptop was balanced, stood a video camera, its unforgiving eye pointing directly towards her.

'I don't want this. I want to go home...'

Still he said nothing, releasing his grip now, as he punched a few more keys. And now suddenly a new voice rang out, tinny and cold.

'Can't you shut her up? Nobody wants to hear her whining.'

Startled, Naomi looked up, taking in the multitude of faces on the laptop's screen. She was clearly the focus of a Zoom call, the participants of which generally seemed happy to be seen, to flaunt their identity, confident that they would not be exposed, unmasked or disturbed. The sea of male faces stared at her now, their expressions filled with anger, menace and a dark desire that made Naomi want to vomit. Her tormentors were of all ages, all sizes, all races, a morass of collective depravity, but even amongst the many faces, Naomi managed to pick out a red-faced, flame-haired blob and a tall, skinny, bald man whose intense expression froze the blood in her veins.

Now, finally, her captor moved away from the laptop, positioning himself directly in front of her. Terrified, Naomi instantly took a step backwards, but her attacker barely reacted. He was calm, collected, in total control.

'Now this is very simple, Naomi. You do exactly what I tell you, when I tell you, and I'll let you live. If not...'

His eyes were ablaze with hatred, his malign presence filling the room, rendering any resistance futile. Naomi had no doubt that he meant what he said, that he'd kill her as soon as look at her. She tried to speak, to answer him, but no words would come out, just a futile, miserable gasp. Instead she nodded dully. Her whole body was shaking now, her senses exploding, utterly paralyzed by fear. She wanted to close her eyes, to make all this horror go away, to save herself from the torment she knew was coming. But even as she shut her eyes, praying for oblivion, a hard, Scottish voice rang out in the lonely cellar.

'Right, then. Shall we begin?'

Chapter 60

'Are you sure you want to do this?'

Helen was leaning over her desk, staring down at her files, but looked up at Charlie now, a look of confusion on her face.

'I think it's a bit late for second thoughts, Charlie. We've done the hard bit, now we have to see what they, what *we*, can turn up.'

Nodding distractedly, Charlie looked back into the incident room, clocking that DC Reid was watching their conversation through the open doorway. Crossing the floor quickly, she pushed the door to and was about to drop the blind, when Helen intervened.

'Leave the blind up – we've nothing to hide. I don't want Jennings and his buddies thinking we're rattled.'

'Aren't we?'

Charlie's question surprised Helen, who'd assumed from her bravura performance in the briefing that her deputy was on board.

'What's eating you?' Helen enquired, keeping her tone light.

'Look, I'm not questioning the direct of travel...'

'But?'

'But I'm just worried we're going to alienate the entire team. Jennings is clearly not the only one who's got reservations about investigating a fellow officer, purely on the basis of circumstantial witness testimony from a dealer and a very green probationer…'

'Careful, Charlie, you're beginning to sound like management.'

'I'm serious, Helen. Discreet background checks and quiet words are one thing, but tasking the whole of the unit with proving that one of their own is a rapist, a kidnapper, a killer even – that's a major step. Which will go down like a bucket of sick with the rank and file, not to mention Holmes. She'll hit the roof when she finds out, accusing you – accusing *us* – of deliberately trying to sully the reputation of this force. That worries me.'

'It worries me too,' Helen replied candidly. 'She hates me enough already, without handing her fresh ammunition. But I'm not going to let that stop me. PC Dave Reynolds is hiding something and I intend to find out what. If there's the remotest chance that he's responsible for Naomi's disappearance, I have to investigate, have to throw everything at it. I couldn't look Sheila Watson in the eye if I didn't. If that costs me my job, well so be it.'

'Don't say that…' Charlie responded quickly, suddenly looking rather ill.

'I mean it, Charlie. I will not be diverted or influenced by station politics. Or by the fact that everyone seems to think Dave Reynolds is a top bloke. I think there's something off about him and I intend to expose whatever it is that he's caught up in. But I would prefer not to do it alone. So can I count on you, Charlie? It's going to get messy, so I need to know you've got my back. Can I trust you to stick up for me, to be loyal at all times?'

'Of course you can,' Charlie responded, agitated. 'You know you can. But I wouldn't be a proper friend, a proper colleague, if I didn't warn you of the dangers, that's all.'

'I consider myself warned, then. And I thank you. But my position remains the same.'

Charlie digested this, gathering her thoughts, before asking:

'So what now then? We need concrete evidence that Reynolds has a history of offending, that he's a danger to women.'

'Exactly, and if my hunch is right, those three historic complainants are just the tip of the iceberg. I'm guessing there'll be more victims out there, which is why we need to make our search bigger and louder, not quieter and more discreet.'

'Meaning?'

In response, Helen hit the speaker function on her office phone and quickly dialled a number. The call rang briefly, then was answered, the operator's voice ringing out clearly:

'*Southampton Evening News*. How may I assist you?'

'I'd like to speak to Emilia Garanita please. It's DI Helen Grace.'

The look on Charlie's face said it all, surprise and alarm wrestling for supremacy. Holding her hand over the mouthpiece, Helen stared intently at her colleague, as she concluded:

'It's time to go nuclear.'

Chapter 61

Teasing open the back door, David Reynolds slipped into the house, Willow darting past him. Crossing the floor of the small utility room, he gave the dog a friendly fuss as she settled down in her well-worn basket, laying her greying muzzle on the floor.

'You're a good girl, aren't you?' he beamed. 'A good old girl.'

Willow side-eyed him from her recumbent position, enjoying the attention. Straightening up, Reynolds washed and dried his hands quickly, before heading towards the internal door. He took care to avoid the loose tile that always creaked loudly, moving noiselessly into the main living area. From outside, the house had seemed dark and silent; with any luck Jackie had already gone to bed, so they could avoid another scene. A quiet whisky by himself would round off his birthday nicely. Opening the door, he left the utility room, stepping into the darkened space beyond, then froze. Instinctively he could tell that something was wrong, that he was not alone. Before he could react, however, the lights snapped on.

'Surprise!'

For a moment, Dave Reynolds was speechless, staggered by the sight in front of him. Jackie, Archie and two dozen friends and neighbours were gathered in the front room, beaming happily at him. Balloons and banners decorated the scene, streamers flew through the air and many of the guests wore colourful party hats. They all looked pleased to have surprised him, none more so than Jackie.

'Told you he hadn't guessed, didn't I? Right then, shall we sing?'

Without further delay, the guests launched into a tuneless, impassioned rendition of 'Happy Birthday'. Reynolds remained stock-still, lost for words. Even as their singing came to a blessed end, he still could not think of what to say or do. Half of him wanted to tell them all to bugger off – he was *not* a man who liked surprises – but the other half of him just wanted to burst out laughing at the sheer craziness of it all.

'Cat got your tongue, mate?' Alan said, thrusting a beer into his hand. 'Not like you to be bashful. What say we give him another little song whilst he composes himself, eh? For he's a jolly good fellow, for he's a jolly good fellow...'

His neighbour ripped into the ditty with gusto and verve, leading the other revellers in song.

As the words washed over him, Reynolds let his eye wander over the assembled crowd. Their enthusiasm was manic, their goodwill overwhelming, a collective throng convulsed with affection and enthusiasm. And there at the heart of it, leading the congregation, was his wife, belting out the words of praise as if her life depended on it. It was absurd, it was hilarious, so now Reynolds didn't resist, throwing back his head and roaring with laughter.

Chapter 62

She lay in the corner of her cell, her face turned to the wall. Her whole body was shivering, though whether this was due to the plummeting temperature or shock was impossible to say. Naomi felt as if she had lost control of herself – her body, her mind, her fate – as if she was freefalling into a vortex from which there would be no escape. How pathetic, how inadequate her earlier attempts to console Mia seemed now. She'd had no concept of what her friend had endured, how brutalized, insignificant and wretched one person could be made to feel. The sisterly affection she'd lavished on her cell mate seemed insulting now, even obscene. Naomi had had no idea what suffering had meant, until now.

Pressing her cheek to the cold concrete, Naomi stared at the drop of water gathering on the joint of the leaky water pipe, watching it grow steadily larger until gravity took over, the liquid falling silently to the floor. Immediately, another drop started to form and she kept her eyes glued to it. If she could just focus on this, the steady, predictable rhythm of accumulation and release, then she could stop herself collapsing inwards, avoid endlessly replaying the horror of her ordeal. But those emotions, those feelings, were hard to push away. She felt like she'd been *destroyed*. Not just by the appalling physical degradation her captor had inflicted upon her, but by the callous refusal to treat her like a human being. To her abuser, to the barbaric crowd of voyeurs, she was just an object, something to be used for their pleasure, then discarded. The most painful, most distressing day of her life had also been the most eye-opening. Until tonight, she'd had no idea that such evil, such cold, pitiless evil, really existed.

Her captor had hardly said a word throughout, taking orders from his audience and responding with cold efficiency. Afterwards, he made her get dressed, then marched her back to her cell, chaining her to the wall, before hurrying off without another word. Even in her confusion and pain, Naomi had noticed an impatience to get away, an urgency, in her attacker's manner. For the first time she suddenly realized that their abductor must have a life, duties to people beyond these four walls, things that he had to deal with, places he had to be. It was shocking and devastating in equal measure. For him, this gruesome ritual of imprisonment and abuse was just one element of his life, whereas for Naomi and Mia, it was their whole existence, their sentence. This was utterly crushing, Naomi projecting forwards to what lay ahead, the ghost of the absent Shanice colouring every dire prediction. Clamping down her terror, Naomi kept her eyes fixed on the growing water drops, hoping, praying, that she could maintain her sanity.

The water continued to ooze from the aged pipework, falling to the floor without disturbing the silence that filled the claustrophobic space. Naomi had no idea if Mia had looked up when they'd returned to the cell, or whether she'd tried to block the whole thing out, hunkering down in her corner of the room. But she was certainly not moving now. For one terrible moment, Naomi thought that something had happened to her, that death had claimed her whilst she was alone, but as the seconds passed, she finally picked up the slow, rasping breathing of her fellow captive, a gentle, fragile intake of air that sounded as delicate and vulnerable as a feather in the wind. But that was the only sign that she was not alone. Mia did not speak, she did not reach out to Naomi, she simply lay where she was, silent and immobile.

Part of Naomi wanted to be angry with her, to berate her friend for not showing any concern or sympathy for her following her ordeal, but the better part of her knew that to do so would be heartless, ignorant and cruel, adding unjust insult to terrible injury. Mia had already been attacked by her captor multiple times, had been broken on the wheel of his perverted desire and had no fight left. Before, Naomi had perhaps judged her for that, angry that she would allow her spirit to be broken, to give up, but now she understood the cause of her submission. They were trapped down here, sentenced to appalling suffering, despite having committed no crime. It was a shattering realization, a dreadful fate, one from which there appeared to be no possibility of deliverance. So, in the end, what was the point in fantasies of escape? What was to be gained by pretending that if they supported each other, things might yet work out well for them? There would be no happy endings, no redemption, which is why tonight they lay still in the silence, their faces turned away from each other, each locked in their own private hell.

Chapter 63

It was nearly midnight and the streets were deserted. It was time for Helen to head home in the hope of capturing a few hours' sleep before the dawn of a new day. But there was one task she still had to carry out before she could rest, an act of penance that couldn't wait.

The dull glow of a single naked lightbulb illuminated Sheila Watson's features as she opened the door, surprised to have a visitor so late at night. Helen glimpsed the momentary hope in her expression, the belief that this unexpected intrusion might herald the return of her daughter, then had to watch on as this transmuted into surprise, then concern.

'Sorry to bother you late at night. I wasn't sure if you were up or not, but the light was on, so...' Helen apologized, nodding to the hallway light.

'I never turn it off,' Sheila conceded bashfully. 'I suppose I feel that if I leave it on, it might light Naomi's way home. It's silly really, but—'

'It's not silly at all,' Helen interjected kindly. 'If I was in your shoes, I'd do exactly the same. You keep it on, until Naomi's back safe and sound.'

Sheila Watson blinked at Helen as she gathered herself, clearly reassured by Helen's words, her manner, that she wasn't the bearer of the worst possible news. Clutching her dressing gown around her, she stepped back, allowing her visitor to enter. Helen moved smartly through to the living room, where the TV burbled in the corner. As Sheila hurried to turn it off, Helen surveyed the cosy space, picking out the innumerable photos of Naomi that graced the mantelpiece and sideboard. It was moving to see the full panorama of her life, from pudgy baby to cheeky toddler and beyond, her childhood played out in a series of carefree smiles. It was cheering to see that Naomi possessed such ebullience, such spirit, yet perversely crushing too, given the misery she must now be enduring, assuming she was still alive. Next to the photos stood a vase, filled with radiant blue and yellow flowers, arresting in their simple beauty.

'They were always Naomi's favourites.'

Surprised, Helen turned to find Sheila standing next to her, starring wistfully at the pretty display of forget-me-nots.

'She loved their vitality, their colour – always put a smile on her face, she said.'

Sheila's desolate tone underscored the poignancy, the irony, of this memory. Happiness seemed a long way off and there was no question of either of them forgetting about Naomi.

'Is there any news?' Sheila continued, her voice suddenly tight with tension.

'Nothing concrete,' Helen conceded. 'We still don't know where Naomi is, or how she's doing, though obviously I've got every officer in my team engaged in the hunt.'

Sheila nodded soberly, but said nothing, sensing that there was more to come.

'No, the reason I needed to see you tonight, Sheila, is that there are going to be some press stories, emerging in the next day or so, which have a bearing on Naomi's disappearance, and which you may find upsetting and alarming.'

Sheila looked so worried that Helen pressed on quickly.

'I wanted to let you know about these developments before you saw them in the press, as they are going to generate a lot of interest and cause major ructions both within our force and beyond. It's ... it's my suspicion, it's my belief, that a serving police officer might be responsible for Naomi's abduction.'

Sheila stared at her wide-eyed, her expression a mixture of incomprehension and horror.

'Please believe me,' Helen continued quickly, 'when I say that this is as distressing and shocking for me as it is for you. But I didn't want to hide this from you. You've got a right to know.'

'Who ... who is this person?' the stunned mother stuttered.

'He's a beat officer, who's been working for Hampshire Police for many years. It's my belief that he's been using his uniform, his authority, to commit criminal offences in plain sight, convincing young women to trust him, before assaulting them. His initial offences seem to have been opportunistic, but I fear he's graduated to abducting and holding his victims captive. I'm so sorry, Sheila, I know this is the last thing you want to hear.'

'But why the hell is he still a police officer? Why hasn't he been booted out if he's committed all these crimes?' Sheila blustered, aggrieved, reeling.

'Because he was never charged. Because none of his victims were prepared to testify against him. Because they were too scared, fearful they wouldn't be supported.'

The middle-aged mother was fighting tears once more, but these were tears of anger, of outrage.

'It's wrong, completely wrong, and believe you me, Sheila, I will work night and day to make sure his crimes *are* exposed, that he is held to account for his actions, and if he *is* involved in Naomi's abduction, that he reveals her whereabouts to us so that we can return her to you.'

'I can't believe it...' Sheila responded, struggling to find the words. 'That someone in uniform could do something like that. It disgusting, it's evil...'

'I totally agree, Sheila. It's beyond disgraceful, a stain on my force, on me, on everyone who wears a uniform or carries a badge. We've let you down, Sheila. We've let Naomi down. And many other young women and girls too. I won't apologize to you because apologies are woefully inadequate. All I can do is promise that I won't rest until we've got Naomi back and that this piece of shit is behind bars. You have my word on that.'

Sheila nodded absently, but Helen knew her words were scant consolation. Previously Sheila had blamed herself, insisting that she'd failed Naomi as a mother. Now it was horribly clear that the fault, the blame, lay elsewhere, that it was a serving police officer, someone whose job it was to uphold the law, who was responsible for the Watsons' ever-darkening nightmare. Helen felt sick, ashamed, hollow. She had nothing to offer Sheila except pain and disillusionment, as the extent of this catastrophic breach of trust became clear. Raising her gaze to meet Sheila's, she saw only disorientation and anguish. This time, Helen maintained eye contact, refusing to avoid the censure that was her due, but inside she was dying. In all her many years of service, she had never felt so ashamed as she did tonight.

Day Five

Chapter 64

Tearing her attention away from her toddler, who was busy dressing and undressing her favourite doll, Tara Bridges downed the rest of her coffee and snatched up her phone. She was due to drop Amy at nursery in fifteen minutes and there were still several domestic chores to complete. She had to do an online Asda shop, pay an electrician's bill and message her mother about arrangements for the weekend, but as the young manager looked down at her phone, her attention was arrested by a news headline that flashed up on the screen, before discreetly disappearing from view.

Troubled, Tara quickly opened up her news app, but her eyes hadn't been deceiving her, the headline as blunt and as shocking as she'd imagined.

Serving police officer suspected of sex crimes

Suddenly all thoughts of domestic duties vanished, as Tara took in the detail. The story had broken locally, courtesy of a journalist at the *Southampton Evening News*, but had now gone national, several news outlets majoring on it, as yet another ingredient in the grim mosaic of crimes and misdemeanours committed by serving members of the police force. It was an increasingly long, increasingly dispiriting list of offenders that encompassed pretty much every force in the country. But today it had landed on their doorstep, the culprit a regular presence on the streets of Southampton.

Breathless, Tara took in his name, her anxiety growing as she read about the historical allegations of abduction and rape, which had later been dropped, following his victims' decision to withdraw their allegations. Tara's hand was shaking, her anger growing, imagining their distress, their fear, as the full force of their attacker's authority was brought to bear on them, crushing their resolve, their resistance, but she read on, determined to find out the full extent of PC David Reynolds' offences, however distressing that might be.

But now, suddenly, she ground to a halt, her finger hovering over the screen. Reynolds' official service photo, gleaned from Hampshire Police's community outreach website, was displayed in the middle of the article and stared out at Tara now. A moment's panic, a sharp intake of breath, then Tara slammed the phone down on the counter, unable to bear his scrutiny for another second. For a moment, she stood there, shaking and speechless, before she was summoned from her trance by a childish voice.

'Mummy, are you OK?'

Snapping out of it, Tara turned to find Amy looking up at her, puzzled.

'Fine, I'm fine, honey,' she replied quickly, just about keeping the emotion from her voice. 'But we *do* need to go soon, so finish up what you're doing.'

Tara turned away, not trusting herself to maintain her composure. Emotions were swirling inside her, feelings she'd kept buried for a long time, feelings she didn't want to confront. That was her *then*, not now. Now things were very different. She had a husband, a child, a good job, a life. *This* was the real her, the person, the success she had become.

The sweat that was creeping down her back, the thickening emotion in her throat, told a different story, however. They suggested that nothing had changed, that the terror, the shame, the humiliation she'd felt all those years ago was as keen, as sharp, as ever. They robbed her of her composure, her confidence, her certainty, insisting now that she pick up the phone and read on, that she thrust herself into the gathering storm. But how could she?

Turning back to look at her daughter playing innocently on the floor, Tara knew that it was an impossibility. She couldn't tear down the fabric of her life, couldn't traumatize those she loved best. The damage would be too great, the impact too devastating. After all, how could she admit what had happened to everyone else, when she had never admitted it to herself?

Picking up her phone, Tara turned it off before dropping it into her handbag and fastening the clasp. Out of sight, out of mind. It was pathetic, shameful, but it was the only way she could survive. So slinging her bag over her shoulder, she walked slowly over to her baby girl, a rictus smile painted on her face, as she piped up:

'Come on, honey. We don't want to be late.'

Amy obliged, scrambling to her feet, pushing her messy, tangled hair out of her face. Normally, Tara would have reacted to this, grabbing the nearest brush to restore some sense of propriety, but there was no prospect of that today. Today she just wanted to cling onto her daughter's hand, to hold her close, hoping that by embracing the present, she might blot out the past.

Chapter 65

'Can I help you?'

The smartly-dressed professional looked Charlie up and down uncertainly. She was obviously annoyed to have been summoned to the door whilst preparing to leave for work and was concerned that she was now facing a lengthy conversation with a saleswoman, a political canvasser or, worse, a religious zealot. Charlie was quick to disabuse her, extracting her warrant card from her jacket.

'DS Brooks, Hampshire CID. Sorry to disturb you so early.'

'That's no problem,' the young woman responded, her scowl swiftly replaced by an awkward smile. 'What can I do for you?'

'It's nothing to worry about, I just wanted to have a quick word. I am speaking to Leanne Gardner, correct?'

The homeowner nodded, intrigued and disconcerted in equal measure.

'Excellent. Could we step inside?'

'Look, to be honest it's not a great time,' the young professional replied, pulling a face as she checked her watch. 'Is it possible you could talk to my fiancé? I'm already running late, so...'

'No, I'm afraid it has to be you.'

'OK then, but please make it quick. I really can't hang about, not today...'

'Fair enough, but I do think it would be better if we stepped inside...'

Leanne made no move to admit her, determined to keep their conversation as short as possible, so Charlie continued:

'I wanted to talk to you about an allegation you made against a serving police officer back in June of 2016.'

Even as she spoke, Charlie saw the colour drain from the young woman's face.

'You alleged that PC David Reynolds detained you on suspicion of possession, then forced you to commit a sex act on him in the back of a police van. Is that correct?'

Leanne nodded slowly, dully, before darting an anxious look behind her.

'You're not in any trouble, Leanne, and I'm here to help and support you in any way I can. I'm just wondering why the case was dropped? Why you didn't take it further?'

'Why do you think?' Leanne fired back angrily, finally finding her tongue. 'I was a fifteen-year-old girl who was off my head that night, and he was a police officer. Who do you think the courts were going to believe?'

'But you still reported it, Leanne, so you must have had some hope, initially at least, that you might be able to press charges...'

'My mum made me do it, I didn't want to. But it wasn't her that had to sit in that police station whilst his mates, his colleagues, made comments about me – about how I dressed, about what I got up to when my folks weren't looking. I knew what they thought of me and I didn't want anyone saying those things about me in public, all right? It would have killed me.'

'I understand. It must have been very hard for you. I'm so sorry you had to go through all that.'

'Well, if you've come to apologize, you've said your piece now, so you can go. Frankly, a letter would have done the job.'

'I'm afraid it's a bit more complicated than that, Leanne. You see, David Reynolds is alleged to have assaulted other girls, both before and after he attacked you.'

The young woman said nothing, appearing shocked that her ordeal was not an isolated incident.

'In fact,' Charlie continued quickly, 'we believe that he may still be committing offences against women and girls, but we need concrete evidence of his wrongdoing. Specifically, and I appreciate this is a huge ask, we need people who've suffered at his hands to speak up, to hold him to account, to make him pay for his crimes.'

'No, no, no, no...'

The young professional was visibly retreating, as if keen to shut the door on Charlie and that part of her life. But Charlie took a step forward, keeping the conversation alive.

'Believe me, Leanne, I wouldn't ask unless it was vital. I have no desire to cause you any pain, or to dredge up the past, but if Reynolds is still a danger to women, to girls, we need to put him away. We need people to have the courage to come forward, to speak out.'

'No, I'm not doing it. And you can't make me.'

Leanne was defiant, but it was defiance laced with hurt, her eyes glistening.

'That part of my life is dead and buried and I want nothing to do with it.'

'On the contrary, Leanne, it's very much alive. David Reynolds is still in post, still walking the streets, still an active threat to—'

'Do you have any idea what you're asking?' Leanne demanded, her voice shaking. 'I'm getting married this year. How do think that's going to play out if I suddenly dig up all that ... all that shit? I couldn't tell my fiancé that. Couldn't tell his family that.'

'I'm sure they wouldn't think any differently of you. I'm sure they'd understand and applaud your courage in seeking justice not only for yourself, but for others.'

'Well, that's bloody easy for you to say. Have you ever been attacked like that?'

'No,' Charlie conceded, suddenly feeling like a fraud.

'Then you wouldn't understand. You don't know the mark it leaves, the shame and humiliation you feel.'

'Leanne, I get that, I really do. And I fee—'

'No, you don't. You can't. Not unless you've been through it. If you had, you wouldn't pitch up here, asking me to turn my life upside down, you wouldn't have the bloody nerve.'

'Please, Leanne, hear me out. Nothing will be decided today, I just need you to listen ...'

Charlie was fighting a desperate rearguard action here, hoping to, at the very least, keep Leanne in the conversation. But the young bride-to-be was not for turning.

'No, I'm not doing it. It's my past, my life. I won't go back there, I just *won't*.'

She was shaking with emotion, but her resolve was clear.

'That's my final decision, so now I'd like you to leave. You're wasting your time.'

Charlie wanted to respond, to plead, but before she could do so, the door was shut firmly in her face. Frustrated, downcast, she breathed out heavily, before turning to walk back to the car. She had come here expecting little, but had got even less than she hoped for. She'd been firmly rebuffed, succeeding only in causing pain and distress in the process. How must Leanne Gardner be feeling now? Would she be able to conceal her distress from her fiancé? Or summon a good enough lie to explain away her tears? The whole thing made Charlie feel shabby and uneasy. She knew why Helen wanted them to track down Reynolds' past accusers, why she felt they *had* to do so, but would it really yield any concrete results? Or would they simply cause untold pain and misery, forcing these poor women to relive horrendous events that they would prefer to bury for good? Weren't they guilty of torturing Reynolds' victims, humiliating and upsetting them all over again?

And yet what was the alternative? To collude in the suppression of evidence, to sanction criminality, to ensure that David Reynolds *won*? Such a thing was unthinkable. So although she knew she was going to rip open many old wounds in the process, Charlie knew she had to persist, to try to persuade Reynolds' victims to come forward. Too many women had been ignored, belittled or intimidated for too long. There could be no question of giving up now, however substantial the obstacles appeared to be. These women deserved justice and, come what may, Charlie was determined to see that they got it.

Chapter 66

'Are you *seriously* telling me you're not responsible for this?'

Helen knew Rebecca Holmes had fire in her belly, but she'd never seen her so incandescent as she was this morning. Breaking eye contact, Helen looked down at the offending newspaper, Emilia's shocking headline leaping out at her. The journalist had been as good as her word, her exposé, her attack, was devastating.

'If you knew the full history of my relationship with Emilia Garanita, you wouldn't even suggest it,' Helen replied evenly. 'We've never exactly been best friends.'

'Oh come off it, Helen. How green do you think I am?'

Her superior's tone was caustic, withering, but Helen said nothing. Emilia had at first been surprised by Helen's call, then only too pleased to help once she discovered what her former nemesis was proposing, but there was no way Helen was going to offer that up.

'You've had it in for PC Reynolds from the off. You're the only one who knew about these past accusations...'

She gestured dismissively to the newspaper.

'And the only one with sufficient brass neck to leak them to the press.'

'I can only repeat what I've already said, ma'am,' Helen

responded carefully. 'Garanita and I hate each other, always have done. The idea of us colluding together is laughable.'

'So where did she get all this from then?' Holmes demanded. 'She's got the lot – dates, times, locations. In fact, I'll bet she's got an actual copy of Reynolds' HR file, the leaking of which I shouldn't have to remind you is a criminal offence.'

'Then I sincerely hope you get to the bottom of it. Nobody likes a leaky ship.'

'I think I've already got to the bottom of it,' Holmes fired back angrily. 'I think the culprit is standing directly in front of me. Motive, means and opportunity, Helen. The holy trinity. And you had all of them, despite your alleged aversion to Garanita.'

'Call her then. Ask her,' Helen demanded stridently. 'My conscience is clean.'

'As if she'd ever reveal her sources. I wouldn't waste my breath.'

'Well then, I presume you have some other evidence that I was responsible for these leaks? After all, *every* member of the Major Incident Team had access to that information.'

'Don't try to cloud the issue, Helen. It was *you.*'

'So why aren't Professional Standards here?' Helen hit back. 'If you're so convinced of my involvement?'

'Look, I may not have the smoking gun,' Holmes countered. 'But that doesn't mean that you can play fast and loose with this investigation or the reputation of Southampton Central.'

'Meaning?'

'Meaning I'm taking you off the case. Effective immediately.'

For a moment, Helen was speechless, staggered by the audacity of this move.

'You have been insubordinate, obstructive and, frankly, wilful from the word go. I'm hoping that DS Brooks values her career more highly than you do, that she can toe the line, set an example...'

'With respect, ma'am, I think that would be a seriously bad move. One you might come to regret.'

'Are you threatening me, DI Grace?' the station chief roared, her eyes blazing.

'No, I'm just thinking of the optics of this situation. And the reputation of this force. The whole city is talking about this story – the local radio and TV stations, the news feeds, not to mention the thousands of concerned citizens poring over the terrible headlines this morning. They are all justly worried about a culture of misogyny and lawbreaking within Hampshire Police, a culture that has fostered rapists and killers, men who think they are above the law, who prey on women and girls with impunity...'

Furious, Holmes tried to intervene, but Helen talked over her.

'Yet you appear intent on removing Southampton Central's most decorated, best-known *female* detective from the case? Sidelining her to shield those very same rapists and killers, all in the interests of protecting your station from "reputational damage". Pull me off this investigation, throw me to the dogs, and I promise you the public outrage will be threefold what it is now. So think carefully about your next move, ma'am. Because I'd hate for you to make a bad situation a whole lot worse.'

Holmes was staring at her, looking for all the world as though she wanted to vault over the desk and strangle Helen there and then. Yet with each passing second of silence, Helen knew she had beaten her, the threat of personal, reputational damage too much for her superior to stomach. Holmes was an accomplished politician, but she was not a street fighter, having spent too long on management courses and too few hours on the front line. If Helen had to fight dirty, she'd have no hesitation in doing so and, in that event, there would only ever be one winner. Holmes might try to clip her wings, but Helen would meet every challenge head-on, using any and all means at her disposable. She would not be sidelined by a pen-pusher like Holmes. She would not be undermined by a snake like Jennings. She would fight tooth and nail to the end, leading this investigation with all the fire, zeal and determination she could muster.

Naomi's survival depended upon it.

Chapter 67

'Get away from me, you piece of shit.'

Naomi was on her feet, ready to fight tooth and nail if she had to. Having lain stock-still for most of the night, desperately trying to pretend that none of this was real, even as her battered body insisted it *was*, Naomi had sprung up the minute she heard their tormentor approaching. Mia had not budged an inch, remaining laid out on the floor across the room, but despite her injuries, despite the deep despair that had gripped her all night, Naomi was not willing to give her attacker the satisfaction of total submission.

So instead, she'd tried to put as much distance between herself and the door as possible, poised to lash out with foot or fist if her abductor came near her. To her fury, however, he seemed at best indifferent, at worst amused, by her hostile demeanor as he hurried into their cell clutching two battered metal bowls.

'Cool your boots. I'm just bringing you breakfast.'

'Go to hell.'

But the words glanced off him as he placed her bowl on the ground, keeping a wary eye on her right foot, which was primed to strike.

'Your shout, but the cockroaches will have it if you don't...'

He was already moving away, turning his back on her as he

hurried over to Mia. Instinctively, Naomi glanced down at the bowl. As usual, it was full of dull grey slops, as alluring as a bucket of sick. And yet her stomach was groaning and she was starting to feel lightheaded, fatigue and hunger attacking her in a pincer movement. She'd have to eat something and as this was the only thing on offer, she had little choice but to comply eventually.

For now, however, her attention remained riveted on the two figures on the other side of the room, a slow, creeping anxiety stealing over her. Mia remained motionless on the ground, as their captor hung over her, slapping her face and pinching her arm viciously. Slowly, Mia was beginning to stir, moaning gently, her body turning slightly in a feeble gesture of resistance. But she was clearly in a seriously bad way, which angered her tormentor.

'Get yourself together, girl. You're no use to me like this...'

But all he received in response was a wheezing round of coughing, Mia's harsh bark replaced now by a soft gasp. It chilled Naomi to the bone, Mia's total loss of power and energy shocking to behold, and it clearly troubled their attacker too, who straightened now, an angry, resigned look on his face. Shaking his head, he departed without another word, locking the door behind him. Naomi watched him go, suddenly beset by fears. Was Mia beyond saving? Had he given up on her? And if so, what did that mean for Mia? And for her?

And now it hit Naomi. Having spent the night plumbing the depths of despair, feeling she couldn't sink any lower, that she was suffering more than she ever had before, she now realized that the worst was yet to come.

Chapter 68

She cupped the cool water in her hands, then threw it into her face. The effect was jarring but revitalizing, so Charlie repeated the trick. Arriving back at Southampton Central, she'd felt uneasy and troubled, as if a dozen different problems, a dozen subtle threats, were crowding in on her. Desperate concern for Naomi Watson mingled with flashbacks to Leanne's tearful anger, before merging with Jennings' snarling hostility. Charlie knew she had to set an example, to support Helen in her dangerous mission to expose one of their own, yet her anxieties persisted. The icy water had a temporarily restorative effect, but couldn't entirely quell her jangling nerves.

Turning away, she grabbed a handful of paper towels, drying her face impatiently with them. There was no point denying her disquiet, yet she was still angry with herself. She wasn't normally this timid, this hesitant. What was it about this case that made her doubt herself? She had to be strong, she had to keep the team in line, she had to *lead*.

'Get it together, girl,' she muttered darkly, staring at herself in the mirror.

The woman staring back at her looked beleaguered and edgy, so Charlie turned away, making for the door. But as she did so, she heard something that made her pause. The sound of sobbing.

Pausing, she scanned the room. The sinks were deserted and only one cubicle door was closed, so she padded over to it, the sound of crying growing steadily louder. Hesitantly, Charlie knocked on the door, causing the sobs to cease immediately.

'Hello?'

No sound came from within, save for short, strangulated breathing.

'It's DS Brooks. Can I help?'

For a moment, silence reigned, a sad, heavy silence, then Charlie heard movement within. Seconds later the lock slid across and the door opened to reveal a tearful Beth Beamer sitting on the loo seat. The young probationer looked wretched, her cheeks stained with tears, so Charlie quickly stepped inside the confined space, closing the door behind her. It wasn't ideal, the two women virtually on top of one another, but the young officer was in a bad way and Charlie was determined that she should not be discovered in this state. Police stations were no better than schools when it came to unkind gossip, female officers picked upon for showing any signs of 'weakness'.

'What's the matter, Beth? What's happened?' Charlie enquired, concerned.

For a moment, Beth Beamer said nothing, staring disconsolately at the floor before slowly raising her eyes to her superior.

'I'm sorry, I shouldn't be crying like this, but... but I don't think I can do this anymore.'

She seemed close to despair, her face white as a sheet.

'Why? Tell me what's happened.'

'It's Reynolds,' the probationer replied, choking on his name. 'He's making my life hell. He... he knows I talked to you about Naomi and he's not going to let me forget it. I've had a dead rat in my locker, my bike tyres slashed, and everywhere I go, everyone I talk to, it's the same. They all give me that look, like they don't trust me, like they don't *want* me here ...'

Charlie could feel a fierce anger rising within her, but she tried to rein it in.

'Are you sure he's behind it?'

'One hundred per cent,' Beamer replied bitterly. 'He's keeping his head down, staying out of my way, but he's got mates in every department, pals who are very happy to put the boot in, to make my life as uncomfortable as possible. He wants me out, I know he does, and he's going the right way about it.'

Collapsing in on herself, Beamer started to cry once more, her anguish and disappointment spewing forth. It was a sight that saddened and enraged Charlie in equal measure.

'Have you spoken to your line manager about this?' she asked gently.

'Yes! And the Chief too.'

'You spoke to *Holmes* about this?' Charlie replied, surprised by her boldness.

'Yes, my manager wasn't prepared to do anything, so I went straight to her. I thought that maybe another woman would understand what I was going through, but ...'

'What did she say?'

'She suggested ... she suggested I might be happier elsewhere.'

Charlie stared at the young probationer, aghast.

'She said *what*?'

'I'm sorry, I probably shouldn't be telling you any of this,' Beamer said quickly, suddenly looking nervous.

'On the contrary,' Charlie reassured the tearful probationer. 'If senior management are not supporting our female probationers, then I need to know about it. And you can bet DI Grace will have something to say about it too.'

The young officer nodded gratefully, but still seemed stricken.

'I just want to be left alone to do my job, you know,' she continued falteringly. 'Wearing this uniform, serving the community, it's all I've ever wanted to do.'

Charlie felt a flush of recognition, remembering her own childish dreams.

'I was so proud when I got my stripes, my parents too. But how can I carry on, how can I do the job when everyone in this station hates me?'

'Nobody hates you, Beth.'

'You don't see how they look at me,' she cried passionately, her voice shaking. 'Like I'm shit on their shoe, like I'm scum. Everywhere I go, I feel their eyes on me, hear their comments, their insults. I just can't do it anymore.'

'Beth, you mustn't give up, not like this. You've worked too hard to throw it away now.'

'No, no, I've made up my mind,' she insisted. 'I'll work the rest of the day, then I'm going to hand in my resignation.'

Charlie stared at the probationer, stunned. Drawing breath, she crouched down, taking the young woman's hands in hers.

'Listen to me, Beth. I know things seem bleak now, that there's no way out of this, but you *have* to hang in there. Young women like you are the future of this force, the brightest and the best. If you let Reynolds and his cronies beat you, then nothing will ever change. I know it's hard, God knows I've been through it myself, but you have to hold the line. I will deal with Reynolds and his pals, DI Grace will too, making it abundantly clear to them that if they so much as look at you in the wrong way, it'll be *them* leaving Southampton Central. All I need in return is that you stay strong, stare them down, that you refuse to be beaten...'

For a minute, it was as if Charlie was talking to her younger self, memories of past battles and indignities looming large in her mind. Which is why she invested her words with real passion, as she concluded:

'You cannot let them win.'

Chapter 69

PC Dave Reynolds marched along the shabby corridor, consumed by dark thoughts. How quickly life changes, how swiftly
triumph turns to disaster. Last night, before anyone had read
the headlines in the local press, friends and neighbours had
been falling over themselves to pat him on the back, shake his
hand, sing to the world what a jolly good fellow he was. It
was a different story this morning. Having been tipped off last
night by a friend about the damning headlines, he'd expected a
reaction, but he had hoped that his standing in the community,
his long history of service, would delay people's rush to judgement. Not a bit of it. These days it was trial by media, mud
sticking to whomever the papers decided to smear. Neighbours
who were partying with him last night studiously avoided his
eye this morning, bundling their kids into the car and racing
away. It was as if he'd gone from saint to sinner overnight, with
no chance of return.

Swallowing down his fury, Reynolds marched on, determined
to front it out.

'All right, Frank?' he shouted to the portly custody sergeant,
a smile painted on his face.

But there was no comeback, no stale joke or cheeky grin from
the station's keeper today. Just a curt nod, before he resumed

gossiping with a colleague. Enraged, Reynolds buzzed himself in, stalking across the lobby, before diverting towards the stairs. There was already a crowd waiting by the lift bank, the volume of their chat audibly dropping as he approached. He wasn't going to offer himself up for their scrutiny, trapped together in a tiny, tense space, so instead he took the stairs, mounting them three at a time.

Pushing out onto the third floor, he hurried down the corridor, nodding to a veteran family liaison officer as he did so. She said nothing, dropping her eyes, before carrying on. Rage flared in Reynolds and he ground to a halt, turning to follow her progress. He wanted to grab her arm, pin her against the wall, force her to admit that there was nothing in these rumours, that they were baseless, vindictive innuendo. But she was already well out of range, increasing her speed with each step. Seething, PC Dave Reynolds turned once more to resume his progress, only to find DI Helen Grace heading directly towards him.

For a moment, he was stupefied. CID never graced the third floor, never mixed with ordinary mortals. Which meant that Grace had come here deliberately, perhaps spying his arrival from her vantage point on the seventh floor, making sure their paths crossed.

'You've got some nerve coming down here!' he barked, advancing upon her. 'Marching straight into the lion's den.'

'On the contrary,' Grace replied coolly. 'Everyone's been incredibly friendly. I only hope *you* get a similar reception.'

Her knowing tone was hard to stomach. Clearly she'd already been turning people – *his* people – against him, doubling down on last night's slander.

'I warned you before to be careful,' Reynolds hissed, his blood boiling. 'And I'll warn you again. I'm part of the fabric of this place, always have been, always will be.'

'I wouldn't bet on it. The place could do with a bit of renovation. Some parts of it seem to be old and rotten, in dire need of repair ...'

'Watch your step, Grace. I won't tell you again. You may think you can trash me in public, blacken my name, but I won't take it lying down, you can be sure of that. Those historic allegations were false, unfounded, proven to be so, yet you seem determined to destroy my career because of some misguided notion of justice. Well, be warned, I will sue, I will seek reparations, and when the dust settles, it'll be your head on the block, not mine.'

He was in her face now, breathing on her, projecting as much violence and venom as he could at the experienced female officer. But to his surprise and alarm, she betrayed not the slightest flicker of anxiety, her eyes boring into his as she replied:

'Let me make one thing very clear, PC Reynolds. You are unfit to wear this uniform. In fact, you are a disgrace to this profession, a cancer eating away at us from within.'

Reynolds stared at her, taken aback.

'Which is why,' she continued, her tone steely and determined, 'I will make it my personal mission to see that you are run out of this force. What's more, I'll enjoy doing it.'

She looked at him, her eyes sparkling, relishing his discomfort. Then, stepping aside, she hurried on, marching purposefully to the stairwell, before disappearing from view. Reynolds remained glued to the spot, however, stunned by her pushback. He'd been hoping to intimidate her, as he'd done so many others before, to scare her into withdrawing her forces, but her determination to destroy him, to hold his feet to the fire, was crystal clear. For the first time in years, PC Dave Reynolds felt a frisson of fear. He'd known there would be battles to fight, colleagues to win over, but suddenly the odds seemed stacked against him, given the appalling implacability of his opponent. He had hoped this would be a disciplinary matter, something he could fudge, obscure and stymie, but actually Grace's attack on him seemed like something far worse, far more threatening.

It felt like a personal vendetta.

Chapter 70

'So what did he say?'

Charlie stood in front of Helen, troubled but intrigued. Helen, by contrast, seemed entirely relaxed as she rounded her desk to confront the mountain of files awaiting her.

'He threatened me, of course. He only knows one way – to attack, demean, belittle and intimidate – but I think he's finally cottoning on that that won't cut it this time. He's got nothing on me and once his cronies turn their backs on him, he'll have nowhere to go.'

'What about Holmes? She's had his back so far.'

'Maybe, but bad headlines are bad headlines. And if – when – she realizes that we're right about Reynolds, she'll drop him like a hot coal. She's new here, doesn't want her first major intervention to be the spirited defence of a serial rapist. He's on borrowed time here, but we need evidence. How did you get on with Leanne Gardner?'

'Not good, I'm afraid,' Charlie conceded. 'Obviously, I'll follow up with her, but she's getting married soon, doesn't want to know.'

'I see. OK, well, let's follow up with the other two victims, see if they are more open to talking to us. What else have we got?'

'Well, DC Wilson's been doing some good work, comparing

Dave Reynolds' historic beat pattern with our missing girls. We know he encountered Naomi on his rounds and records show he would have been patrolling Portswood around the time Mia went missing.'

Helen nodded, pleased, but there was more to come.

'Plus, we think he was working the St Denys beat when Shanice Lloyd vanished. She was last seen outside the New Testament Church on Priory Road.'

'OK, so we've got a potential pattern,' Helen responded, excited. 'He encounters them, talks to them, scopes them out, then returns to pick them up after hours.'

'Makes sense.'

'And what about his current movements? After hours, I mean. Has he visited anywhere remote, out of the way, somewhere he might be keeping Naomi and Mia?'

'Not that I can see,' Charlie replied, grave. 'We've triangulated his movements and he's either here, on the beat or back at home.'

'So either he's keeping them at home...'

'Which seems unlikely, given that he's got a wife and kid.'

'...or he's leaving his phone at home when he goes out to avoid being tracked.'

Charlie nodded in agreement, before replying:

'Do we want him put under surveillance?'

'In time, yes. But we'll need more, something concrete, before Holmes will agree to that. I'd like to do a bit more digging, find out what we're dealing with here. Reynolds is going to resist all the way, saying that black is white, that this is a deranged personal attack, but I'd like to look closer at Jackie Reynolds. She could be our way in. She looked nervous as hell when I spoke to her yesterday. I think she's scared of Reynolds, is worried what the fallout might be for her, for her son, if the sky falls in.'

'Could she also be a victim?' Charlie queried.

'Very possibly – she's certainly a lot younger than him.'

Helen picked up her file and was already leafing through it.

'They got married when he was twenty-five and she was seventeen. Allegedly they were together from when she was sixteen, but who's to say that's true? He could have met her when she was underage, groomed her. She fell pregnant soon after they got married and has never worked. She plays the loyal wife, kept in her little box where Reynolds wants her, but there's something fishy about the whole thing.'

'What do you mean?' Charlie queried.

'Well, I was in their house yesterday,' Helen continued, ignoring Charlie's look of surprise. 'And they are minted. The house is immaculate, they've got a huge Sky Glass TV on the wall, not to mention a new BMW X5 on the drive. They go on luxury holidays apparently, send their son to private school. Now how does Dave Reynolds afford all that on a PC's salary? He's got no family that we know of, nor does she, so where's the money coming from?'

'You think... you think he's somehow *profiting* from these girls' abductions?' Charlie asked, shivering inwardly. 'That he's monetizing his crimes?'

'It's got to be a possibility. Jackie Reynolds had a purse stacked with notes, a huge wad of £20 notes. Who the hell uses cash these days? Dealers and criminals, that's who. I've got Meredith examining a couple of the notes as we speak...'

The two women stared at each, lost in their own thoughts, before Helen added:

'Reynolds is a bad man. I'd bet my life on it. The only question for me now is how *far* does his criminality extend?'

Once more, both women lapsed into silence. It was a sobering thought, which only raised their anxiety levels further. What the hell were they dealing with here?

Chapter 71

'What are you going to do about DI Grace?'

Flanked by his police union representative, Dave Reynolds wasted no time in getting straight to the point. Chief Superintendent Holmes had been unwilling to see him, claiming her packed diary schedule wouldn't allow it, but in the end it was *he* who'd proved unwilling to budge, kicking up such a stink in her office that eventually she was forced to relent. She sat opposite him now, looking distracted and stressed.

'She's completely lost the plot. There are genuine crimes out there that need investigating, significant threats to public order that require our attention, yet instead Grace seems determined to pursue this unjustified witch hunt.'

'By any means necessary,' his union rep added pointedly. 'DI Grace has always treated the rules, well-established protocols, with disdain. I've crossed swords with her many times over the years in this regard. But I must say her behaviour over the last few days has plumbed new depths.'

'What specifically are you referring to?' Holmes asked testily, annoyed by his prim tone.

'How about dragging my name through the mud? Hanging me out to dry as ... as a bloody sex offender?' Reynolds responded, looking aggrieved and bewildered. 'But that's only the half of it. Yesterday, she tricked her way into my home on the grounds of pursuing some bogus traffic offence, then quizzed my wife about me, our family, my career history. There was no other officer present, my wife had no representation, but DI Grace doesn't care. She's been running a covert investigation into me, my past conduct, for days now, without any authorization from you or anyone else at this station. It's personal, it's nasty and it's completely out of order. She accuses me of being a law-breaker, yet *she's* broken every rule in the book.'

'As you can see, Chief Superintendent,' Reynolds' rep chimed in, 'a persistent and flagrant disregard for due process.'

'You have to suspend her immediately,' Reynolds persisted. 'And if I were you, I'd do the same to DS Brooks. Those two are like peas in a pod, as bad as each other...'

Holmes regarded Reynolds curiously, intrigued by this blatant push to banish fellow officers.

'I take it then that you're denying there's any truth in her accusations?'

'Absolutely and categorically,' Reynolds insisted, aggrieved. 'My record's clean and so is my conscience.'

His representative nodded vigorously, but Holmes ignored him.

'In which case I can see why you're so troubled, so angry, about recent developments.'

'Let's call it what it is. A witch hunt,' Reynolds repeated.

'And in many ways, I share your outrage. Indeed, I had DI Grace in here this morning and during our conversation I let her feel the full weight of my displeasure. I don't like mavericks and DI Grace seems intent on pushing everything to the limit, with scant regard for the consequences, either for individual officers or the reputation of this station.'

Reynolds nodded eagerly, waiting for the coup de grace.

'However, as things currently stand, I can't possibly sanction suspending the head of our Major Incident Team.'

'You can't spare her just because of her status, her position. If she's broken the rules, she needs to go,' Reynolds fired back, looking like he might be about to explode.

'But has she?' Holmes returned, her tone even.

'I thought we'd just agreed—'

'DI Grace flatly denied leaking anything to the *Evening News* and frankly I can't prove that she did. So unless you have evidence to the contrary...?'

'Well, no,' Reynolds said angrily. 'But you know as well as I do that she was responsible for the leak.'

'And as for the incident with your wife, did a traffic offence occur or not?' Holmes asked, ducking the accusation.

'Well, there was no bulb in the rear brake light,' Reynolds conceded, bristling. 'But *we* didn't take it out.'

'So DI Grace was within her rights to sanction your wife and issue a ticket?'

'Technically, yes, but she used it as an excuse to enter my home.'

'Did she force her way in, or was she invited in?'

'The latter, I guess, but the fact remains that it was just a ruse. A way of gathering information, of playing mind games with us.'

'None of which can be proved, PC Reynolds. So you see the bind we're in?'

'Why the hell are you defending her?' Reynolds burst out. 'She's a dangerous renegade who you should be clamping down on, making a public example of. What's she got on you?'

A frown creased Holmes' expression, but she maintained her cool.

'Instead of trading insults, can I suggest that we all just get on with doing our jobs. As for DI Grace's investigation of your

conduct, well she's obviously at liberty to do so during the execution of her duties. There is no special dispensation for serving
officers, as you well know. And if, as you say, there is nothing in
her accusations, then hopefully everything will be resolved in a
timely fashion to everyone's satisfaction.'

'And in the meantime, she gets to trash my reputation? A
reputation I've spent years building, *earning*, through solid,
dogged, loyal policing...'

'I understand your anxiety, PC Reynolds, I really do, but she
has to be allowed to do her job.'

'Ah, this is horseshit.'

Reynolds rocked back in his chair, before turning to his representative, exasperated.

'Come on, let's get out of here.'

Livid, Reynolds rose to his feet, but as he did so, Holmes'
voice cut through.

'I would remind you, constable, to treat senior officers with
the respect they deserve. Whatever my feelings about DI
Grace's conduct, there is no doubting that her line of enquiry
is valid and necessary. You omitted to mention meeting Naomi
Watson on the night she went missing and there are grounds
for questioning your conduct whilst serving as a police officer,
whether or not those questions ultimately prove to be valid. So
I would suggest you do your job and allow DI Grace to do hers.
Hectoring senior officers, whilst pushing for your colleagues to
be suspended, is not the way to win friends round here. Is that
understood?'

'Perfectly,' Reynolds responded, not trusting himself to say
more.

'Then get out of my sight.'

This time there was no mistaking Holmes' anger. Defiant to
the last, Reynolds glared at her, before marching away, head held

high. But inside, his guts were churning, his brain feverishly trying to process this latest turn of events. It was well known that Holmes and Grace had a difficult relationship and he'd been convinced the station chief would take his side against the rebellious CID officer. But he'd misjudged the situation badly, earning only Holmes' anger in the process. Clearly this most political of station chiefs was determined not to ally herself with *anyone*, to keep her hands clean and her options open, should a suitable scapegoat be required further down the line. Once more Dave Reynolds felt the ground shifting beneath his feet, old certainties giving way to fresh doubts. Where would it all end? Would he see off this latest challenge? Or had he finally met his match? Only time would tell, but for the first time in years, PC Dave Reynolds felt under pressure, every passer-by viewing him with suspicion, watching and waiting for him to slip up.

The hunter had become the hunted.

Chapter 72

His attacker came up fast behind, giving Brent Mason no time to react. Finally released from custody, the dealer had hurried away from Southampton Central, determined that none of his associates should see him tripping happily down the steps of Southampton Central. That's how rumours started, rumours that could get you killed.

Head down, Brent moved swiftly away down the street, avoiding the gaze of passers-by. He was determined not to run or appear uneasy; in fact he wanted to draw as little attention to himself as possible. But his measured pace cost him now, as heavy footsteps hurried up behind him, catching him off guard.

He had no weapon, nothing to defend himself with, but if one of his rivals, or indeed one of his associates, wanted rid of him, he wasn't prepared to go down without a fight. Spinning, he advanced on his nemesis, snarling, only to stay his raised fist at the last second. His shadow was not a dealer or a hired hood, but a police officer, somebody he knew by name, someone who he'd had dealings with before.

'DC Jennings? What can I do for—'

But he didn't get to finish, Jennings grabbing him by the shirt and dragging him down an alleyway, out of sight.

'Hey, what hell are you doing, man? Your lot just let me *go*.'

'Maybe so, but I wanted a quick word.'

'Then get your bloody hands off me. You can't mess me around like this.'

'When we've finished our chat. I let you go now and I won't see you for dust.'

Annoyed, Brent tried to wrench himself free from the officer's grasp. For a moment, Jennings appeared to relinquish his grip, but it was only a ruse, Jennings allowing the dealer to take a step forward, before slamming Brent back into the brickwork.

'Play nice, Brent, or this could go very badly for you...' his attacker breathed menacingly, his malodorous mouth just inches from the young man's face.

'All right, all right,' Brent wheezed. 'You've made your point.'

'Good, then I'll cut to the chase. I need information.'

'About what?' Brent asked, suspicious.

'The Freemantle shooting.'

Already, Brent was shaking his head. There was no way he'd risk that. Jennings' reaction was immediate, his hand sliding up from Brent's chest to his throat, pressing down hard on his Adam's apple.

'Get off, you're hurting me,' the dealer gasped.

'I'll do a lot worse if you don't give me what I want. I know you know who organized the ambush, who took the money. I want names, I want locations, I want the whole lot.'

'Get out of here, you must be mad.'

'You better believe it,' Jennings continued, pushing still harder on the young man's throat. 'Which is why I'm not walking away from here until I've got what I need. I want to know the who, why, where. I want an arrest.'

'I've said I can't,' Brent protested. 'I'll be a dead man walking if the Main Street boys know I grassed them up.'

'Not if they're all inside, Brent. And I can make that happen.

In fact, I'm determined to make it happen. Which presents you with an opportunity. Think about it, if I can take down the rest of the Main Street crew, if I can nail them for attempted murder, then a space opens up in the drugs market. A space you could fill.'

Now Brent paused, perplexed. A serving police officer appeared to be encouraging him to deal drugs. It had to be a set-up, a trap, yet Jennings seemed completely sincere and would hardly be strangling him if their conversation was being recorded. Even so, ratting on fellow criminals, your own paymasters, was a massive ask, casting a permanent cloud over your character, your loyalty, your reliability.

'I'm sorry, man,' Brent replied, twisting his neck in order to try and get a bit more air in his lungs. 'I can't do it, there are some things that just aren't right.'

But Jennings could tell he was wavering, so he went in for the kill.

'What if I was to sweeten the deal a little further?'

Brent looked at him, surprised.

What can you possibly offer me? I'm in the clear. Grace let me go.'

'How about the stash they took off you when they picked you up?'

Jennings dug into his jacket pocket, producing a handful of small, clear plastic bags, each containing a good measure of cocaine. Brent stared at it, disbelieving. It looked like his stash, but was this guy really going to give it back to him?

'What's more,' Jennings added, grinning wolfishly, 'I can supply you with a steady quantity of this, gratis, if you supply me with the information I need. Who ordered the shooting, who pulled the trigger, where are they likely to be now. If you do that for me, if you can lead me to them, then I will give you protection, I will provide supply. Think about it, Brent, you could be a solo operator if you wanted to be. The next Mr Big...'

Brent eyed him, saying nothing, his vision clouded by dreams of riches.

'Now what do you say?' Jennings continued urgently. 'Do we have a deal or not?'

Chapter 73

The door opened a crack and a pair of eyes peered nervously out over the safety chain.

'Yes?' the inhabitant demanded, suspiciously.

'Mr Malcolm Cartwright?' Charlie enquired.

'Yes,' the elderly man repeated curtly.

'I'm DS Brooks. I was wondering if I might have a quick word?'

His eyes now drifted to her warrant card, taking his time to examine the detail carefully before reluctantly removing the chain and ushering Charlie inside.

'I've already spoken to a member of your team,' the pensioner complained as he led his visitor slowly into the living room. 'Big chap, blond hair, a DC, I think...'

'DC Jennings.'

'That's the fella. I'm really not sure what I can tell you that I didn't tell him...'

He shuffled across the room, before collapsing into an armchair. Turning the TV off, he gestured for Charlie to seat herself on the sofa opposite. She obliged, noting that her host continued to avoid eye contact. Was that because he was annoyed? Or did something else lie behind his circumspection?

'I wanted to go over the details of your statement,' she

responded purposefully. 'Just to make sure we've got everything correct, if that's OK?'

Cartwright shrugged reluctantly, but didn't refuse.

'You drive a dark blue Mazda 5, registration DB14 HTE. Is that correct?'

'I imagine you walked past it on the drive, so...'

Still no eye contact and now a flash of irritation. Intrigued, Charlie continued.

'And you were driving it through the Lordship Road under-pass on the night of the ninth of November, correct?'

'Yes. As I said before, I was returning from visiting my brother-in-law. We're not terribly close, but since my wife's death, he's the only family I've got.'

'I see. And you passed through the tunnel at around 9.45 p.m.?'

A brief nod of the head.

'An on-site traffic cam shows that it took you upwards of five minutes to exit the tunnel, a journey which should take no more than thirty seconds. Can you tell me why that was?'

'As I explained to your colleague,' Cartwright replied impatiently, 'I received a phone call from a friend, so I did the sensible thing and pulled over to take it. We spoke for a few minutes, then I drove on. That's really all there is to it.'

'Well, that certainly would explain it,' Charlie replied, smiling. 'The only problem is that there's no record of you having received a call at that time.'

Now there was no pushback. No condescension, no irritation, no fatigued shaking of the head. The old man sat stock-still, staring determinedly at the carpet.

'You have a mobile registered with Vodafone, phone number 07768 037608. Is that the phone you're referring to?'

He continued to stare at the floor, unwilling to respond.

'Is that your phone, Mr Cartwright?'

'Yes, yes,' he muttered unhappily.

'Well, I've got your call log here,' Charlie said, pulling a sheet from her file and handing it to him. 'As you can see there's a call at 17.00 hours, but after that nothing until 10.15 the following day.'

Cartwright held the piece of paper, but didn't bother looking at it.

'In light of that information, would you care to revise your statement?'

Her tone was firm, even a little aggressive, and now finally the pensioner raised his eyes to meet hers. Instantly, Charlie saw it – fear.

'I would advise you to think very carefully about your response, Mr Cartwright. As I'm sure you're aware, misleading the police in the execution of their duties is a criminal offence.'

Charlie noted that the piece of paper was shaking in his hands now, his discomfort rising with each passing second.

'Malcolm, what really happened that night?'

'Look, I don't know what all this is about, but I've done nothing wrong, OK?'

'Perhaps you'll let me be the judge of that. What happened?'

'I… well… I didn't go out that night. It wasn't me driving.'

'So who was at the wheel that night?' Charlie asked, surprised.

'An old friend. Well actually, an old neighbour. Used to live two doors down.'

'A name, please?'

Malcolm Cartwright shifted uneasily in his seat, before murmuring, 'Dave Reynolds. He's one of your lot, a beat copper.'

'I see,' Charlie replied carefully. 'It's my understanding that Mr Reynolds and his family have two cars of their own, so can you tell me why he'd need to use yours?'

'Do we really have to do this?' the pensioner suddenly protested. 'I'm sure Dave's done nothing wrong and I'd hate to—'

'Can you just answer the question, please?'

There was a brief silence.

'Look, the truth is that I don't use the car much anymore. My eyesight's not what it was, I probably shouldn't be using it at all. Since Covid, I… I get a lot of things delivered – food, prescriptions and so on – but I don't want the car to go to rack and ruin. I paid enough for it and would like to get something back, when I eventually do decide to sell.'

'So…?'

'So, as a favour to me, Dave pops round once in a while, takes it for a spin.'

Charlie's heart was pounding now, but she kept her voice even as she replied, 'And he did that for you on the evening of the 9th June?'

'Yes.'

Charlie stared at the pensioner, her eyes sparkling fiercely. She was thrilled at having elicited a potentially major breakthrough from the reluctant witness, but also angry that he had kept this vital information to himself for so long.

'And can I ask why you lied to my colleague when first asked about this?'

The elderly man shifted uncomfortably in his seat.

'Look, I didn't mean any harm by it. The truth is, I didn't really believe that Dave drove the car purely out of the kindness of his heart. I suspected… well, I suspected that maybe he had a fancy woman on the go, someone he didn't want his wife knowing about, and that it would be easier, better, for him if he didn't take his own car. Honestly, I didn't pry too deeply, it's none of my business really…'

'I wish you had,' Charlie countered, pointedly.

'Why? What on earth has he done?'

'David Reynolds is the prime suspect in an active investigation concerning the abduction and false imprisonment of an underage girl.'

Perhaps she could have kept this to herself, but Charlie wanted to see the old boy's reaction when he realized what kind of animal he'd been covering for. But to her annoyance, Malcolm Cartwright reacted not with regret or horror, but pure astonishment.

'Dave? Mixed up in something like that? No, no, no, I think you must have got the wrong end of the stick, dear.'

He leaned forwards, smiling, enunciating his words clearly as if speaking to a child.

'David Reynolds is one of the nicest people I know.'

Chapter 74

'What the hell's going on, Dave? I don't understand...'

Jackie Reynolds stared at her husband, stupefied, craving re-assurance. But there was none to be had today, David Reynolds taking a step towards her and jabbing a finger in her face.

'Stop twittering and listen to what I'm saying. I want you to take the cash, all of it, and put it in that bag.'

Still she made no attempt to move, so Dave Reynolds snatched up the empty holdall and marched into the utility room. Once inside, he teased up the loose floor tile and reached down into the void, swiftly retrieving a thick jiffy bag full of cash. Staring down at the contents, he paused momentarily, horrified by the waste, then stuffed the full envelope into the bag. Straightening up, he marched back into the kitchen, shoving the holdall into Jackie's arms, rocking her back on her heels.

'You'll need to throw in your gold watch, the engraved lighter and your diamond earrings too. In fact, put all your bloody jewellery in there.'

'Why? What's happened?'

'Then I want you go out the back way, take a bus to the docks. My car's parked down there. Pick it up, drive down to Calshot and then throw the bloody bag in the sea.'

'You can't be serious?' Jackie protested, aghast.

'Deadly,' her husband hit back, staring fiercely at her.

'But that stuff must be worth a fortune.'

'Which is why we have to get rid of it. That bitch Grace will be sniffing around here soon enough and if there's anything here we can't account for through our own funds, then we're done for.'

'Well, I'm sorry, I'm not doing it,' Jackie replied, stepping away from him.

'I beg your pardon,' Reynolds hissed, his tone suddenly menacing.

'I've spent years putting that collection together, plus there's loads of sentimental stuff there, from birthdays, anniversaries...'

'I don't give a shit. Get rid of it.'

But still Jackie made no move to comply, shaking her head angrily.

'I said this would happen. Buying stuff with hooky money. I told you it would come back on us, didn't I?'

'Yeah, you put up a great fight, love,' he responded witheringly. 'You really worked hard to stop me buying you the rings, the bracelets, the earrings...'

'You said it was safe, that nobody would know,' Jackie hissed.

'Well now it's not, so get your coat on and get cracking, before I lose my temper.'

'So that's it, is it? Everything we've built up, the nice life we have, gone just like that?' she replied, bitter, accusing. 'Just because *you* say so?'

She stood directly in front of him now, her eyes blazing, her face flushed. For a moment, her husband appeared to regard her with incomprehension, before fury gripped his features.

'Do you remember what you were when I found you?'

'Don't you dare, Dave. I won't stand for it,' his wife retaliated, her voice rising sharply.

'Well, do you?'

Taking a step forward, he shot out an arm, grabbing his wife by the throat.

'You were a whore in the gutter. A dirty little whore.'

Jackie struggled wildly, but his grip was too tight, robbing her of breath, of defiance.

'But I took pity on you, raised you up, didn't I? Now look at you. A big house, plenty of money, married to a pillar of the community. You've made it, girl.'

Tears were creeping down her cheeks, but he made no move to loosen his hold on her.

'But, be careful, eh? Because I can toss you back onto the streets anytime I want. Is that what you'd like?'

Even under his tight stranglehold, Jackie managed a tiny shake of her head.

'You bet, you don't. Because who on earth would want you now? You're a scraggy piece of old mutton, dressed up as lamb. No man in his right mind would even want to look at you, let alone fuck you. You're all washed up, Jackie...'

But now his victim's expression suddenly changed, fear and alarm in her eyes, as she darted a glance towards the front door. Turning sharply, Dave Reynolds saw Archie standing in the doorway, glaring with shock and fury at his father.

'Take your bloody hands off her.'

The teenager was already crossing the floor towards them, determined, enraged.

'Stay where you are, boy. This is nothing to do with you.'

'I said, take your hands off—'

Dave Reynolds' fist crashed into Archie's chin without warning, sending him staggering backwards. For a moment, the teenager looked like he might steady himself, respond in kind. But then suddenly the boy seemed to lose his balance, crashing heavily to the floor. Now, finally, Reynolds relaxed his grip, his wife staggering across the floor, clutching her throat, before falling to her knees next to her son, pulling him to her. Livid, Reynolds crossed to them, glowering over the terrified pair. For a moment, it seemed that he might inflict more pain on them. But then, pulling himself up sharply, Reynolds turned, snatching up the holdall before heading for the stairs.

Pausing at the bottom of the stairwell, he turned to face his floored family once more, hissing at them:

'You two deserve each other.'

Chapter 75

The phone buzzed angrily in her hand. Darting a look at the caller ID, Helen clocked that it was DC Jennings calling, so rejected the call, returning her attention to Meredith Walker, Southampton Central's chief forensics officer. Helen had no desire to be disturbed, not now that they finally had a concrete lead.

'Can you show me?' she asked Meredith eagerly.

Nodding, the experienced officer beckoned Helen over to the microscope. Illuminated on the slide was a £20 note, the strong fluorescent beam picking out strange swirling patterns below.

'There are two matching fingerprints. One partial here...'

She indicated a half-moon of tight elegant lines on the edge of the note.

'...and a full one just here.'

As she spoke, Meredith flipped the note over, revealing the other side. Half an inch in from the edge, a complete fingerprint could be seen.

'We've run the comparison test a couple of times to be sure, but they're definitely the same person. Left index finger.'

'And you're sure about the match?'

'One hundred per cent. The lines are crystal clear, he must have been clutching the note quite tightly and, look, you can see that the finger has a slight abrasion on it, maybe a historical cut or nick, which is mirrored on both prints.'

Helen nodded eagerly, the excitement rising inside her.

'So who is he? You said he was known to us already?'

'Graham Armstrong. Edinburgh-born, but been living down here for the best part of forty years. He's a convicted paedophile, who returned to the Southampton area following his release from prison after a fifteen-year stretch.'

Helen took this in, intrigued and troubled in equal measure.

'What exactly did he serve time for?' she demanded.

'Possession and distribution of indecent images of children and teens. He was also convicted on an international warrant of directing and facilitating live online abuse of children and teenagers in Thailand and Indonesia.'

Helen blew out her cheeks. It was worse, much worse, than she'd feared.

'Do we know where he is now?'

'Well, you'd have to check with the probation service. There's an address in Weston on his file, but I don't know how diligent Armstrong's been in sticking to the rules of his licence.'

Helen nodded, deep in thought.

'Can I ask where you found the note?' Meredith enquired.

'In a suspect's wallet. Well, his wife's purse actually...' Helen replied, her mind whirring.

'So you're thinking there's some kind of financial relationship between this guy and the suspect in the Naomi Watson case?'

'Possibly. She had a stash of these notes, more than you'd usually take out of a cashpoint and if we can prove they came from Armstrong, then we've got our first proper link between David Reynolds and a wider paedophile network.'

Helen was not as coy as Meredith in using the suspect's name, earning a half-smile from her colleague.

'But first we have to find Armstrong. If he can give us Reynolds, then hopefully we can bring this case to a swift conclusion. Was there anything else on the notes? Drug traces, sweat, anything like that?'

'No, just the prints. Isn't that enough for you?'

'It'll do for now,' she replied gratefully, patting Meredith on the arm.

Turning, Helen departed, pushing through the doors and away down the corridor towards the exit. She felt alarmed, excited and tense all at once, this latest development suggesting a much bigger, more complicated crime than she'd at first suspected. It concerned her, her mind raging at the thought of what Naomi and Mia might be being forced to endure, but it also raised her hopes that they were both still alive.

Would they find them in time? Could they rescue them before any further violence was meted out on them? It was a tantalizing prospect, more so now that they could potentially link the Reynolds family to a convicted paedophile. Helen felt a shiver of excitement as she walked back to her bike, the sense that perhaps finally the wheel was about to turn.

At long last, they had their first real break in this troubling case.

Chapter 76

'These two men hold the key to finding out what happened to Naomi Jackson and Mia Davies.'

Helen placed a mugshot of Graham Armstrong next to the photo of David Reynolds that was already fixed to the board. The team had returned to base to hear the latest developments, all that is except DC Jennings and DC Reid, who had apparently gone rogue, busting heads on an industrial estate across town in pursuit of the Freemantle shooters. This blatant act of rebellion made Helen's blood boil, but she couldn't afford to let herself get distracted by it now. Every second counted in the hunt for the missing girls.

'Having thought that Naomi's abductor was a lone wolf, it's now my belief that David Reynolds is part of a wider paedophile network. If we can break Reynolds, if we can locate Armstrong, then I think we find Naomi and Mia.'

'We're sure we can make that link based on a bank note alone?' DC Malik queried. 'Jackie Reynolds could have got it out of a cashpoint; we can't prove that it was payment from Armstrong.'

'Not *yet*,' Helen counselled. 'But to me the coincidence of the connection is too great to overlook. I spoke to Armstrong's probation officer earlier, turns out he's been off grid for upwards of a year, no contact at all. We can assume, I think, that's he's not honouring the terms of his licence in any way and that he's gone underground for a reason. PC Reynolds is a different animal, he prefers hiding in plain sight, but I believe he has a secret side too, a secret life that's entirely concealed from the world around him – his colleagues, his neighbours, perhaps even his wife too.'

'As evidenced by his manipulation of Malcolm Cartwright,' Charlie overlapped, sticking a picture of the blue Mazda 5 on the board just beneath Reynolds' picture.

'Could Cartwright be in on it too?' DC Edwards asked. 'Is he an offender?'

'We don't think so,' Charlie replied quickly. 'There's no history of criminality and no evidence that he has an online life. There's no internet connection at his house and his phone is from the ark, so for now we're saying he's just a gullible stooge.'

'Obviously Meredith and her team are poring over the impounded Mazda now, to see if there's any forensic link to Naomi Watson. In the meantime, we need to pin down the Mazda's movements on the night she was abducted. DC McAndrew?'

The loyal officer stepped forward, taking her place in front of the team.

'The traffic cams at the tunnel exit show the Mazda leaving the tunnel at 9.51 p.m. Impossible to see who's in it because of the angle, but we do pick it up again later. I've sent a couple of officers out to do a major CCTV trawl, as we're really just getting to grips with this, but currently we have two more shots of the vehicle. First on Marine Parade, and then again on Chapel Road. After that, nothing until it reappears the following day on Endle Street on its way back to Malcolm Cartwright's house in Itchen.'

'So we're saying he stashed it in Midanbury for the night?' DC Wilson suggested. 'That that's where Naomi is being held?'

'That's certainly a strong possibility,' Helen concurred. 'That she, and maybe Mia too, have been imprisoned in the eastern part of the city. That obviously doesn't narrow it down very much, but I've asked uniform to do a sweep of that area, looking for any locations that might fit the bill. If I'm right that Armstrong is involved, that there is a wider global audience for Reynolds' horrific crimes, then that suggests to me that he needs a discreet base, away from heavily residential areas perhaps, with a decent internet connection, electricity and so forth. So it's not going to be somewhere totally derelict, nor some shack on waste ground. Perhaps a building that's awaiting renovation, or due to be sold.'

'Or some tasteful suburban semi with a bloody dungeon,' DC McAndrew offered bitterly.

'Possibly, but Reynolds is very careful, very cautious, and I think he'd be wary of any location where the girls might be heard. DC Edwards, I'd like you to take point on this, please, running the rule over possible locations and liaising with our colleagues in uniform.'

'Of course, boss.'

Nodding her thanks, Helen was about to continue when the door banged open. Looking up, Helen saw DC Jennings and DC Reid strolling towards them, oozing self-satisfaction. On her ride back to Southampton Central, the news had broken that the pair had scrambled tactical support to an industrial estate in Townhill Park, unearthing a drugs factory *and* the two Main Street members who Brent Mason alleged were responsible for the Freemantle shooting. No wonder Jennings and his sidekick looked pleased as punch.

'Ah, DCs Jennings and Reid. How nice of you to join us.'

Jennings nodded, but said nothing, his eyes sparkling and shrewd.

'If you could perhaps apologize to the rest of the team, then we can get on?'

'Apologize?' Jennings blurted, confused and wrong-footed.

'The team summons was not a request. It was an order. You've shown considerable disrespect to myself, DS Brooks and the rest of the team by electing to ignore it. I think we all deserve an apology, don't you?'

'But you know where I've been, what we've achieved,' he pushed back, bristling.

'Yes, you've been out playing cops and robbers.'

'I've been out doing *proper* policework,' Jennings fired back. 'Catching dangerous criminals, busting drug rings, pulling in street gear that's worth more than half a million quid.'

Helen broke into a smile, giving him a sarcastic round of applause.

'And I bet the Chief Super is thrilled. It'll play well with the press for sure. And who knows, you might even get a little medal for it.'

Jennings glared at her, enraged by her mocking tone.

'But I'm *not* impressed,' Helen continued, stern. 'And neither is DS Brooks. When a superior officer gives you a direct order, I expect you to follow it.'

'Even if those orders are wrong-headed, misguided?' Jennings countered aggressively.

'I beg your pardon?'

'This whole unit is back to front,' Jennings continued, undeterred. 'It's priorities all wrong. I've said it from the off and I know half the officers here agree with me. The senior leadership team need to take a long hard look at themselves. Or step aside and make way for those who know how to run a Major Incident Team.'

It was so preposterous, so jumped up, that Helen could have laughed. But it was a serious challenge to her authority, however, and had to be dealt with.

'Well, I'm certainly impressed by your ambition. Perhaps you moved to this station, this unit, specifically to shake it up?'

'That's about the size of it,' Jennings replied, standing taller.

'Well, that's odd because I had a private word with your old boss last night. DI Bentham, down in Dorset. Turns out the reason he gave you such a good testimonial, the reason he bigged you up so much, was that he was *desperate* to get rid of you.'

Jennings glared at Helen, suddenly looking less cocksure.

'Apparently when you worked for him, you were ... now, let me get this right ... yes, you were "lazy, arrogant and entitled". Those were his exact words. Good to see things have changed, DC Jennings.'

'You've got no right to talk to me like that.'

'I've got every right,' Helen cut in angrily. 'You've been nothing but trouble since the moment you got here. Ducking your responsibilities, resisting authority, taking credit for other people's work. But it stops today, otherwise you're out. Is that clear?'

He stared at her, his eyes blazing, but he said nothing.

'I said, is that clear?' Helen continued, raising her voice still further.

Reluctantly, Jennings shrugged, backing down.

'DC Reid?'

'Ready and willing to serve, ma'am. And apologies for earlier, apologies to you all ...' he piped nervously.

'Well then, let's see if we can make use of you. DC Reid, you can assist DC Edwards, and as for you, DC Jennings, I've got a special task that will suit you down to the ground: Graham Armstrong, retired firefighter and known paedophile. I'd like you to find him for me, before the day's out, please.'

'On my own?'

'I'm sure an officer of your unquestionable gifts won't find it a problem. The rest of you will accompany DS Brooks to the Reynolds' residence to assist with his arrest and the subsequent search operation. So, game faces on please. We've been too cautious, too respectful up until this point, now it's time to get serious. It's time to shake the tree.'

Chapter 77

'David Reynolds, I'm arresting you on suspicion of abduction and false imprisonment.'

Charlie stood opposite the decorated officer, who was eyeing her with naked hostility. As she continued to read him his rights, Reynolds never once broke eye contact, his gaze burning into hers, challenging her to stutter, to stumble, to give up. He was determined not to make this easy for her, yet it was *he* who was in the dock here, standing alone in his living room, surrounded by family photos and police commendations, even as a dozen fellow officers were preparing to turn this place, his life, upside down. Concluding the speech that she'd made so many times before in her career, Charlie took a step towards the suspect.

'You know the drill,' she continued briskly. 'So if you could turn around for me...?'

But Reynolds remained where he was, his eyes glued to Charlie. She saw anger there, but also incomprehension that he was about to be led out of his own house in handcuffs. Already a crowd was gathering outside, ensuring his departure would be a very public event, no doubt to be recorded and circulated on social media within minutes. There was no such thing as quiet justice these days.

'PC Reynolds, I'm asking you to submit to being handcuffed.

If you refuse, I will have to add resisting arrest to your already lengthy charge sheet.'

He remained as still as a statue, only the sound of his breathing confirming that he was actually alive.

'Fair enough, have it your way ...'

She moved to circumvent him, but as soon as she was halfway there, he finally turned around, joining his wrists together. Annoyed, Charlie returned to her initial position, sliding the cuffs on and securing them tightly. There was a brief reaction, pain morphing into anger, as the metal bit his skin, but Reynolds kept his counsel. Placing a hand on his back, Charlie guided him forwards, manoeuvring him towards the uniformed officers by the door. On cue, both officers dropped their gaze, clearly deeply uncomfortable about arresting someone they shared a locker room with on a daily basis.

'Yeah, you might well look ashamed,' Reynolds hissed. 'All of you. This is a stitch-up, a bloody witch hunt.'

'All right, Reynolds, that's enough,' Charlie warned.

'But let's see who's still standing when this is all over, eh?'

All present avoided his eye, his aggressive presence seeming to fill the room. Reluctantly, he walked on, pausing only at the doorway, turning back to look at his wife and son, who had appeared to watch his departure.

'I'll be back for dinner,' he announced. 'Make sure you cook me something nice.'

Jackie Reynolds said nothing, staring at her husband, distressed and concerned. His son remained silent and, given the livid bruising that was starting to blossom on his cheek, Charlie could guess why. Having said his piece, Reynolds now disappeared from view, led away by his colleagues. On cue, Jackie and Archie vanished too, hurrying back upstairs to cleave to each other and lick their wounds. This was tough on them, but

Charlie knew there was no question of sparing their feelings, of diminishing their embarrassment or pain. They had a job to do, so raising her voice once more, she declared:

'Right then, let's get to it. Let's tear this place apart.'

Chapter 78

'Please, Mia, I'm *begging* you. Don't leave me ...'

Naomi could barely speak through the tears, but she had to make one last desperate effort. She was holding the unresponsive girl to her chest, her tears falling onto Mia's pallid cheeks, but nothing she did seemed to have the slightest effect. Her caresses, her encouragement, her singing, had all fallen on deaf ears, her ailing friend having exhausted her last vestiges of energy. Mia lay heavy and hopeless in her arms, silent and immobile, save for the erratic rise and fall of her chest. She was clearly not getting sufficient oxygen, but appeared powerless to do anything about it, her shattered lungs useless and inert. There was no point in urging her to do anything to help herself – Mia had lost consciousness some time ago – nor anything to be gained by howling for assistance. They were quite alone down here. So, with no other recourse, Naomi had resorted to pleading, desperately begging her friend to find something, some spark of life, to avoid ending her days in this awful place.

'Come on, Mia. We made a deal remember. We were going to get out of this *together*. You were going to find Freddie, I was going to see my mum ...'

She nearly broke down, but somehow kept going, even through her cascading tears. If she just kept talking, if she kept her hope alive, then somehow Naomi felt sure that nothing would happen, that she could delay the inevitable by sheer force of will alone.

'Maybe they can meet, we can have a little party to celebrate, it'd be fun...'

Now Mia *did* respond, shifting suddenly in Naomi's arms. Buoyed up, Naomi looked down at her friend with wild, zealous encouragement. But immediately Naomi caught her breath, shocked, devastated. Mia was not responding to her pleas, instead her body was spasming wildly, bucking in Naomi's arms, as the sound of a hideous, desperate wheezing filled the small room. This was it, the crisis Naomi had known was coming all along, but now it was here, all she could do was watch on as her friend slowly suffocated.

'No, Mia, *no...*'

Naomi's voice was cracking, her composure deserting her, as she witnessed her friend's agony. Mia's body jerked again, more violently this time, propelling the breathless teen upwards briefly, before she collapsed into Naomi's arms once more. Then she lay there, languid and still, the fight seemingly at an end, before she took one last, desperate gasp.

'Mia?'

Naomi couldn't process what she was seeing. It was beyond her worst nightmares.

'Mia, please...'

But looking down at her motionless friend, Naomi knew for sure that she was dead. Mia's chest had stopped rising, and she felt heavier in Naomi's arms. Perhaps Naomi should have felt relieved that her friend's torment was over. Happy that she was finally at peace. But Naomi felt none of these things, instead gripped by crushing desolation and fierce, terrifying loneliness.

'No...' she howled, screaming as if her lungs would burst. 'No, no, no, no...'

But her horror, her defiance, was as pathetic as it was point-less, her cries bouncing off the cold brick walls before slowly dying away. There was nothing to be done, no redemption to be found here, no victory to be snatched from the jaws of death. Her friend had died and Naomi suddenly knew with terrifying certainty that the same fate awaited her.

Chapter 79

What had he done to deserve this? It was unfair and it was unjust, revealing a vindictiveness in Grace's character that had been well concealed until now.

Cursing his luck, DC Jennings trudged along the run-down third-floor walkway, his spirits descending further with each step. Looked at objectively, his actions had been justified, successful and ultimately beneficial to the unit. Everyone knew that Holmes thought they were dragging their feet on the Freemantle investigation and that Grace was getting grief from the station chief as a result. By seizing the initiative himself, by getting off his arse and actually *doing* something, screwing the necessary information out of Brent Mason, he'd resolved that problem in an instant. The case was off their books now, leaving his immediate boss to pursue her pet projects to her heart's content. But was Grace grateful? Was she prepared to concede that he was actually an asset to the team? A leadership candidate in the making? Jennings knew the answer to those questions, her low opinion of him made explicit by his dispatch to this crumbling housing estate, sent on a wild goose chase that would yield little glory.

His day had started well, but had descended to this lonely pilgrimage to the Southford Estate, once a shining example of modern town planning, now a ramshackle haven for dropouts and illegal immigrants. If Graham Armstrong was hiding out here, it was a sorry place to end up, though perhaps it was all he deserved. Still, it was annoying to be making this journey alone, DC Reid having at least been handed an active role in proceedings. Reid was no bigger a fan of Grace or Brooks than he was, though of course he kept those opinions to himself, rolling over as soon as he was directly challenged. Such were the perils of leadership, Jennings mused bitterly, the price of sticking your head above the parapet.

Nearing the end of the walkway, Jennings paused, tugging the photocopied sheet from his jacket and checking the address. When Graham Armstrong had been released from prison, he'd been given a flat here, his family and friends having either turned their backs on him or moved away. This was the reward for his infamy – Flat 27, Block C, on the Southford Estate. Staring at the graffiti-smeared door, Jennings pondered the madness of some people. Armstrong had been set for life, a well-known figure in the fire-and-rescue community, with an exemplary work record and a generous pension in the offing. And he'd thrown it all away, tossed thirty years of diligent work down the drain, all because of his pathetic predilection for Thai girls. Some people were beyond saving, they really were.

Exhaling theatrically, Jennings rapped sharply on the door. Sliding out his handcuffs, he braced himself for action. It would be just his luck if Armstrong tried to make a break for it, or decided to put up a fight, so there was no point in being taken off guard. But his knocking elicited no response, so stepping forward, he tried again, this time pressing his ear to the door. At first, he heard nothing, the flat appeared lifeless and still, but then he heard a floorboard squeak inside, not five feet from where he was standing. Straightening up, he pressed his face to the door, peering down the spyhole, only to see an eye staring straight back at him. Instantly, the eye disappeared and he heard footsteps hurrying away.

Jennings' fist slammed into the door once more, paint flying off as he did so.

'Hampshire Police, open up!'

Jennings listened for a second, then slammed the door again.

'Armstrong, I'm giving you ten seconds to open the door or I'll kick it down.'

He took a step back, preparing to launch himself at the door. 'Ten, nine, eight...'

Setting himself in an upright runner's stance, he prepared to charge, confident the door would buckle on first impact.

'...seven, six, five, four... oh what's the point?'

Springing forward, Jennings hurled himself at the door. But as he did so, the door swung open, his target swiftly receding. Off balance and in mid-air, Jennings tripped and fell, crashing to the floor, before sliding into the hallway. He saw a pair of feet spring back to avoid him and he was quickly back up again, preparing to confront Graham Armstrong.

Only to find a confused Asian pensioner staring back at him, flanked by a multitude of startled faces behind her.

Chapter 80

Now that Reynolds was in their sights, there was no question of leaving anything to chance. Locked away alone in her office, Helen was surrounded on all sides by files, the result of many hours dogged graft by her team, who'd done heroic work unearthing everything that was on record about the Reynolds family's health, wealth and personal history. Helen was beginning to feel that she knew Reynolds and his dependents better than she knew herself, but this was just as well. The suspect had been arrested, cautioned and was already downstairs, being processed for questioning in the bowels of the building.

Their first chat had been a skirmish, Helen sounding Reynolds out, attempting to confirm her suspicions that he was a bad egg. This second conversation would be all-out war. Reynolds was fighting for his life, his liberty, teetering on the edge of an abyss that might destroy him. Even putting aside the professional disgrace and attendant personal shame, his conviction would usher in the grimmest period of his life, a paedophile policeman at the very top of the list for 'honour' attacks amongst prison inmates. Reynolds would resist her accusations forcefully and with passion, so it was up to Helen to use whatever leverage she possessed to crack him, whilst hoping the painstaking search of his property and vehicle revealed compelling evidence of his connection to these awful crimes.

Sifting through the details of his life, Helen had satisfied herself that there was no way Reynolds could have paid for his and family's lifestyle through legal means. Even putting aside the material wealth and the brand new BMW, there were a number of exotic foreign trips he'd treated the family to – jaunts to Barbados, St Lucia and Florida, which he'd conspicuously failed to mention to his colleagues. Other chaps in the locker room used to tease him, calling him sunbed Dave, but the joke had turned out to be on them, Reynolds presumably having never set foot in a tanning centre. But where did all this wealth come from? And how was it acquired? There were no obvious purchases from electrical outlets or online retailers, so had he required all these high-value goods via cash, possibly from criminal suppliers? There seemed no other obvious explanation.

As illuminating as his financial records had been, his medical history was also intriguing. Three times in the last ten years he had been treated for a sexually transmitted infection, his GP's notes recording in detail both the complaint and the treatment provided. Three times in a decade was a high hit rate for a happily married man, suggesting his real sexual interest lay outside the marital home, especially as there were no recent instances of Jackie Reynolds having to receive similar treatments, according to her medical files.

Helen was still digesting these details, when DC Wilson approached, a serious look on his face.

'Just heard back from Meredith Walker.'

'And?'

'The Mazda is clean as a whistle, inside and out. By the look of it, it had a thorough valet before it was returned to

Cartwright. No hairs, no DNA, no prints, even on the exterior, it's like it's brand new.'

Helen slumped, deflated by this surprising news. Concrete forensic evidence of Naomi's presence in that car was their best bet of forcing a confession from Reynolds. Wilson must have read her mind, because he now added:

'Oh, and DS Brooks wanted me to tell you that the suspect is ready for interview. Shall I let her know you're coming?'

Chapter 81

'I'd like to remind you that you are being interviewed under caution and anything you say during this interview may be used in evidence against you. Also present in the room are DI Grace, DS Brooks, and solicitor for the accused, Eleanor Higham.'

Helen completed the caution, raising her eyes to take in their prime suspect, who sat bolt upright in his chair, flanked by his expensively tailored solicitor. Whereas Reynolds had been relaxed and convivial during their initial chat, now he seemed focused and alert. According to Charlie, he hadn't uttered a single word during his arrest, other than to confirm his name to the custody sergeant, presumably saving his energy for the battle ahead.

'I'd like to take you back to the ninth of November, if I may,' Helen began, opening her files. 'Can you confirm that you were on duty that evening, walking the Hoglands Park beat with PC Beth Beamer?'

A curt nod from Reynolds, his eye drifting slowly from Helen to Charlie, then back again.

'According to PC Beamer, during your rounds, you encountered Naomi Watson, who was apparently sleeping rough in the Lordship Road underpass. Can you confirm that?'

'I believe we had a brief conversation,' Reynolds replied cautiously.

'You believe?' Charlie queried.

'I'm afraid my memory of that night isn't terribly clear,' the suspect continued. 'We were involved in a number of different encounters and altercations, lots of faces, lots of places.'

'So you've no recollection of what you discussed with her?' Charlie persisted.

'Probably just checking that she was in the land of the living. I've found dead bodies in that underpass on more than one occasion over the years, I can tell you…'

He smiled briefly, his whole bearing genial and friendly. Helen wasn't convinced for one minute, so resumed her attack.

'What about your second encounter that evening?'

Reynolds said nothing, but adopted a pointedly quizzical expression.

'My client has made it clear that he only met her once,' his brief intervened. 'And he barely remembers that.'

'Except you did go back, didn't you, David?'

A slight reaction from Reynolds, who seemed to take exception to her using his full name.

'You borrowed an old neighbour's car and drove back to the tunnel. I'm referring to a Mr Malcolm Cartwright, resident of 45 Blossom Drive, who's confirmed that he lent you his Mazda 5 that night, a vehicle which you subsequently returned the following day. I'm showing Mr Reynolds a still from a CCTV at the mouth of the underpass, showing that same car, entering the tunnel at 9.45 p.m. on the ninth of November and leaving it at 9.51 p.m.'

She slid a copy of the photo across the table towards him. He refused to even look at it, but his solicitor examined it swiftly, before replacing it on the table.

'Can you confirm that you were driving Mr Cartwright's Mazda that night?'

'Absolutely not,' Reynolds pushed back. 'I have two cars of my own, why would I need his?'

'He confirmed that he lent it to you. I have his written testimony here,' Helen persisted. 'In fact, you've borrowed it a number of times over the years, apparently.'

'Do you have any evidence to support that outlandish claim?' the lawyer butted in. 'As you can see, the driver is not visible in that photo, so unless you have other evidence, an independent witness placing my client there...'

'So Mr Cartwright is lying? Deliberately misleading the police?'

'Look, I don't know him that well, to be honest,' Reynolds answered calmly. 'But I certainly wouldn't put it past him. He's old, he's crabby, he's confused. When we lived there we did have a bit of a falling out actually – he objected to my boy playing football in the street with his pals. Maybe he's still pissed off about that, I don't know. But, honestly, he's talking through his hat.'

It was a convincing performance, reasonable, credible and with sufficient annoyance to suggest he might be telling the truth. But Helen knew in her heart that Reynolds was lying, so dismissed his explanation out of hand.

'We take a very different view. We feel he is a very credible witness, with no reason to lie, especially as he seemed oddly fond of you. Said you and your family had done loads for him over the years...'

Reynolds shook his head, looking bemused, but Helen wasn't distracted.

'It's our firm belief that you were in the underpass that night, that you persuaded Naomi Watson to get into the Mazda, that you then abducted and imprisoned her.'

'Why on earth would I do something like that?' he protested. 'I'm a serving police officer.'

'For your own sexual gratification,' Helen fired back.

Reynolds sat back in his chair, throwing up his hands in an extravagant gesture of disbelief.

'You have, after all, been accused on three separate occasions of sexually assaulting underage girls.'

'Really?' Reynolds exclaimed, withering. 'You want to go over all that *again*? They were liars, attention-seekers. They objected to getting pulled in for drinks, drugs, what-have-you, so they tried to make life hard for me. But it was all hot air from start to finish, which is why they never got anywhere.'

'You didn't attempt to persuade them to drop the charges? Pressure them into retracting their statements?'

'That's a very serious allegation, Inspector,' Eleanor Higham complained, frowning. 'I hope you have firm evidence to support your accusations.'

'There's another reason why you might have abducted Naomi,' Charlie intervened, trying to draw the solicitor's fire. 'Money.'

'I'm sorry?' Reynolds queried, once more appearing bemused.

'We recovered a bank note recently during an encounter with your wife, Jackie.'

'An illegal intrusion of my property.'

'No, the legitimate settling of a fixed penalty notice for a traffic violation,' Helen countered. 'Subsequently that note was tested in the police forensic lab and found to have two finger-prints on it belonging to a man called Graham Armstrong, a convicted paedophile.'

This provoked an instant reaction from his solicitor, a marked furrowing of her brow, but Reynolds was swift and cool in his response.

'Do you always send parking payments to the forensics lab?' he asked knowingly.

'When I feel such action is justified and necessary,' Helen replied curtly.

'Is that right?'

'From memory, your wife had a considerable bundle of notes in her purse, which struck me as odd. Any reason she might need to carry so much cash?'

'You'd have to ask her,' Reynolds replied carefully. 'But we have been doing a lot of work on the house recently, and the builders like to be paid in cash. Hide it from the taxman and all that? I don't condone it, but it's the way the world works…'

Again, Reynolds appeared both reasonable and composed. Helen knew she had to keep pushing.

'I'm glad you've mentioned the work on your house,' she continued. 'You've obviously piled loads of money into your property. This over and above the large amounts you've spent on luxury cars and foreign holidays. Now, we've done a deep dive on your finances, your income, and guess what? They don't tally. You couldn't even come close to affording all that on a PC's salary. What's more, I don't see digital transactions between yourself and travel agents, airlines, hotels, electrical retailers or car showrooms. Suggesting to me that you paid for lots of these big-ticket items *in cash*. Now who does that these days? Who buys a new car with cash? Pays for £20k holidays in cash? Criminals, that's who.'

'This is utter madness, Inspector Grace, even for you,' Reynolds' lawyer protested.

'Perhaps your client can explain the anomaly then? Where

did the money come from? Did Graham Armstrong give it to you for services rendered?'

'Look, we've had a bit of inheritance over the years, from my parents, from Jackie's. And often you can get better deals with cash. There's nothing sinister about it.'

'And you'd be able to prove that, would you? You'd be able to provide us with bank statements, legal documents showing us exactly where the funds came from to finance your lavish lifestyle? This inheritance you claim to have received?'

And now for the first time, Reynolds hesitated. Helen reasoned that if he hadn't ever envisaged getting caught, he wouldn't have constructed such an elaborate artifice, and was poised to pursue this, when Eleanor Higham again cut in.

'I must say this all seems very convoluted, Inspector. What exactly are you accusing my client of, other than providing a good life for his wife and son?'

'I'm accusing him of abducting underage girls for sexual exploitation and financial gain. Shanice Lloyd, Mia Davies, Naomi Watson, Laura White...'

Again, a marked reaction, the names appearing to land with Reynolds and fluster his brief, who'd no idea that other victims were potentially involved.

'Of falsely imprisoning them, abusing them, monetizing their pain for the "enjoyment" of other men.'

'That's total crap,' Reynolds exploded, shaking his head violently.

'On the contrary, you have a history of sexual crimes against women, of using your knowledge of the streets and the power of your uniform to intimidate, trick and assault young girls. My belief is that over the years, your offending escalated to keeping your victims captive, exploiting them over a sustained period of time. I am in no doubt that you represent a profound threat to women and that you are guilty of preying on the most vulnerable members of society, young girls with nowhere to go, who feel they can trust you. You are the very worst kind of offender and I intend to ensure that you are made to pay for your crimes.'

She finished, breathless and angry, staring directly at Reynolds. He eyed her for a moment, shaking off his discomfort as he gathered himself, replying:

'What have you got? Statements from a bunch of liars, a confused old man, a Mazda with a phantom driver and a few bank notes which probably came from a cashpoint. If Armstrong's fingerprints *are* actually on them, it's nothing to do with us.'

'I disagree. No smoke without fire, Dave ...'

'I'd never harm anyone,' the suspect continued, aggrieved. 'In fact, I've never hurt anyone in my life. And I certainly have no interest in teenage girls. I mean, what do you think I am?'

'Do you really want me to answer that?' Helen replied darkly.

'There you go,' Reynolds burst out, gesturing at Helen. 'You see that? It's a hatchet job, an attempt to frame me, to ruin me. Well, it won't work and you know why?'

He leant in closer to Helen, eyeballing her viciously.

'Because you've got *nothing* on me.'

Chapter 82

'Well, that was a bloody disaster.'

Heads turned, various officers looking up from their desks, as DC Jennings stalked past. He'd endured a completely pointless journey to Weston and he was not prepared to suffer in silence. Better that the team know that he was being victimized, that Grace was a mean-spirited and petty dictator.

'No sign of Armstrong then?' DC McAndrew replied over her shoulder, chewing her pen as she stared at her screen.

'Not a dickie bird. A new family moved into that flat two weeks ago. Before them it was a teenage boy, just out of Winchester Prison. And before him, it was a bunch of ravers who kept the estate awake all night.'

Nodding, McAndrew pulled a face, but remained glued to her screen. Annoyed by the lack of sympathy, Jennings continued his complaint.

'I reckon Armstrong hasn't been there in well over a year. And, guess what, he didn't leave a forwarding address. It'll be like looking for a needle in a bloody haystack trying to find him.'

'Then you'd best get on with it,' McAndrew replied dryly. 'You heard the boss – if we find Armstrong, get him to cough up what he knows, then we're home and hosed.'

'Not bloody likely. You ever interviewed these people?'

Jennings countered dismissively. 'They'll deny until they're blue in the face that they've done anything, that they've got any interest in underage kids, even when the evidence against them is overwhelming...'

'We can but try,' his colleague responded wearily, shutting down the conversation.

Jennings stared at her, aggrieved. McAndrew's lack of interest, her lack of sympathy, felt like a direct snub. And scanning the rest of the room, he was surprised to see most of his fellow officers were also head down, diligently doing Grace's bidding. Having felt sure the tide was turning against their maverick leader, now Jennings wasn't so certain. Did they actually believe her wild theories? Did they believe that Reynolds was some kind of psycho pervert? Or were they just keeping their heads down in the hope of future promotion? If so, it was clear who was going to be the sacrificial lamb, who was going to be cast out into the cold.

'Well, I still say it's a giant waste of time,' he muttered, resentfully heading on his way.

He stalked back to his desk, ruing the day he'd ever put his name forward for this unit. He'd hoped it would be the making of him, his shot at glory, yet here he was faced with the prospect of filing his report, his failed venture, then twiddling his thumbs until Grace dreamt up some new humiliation for him. Bearing down on his work station, fizzing with anger, he spotted his waste paper bin, empty and beckoning. He didn't hesitate, swinging his left leg at it and watching with satisfaction as it sailed across the room before landing in Helen Grace's private office with a heavy clunk.

Chapter 83

She looked down from her lofty vantage point, watching as the tiny figure of PC David Reynolds hurried away from the station, deep in conversation with his lawyer.

'So what do you want to do next?'

Helen didn't reply immediately, savouring the fact that for once Rebecca Holmes wasn't questioning her judgement. The station chief seemed troubled and uncertain today, no longer querying the direction of travel.

'Well, with your permission, I'd like to keep the heat on Reynolds,' Helen replied diplomatically.

'You're *convinced* he's responsible for these girls' disappearance?'

Holmes' tone suggested she was desperately hoping that Helen might retain some doubt, so she was quick to put her superior straight.

'Completely. I know that's not the answer you want, that this will make things very difficult for us, for the Force...'

'You think? I've just spent the past half-hour trying to convince the local press that we're not rotten to the core.'

'Even so, we can't risk any suggestion of a cover-up, of special treatment, we have to see this through to the end.'

Holmes nodded soberly, but looked deeply unhappy.

'So what now?'

'Well, we're going to mount round-the-clock surveillance on him,' Charlie chipped in, keen to change the mood. 'If he's rattled, if he feels we're closing in on him, he might try to take action to cover his tracks, which could lead us to Naomi.'

'It's a big risk. What happens if he shakes off his tail? Or, conversely, does nothing at all?'

'We don't have a choice,' Helen replied quickly. 'Reynolds has been cautious, careful. So far, we've found nothing in his vehicles or property to link him with these crimes...'

Holmes looked up sharply, concern clouding her expression, so Helen continued briskly:

'...but we will, in time. We're also widening the search for Graham Armstrong, following up every past friend or associate, every family member, investigating anyone who might be shielding him. I'm convinced he's still local and in contact with Reynolds, so if we find him—'

'There's a lot of "ifs", Helen. A lot of hunches...'

'I'm not wrong about him. I just need to prove it. I'd like to draw in his family too, up the pressure that way. I'm convinced Jackie Reynolds knows more than she's letting on, perhaps was even abused by her husband when younger. There's obviously violence in the family too, we can use that as well.'

'His son had a stonking great bruise on his face when we pitched up earlier,' Charlie concurred, provoking a further grimace from the station chief. 'A fresh one at that.'

'However we skin it,' Helen added, 'I think our best bet now is to keep a close watch on Reynolds, apply pressure to the family, let him know that we're not going to give up. He's been used to operating with impunity – let's see how he reacts now that the heat is on, when everyone's gossiping about him, when nobody will look him in the eye...'

Holmes looked sick at the mention of the word gossip, as if

the very concept offended her, so Helen returned her gaze to the car park, watching on as Reynolds shook hands with his lawyer, before taking his leave. Moments later, two plainclothes officers emerged from a parked car, separating quickly and setting off in pursuit of him.

'I'm convinced he'll crack,' she continued firmly. 'Convinced he'll finally give himself away. And when he does, we'll be waiting for him. PC David Reynolds is living on borrowed time.'

Chapter 84

He marched purposefully along the street, staring straight ahead of him, a man seemingly bent on getting home after a busy day's work. Passers-by nodded and smiled at him, reacting to the uniform, and David Reynolds returned the favour, even though in reality his attention was glued to the scene behind him, to the two casually dressed figures who were now dogging his heels on opposing sides of the street.

He'd been expecting nothing less. Grace had sufficient evidence, sufficient grounds for concern to have questioned him for longer, perhaps even to have extended his custody, but instead she had let him go. At first, he'd been buoyed up by this, swayed by his solicitor's conviction that the investigating officers had failed to land a punch, but as he walked from the station, cutting a swathe through fellow officers who avoided him like the plague, doubts began to set in. Grace was a formidable opponent, a woman who'd brought countless devious criminals to book, who never willingly let her opponents off the hook. Add to the mix the fact that this was *personal* for her, that she clearly loathed him, and there could be no question of her having thrown in the towel. Maybe she didn't have the evidence to charge him yet, but she would keep probing, keep digging, ramping up the pressure all the while. Hence the sudden appearance of his tails, who continued to shadow him, keeping a watchful eye on his progress.

They were presumably experienced officers and were handling their pursuit skillfully enough, the female officer laden down with shopping bags, her male counterpart talking animatedly on his phone, but Reynolds had been expecting them and they were easy to spot. When he slowed, casting an eye at their reflection in shop windows, they slowed. When he sped up, they responded. In a perverse way he almost enjoyed their presence, pleased to have clocked them so quickly, to be toying with them, pausing occasionally to tie up his shoe laces or consult his watch. But in truth, their pursuit made him feel distinctly uneasy, their constant scrutiny unnerving him.

He realized now how easy his life had been up until this point. Not his very early years, of course, they had been hateful and best forgotten, but since he first put on his police uniform, things had been plain sailing. He'd had close scrapes before that could have landed him in hot water, teenage girlfriends who'd promised much before suddenly attempting to withdraw their charms, but from the point that he'd graduated from Hendon, he'd never looked back. Girls love a man in uniform and they'd been easy to find, some of them seemingly very willing to comply with his particular tastes. Others had been more resistant, some even downright hostile, yet the respect and awe his badge inspired had kept him safe from harm, intimidating even the most defiant of his victims. Over the years, he'd got his speech down to a fine art and always enjoyed delivering it, watching his pointed threats, the promise of maximum shame and exposure, land on his playmates as they cowered half naked in the back of the police van.

Such was his invulnerability, his feeling of power, that in recent years he'd taken his interests a stage further. His first abduction had been ham-fisted and awkward for both parties, but since then he'd refined his technique, winning their trust, charming his victims, before striking. Only a few days ago, he'd felt set fair for life, congratulating himself on his good fortune, the fact that he could satisfy himself, whilst also turning a handsome profit. All without a single soul having a clue what he was up to, without the disappearance of his victims even occasioning a proper, sustained search. He had chosen wisely, acted carefully and continued to commit his crimes completely under the radar.

Until now. His targeting of Naomi Watson had been his undoing, her mother's persistence and Grace's obsessive interest combining to disastrous effect. Was it the bite mark on his hand that had given him away, that had aroused Grace's suspicions? Naomi had given it to him that first morning, when she'd fought him off, refusing to eat her breakfast. Had *that* been the signal to Helen to investigate? Was it Naomi herself who'd unwittingly brought all this heat down on him? Either way, it was clear now that the carefully constructed edifice of his double life was threatening to collapse, with potentially catastrophic consequences. There had been a moment when he thought he might get away with it, when he felt sure he could frame Ryan Marwood for the crime. But it had proved a fond hope, Grace slowly and methodically working her way towards the true culprit.

Would she ever give up? Would he ever manage to convince her, convince the world, that he'd been falsely accused? Her bearing in this morning's interview, the coiled energy and determination that she gave off, suggested not. As did the pair of shadows, who drifted in and out of view behind, without ever losing sight of him. Was that his fate now? To be spied on, followed, pursued? Invisible and invincible for so long, David Reynolds felt the wheel of fortune beginning to turn. For years, he'd had the wind on his back, the sun on his face, but now at long last, he felt the net beginning to close.

Day Six

Chapter 85

'Where are you, you piece of shit?'

Spittle flew from Naomi's dry mouth as she bellowed out her anger.

'I'm still down here, you know! I'm still alive!'

Fury and desolation wrestled for supremacy, as the teenager's voice shook.

'Show yourself, be a bloody man. See what you've done...'

Naomi angled a glance towards Mia's corpse, then swiftly turned away. Her friend looked more waxwork than human, a sight that crushed her.

'This is *your* fault! *You* did this!'

Raging, she pointed her finger at the door, as if her censure, her hatred, could somehow summon her captor, calling him to account.

'Come down here and look at her. Just *look* at her...'

She petered out as emotion mastered her, a heartfelt sob erupting from her.

'Just look...'

She whispered the last words, before collapsing to the floor and burying her head in her hands. Naomi was beyond exhausted, having spent the entire night fighting off scavengers who relentlessly circled Mia's body, and now her fury and defiance was inexorably turning to despair. It was inevitable that her resistance would be broken soon, that the determined vermin would finally gain their prize. If only *he* would come back, if only he would see what he'd done to her, then maybe she could still be saved this torment. He could take Mia away, bury her, save her from the slow decay that surely awaited her...

But there was no sign of him. In fact, he had been gone for over a day, a delay, an aberration that had proved fatal. Would he ever return? Even if he did, how would he react? Would he somehow blame *her* for Mia's death and punish her accordingly? Would he simply take the poor girl away in silence, leaving Naomi all alone? Or, worse still, would he find another companion for her, some poor innocent who even now was going about her business, unaware that a fate worse than death awaited her?

These horrific possibilities spun round Naomi's brain, pitching her further into despair. Each day seemed to bring fresh punishment and this morning was no different. Last night she'd found herself cradling a dying girl, fighting off the relentless pests. This morning, she found herself screaming wildly into the ether, hopelessly summoning a phantom who refused to appear. Exhausted, dizzy and hollow, she wondered now where her torment would end. Yesterday she'd been convinced she knew the worst, understanding with total certainty that she would die in this dark vault. But now she wondered if life, this shitty, unfair, cruel life had other plans for her.

Was it possible that instead of losing her life down here, she would first lose her mind?

Chapter 86

'I appreciate this is difficult for you, but please know that this is a safe space. I'm on your side and I can promise you that if a crime's been committed, I *will* act.'

Helen's tone was gentle, but her conviction strong, which seemed to have an effect on the witness. Tara Bridges had been diffident and uncomfortable from the start, clearly deeply uncomfortable at being in a police station. On more than one occasion, as Helen led her from the waiting area in the lobby to their most remote, most discreet interview suite, she'd been convinced that the young woman would change her mind, would turn on her heel and flee, having thought better of her rashness. Helen was working overtime to present herself as a benign, trusting, sisterly presence, but still Bridges seemed jumpy and distressed. Helen knew, however, that she had to keep her onside – something in Tara's bearing, the fire in her eyes, told Helen that Bridges had something important to say.

'Also, please know that I'm not here to judge you, or shame you, or belittle you in any way,' Helen continued kindly. 'I'm just here to listen.'

Bridges nodded gratefully, tugging distractedly at her watch strap, before running a hand through her long, silken hair. She was obviously trying to find the words, find her voice perhaps, so Helen said nothing, letting the young mum gather herself.

'I ... I saw the article in the newspapers, about PC Reynolds ... so I got in touch with the journalist. We spoke and she said I should contact you directly.'

'I'm very glad you did,' Helen said encouragingly.

'My ... my name's Tara Bridges and I'm the manager of the homeless centre on Lime Street.'

'I know it well, a very fine institution. Been there long?'

'Five years now,' the manager responded, sounding a little more confident now. 'And I've been working in the sector for over ten. It's very close to my heart.'

Helen smiled, but said nothing, convinced there was more coming.

'You see, fifteen years or so years back, I was homeless myself,' Bridges continued. 'My dad ... well, he drank a lot, and Mum never called him on it, never pushed back, so in the end I had to go.'

Helen digested this, echoes of her own past punching through.

'I was on the streets for eighteen months or more.'

'How old were you at this time?'

'Fifteen.'

'That must have been very hard for you.'

Tara Bridges nodded but said nothing, suddenly looking anguished. It was obvious that this trip down memory lane was going to be difficult, even traumatic.

'I ... I went through a lot, every day was a fight to stay warm, to find enough to eat. Some people helped, some amazing kind-hearted people, but loads didn't.'

She was building herself up to something, willing herself to have the courage to speak, so Helen remained quiet but supportive, silently urging her on.

'One night...one night I was looking for a place to bed down near the docks when...when a police car pulled over. The officer got out, came over to talk to me...'

'Did you catch his name?'

'No, I never knew his name. Well, not until I saw the newspaper article. It was PC Reynolds.'

'I see,' Helen replied calmly. 'And this was fifteen years ago?'

'Yup, more or less.'

Helen digested this, deeply saddened for Tara, but also shocked by the extent of Reynolds' criminality.

'And what happened then?'

'He...er...he asked me about myself, asked if I had family or friends who could help, and when I told him I didn't have anybody, he said *he* would.'

Helen didn't react, not trusting herself to speak. She could sense where this was heading.

'Obviously I believed him. He seemed nice enough, plus he was a policeman. And I was desperate, really desperate. It was a freezing cold night and I hadn't eaten in days...'

'Did he offer to take you somewhere?'

Another brief nod.

'He said he knew a hostel that would take me. That we could pick up some food on the way...so I got in the car. We...we drove for only a couple of minutes, then he pulled off into... into a side street.'

Her breathing was short now, as the memories gripped her, long-buried emotions surfacing.

'Can you tell me what happened then? If you're able to...?' Helen prompted.

'Well, then...then he got in the back with me, told me he wanted to chat. He...started pawing at me, trying to get me to kiss him. I said no, I screamed at him, tried to push him off, but he was too strong for me ...'

She hung her head, gasping back a sob. Helen longed to pull Tara to her, to try and comfort her, but she knew she needed more.

'Did ... did PC Reynolds rape you, Tara?'

She nodded, but said nothing, unable to speak.

'For the tape, the witness is nodding.'

Looking up, Tara's tear-rimmed eyes spotted the recording device for the first time.

'Yes ... yes, he raped me,' she confirmed. 'More than once.'

Helen felt a wave of nausea, of anger, sweep over her. Struggling to maintain her composure, she asked:

'How long were you in that car, do you think? If you can recall?'

'A couple of hours, maybe more. I couldn't fight him off, he'd put his cuffs on me, shoved a rag in my mouth ...'

'No one's saying you should have, Tara. He was bigger than you, stronger ...'

Tara nodded, but said nothing, suddenly right back in that car.

'I'm sorry to have to ask you this, Tara, but what happened after that?' Helen persisted.

'Well, he drove me around a bit, then threw me out on the street again. I was in pieces, couldn't believe what had happened, but I still told him what I thought of him. He didn't seem to care though ... He was totally relaxed, found the whole thing, found *me*, funny. I told him that I'd dob him in, but he just laughed. He said that I wouldn't have the nerve to come forward and that if I did, I wouldn't be believed. So in the end ... I didn't.'

This seemed to grieve Tara almost as much as the assault itself. Helen was depressed to see shame in her expression, as if she had somehow done something wrong.

'I've never ... I've never spoken about it until now,' Bridges continued falteringly. 'But if he went on to attack other girls, other women, all because I didn't have the courage to come forward—'

'No, Tara, none of this is your fault,' Helen interjected firmly. 'It's his and his alone. You've been incredibly brave, in getting through this, in making a life for yourself, in coming forward now. Honestly, if it wasn't for the courage of people like you, these people would never be called to account. You've got *nothing* to reproach yourself for.'

The young manager nodded, but didn't seem entirely convinced, clearly riddled with guilt.

'PC Reynolds is the only person to blame here,' Helen continued. 'He alone is responsible for all this pain, all this heartache, but now, thanks to you, he is going to pay for his crimes, I can assure you of that.'

Now Tara Bridges did look up. Her expression was still troubled but Helen now saw something else there too – hope. Helen felt a surge of adrenaline. From the off, people had questioned her judgement, queried her suspicions, but now she felt fully vindicated. She had appealed to other victims to come forward, convinced there would be other women who'd suffered at Reynolds' hands, and Tara Bridges had the courage to do just that, to find her voice. It made Helen all the more determined to ensure Tara and others like her received the justice they deserved, to bring an end to Reynolds' long reign of terror.

'You will get him, won't you?' Tara asked, pulling Helen back to the present.

The young manager suddenly looked scared, fearing perhaps that Reynolds might seek her out, so Helen was quick to reassure her:

'You have my word,' she insisted, reaching out to take Tara's hand in hers. 'I will not rest until PC David Reynolds is where he belongs. Behind bars.'

Chapter 87

'There's your evidence. There's your smoking gun.'

Helen pointed angrily at Tara Bridges' statement, forcing Rebecca Holmes to look at it.

'That's the true face of your "experienced, well-respected beat officer".'

'All right, Helen, you've made your point,' the Chief Superintendent replied testily.

'He's a predator. He's a rapist. What's more, he's been protected and shielded from justice by members of this police force.'

'Look, Helen, I understand why you're angry,' Holmes replied, looking shaken by the force of her colleague's attack. 'But that is simply *not* true. Nobody covered up for him.'

'Rubbish. People must have known, must have had their suspicions,' Helen scorned. 'But they weren't brave enough to stick their neck out, weren't brave enough to ask the difficult questions.'

'Well, I concede that mayb—'

'There was a culture of silence at this station. And this is what it breeds.'

She gestured at Tara's statement once more.

'Suffering.'

Holmes stared at Helen, but said nothing. Helen knew that in normal circumstances she'd have been hauled over the coals for speaking so aggressively, so disrespectfully to her superior, but there was no pushback today. Holmes was bang to rights and she knew it.

'So what do you want to do, Helen?' Holmes asked, fighting hard to conceal her discomfort.

'I want Reynolds formally suspended from the Force, pending the completion of our investigations. We've clear evidence now, first-hand testimony, that he's committed serious crimes against women whilst on the beat, so it's vital he never sets foot on the streets in uniform again.'

'OK, I can agree to that. Are you going to bring Reynolds in? Question him about the attack on Tara?'

'In time. But I want to keep him under surveillance for now, see what his next move is. However, in the interim, I want us to reach out to Tara Bridges, see if she wants any protection, whilst we construct our case against Reynolds.'

'Again, not a problem.'

'And finally, I want to be left alone to do my job.'

Her last request was terser, more pointed.

'We should have moved quicker to rein this guy in. We might have done so too had I not met with resistance and suspicion. Well, that stops now. I'm to be given your full backing and all the resources I require to nail this bastard. Yes?'

What else could she do? Holmes was beaten and she knew it. Maintaining eye contact, determined not to appear diminished, her superior nevertheless conceded immediately.

'Of course, Helen. You can have whatever you need to bring this case to close.'

*

Striding back to the incident room, Helen tried to get a grip on her swirling emotions. She was resolved and excited, relieved that they finally had concrete testimony of both Reynolds' former crimes and his prevailing modus operandi, targeting the most vulnerable sections of society for his own depraved ends. The details in Tara Bridges' account tallied perfectly with those of Naomi's abduction, dispelling any doubt in Helen's mind that David Reynolds was responsible for the teenager's disappearance. But underlying Helen's sense of purpose, of personal vindication, was a growing fury that Reynolds had been allowed to offend for so long. Too many people had turned a blind eye, allowing the decorated officer to offend in plain sight. What's more, his actions would shatter trust between Southampton Central and the people they were duty-bound to protect for years to come. What young girl, what woman would trust the police now, given Reynolds' monstrous crimes and the impunity with which he committed them? It would be a long, long road back from here.

Pushing angrily back into the incident room, Helen marched towards her office, but as she did so, Charlie intercepted her, hurrying over. Pausing, Helen gathered herself, clamping down her fury and turning to her deputy.

'Might have a lead on Graham Armstrong,' Charlie offered, excited.

'Go on.'

'Well, DC Malik was running the rule over his family members, associates, et cetera. Most people dumped Armstrong after he was arrested, but prison records show that his mother never did so, visiting him constantly throughout his sentence.'

'So where is she now?'

'Well, she's been pretty hard to find. She reverted to her maiden name after her son was convicted, and has moved three times since then.'

'I see...'

'But we've now found a current address for her. A two-up, two-down terraced number in Shirley.'

'Then what you waiting for?'

Helen was already gesturing DC Malik and DC McAndrew to join them.

'Let's bring him in.'

Chapter 88

Graham Armstrong breathed a sigh of relief and closed his laptop. The computer's memory and hard drive had been wiped clean, providing him with a measure of reassurance, but there was still work to do. Secreted in a false bottom in his wardrobe, he had an external hard drive, which he'd used to back up his recordings. This would also need to be destroyed before he could count himself as totally safe.

He'd woken this morning in a state of high anxiety, after a fitful night's sleep. It had been over a day since the outing of Dave Reynolds in the *Southampton Evening News* and Armstrong was still reeling from it, terrified of the potential consequences. The breaking scandal explained why Reynolds had missed a scheduled Zoom meet, but little else, as the police officer had proved impossible to raise, despite several attempts to contact him. This morning, seized by panic once more, Graham Armstrong had checked his burner phone straightaway, anxious for news. Immediately, he wished he hadn't, dropping the device as if scalded. On it was a text message from another member of their fraternity. This in itself was bad enough, the protocol being to keep communication to a minimum, the phone being primarily for voice calls only. But worse still was the content, his correspondent asking him if he'd heard that Dave Reynolds had been arrested and questioned in connection with missing teenager Naomi Watson.

The news knocked Graham Armstrong for six. Now he knew why Reynolds hadn't attended their meet, but this knowledge made him feel worse, not better. Was Reynolds still being questioned? Had he confessed to anything? Armstrong found that idea hard to credit, but how could you tell for sure? With his back against the wall, faced with losing his job, his reputation, his family, who knows what – or who – Reynolds might offer up.

Crossing the room, Armstrong opened the door to his wardrobe and dropped down onto his knees. He knew this amateur secret hiding place was sufficient to fool his mother, who barely set foot in his room anyway, but it wouldn't take a police search team long to discover it. Teasing his fingers into the small holes he'd made in each corner, he lifted the bottom clean off to reveal a dusty space beneath. Tossing the wooden board aside, Armstrong reached down into the void, pulling out the heavy hard drive.

Straightening up, he began ferreting around on top of the cupboard. He didn't possess the technology or know-how to wipe a hard drive, so he'd have to do this the old-school way. Impatiently, he groped the top of the wardrobe before his fingers alighted on the old hammer he'd left up there. He always kept it close by, just in case the neighbours worked out who he really was or some have-a-go vigilantes tracked him to his new address. He was glad of it now, enjoying the weight in his hand. Crossing to the bed, he pulled the pillow into the centre of the duvet, placing the hard drive on it. Slowly, he lowered the head of the hammer, placing it in the centre of the drive, taking aim. Then he carefully raised his weapon, before slamming it down with all his might.

The effect was electrifying, a huge crash seeming to echo

through the house. Armstrong stared at the hammer, stupefied, wondering if he had suddenly metamorphosed into Thor. But then loud thumping on the stairs brought him to his senses. He could hear shouting, footsteps getting louder, and now to his horror he realized the source of the almighty crash. Their front door had just been kicked in.

Even now, he could hear his mother wailing, brutish police officers hollering to each other as they stormed the premises. Armstrong was frozen, terrified, barely able to react, before the door burst open. Turning, Armstrong raised his hammer once more, determined to destroy this one last piece of evidence. Bellowing, he swung it down with all his might ... but before he could connect, he found himself flying sideways, tackled by one of the intruders. He crashed to the ground, skidding into the far corner, his head striking the skirting board hard. Dazed, he was powerless to resist, dragged to his feet, his face pressed against the peeling wallpaper as he was aggressively cuffed. Satisfied, the officer now spun him round in order to pat him down, but Armstrong had nothing dangerous or incriminating on him. No, the really damning evidence, the one item that would surely ensure his ruin, was firmly clutched in the hand of the lead search officer, whose expression was one of pure triumph.

Chapter 89

Their task was simple: to remain invisible and undetected, whilst never taking their eyes off their prey. DC Japhet Wilson and DC Mark Edwards sat in silence, newspapers open in front of them, but neither had taken in a word of the articles. Their sole focus was the impressive detached house a hundred yards down the street, home of the Reynolds family. Husband, wife and their teenage son had been hunkered down in there since the accused officer had returned home last night. The lights were off, the curtains drawn and the milk delivery remained untouched on the porch. The lack of activity, the all-pervading silence that gripped the house, unnerved Japhet Wilson. He'd been involved in cases where men who were close to exposure or ruin had destroyed both themselves and their families, rather than face arrest. He didn't think that would be the case here, and certainly there had been no sounds of violence within, but how could you tell for sure?

'What do you think they're up to in there?' Edwards asked quietly, as if reading his mind.

'God only knows,' Wilson responded quickly. 'But I'd love to be a fly on the wall.'

'Too right,' Edwards concurred. 'I mean, how do you talk your way out of this one?'

It was a good question, one Japhet Wilson longed to know the answer to. Up until now, Dave Reynolds had led a charmed life, popular and successful at work, able to provide a very comfortable existence for his family. But what did they make of him now? He'd been arrested, very publicly arrested, in connection with the disappearance of a teenage girl, marched away to Southampton Central in handcuffs. The neighbourhood would have been alive with gossip and speculation thereafter, but presumably Jackie and Archie would have seen none of it, holed up inside, going out of their minds with worry. Dave Reynolds would have returned home to a blizzard of questions, the family's fear of imminent ruin driving their scrutiny. Had he had his answers prepared? Had he somehow managed to explain away his arrest? Or was he even now confessing all? It seemed unlikely, given Reynolds' history and personality, but how Wilson would have loved to have listening devices inside just in case.

'Funny old thing though, isn't it? All this?'

Edwards gestured towards the Reynolds' residence.

'I mean I'm happy sitting in judgement on the usual crooks and thugs we pull in, but this is different. Keeping tabs on one of your own, potentially having to bring him in: well, it's not very comfortable, is it?'

Japhet shrugged, though in truth he knew exactly what his colleague meant. It did seem strange and was disquieting, the idea of arresting and charging a serving officer seeming to be almost an act of self-harm. Yet there was a growing conviction within the team that Reynolds was not just an offender, but a serial offender, sullying the name and reputation of Hampshire Police over many years. If that was true, if he had fooled them all for so long, then the sooner this was over, the sooner this boil was lanced, the better.

Picking up the radio, he pressed down the call button as he resumed his rounds.

'This is Team A. Are you receiving, Team B, over?'

There was a brief silence, then his radio sparked into life.

'Team B receiving, over.'

'Any movement out back? Over,' Japhet persisted.

'Negative, over.'

Logging this, Japhet continued, checking in with the other teams, all of whom lingered close by, cutting off a possible escape route. But the answer from all was the same. Reynolds and his family had gone to ground. On the one hand, he felt reassured by this – he was in charge of this elaborate surveillance operation. If anything *did* happen, if Reynolds made a break for it, it would be on his shoulders to bring him in safely. On the other hand, the waiting made Japhet profoundly nervous, a stakeout being a horrible mixture of boredom and tension. He always had the sense that it was simply the calm before the storm, that somewhere, somehow, trouble was brewing.

And now he *did* notice something. Movement by the front door. Craning forwards, Japhet Wilson saw a figure striding down the pathway. Who was it? It was too tall for Archie, so who then? Jackie? Reynolds himself? Tensing, he leaned forwards in his seat, scrutinizing the fugitive who now hit the street, hurrying away in an easterly direction.

'It's Reynolds...' he breathed, as much to himself as to Edwards.

There was no doubt about it. The receding figure was athletic with a long stride and short, dark hair, in contrast to Jackie's, which was long and curly. Reynolds was dressed in jeans, muck boots and a faded North Face puffa, his cap pulled down low. He clearly didn't want to be recognized by his neighbours and was dressed for rural rather than urban terrain. Was he going to try and make a break for it through the nearby woodland? Perhaps following the route he'd taken so many times with his dog?

Concerned, Japhet Wilson teased open the door, snatching up his radio.

'I'll alert the other teams, you report back to base,' he told Edwards. 'Tell them, tell DI Grace, that our suspect is on the move.'

And with that Japhet was gone, crossing quickly to the other side of the road and padding quietly away after his quarry.

Chapter 90

She paced back and forth in her cramped cell, her chain clanking noisily. Naomi was dizzy with fear, but she couldn't keep still, her nervous energy demanding that she scream, shout, jump about, anything rather than lapse into despair. She knew if she did so, stuck down here with her friend's rigid corpse, that she would go mad, stark staring mad.

From the minute Naomi had found herself down here, she'd longed to escape. But now it was a necessity, her sanity, her health, hanging by a knife edge. Her mind was whirring, full of the direst scenarios. Come what may, she had to get out of here. But how could she even contemplate such a thing when she was so firmly attached to the wall?

She had to try again. Putting one foot on the wall, she bent her leg forwards, then suddenly straightened it, pulling against the chain with all her might. Nothing. She tried again, screaming out in agony as she heaved with all her might. But the plate on the wall remained secure, the chain links intact, and Naomi slumped to the floor, disappointed. She sat there for a moment, gathering herself as she caught her breath, then scurried over to the wall. Fear and desperation were driving her now and if brute force wasn't going to work, she would have to try and find another way. Crawling over to the wall, she examined her bond.

The chain was secured to a hoop on the wall plate. In theory, the hoop should have been the weakest link, but as hard as Naomi yanked at it, it refused to budge, so instead she turned her attention to the wall plate itself. This was secured to the wall with four heavy-duty screws, which had been painted over some time ago and which had not budged an inch in all the days Naomi had been down here trying to loosen it. But it remained her only option, so digging her thumbnail into the groove on the head of the screw, she started to rub away at the flaky paintwork. It was old and dry, quickly coming away to reveal the screwhead proper. If only she had a screwdriver, Naomi felt sure she could have freed herself in seconds, however hard the screws had been tightened. But obviously they'd been left with nothing but their clothes, a couple of dusty water bottles and their empty food bowls...

Now Naomi paused, before scrambling over to her bowl. Was it a camping accessory or a dog's bowl? Either way, it was solid, with a firm metal lip at the top to avoid spillage. Snatching the bowl up, Naomi hurried back to the wall plate. With a shaking hand she attempted to jam the thin lip of the bowl into the groove of the nearest screwhead. For a moment, she thought it was going to slide in cleanly, but at the last second, it caught on something.

'Shit...'

Removing the bowl, Naomi re-examined the groove, spotting that a small amount of paint remained at the very bottom. Digging her nail in once more, Naomi began to work away at the remaining obstacle. Her nail cracked almost immediately and she could tell by the increasing stickiness of her finger that she was bleeding, but still she didn't relent, working away as if her life depended upon it, which in truth it probably did.

Withdrawing her finger, she peered at the groove once more.

It appeared to be free of paint now, so she picked up the bowl once more. This time the lip slid into the groove smoothly and, turning it slightly, Naomi felt it bite. Sweating, excited, she increased the pressure, only to feel the bowl start to bend and warp, as the aged screw resisted. Panicking, she paused, rotating the bowl in her hand to ensure a hard, straight lip nestled in the groove once more. Now she proceeded with more caution, pressing her fingers close to the lip of the bowl to stop it bending, rocking it back and forth to see if she could fashion any movement.

And now, to her delight, Naomi felt the screw shift. Only a millimetre, but it was movement nevertheless. Resisting the urge to yank the bowl round with all her might, she continued with her patient back-and-forth motion, the screw slowly loosening all the while. She counted to ten then, confident that the screw was starting to give, started to turn the bowl in a steady anti-clockwise direction. Slowly, reluctantly, the screw gave up the fight, turning, turning, turning, until eventually half the screw was visible, sticking out proud from the wall plate. Now Naomi dropped the bowl with a clatter, seizing the screw and rotating it as fast as her brittle fingers could turn. Less than a minute later the screw was in her hand, her emotions in riot as she looked down at her prize.

Naomi could scarcely credit it. This was the first – the only – good thing that had happened since her captor had brought her here. Gripped by hope, Naomi now set to work in earnest, cracking nearly all her nails as she drove the flaky paint from the grooves of the remaining screwheads. Once they were clear, she set to work with the bowl once more, teasing first one, then two, then the final screw from its mooring. As she did so, the metal plate fell to the floor, a dull thud reverberating around the walls. Elated, Naomi seized the chain, lifting the plate from the floor, free now to roam the constraints of her tiny cell. This was not how she'd imagined finally liberating herself and she would dearly have loved to free her ankle from the clasp that pinched her skin every time she moved, but at least she could move around at leisure. Moreover, she now had a weapon.

Swinging the chain, the plate – heavy, bulky with nasty pointed corners – began to rotate in the air. If she could secure one proper hit, she felt sure she could do her captor some serious damage. Suddenly she was seized with the idea of hurting him, of raining all her rage, vitriol and bile down on him, crushing him, destroying him. But in her heart, she knew that she would have to be sensible, cautious, precise if she was going to make her advantage count, if she was going to secure her freedom. The important thing now was to ambush him effectively, lay him out cold, then put as much distance between herself and this awful place as possible.

Timing was everything now, preparation key. So, slowing the swirling plate, she began to pace back and forth, considering her options. If and when her captor returned, she would need to be ready. Taking up a position to the right side of the door, she disappeared into the gloom. Here she would wait, listening carefully for his descending footsteps, primed and ready to strike.

Chapter 91

'Is he talking?'

Charlie's question was earnest, impassioned.

'You bet he is,' Helen replied darkly. 'He's not going to give us everything straightaway, but Graham Armstrong knows he's done for now. His only hope is to co-operate, in the hope of obtaining a lighter sentence. Honestly, I'm not sure it's going to wash, given the severity of his crimes, but he's got no other option.'

Charlie nodded purposefully, exhaling slowly, realizing now that she'd been holding her breath whilst awaiting Helen's response. The arrest of Graham Armstrong was potentially a game-changer, so much hanging on whether he co-operated or not, and she was profoundly relieved that this reptile had chosen to do the right thing.

The pair of them were closeted away together in the station's viewing suite, a technician sitting close by, silent but attentive. Charlie felt a little awkward discussing such sensitive matters in front of him, but she had no choice. The clock was ticking.

'What's he coughed to so far?' she asked.

'He's admitted that he was the main driver behind the whole thing, organizing "live" sessions for paying customers. Apparently it was a very profitable business, they even had a waiting list...'

Charlie grimaced, sickened by the thought of such depravity. 'And will he give up Reynolds?'

'Looks that way. He claims he paid Reynolds large sums of cash to abduct, imprison, then abuse teenage girls on demand. Used to send the cash in a jiffy bag to a PO box in Harefield, in order to conceal the transaction.'

'Have we got enough, then? To charge Reynolds, I mean?'

'Probably, but I'd like to look at the footage first. Though "like" might be the wrong word ...'

She nodded at the screen, pulling a face. Charlie knew exactly how she felt. The idea of watching a young girl being assaulted turned her stomach, especially as she had two little ones herself.

'Ready?'

Charlie nodded in response to Helen's question, though in truth she wasn't.

'OK, run it please,' Helen intoned sombrely.

The technician obliged and suddenly the screen sprang into life. The recording revealed a messy, dirty room, with bare boards and crumbling brickwork, a scattering of building equipment lying in the background. The foreground was powerfully lit, a neat circle of illumination, which for the moment remained empty. Charlie leaned forward, taking in the details, attempting to see if she could 'place' the setting, but her interrogation was interrupted now by voices off camera. She strained to hear, but couldn't make out the words. She could, however, read the tone – the man's voice was rough and brutish, the girl's anguished and fearful. Now suddenly the two figures came into view, a teenager in a grey tracksuit and a tall man in dirty jeans and a T-shirt. Stepping forward, the man gripped his prisoner by the neck, turning her round to face the camera. Pinioned, in pain, Naomi Watson blinked at the camera, terrified, powerless.

'Dear God,' Charlie said, putting her hand to her mouth.

The man was barking at her now, but Charlie couldn't take in the details, her attention fixed on Naomi's protests, her doomed attempts to resist. Her captor was having none of it, moving forward angrily and tugging her jumper off.

Charlie wanted it to stop, didn't want to see the outrage that she knew was about to follow, but as ever, Helen was focused purely on the evidence.

'Is that definitely him?' she demanded urgently. 'Is that Reynolds?'

Wrenching her attention away from the unfolding horror, Charlie took in the toned, athletic figure.

'Looks the right build, right height, and he's got a tattoo or something on his right arm.'

Charlie tried to focus on the man's arm, but he was in constant motion as he worked swiftly to expose the trembling girl to the camera. Frustratingly his head remained out of shot, presumably by design.

'Slow it down a bit...' Helen suggested.

The technician obliged, the awful scene playing out in slow-mo. And now they both saw it, Naomi's attacker leaning down to force her to remove her jogging bottoms.

'There,' Helen cried out.

The screen froze on command, the trio staring at the image in front of them. It was a side angle on the abuser's face, but no one present was in any doubt as to his identity now.

'That's him, that's Dave Reynolds!' Charlie virtually shouted, unable to contain herself.

She was relieved beyond measure that they didn't have to watch any more, turning to Helen swiftly with a follow-up question.

'So what now?'

'Look at the time code,' Helen replied quickly, directing her deputy's attention to the bottom of the screen. 'If it's accurate, it proves that Naomi was still alive two days ago, in some local basement. Obviously we need to throw everything at finding her. I'd like you to take the lead on that.'

'Of course.'

'And Reynolds?'

'Well, it's time to bring him in,' Helen replied fervently, her eye drifting to the frozen face on the screen in front of her. 'We've got enough evidence here to put that bastard away for a very, very long time.'

Chapter 92

Where the hell was he going? What was he doing?

DC Wilson continued to dog David Reynolds' footsteps, his invisible shadow watching over him, but his mind was full of misgivings. Having been convinced that the suspect was about to make a break for it, given the urgency of his sudden departure from the house, now he wasn't so sure, bewildered by his choice of route. The disgraced constable hadn't headed for the train or bus station, nor had he hurried towards any secreted vehicle, instead cutting down a series of unremarkable residential roads, moving at a pace down the quiet pavements. Convinced that his true destination was the thick woodland that fringed this part of town, Wilson had been certain he would at some point veer off down a cycle path or bridleway, disappearing in the murky woods beyond, but he was mistaken. Reynolds kept up a brisk, steady pace, apparently heading for the local shopping precinct.

This made Wilson nervous, his brain scrolling ahead for any possible avenues of escape. Did Reynolds have friends locally? Did he know a shop owner who would allow him to slip out the back door? It seemed unlikely, and even if he did manage to do so, what would he achieve? He'd still be in the heart of suburban Bitterne Park, an easy spot for the other teams who continued to flank, and predict, his progress. Surely there was no way out for him, so perhaps escape was not his plan? Was he perhaps even now hurrying to the grim basement where Naomi, Mia and God knows who else was being held? That remained a tantalizing prospect, Wilson longing to rescue the poor girls from their awful captivity, but surely Reynolds wouldn't be so reckless? He must have guessed that he was under surveillance, even if he hadn't clocked the individual officers? To lead them straight to his captives would be an act of suicide. So what was his plan?

Suddenly Reynolds changed direction sharply, hurrying along a side road, before cutting back right onto the main road east. Confused, Wilson kept up his pace, wondering why Reynolds now appeared to be doubling back on himself, perhaps even heading home. Had he simply come out for a long walk? If so, why the urgency? And why the muck boots and thick puffa jacket for an urban stroll? Was he leading them a merry dance on purpose, perhaps trying to clock how many surveillance officers were in attendance before making his next move? If so, what might it be?

A voice in his pocket brought DC Wilson back to the present, his radio springing to life.

'Base to DC Wilson. You are cleared to bring the suspect in. Repeat, you are cleared to bring the suspect in, over.'

'Understood, over,' he answered, having retrieved his radio.

Changing the band, he spoke crisply and clearly to his fellow officers.

'OK, it's a go to pull him in. Repeat it's a go!'

Breaking into a run, Wilson raced towards the suspect. Hearing his footsteps, Reynolds seemed to hesitate, then began to speed up, but it was too little too late, Wilson on him in a flash. Grabbing him by the shoulder, he span him round.

'David Reynolds, I'm arresting you on suspic—'

But the words died in his mouth, as he took in the startled, female face in front of him. Shocked, angry, he tugged off the suspect's cap, releasing a cascade of thick, brown curls. Jackie Reynolds stared back at him, scared, nervous, but triumphant. They'd been duped – Dave Reynolds had set a trap for them.

And they'd fallen for it – hook, line and sinker.

Chapter 93

It had been an arduous, dangerous journey, but he had made it.

Since his release from custody, David Reynolds had been going quietly mad, racking his brains for a solution to the terrible bind he found himself in. His mood had soured further when his source at Southampton Central confirmed that Graham Armstrong had been arrested, the danger ramping up still further. Grace would be coming for him soon, there was no question about that, and this time there'd be no bail, no possibility of escape. He had to act *fast*.

Before he could do anything meaningful, he needed to shake off the surveillance officers who surrounded the house. He'd spotted a pair of officers out front, two out back, and he presumed there were at least four more in positions close by. Somehow he had to lead them away from the property, lifting the stranglehold on his movement, and there was only one way of doing that. Jackie had taken a little persuading, but she knew not to resist him when he had fire in his eyes, and she made a convincing decoy, being tall for a woman and as athletic and toned as her husband. Even so, there was no guarantee that their simple trick would work and Reynolds had watched with bated breath as Jackie had hurried down the path, head bowed. Pressed against the bedroom wall, he had his attention not on her, but on the car parked further up the road. Happily, as soon as she'd gone a short distance, one of the officers – was it Wilson? – had climbed out of the car and set off in pursuit, his colleague following moments later.

Abandoning his position, Reynolds had crossed the room, keeping close to the wall, before exiting onto the landing. Hurrying past Archie's room, whose door remained defiantly closed, Reynolds made his way to the back bedroom, teasing open the curtains to peer beyond the fence to the pathway beyond. Thankfully, this also appeared to be deserted.

Emboldened, he'd hurried downstairs, crawling across the kitchen floor and out into the utility room. Staying low, he grabbed a jacket and slinging it on, eased open the back door. Now he paused. This was the moment of maximum danger, when he broke out into the open for the first time, but something told him it was now or never, so closing the door quietly behind him, he crawled along the side access, pausing as he reached the garden. Once more, he scanned the scene in front of him, searching the trees for signs of life, but seeing no one, he pressed on, crawling down the back of the flower bed to the end of the garden. His hands were now dirty, his wrists scratched, but he didn't care. All that mattered now was his bid for freedom.

Reaching the back gate, he turned to look back at the house. To his surprise and horror, Archie was standing in the back bedroom. He'd opened the curtains and was staring at him, as if flagging his escape to any onlookers. He half expected his son to open the window, to cry out, but the boy just stood there, looking at him. Discomfited, Reynolds turned away, opening the back gate and peeking out. The alleyway beyond was lifeless and quiet, so he hurried on, making it into the woodland beyond in a matter of seconds.

Relieved, he proceeded now as if on autopilot, following the paths he knew so well, until eventually he emerged, tired and sweaty, on the back streets of Midanbury. Danger lay here too – a passing squad car, an alert colleague, could pass by at any moment – so pulling his cap down Reynolds hurried on, avoiding any human contact as he scurried to the fenced-off building that had become his home from home. Teasing open the dilapidated metal fence, he hurried on to the main entrance. Here he paused, glancing behind him to check he hadn't been followed, then teased the key into the padlock. Then, with one final look behind him, he stepped inside the gloomy building, pulling the door firmly shut behind him.

Chapter 94

Naomi scrambled to her feet, her heart pounding. She had been waiting, waiting, waiting, going out of her mind with worry, convinced she'd been abandoned for good, but then suddenly she'd heard it. The familiar sound of the door opening and closing above. Her captor had returned.

Positioning herself to the right of the door, she readied her weapon. Slowly, she started to turn the chain, the heavy metal plate starting to spin in the air. She knew from experience that it took her abuser about a minute to open the secret door to their cell and when he stepped inside, she had to be ready for him. She had the element of surprise on her side, but still she had left nothing to chance, moving Mia's corpse close to the entrance, where it lay blocking his path. Her plan was simple: her captor would step inside, see the prone teenager in front of him and react. In an ideal world, he would bend down to check on her, but even if he paused, Naomi felt it would be enough. She could then let him have it, swinging the plate at him with all her might. Hopefully that would lay him out, but if it didn't, she'd be quick to follow up with more blows, a kick, a fist, whatever was required to subdue him. And then she'd run, carrying her heavy chain with her, attacking any obstacles in her path until she was free of this awful place.

The thought made her dizzy with anticipation. Her ordeal was nearly over. It had come too late for Mia, but she could get out, she could alert the police, she could bring the curtain down on this hideous nightmare. She just needed to be brave, to be focused.

She just needed to land one killer blow.

Chapter 95

'What do you mean he's escaped?'

Helen was aware that she was shouting, that the rest of the team could hear, but she couldn't contain herself.

'Have you searched the house? He's definitely not in there?'

A crestfallen DC Wilson shook his head, angling a glance at the open door of her office to the officers beyond, many of whom were clearly eavesdropping. This was still preferable to looking at a stupefied DS Brooks or his incandescent boss.

'Yes, we searched it top to bottom, twice. Besides, the son, Archie, confirmed that Reynolds left. Crawled on his hands and knees down the garden, then out the back gate.'

'But why on earth weren't there officers there, covering the rear passageway?'

'I felt...' Wilson continued, stumbling. 'I felt that it was important to stay on the main suspect. It looked like he meant business, that he had a plan, and as he knows the area much better than us, I felt we needed all officers in pursuit.'

'Except it wasn't him, was it?' Helen hissed.

Charlie shot a warning look at her, but Helen was not to be appeased.

'Look, I'm sorry if I seem angry, but our main suspect has

vanished. He could be doing a bunk, he could be heading to Naomi, he could be bloody anywhere.'

Wilson said nothing, shamefaced.

'Did he spot you?' Helen demanded. 'How careful were you?'

'Very careful,' Wilson emphasized. 'But he must have known he was being watched.'

'Why take the risk then?' Helen countered. 'If we'd seen through his ruse, there would be no easy way to explain this whole stunt. It would have been clear he was trying to do a bunk.'

'Maybe he felt he had to,' Charlie intervened.

'Why?' Helen demanded, before a thought landed. 'Because of Armstrong, you mean?'

Charlie nodded cautiously, as if unwilling to offer this thought.

'If he'd got wind of Armstrong's arrest somehow,' she continued carefully, 'then he would have known the game was up, and that all that remained was to get out of Southampton as fast as he could.'

'But he could only have known that if someone tipped him off,' Helen muttered angrily. 'It wasn't like Armstrong's arrest was in the press or anything...'

'Well don't look at me,' Wilson protested, also keeping his voice low. 'No one wants to nail this guy more than I do.'

'It's all right, DC Wilson, no one's accusing you of anything. I know you did your best.'

Her junior colleague looked mightily relieved, as Helen pressed on decisively.

'OK, DS Brooks, I want you to run the rule over Reynolds' comms – phone, email, social media, the works – to see if he had any advance warning. DC Wilson, you're with me. We're going to liaise with uniform, with traffic, the eye in the sky. All our efforts have to go into tracking our fugitive now.'

She was already on her way to the door, Wilson scurrying after her.

'We *have* to find Reynolds.'

Chapter 96

He gripped hold of the metal shelves, yanking them roughly off the wall, before hurling them across the room. They clattered noisily to the floor, the sound echoing off the bare brick walls, but he didn't care. It was speed, not stealth, that mattered now.

David Reynolds set to his task energetically, systematically working his way along the false wall, removing the shelving units that had been put there to conceal the real purpose of the partition. Had anyone stumbled down here previously – squatters, junkies, police officers or council workers – they would have found only an old storage room, a forgotten basement full of junk, before hurrying on their way. They would have no concept of the tiny cell concealed just beyond this specially constructed barrier.

It seemed strange to be pulling it apart now, given how carefully and painstakingly he'd constructed it. He had fussed and fretted over the details, and on more than one occasion had misjudged the strength of the plasterboard, the loaded shelves too heavy for their mooring. Eventually, he'd got it right, however, and had been justifiably proud of his endeavours, but he cared little for past successes now. His sole focus today was protecting himself, of destroying the evidence that could damn him forever in the eyes of the world.

Pausing to breathe, Reynolds took in the unadorned wall in front of him. Stripped of its shelving, it looked strange and intriguing, the thin line that ran down the centre of the wall, where the two hinged doors met, now obvious to the eye. For a moment, he was lost in memories, of the many times he'd snuck here, throwing open the doors to reveal his cowering captives beyond. Those days were gone now but the remembrance would linger long, and fondly, in the memory.

Stepping forward, he cast around him as he prepared to finish the job. He half expected to hear muffled cries from behind the wall – he'd been away from the girls for a long time now and they must have heard the din he was making – but oddly all was silent within. This both unnerved and intrigued him, but this was no time for idle curiosity. Walking purposefully across the floor, he found a large, plastic bucket. Placing it directly in front of the hinged wall, he then grabbed the sack of powdered plaster. This he emptied into the bucket, before picking up a six-pack of water bottles, emptying them inside, one after the other, before tossing the empties away. Then, grabbing an offcut of wood, he begun to stir, happily watching on as the plaster mixture slowly thickened. Taking a break, he dipped his finger in it. Pleased with the consistency, he scanned the room for the last piece of the jigsaw. For a moment he couldn't find what he needed, panicking that he would be frustrated at the last, but then his eyes alighted on a plasterer's hawk lying discarded in the far corner. Hurrying over to it, he returned to the wall with his prize.

Taking a breath, David Reynolds composed himself, suddenly overwhelmed by a wave of regret, then he plunged the hawk into the bucket, making sure the surface was fully coated with soft, pliable plaster, before he lifted it to the hinged doors, smearing the thick substance carefully over the join.

Chapter 97

Naomi was poised to strike, the metal plate spinning frantically round in the darkness. But her arm was getting tired and her resolve weakening, gripped by a sudden fear that something had gone badly wrong.

Why had her abuser not come in already? Usually it took him no more than a minute to unlock and unseal the doors. But tonight he seemed in no hurry, spending five minutes or more making the most god-awful racket. What was he up to out there? Was he constructing something? Or destroying it? And why had he suddenly grown so careless? Normally he was scrupulous about slipping in and out as quietly as possible, but now he was banging doors, tossing things around, as if all caution had been thrown to the winds. Why? What had happened in the interim to occasion such a change in his behaviour? And was there method in his madness or had he just lost his mind?

This unexpected change in routine made Naomi profoundly nervous. Suddenly she was desperate for answers, for certainty. She'd been so buoyed up, so exhilarated at the thought of attacking her tormentor and gaining her freedom, but now she sensed that she wouldn't get the chance, that something significant had happened, altering the fate of both herself and her captor. The thought made her lightheaded and fearful, robbing her of her energy and resolve. Gradually, she slowed the spinning of her chain, gripping the plate gratefully, glad of the rest. She was overheating massively, the temperature seeming to have risen exponentially, the atmosphere much more cloying than usual. And it was now, leaning on her knees, exhausted and dejected, that Naomi noticed something else. She could no longer see her feet, her dirty socks swathed in darkness. Looking up in alarm, she realized that the thin slivers of light that peeked under the door, and through the join itself, were slowly vanishing, as if a giant hand was blocking them out. Terrified, she scuttled towards the door, but she was too late, the last vestige of light dying out as she reached it.

'What the hell?'

She hammered on the door, desperate, confused, scared.

'Please! Don't leave me here! I won't talk, I won't do anything bad, please don't leave me here...'

But no answer came, except for the sound of receding foot-steps, then the main door slamming above. Distraught, frantic, Naomi stood stock-still, her thoughts of escape now in ashes. Something *had* changed, something *had* gone wrong, prompting her captor to take desperate action. Lost in the darkness, the horror of Naomi's predicament suddenly hit home with full force, rendering her speechless with terror.

Her prison was now her tomb.

Chapter 98

The atmosphere in the room was heavy and hostile. Jackie Reynolds's mood had veered from outrage and indignation to despair and self-pity, before lapsing into sullen silence. She seemed determined to resist any and all enquiries, but Helen's blood was up and she was determined to hold her feet to the fire.

'You've known all along, haven't you?'

'Known what?' Reynolds' wife returned truculently, folding her arms.

'That your husband is a rapist and a killer.'

'Don't be absurd. Do you really think I'd live with a man like that?'

'Absolutely I do,' Helen returned firmly. 'I think you're his willing partner in crime and I'm going to see that you pay for it.'

'Are you out of your mind, woman?' Jackie replied, aghast. 'All I do is go for a bloody walk and suddenly I find myself in the back of a patrol car, trussed up like a turkey. I should bloody sue...'

'Do that, see how far you get. Often go out for a walk in your husband's coat and boots, do you?'

'They were the nearest things to hand.'

'Pull the other one, Jackie. You deliberately deceived us.

Wearing your hair up, keeping your head down, leading my officers a merry dance...'

For a second, a smile seemed to tug at Jackie's mouth, before she quickly swallowed it.

'You're hallucinating, DI Grace. Perhaps you've been working too hard. Like I said, it's been a tough day, so I thought I'd go for a long walk and—'

'Where were you going?'

'I'm sorry?'

'Where were you headed?' Helen persisted testily. 'On this "walk"?'

'Oh, I don't know. Just to the parade, I suppose. I had a couple of bits to get.'

'So why did you double-back on yourself? Why head away from the shops, back in the direction of home, before you'd even got there?'

A moment's hesitation now, Jackie Reynolds turning to her solicitor, who shook his head.

'No comment,' Jackie declared, turning back to Helen defiantly.

'Where is he, Jackie?' Helen demanded, cutting to the chase.

'I've no idea – he was gone when I got back.'

'Sorry, that's not going to cut it, Jackie. I am going to charge you with obstructing police business and I may well add per- verting the course of justice and assisting an offender to your charge sheet. That's serious jail time, so I'll ask again, where is he?'

'Please don't threaten my client,' her solicitor cut in.

'I'm just stating the facts. She actively assisted in Reynolds' escape from the family home, drawing officers away from their surveillance in order to facilitate his flight.'

'Can you prove that?' the lawyer persisted.

'Yes, I can. What's more, I can prove that she's been actively involved in the abduction and rape of a number of underage girls.'

'That's completely ridiculous,' Jackie exploded. 'Dave would never get mixed up in anything like that. *I* would never get mixed up in anything like that.'

'No, no, no, don't play the betrayed wife with me, Jackie. You knew – or you suspected – what he was doing and you did *nothing*.'

'No, no, I don't know anything about any girls...'

'Yes, you do, because you were one, weren't you? You were a victim too.'

Now Jackie's gaze rose sharply to meet Helen's, alarmed and surprised.

'We know Reynolds pulled you in when you were fifteen,' Helen continued, softening her tone slightly. 'Drunk and disorderly, underage drinking, resisting arrest. I bet he laid it on with a trowel, painting a picture of the world of shit that you were about to descend into. I bet he threatened to throw the book at you, tell your parents... unless you did something for him. Am I right?'

Jackie shook her head, but it was a second too slow and lacked conviction.

'I'm not having a go, Jackie. I'm not here to shame you,' Helen continued. 'What he did was criminal and immoral, you were the victim in all this. And maybe to some extent you've been the victim ever since. You *and* Archie. I know there's violence in the family, coercive control, perhaps even sexual assault. Has he raped since you were married, Jackie?'

'No, no, nothing like that...' she replied, breaking eye contact and dropping her gaze to the floor.

'Because if he *has*, we can call him to account for that,' Helen persisted, convinced she was on the right track now. 'And if you and Archie don't feel safe, there are places you can go, accommodation we can provide for you where you'll be free of fear, free of his presence.'

Jackie didn't respond, her eyes glued to the floor.

'This is your chance to get out, Jackie. You and your son. We can make that happen, but I do need something from you. I need you to tell me where Dave has gone.'

Helen stared at the crying woman in front of her, praying that she would finally see sense. Slowly, Jackie lifted her gaze once more, looking beaten and hollow.

'I've told you, I don't know where he's gone, he wouldn't say.'

'Jackie, please…'

'But even if I had, I wouldn't tell you…'

Now her eyes met Helen's, defiance wrestling with desolation, as she added:

'He's all I've got.'

Chapter 99

It was time to disappear.

So far, everything had gone according to plan. He'd escaped the family home, concealed all trace of the girls, hidden the laptop and camera equipment in an overflowing skip, done everything he could think of to distance himself from the unfolding catastrophe, but Dave Reynolds still knew he was on borrowed time.

Graham Armstrong was probably talking, no doubt some others too, the full scale of their operation slowly becoming apparent. And what of Jackie? He hoped, he expected, her to be loyal, but who could say that she'd be able to hold out? She'd always been weak and he wouldn't put it past her to fold under heavy pressure from Grace. If so, Reynolds' name, his flight from justice, would have been disseminated to every officer, every border official, perhaps to the press too. His face would grace the news tonight, making him a hunted man. It was imperative therefore to move swiftly, to vanish from the city as fast as possible, to put as much distance between himself and his crimes as he could. Perhaps if they never found the girls, perhaps if they never found him, their investigation might eventually run out of steam. A lot of hearsay, a lot of lurid allegations, but no smoking gun. Perhaps they would hit a brick wall and reluctantly move on, distracted by fresher, more urgent offences?

That was for the future, however. Now it was all about survival. Keeping his cap pulled firmly down, Dave Reynolds hurried on his way, avoiding the gaze of passers-by by pretending to be messaging on his phone. He knew his route by instinct, had played out this exact scenario a dozen times, future-proofing his escape plans. But now it was actually happening, now it was *real*. He prayed that his preparations would prove adequate, that he hadn't overlooked any obvious flaw in his planning, but how could he be sure? In the past, when he'd role-played his retreat, he'd been confident, in command, purposeful. But now that it was actually here, he felt exposed and ill at ease, seeing danger everywhere.

He felt sure that the streets would be swarming with uniformed officers, that scores of his old colleagues would be searching high and low for him, each keen to be the one who finally brought him in. Could he risk sticking to the pavements and walkways? He had no choice really, but the thought still made him extremely nervous. His destination was nearly thirty minutes' walk away, half an hour out in the open, exposed to God knows what. Surely that was too big a risk to take? Especially when the stakes were so high. Exposure now would lead to a lifetime behind bars, *if* he was lucky to survive that long at the hands of his fellow inmates, who'd be itching to have a crack at him. Such a fate was unthinkable, so changing direction sharply, Dave Reynolds made a decision. Speed was of the essence now, so hurrying across the road, he made his way towards a nearby taxi rank. Hailing a cab would be risky, but at least it would be quick, his nerves already shot at the thought of continuing out in the open. Hurrying to the nearest taxi, he bent down by the open window, dropping his voice half an octave as he said:

'Woolmer Road, please, quick as you can, mate.'

Was it the tension in his voice? Some hint of anxiety in his expression? Either way, the cab driver was clearly intrigued by his request, staring at him with open curiosity, running his eyes over his face. Did he recognize him? Was his photo already doing the rounds? Or had this driver read Garanita's hatchet job a couple of days back?

'Actually, on second thoughts, it's a nice day, so ...'

He straightened up as he spoke, patting the roof of the car, before heading on his way. Despite his jaunty tone, Reynolds' heart was thumping, beads of sweat creeping down his temple. Was it his imagination or could he feel the cab driver's eyes on his back even now, drinking in his hasty retreat? It had been foolish to engage with him, weak even, and he might yet pay a heavy price for his rashness. For so long able to offend in plain sight, David Reynolds had never felt so visible, never felt such a marked man, as he did today.

Chapter 100

'He was definitely tipped off, no question about it.'

DC Wilson was standing by Charlie's desk, excited and breathless. But his tone was tinged with anger too, clearly furious that someone within the wider community had encouraged PC David Reynolds to flee.

'Show me,' Charlie demanded.

Wilson handed her the tablet, on which were listed recent WhatsApp messages that had been received and read on Reynolds' mobile phone.

'Check out this one,' Wilson continued, 'sent just after 4 p.m. today. "Your cards are marked, better fold now." I mean it's on a WhatsApp group set up to organize poker meetings, so I guess you could kind of explain it away, but—'

'But it wasn't like Reynolds was involved in a poker game in the middle of the day,' Charlie cut in, shaking her head. 'Not when he was fleeing the bloody city...'

'Exactly. Everyone in the group has a nickname, so it's hard to know their identities. Reynolds calls himself Alpha Boy and the message was sent by Big Dog. Obviously I can run the phone number, but it'll take me a little while to get a match.'

'No need,' Charlie said, anger surging within her. 'I'm pretty sure I know who that is.'

Turning away from her surprised colleague, Charlie called out to the rest of the team.

'Right, listen up, people, we have a further development in the Reynolds case.'

A dozen heads looked up sharply.

'DC Jennings, how long have you been part of a poker group with PC Dave Reynolds?'

A shocked silence permeated the room, as several of his colleagues turned to face him.

'I'm sorry?' Jennings blustered. 'I'm not sure I kn—'

'You are Big Dog, I take it? You referred to yourself by that nickname the other day when bragging to your pals about your winnings. "Alpha Boy couldn't handle the Big Dog" was the exact phrase you used, I think.'

The colour drained from the DC's face, as the anger and shock in the room started to grow.

'And Reynolds is Alpha Boy, correct?'

'Well, I ...'

'I'll ask you again, how long have you been part of poker group with Dave Reynolds?'

'Well, it's nothing major ... just a few of the lads, well, we meet most Wednesday nights after work at the police social club. No big deal, just small stakes, a friendly thing.'

'So friendly, in fact, that you felt honour-bound to warn your old mucker that he was about to be arrested. The chaps sticking together and all that ...'

Furious, she passed the tablet to DC Malik, who took in the message with evident horror.

'It's not what you think,' Jennings protested weakly.

'It's exactly what I think. Which is why I'm going to have to ask you to step away from your desk, surrender your phone and devices and wait in the interview suite until I've had time to contact Professional Standards.'

'Now come on, there's no need to be like that.'

'There's *every* need, DC Jennings. Aiding and abetting a wanted felon is a very serious offence. I'm not sure we can dismiss this as lads' banter, can we?'

Jennings had nowhere to run and he knew it. He was scowling at Charlie, but his anger, his defiance, was just desperation and humiliation.

'Right then, the rest of you back to your desks...'

Charlie turned away, but then paused, as an uncomfortable thought landed.

'Actually, hold on a minute,' she continued, turning back to the team. 'Before you resume your duties, is there anyone *else* in this unit who participates in this weekly poker game?'

A long, long silence followed, Charlie's gaze scanning the team, even as Jennings stared at the floor, and then slowly, reluctantly, two more hands crept up.

Chapter 101

'I want names. And I want them now.'

Graham Armstrong stared at Helen, startled and scared. He'd been knocked off his stride by her unheralded arrival in the interview suite, seating herself alongside his persecutor, DC McAndrew, but even more taken aback by her attitude. She'd clearly jumped straight from one interrogation into another and was *not* in a mood to take prisoners. She was brooding, hostile and aggressive, leaning over the table and glowering at him with visible distaste.

'I've already told your colleague...' Armstrong responded as politely as he could, his crisp Edinburgh accent punching through. 'I don't know their actual names. They used false identities to deter—'

'Enough!' Helen barked, slamming her hand on the table. 'Enough of the lies and the obfuscation. You've already admitted to my colleague that you set up and organized these Zoom meetings, that you basically recruited every single one of these perverts.'

'Not his exact words, but yes,' DC McAndrew confirmed darkly.

'And I don't believe for a minute that you would have let anyone into your little circle unless you knew *exactly* who they were. Where they lived and worked, that they were good for the "fees", that they wouldn't go soft and rat on you. So cut the crap and give us names. It is your only, your last, hope of any mitigation against what will otherwise be a seriously long sentence...'

The accused turned away, looking agonized, but kept his counsel.

'The rest of it's done and dusted, Graham,' DC McAndrew added, taking up the baton. 'Everybody knows what you've been up to. Your mother, your ex-wife, all of your former colleagues in the Fire Service. If they didn't want rid of you first time around, they certainly will now. There will be no bail, no parole and after you've been convinced and sentenced, no hope of early release. You're done, Graham, a busted flush.'

'So you can either sit there and stew in your disgrace,' Helen continued pointedly, 'or you can do yourself a favour and co-operate with us.'

Armstrong sat back heavily in his chair, running his hand over his face. A quick angled glance to his lawyer, then he eventually replied:

'OK, fine, have it your way. There was Alexander Coulter, also ex-Fire Service. James Peters, he works for Hampshire County Council; Eric Bateman, he's a small businessman and part-time magistrate...'

Helen stared at the disgraced firefighter in dismay as he reeled off a long list of offenders, co-conspirators in his vile enterprise, all of whom had status, power and responsibility. It was a rogues' gallery of degenerates who'd asked for the public's trust, then betrayed it in the most egregious, most repellent fashion. Teachers, charity workers, bank managers... the names tumbled out, each one sharpening Helen's anger.

'...and Simon Reeves, he's a retired journalist, lives near Calshot, I think. I swear that's it, that's the lot.'

Armstrong pulled a handkerchief from his pocket, mopping his brow. He looked exhausted, washed out, as if the act of betraying his associates had cost him physically.

'See, you can do it when you try,' DC McAndrew offered, receiving only a scowl in response.

'Next question, where's Reynolds?' Helen added, keen to keep the pressure on.

'I'm sorry?'

'You heard me, where's he gone? Where is PC Reynolds?'

'You haven't pulled him in yet?' Armstrong questioned. 'I assumed he was already in the building.'

He appeared genuinely surprised, but Helen wasn't prepared to let him off the hook that easily.

'He must have a bolthole. A flat, a lock-up, a static caravan he hides out in. Where is it?'

'I've no idea,' the firefighter protested. 'Honestly. I've never even met the guy. Everything was done either online or by post. That was the whole *point*.'

For once, Helen was inclined to believe him, changing tack sharply.

'What about Naomi then? And Mia? Where are they?'

'I don't know.'

'Graham, I'm going to ask you again,' Helen growled, 'and this time you better tell me the truth or so help me God...'

'I *am* telling you the truth. That was Reynolds' business, not mine. My job was to recruit people, to set up the meets. His job was to secure the... well, you know what his job was.'

'Don't we just,' McAndrew replied bitterly.

'I don't know where he found the girls or where he kept them. Do you think he'd tell me? Or the others? Reynolds insisted on total secrecy in case anyone else was ever pulled in. I only know *his* name because one of the other guys had been picked up by Reynolds for kerb-crawling, recognized him during one of the sessions. It was a total information lockdown.'

Helen dearly wanted to squeeze the information out of him, but again the suspect seemed convincing.

'What about the others? Would they know?'

'Unlikely, but I suppose anything's possible,' Armstrong replied, clearly keen to shift the focus away from himself.

'All right, get this one charged and into custody,' Helen tasked McAndrew, as she rose purposefully to her feet. 'And as for the others, bring them in. Bring them *all* in.'

Turning, Helen departed, wrenching the door open and hurrying away. They had cracked Armstrong, unravelling a major paedophile network in the process, but it wasn't enough. PC Reynolds, the vilest member of this hideous fraternity, was still at large and Naomi Watson was missing, her whereabouts still unknown. Helen knew only too well that Reynolds' flight from justice spelled real danger for the missing teen. The longer he remained free, the longer she remained concealed, the greater the jeopardy became.

Every second counted now.

Chapter 102

Grasping the metal plate tightly, Naomi smashed it against the sealed doors, determined to blast her way to freedom. With each passing second it was getting hotter in her cell, the air noticeably thinner. She knew that she had to escape fast or face an agonizing death in the suffocating darkness.

For a few minutes after her captor had departed, Naomi had been paralyzed with panic, the horror of being sealed in a pitch-black tomb with a decaying corpse too awful to comprehend. Gradually, however, Naomi had become aware of the heavy weight of the chain in her hand once more. She still had a weapon. Which meant she still had hope.

Her initial attempts to free herself had gone badly. With no light creeping under the door anymore, it had taken her a while to get her bearings. Stepping back, she'd swung her chain, revolving it faster and faster, but at the crucial moment, she misjudged her throw in the darkness, succeeding only in skimming the top of her head with the heavy metal plate as she let go of the chain, crying out in pain as she did so.

Cursing, she'd crawled across the floor, accidently squashing more than one bug as she scrabbled to locate the chain. Increasingly desperate, increasingly scared, Naomi now decided on a change of tactic, grasping the plate by the hook that secured it to the metal links, and using it as a makeshift axe. Summoning all her resolve, all her courage, she brought it down, once, twice, three times, slamming it into the doors. She heard the corner of the plate bite, felt specks of chipboard hit her face on impact, but the heavy weapon rebounded sharply each time, throwing her off balance. Breathless, her long hair sticking to her sweaty face, Naomi tried a few more, increasingly lethargic, attacks before giving up.

'Think, think...'

Naomi urged herself on, gratefully sucking in what air she could find, whilst trying to still her pounding heart, trying to regulate her breathing. She had to get out of here, but she had to play it smart, given that her supply of air was diminishing steadily. Stepping forward, she now ran her hands along the surface until she felt a slight bump in the darkness. Here she paused, locating what had once been the join of the two doors, which was now part of a wider, more comprehensive seal. If she could somehow slide the sharp edge of the plate between the two doors, then was there a chance she could jemmie it back and forth, eventually forcing the two doors open?

Using her left hand to guide the tip of her weapon, Naomi placed the sharp edge on the join. Placing one hand on the back of the plate, she now pushed with all her might. She strained every sinew, her feet digging into the floor, her body weight thrown totally forward... but the plate refused to move. Breathing heavily now, she changed tack, banging heavily with her hand on the back of the plate, but before long her palm was smarting and she had still made no progress. Panicking, her strength fading, she pulled the plate back and hurled it forwards, hoping against hope that it would bisect the join cleanly, opening up a wound to attack. But in the all-pervading gloom, her aim was off and the plate rebounded sharply off the chipboard, cannoning into her face. In her shock, she lost her balance, falling backwards, before the final indignity, the plate landing heavily, painfully, on her knee.

'Shit, shit, shit...'

Naomi swore so as not to cry, desperate not to break down completely now. But her resistance was weakening, her strength dissipating and with it her resolve. She was trapped, utterly trapped, with ever-dwindling oxygen. Lying on the floor, Naomi tried to suck in the air as she had before, but there was none to be had, the cell now completely sealed. All she could feel was her own hot breath rebounding onto her.

Tugging off her top, Naomi tossed it away, careless of her dignity now. For a moment, she felt slightly refreshed, her exposed skin kissing the rough floor, but she knew the respite would be temporary. The temperature was rising all the time, hot breathy carbon dioxide replacing precious oxygen, spelling only doom. She was stuck down here with no chance of escape, no hope of salvation, no prospect of ever seeing another human being ever again.

She would die down here. And she would do so alone.

Chapter 103

The solitary figure crept down the narrow gap, his eyes darting this way and that, sensing danger. It had taken David Reynolds over half an hour to get here, sticking fast to the back roads, bridleways and cycle paths, away from city-centre cameras and large crowds. It had been a tense, frustrating journey, but now he was within touching distance of his destination. From here on in, if luck was on his side, things would become easier, but still on the cusp of his deliverance, he nevertheless took the last few steps slowly, cautiously, as if expecting an ambush. Approaching the tired wooden hall from the rear, he crept down the small space between building and boundary wall, squeezing his way along, before emerging at the far end. From here, he could cut round to the main entrance, but he paused, casting a wary eye up and down the street. He could see no one loitering in the quiet residential street, no manned vehicles, no passing patrols, so quitting his hiding place, he scurried round to the front door.

The police social club in St Mary's was a relic of yesteryear, when hard-working men could repair here for a pint after a shift, without fear of getting an earful when they returned home. Now it was a bit of a sad place, unloved and untended, with peeling paint and creeping damp. That said, it was a discreet place for high-stakes poker games and more besides, and Reynolds had made it his home from home, a place to bolt to whenever things got on top of him. He always kept a healthy stash of booze behind the bar in one of the locked chipboard cupboards, but today he'd come here seeking a different prize.

Slipping the key into the padlock, he arrowed a look over his shoulder, but the coast remained clear. Pocketing the lock, he slipped inside, closing the door quietly behind him. Now he didn't hesitate, hurrying straight to the old storage room at the rear. Although this would be his last visit to the club, maybe even his last day in Southampton, there was no time for nostalgia or sentimentality.

Pushing into the tiny room, he tried to ignore the cloying smell of mildew. The place was stacked full of cardboard boxes, broken chairs and other junk. To the rear was a pile of old dust sheets and Reynolds hastened there now. Hauling them roughly off, he unearthed a large cardboard box, which unlike the others was sealed shut with gaffer tape. He tore the tape off efficiently, opening the box to reveal a hiking rucksack inside. Lifting it clear, he undid the strings at the top and ferreted inside. The contents quickly revealed themselves – ration packs of food, a two-man tent, an inflatable mattress, a torch, a water canister and, in the zipped pocket on top, a fake driver's licence and a bundle of £20 notes. It wasn't much but it was all he needed to make good his escape from Southampton before plotting his next move. Where would he end up? The North? Scotland? Ireland even? He wouldn't perhaps have chosen these locations normally, but now he suddenly felt excited about starting afresh, away from Jackie, away from his son, away from all the stresses and strains of his life. The last few days had been fraught, but now deliverance was at hand.

Smiling, Reynolds hoisted the rucksack onto his back. But as he did so, the overhead lights snapped on. Shocked, alarmed, the fugitive span quickly … to discover DS Charlie Brooks standing in the doorway.

'Hello, Dave. We thought you might turn up here. I'm sorry the rest of your poker buddies aren't here to welc—'

He didn't let her finish, charging directly at her. She must have been expecting this move, for instantly she flicked out her baton, raising it to strike. Reynolds was too quick for her, however, his shoulder crashing into her chest, sending her flying backwards. She cannoned into the wall, and clawing his way past her, Reynolds pushed out of the door. As expected, fresh danger awaited him here, two burly colleagues bearing down on him. Instinctively, Reynolds lashed out with his fist, catching the first on the jaw, before climbing over him to ram his forehead into the second officer's nose. Reynolds felt blood splash across his cheek, heard a howl of pain, but he kept going, launching his shoulder into a third officer, who'd just appeared at the mouth of the corridor.

As this third officer crashed to the floor, Reynolds raced on. The cavalry had arrived undercooked, undermanned, meaning that the way to the exit was now clear. Picking up his speed, a jubilant Reynolds raced towards it. If he was fast, if he was lucky, he could still make it away from here, frustrating his pursuers even at their moment of triumph. Laughing, he sprinted towards the door, reaching out his hand to grasp the handle and propel himself to liberty. As he did so, however, his world turned upside down. He felt the impact, his legs sliding out from underneath him, as he seemed to somersault in the air. Then gravity took hold and he slammed down onto the hard wooden floor. Stunned, he barely had time to get his bearings before he heard a familiar voice ring out.

'Oh no, you don't. Not this time …'

Craning round, Reynolds realized that he'd been side-swiped

by PC Beth Beamer, who'd executed a perfect rugby tackle on him. Even now, she was pinning him down, breathless but triumphant. Reynolds tried to throw her off, but he was a second too slow, DS Brooks coming up fast to assist her colleague, throwing herself on top of him. Still he bucked, but the battle was lost and he once more felt the unforgiving bite of police-issue handcuffs.

'Sorry, Dave,' Brooks crowed, snatching up his rucksack as she rose. 'It's not time for your holidays just yet. There's someone at Southampton Central who wants a word with you.'

Chapter 104

They filed into the room silently, heads bowed, mouths shut. Was this purely a defensive tactic, not wishing to incriminate themselves further, or did their bearing denote embarrassment, even shame? Chief Superintendent Rebecca Holmes sincerely hoped it was the latter, wanting to believe that there was *some* goodness in these officers, but privately she feared it was the former. The trio of DCs had proved to be wholly unreliable, utterly unsuited to the position of responsibility they'd been given and, frankly, she now expected nothing of them.

'Right then,' she said firmly. 'This is your new home for the foreseeable future.'

DC Jennings looked around the musty, dimly lit room in horror, his shock and mortification evidently shared by DCs Reid and Edwards. They were in a resources room on the third floor, a holding pen for whiteboards, old office furniture and a couple of photocopiers. The curtains were drawn, dust danced in the air and the room had a strange odour, which was a mixture of decaying fabric and photocopying chemicals. It was clearly not intended for human habitation, but perhaps that was the point. The suspended officers had caused Chief Superintendent Holmes professional embarrassment, a cardinal sin.

'It will take us a little while to process this "situation", partly

399

as Professional Services already have their hands full dealing with other problem officers.'

DC Jennings looked up sharply, clearly not appreciating that description, but Holmes ignored him. She little cared what he thought or felt now.

'You are not to set foot outside of this room without my say-so, and obviously you are not to communicate with anyone else in the building. Is that clear?'

Two of them nodded reluctantly, Jennings merely scowling.

'On a personal note, I'd like to say how disappointed I am in all of you. I must confess I hadn't truly appreciated how deeply entrenched the boys' club culture was at this station. It could have cost us dear, especially if PC Reynolds had managed to make good his escape. Fortunately, DS Brooks and PC Beamer were on hand to ensure he didn't. Once he's been interviewed and charged, we will address your connection to him, and your unhelpful intervention in this investigation.'

Once more Jennings reacted. He was clearly itching to push back, but at the last minute thought better of it, biting his tongue.

'In the meantime, I shall leave you to reflect on your actions. I imagine in the next few weeks and months you'll have *a lot* of time and space to consider what you've done, the damage you've inflicted on both your unit and this station. I'm afraid this is it, boys...'

She gestured to the uninspiring surroundings, sucking in the prevalent air of decay.

'...this is your reality now. It will take me a while to get you out of this building, out of this force, so there'll be plenty of time for introspection, for personal growth. You will spend every day here, under my direct supervision until that process is completed and I would suggest you use that time to consider what your next career might be, *if* you are lucky enough to have one.'

She paused now, taking a moment to look at each transgressor in turn, letting them feel the full weight of her disappointment and anger, before she moved off smartly, walking fast to the door and slamming it shut behind her, leaving the trio of prisoners in the airless room.

Chapter 105

She gasped desperately, her chest heaving as she tried to suck in the last remaining vestiges of oxygen, but could find no relief. The temperature in her tiny, airless cell seemed to have rocketed in the last few minutes and even though Naomi was now lying on the floor, she still felt as if she was suffocating, overwhelmed by a steadily growing cloud of carbon dioxide. Each breath she managed to take only seemed to make things worse, her attempt to live only serving to ensure her imminent death.

She was past hope, past dreams of salvation; now all she could do was prepare for the end. Naomi felt crushed by despair, paralyzed with terror, but she tried to push these feelings away. If this was it, as it surely must be, she wanted to die bathed in happy thoughts, clothing herself in memories of a time when things were good, when life seemed full of possibilities. She remembered Christmas presents when she was a kid, her first surfer Barbie. She recalled the rescue dog, Pickles, that they'd had for a few months back in the day, before it became too infirm to walk. Naomi even managed to dredge up fleeting images of her dad, kissing her softly on the head, as he slipped her a fiver.

But mostly Naomi thought about her mum. It was hard not to imagine Sheila's desolation, her fear, her sadness, especially as Naomi was now convinced there would be no discovery, no justice, no funeral. The world was cruel and Reynolds would win, that seemed clear to her, but by sheer force of will, Naomi pushed these negative thoughts aside. She would not go there; she would not let her last thoughts be these dark images of a grieving mother. Instead, she would remember the love, the cuddles, the kisses. Sitting on the sofa together watching *I'm a Celebrity*, playing with the sprinkler in their tiny garden, walking through Westquay at Christmas time, taking in the sparkling window displays. These were the moments when she'd felt happy, safe and loved. This was her legacy, as limited and unremarkable as that might seem. This was her.

It was time to make her peace with that, to acknowledge that there were some paths you shouldn't take, some mistakes you can't recover from. Naomi was finding it harder to focus now, the thinning oxygen robbing her of composure, of clarity. She knew she had to keep still, had to conserve energy and breath, but her body felt clammy, sweaty, itchy, as if she was slowly cooking in this awful hell. She wanted to fight it, she wanted to stay alive, but she wasn't even really sure which way was up anymore, couldn't tell if she was still awake or merely dreaming now. She kept her eyes open, straining in the gloom to see something, anything, some object, some sign that would confirm that she was still present, still alive. But her resolve, her resistance was at an end and now, suddenly, everything went black.

Chapter 106

'Tell me where she is.'

Helen leant forward on the table, her face just inches from the suspect. Normally, she would have taken her time to work her adversary over, luring him into a trap before confronting him with the evidence, but there was no time for that today. Every second counted now if she wanted to find Naomi alive.

'You're beaten all ends up, Dave. And the road in front of you is not a pretty one. But if Naomi dies, your situation, your life, gets a whole lot worse. So tell me where she is.'

Reynolds remained unmoved, lifting his eyes briefly in the direction of his lawyer, Eleanor Higham, before returning them to rest on Helen. Having kicked and screamed during his arrest, he'd now lapsed into sullen silence.

'Why won't you talk to us, Dave? You must see the hole you're in,' Helen persisted, her passion clear. 'The evidence is overwhelmingly stacked against you. We have footage of you raping Naomi. Statements from Graham Armstrong and James Peters, specifically naming *you* as a serial abductor and abuser of women. This is seventh circle of Hell material, the stuff of nightmares... and yet you can still be the hero, Dave. You can still do the right thing. Naomi's mother is desperate to have her home safe, to help her heal, to help her embrace the long life she has ahead of her. You can make sure that happens. At the eleventh hour, you can prove to the world that there *is* good inside you, that those same instincts that prompted you to become a police officer in the first place remain undiminished. Show them, Dave, show them what you can do, how you can make a difference, how you can *save* the day.'

Reynolds' right eye twitched slightly, but otherwise the disgraced PC seemed inured to her compliments, her bribes. Maybe he smelt a rat, knowing that his image was already tarnished forever, his future in ruins, or maybe he just enjoyed frustrating her. Either way, Helen was no further forward, the fate, the location, of Naomi remaining oblique.

'What's this about, Dave?' Helen said, maintaining her total focus on the suspect opposite her. 'Is it about control? About power? Did you enjoy making Naomi suffer? Do you enjoy frustrating me? Is that what's happening here?'

His eyes narrowed slightly, his expression intensifying, as if he wanted to respond but clearly didn't trust himself not to give too much away.

'Don't get me wrong, I can see why. I mean I've looked at your background, your upbringing and I *do* understand. I went through something similar myself. Abandoned by your parents, brought up in a number of children's homes, one of which was later found to have been run by a serial sex offender ... I can appreciate what you've been through, what that must have been like. No control, no sense of security, no *love*. Who knows, perhaps you were even a victim of abuse yourself?'

Reynolds' expression hardened slightly, encouraging Helen, who felt sure she was on firm ground here, his chaotic, hurtful upbringing still biting.

'I don't know what happened to you in those homes, and I don't need to know. My experiences were not dissimilar and, honestly, they scar me to this day. I understand the anger, the pain, the desire to make people suffer for what you went through, but there is another way, a better way. Rather than hurting people, of behaving like your tormentors, you can offer the helping hand that you were never given. Think back, Dave, think back to how you felt all those years ago – helpless, hopeless, doomed to suffer. If someone had offered to help you then, to pull you out of that awful place, taking you somewhere warm and safe, you would have seized that offer. Don't use your power to hurt, to degrade, to kill. Use it to save Naomi, to save Mia. Do it to save *yourself*.'

Helen came to a halt, breathless and impassioned. Reynolds digested her words, toying with his wedding ring nervously, before looking up once more.

'Mia who?' he offered casually.

Immediately, Helen felt anger surge within her.

'Don't play games with me, Dave. Mia Davies, who you abducted three months ago, before you kidnapped Naomi Watson.'

'I'm sorry, you've lost me ...'

'Don't you *dare* deny it!' Helen cried, jumping to her feet. 'We have video evidence, PC Reynolds, footage that you shot yourself of you attacking Naomi Watson—'

'That's not me,' Reynolds interrupted, shaking his head.

Helen stared at him, aghast.

'It's one hundred per cent you,' she fired back. 'And it is very clearly Naomi Watson too. That footage was taken not two days ago—'

'It's fake,' the suspect intervened once more. 'These things are easily done. Where did you get it from?'

'That's not your concern,' Helen countered angrily. 'The point is—'

'I mean, if you got it from this Armitage guy—'

'Armstrong.'

'Whatever, if you got it from some nonce who's into internet abuse and whatnot, then it's highly likely *he* created it, either to deflect blame from himself, or distract attention from the case.'

'Can you even hear yourself?' Helen raged, aghast. 'We have money recovered from your wife's purse with Armstrong's fingerprints on it, plus very detailed testimony from the man himself as to your longstanding criminal association—'

'He doesn't sound a very reliable witness to me; hard to make his testimony stick, I would have thought,' Reynolds goaded.

'On the contrary,' Helen responded. 'He's been very accurate, very detailed in his statement. Times, dates of your various sessions, plus details of the money he gave you, including the PO box address he sent it to. I'm assuming the post office in question has CCTV that will have picked up yourself, or your wife, collecting those envelopes of money. Suddenly she gets dragged into it then, your own wife, maybe even your son. What then?'

Reynolds was about to spit back some curse, his mouth suddenly curling up into a snarl, before he caught himself.

'They know nothing about any wrongdoing. And neither do I. As I've said from the start, you're barking up the wrong tree on this one, DI Grace, serving only to make yourself look foolish in the process.'

'Bullshit. You've been lying to me since day one. Lying to your colleagues, your family. And we can prove it. We've got you trapped, Dave. You're on a one-way ticket to a whole life sentence and I will personally make it my mission to—'

'OK, you say I've taken these girls, hurt them?' Reynolds interjected forcefully. 'So where's the evidence? Where's the tangible, physical evidence that I had anything to do with these alleged crimes?'

Helen glared at him, her fury rising with each passing second.

'Go on, show me,' Reynolds persisted. 'Where are they? Where's this secret lair they are supposed to be being held in? Where?'

Helen stared at him, not trusting herself to speak.

'You say I'm all these things, but I don't recognize your version of events *at all*. I'm an honest copper, a good husband, a decent guy. I've done nothing wr—'

But before he could finish, Helen was upon him. Launching herself over the table, she grasped a surprised Reynolds by the throat, dragging him physically backwards. As his chair clattered to the floor, the suspect staggered back under her attack, before slamming hard into the wall. Gripping his bulging throat, Helen hissed at him.

'You are a rapist and a killer. And you *will* tell me where Naomi Watson is.'

Reynolds' lawyer was clawing at her, trying to pull her off, but Helen maintained her grip.

'This is your last chance, Reynolds. Or I promise I will send you to Hell.'

She increased the pressure, the suspect gasping under her attack. But now finally Eleanor Higham found purchase, yanking Helen's hand from Reynolds' throat and thrusting the police officer away from her spluttering client.

'DI Grace, this is wholly inappropriate and unacceptable. I demand that you suspend this interview immediately.'

Breathless, consumed by red mist, Helen glared at the outraged solicitor, before turning and walking back to the table.

'Interview suspended at 14.52,' she barked, before stabbing the stop button.

Enraged, Helen hurried to the door, turning on the threshold to look back once more at the suspect. Reynolds remained pinned up against the wall, shocked but triumphant, a smile slowly spreading across his face. Helen had felt sure she had the evidence, the momentum, to finally break him, to reveal his depravity for the whole world to see. But looking at him now, his eyes blazing, his expression victorious, Helen realized with a shudder that PC Dave Reynolds would rather let Naomi Watson die than admit his guilt.

Chapter 107

'OK, guys, the clock is ticking here, so give me something...'

Charlie was pacing back and forth in front of the board, surrounded by the rump of their team. Losing three officers at such a crucial time in the investigation was a disaster and might well cost them dear, but they'd had no choice but to exile Jennings and his cronies, meaning Charlie had to work with the core of decent, hard-working officers who remained.

'Reynolds is admitting nothing, will presumably "No Comment" all the way until he's charged, so *we* need to work out where he's keeping those girls. Are we any further on with triangulating his recent movements?'

'We've double- and triple-checked,' DC McAndrew responded gravely. 'His phone position shows him as either being here, on the beat, or at home. Nothing else. Certainly nothing out of the ordinary, nothing suspicious.'

'What about his family?'

'Their movements are even more contained. Home, school, shops, that's it.'

'What about wider reports of suspicious activity, unusual noises, cries for help. Have uniform reported back on that front?'

'We've had lots of reports since the newspaper article about

Naomi,' McAndrew continued. 'But they've all been dead ends. Trapped cats or hoaxers having a bit of fun ...'

'Strange bloody idea of fun,' Charlie cursed. 'What about our property search? Large buildings in or around the Midanbury area that are lying vacant or have been mothballed or are await-ing development ...'

'We're still compiling a list,' DC Malik said, looking visibly stressed. 'But because of the economic downturn there are lots of developments that have been shelved, or leases that have been given up. We're working our way through them, but—'

'Can we link any of these properties to the suspects connected with Reynolds, people we already have in custody?'

Malik paused, caught off guard.

'Well, we've only just started cross-referencing them.'

'OK, well, drop the other stuff and focus on that,' Charlie demanded. 'It might be a blind alley, but it's probably our best bet. I'm assuming Armstrong doesn't own any property? Somewhere he could have secreted the girls?'

'Not that we know of.'

'What about Eric Bateman, the magistrate entrepreneur guy? He's got resources, so—'

'I had a look at him,' DC Wilson offered quickly. 'He owns three properties, one here, two abroad. We've already turned over his house here though, no sign of anything.'

'What about James Peters? The council guy?'

'No, just a two-up, two-down in Shirley Warren that's already been searched.'

Frustrated, Charlie was about to move on to the next suspect, when she paused.

'Remind me, what does Peters do for the Council?'

There was a brief pause, then DC Wilson's face seemed to light up.

'He works in housing, with special responsibility for the council's fixed assets, properties they either own or have a long lease on.'

'So, presumably, he'd have an overview of which council properties were being used, which were awaiting development or sale?' Charlie replied, suddenly excited.

'Absolutely. But it's a very long list, dozens, possibly scores of properties...'

'I don't care,' Charlie replied, turning to face the rest of the team. 'I'll talk to Peters when they bring him in, see what I can screw out of him. In the meantime, I want the rest of you to work through those vacant council properties one by one, concentrating on those in the Midanbury area. If Naomi is being held in one of those buildings, it's in our gift to find her now, so we do not rest until every single one has been properly investigated. Understood?'

A sea of faces nodded purposefully out her. Charlie felt suddenly moved, buoyed up by the realization that the remnants of the team were honest, hard-working and true.

'Then let's get to it. Don't let anyone or anything stand in your way. We *have* to find those girls. You're their only hope now.'

Chapter 108

Helen stalked along the corridor, her tormentor in hot pursuit.

'I will have your badge for this, Inspector. You may think you're untouchable, but you've really crossed the line this time.'

Eleanor Higham wasn't bluffing, clearly enraged by Helen's assault on her client, but the latter paid her no heed. Her only concern now was locating Naomi Watson. With Reynolds refusing to acknowledge his role in her abduction, Helen would have to find another way to locate the missing teenager, though at present this seemed a remote possibility. The longer Reynolds held out, the bleaker Naomi's prospects became.

'I'm going straight to the Chief Superintendent about this, demanding she take disciplinary action. With any luck there might even be criminal charges too. Assault, threatening behaviour...'

'Knock yourself out, Eleanor,' Helen replied tersely. 'See what kind of reception you get. I know you're not averse to representing low-lives, but you've really excelled yourself here. The most hated man in this force, soon to be the most hated man in Southampton, and you take on his case like a shot.'

'Every man has the right to a proper defence, Inspector.'

'And you're going to give it to him. Still, when the papers go large on how you, a young, female lawyer, are happy to speak up for a multiple rapist, a prolific paedophile who's preyed on underage girls for years, let's see what that does for your standing in the community.'

They were halfway down the corridor towards the incident room, but Higham clearly had no intention of giving up the chase yet, jabbing her finger at Helen.

'You may think you can frighten me, but I'm not going to be the one with egg on my face at the end of all this, Inspector. My client is going to prove his innocence, be acquitted of all charges, whilst you are going to be revealed as the vengeful harpy you are.'

Helen ground to a halt, stunned by what she was hearing, turning on her attacker.

'Absolutely incredible,' she replied, shaking her head. 'You've seen the footage – that is *your* client assaulting Naomi Watson.'

'It shows nothing of the sort. The picture quality is hopeless, it's impossible to tell who the victim is, who her attacker is…'

'I think you better get your story right, Eleanor,' Helen fired back. 'Your client seems to think the whole thing was faked to look like him.'

'You provoked him, but don't worry, we'll be ready and waiting, primed to quash these ridiculous, trumped-up charges.'

'Well, good luck to you.'

'No, good luck to you, Helen. I mean, really, what have you got? The word of a bunch of convicted paedophiles, some grainy footage and a whole lot of circumstantial that I will enjoy picking apart, piece by piece. Against that, we have PC David Reynolds. Experienced, respected, a hero cop of many years standing. A pillar of the community, known and liked by people all over this city. What's more he's a loving husband and doting father. Throw in his dog too and he's the complete package. Simple, wholesome, steadfast. Honestly, the chips are stacked up on my side of the table, so I would seriously...'

But Helen was no longer listening, her mind suddenly whirring. Eleanor Higham ground to a halt, wrong-footed, confused by Helen's thoughtful expression.

'Did you hear what I said, DI Grace?' she demanded.

'Yes, I did,' Helen replied quickly. 'And you've been very helpful. Thank you, Eleanor.'

And with that, she sprinted away down the corridor, leaving the confused lawyer staring after her, open-mouthed.

Chapter 109

'Look, do we have to do this now? It's a *seriously* bad time.'

Archie Reynolds's voice shook as he looked up at Helen, angry, hostile and upset. Helen didn't need to ask why – the young man's bruise was in full bloom, his mother could be heard sobbing upstairs and his father was facing a lifetime behind bars. In one sense, the latter might ultimately prove to be a blessed liberation, freeing them from Reynolds' toxic and domineering presence, but it was hard for the distraught young man to see that now. They had lost their only breadwinner, the axis round which family life revolved, and all that seemed to await them now was infamy, recrimination and ruin. Archie may have disliked his father, may have hated him for all Helen knew, but he was clearly close to his mother, itching now to be rid of Helen's presence so he could go and comfort her.

'I do appreciate that and I'm sorry for barging in on you like this. I wouldn't do so unless it was a matter of life and death.'

This seemed to sober the teenager, who turned away, embarrassed and ashamed.

'Look, Archie, none of this is your fault. No one blames you in the slightest, but I do need your help. There is still a chance we can find Naomi, save her, but I can't do it alone.'

The boy nodded briefly, but didn't look up.

'We're having trouble tracking your dad's movements. He seems to have either been at work or in this house, but I...'

Helen hesitated, aware she was about to reveal that she'd been stalking Reynolds, then pressed on regardless.

'...I followed him one night when he took the dog out.'

'Willow? Yeah, he dotes on her.'

'Yet triangulation suggests that he must have left his phone here. Was that normal when he took the dog out?'

'Sure,' the teenager nodded. 'I asked him about it once and he said his dog walks were his one chance to switch off. Said he didn't want to be bothered by calls or messages.'

Helen nodded, hope surging within her. Suddenly she felt sure she was onto something.

'And who does the dog walking in your family? Do you share it out amongst you or—'

'No,' Archie interrupted firmly. 'It's just Dad, won't let anyone else near her.'

'And how often does he take her out?'

'First thing in the morning and last thing at night.'

'I see.'

Helen said this so firmly, so purposefully, that Archie immediately reacted.

'Why? What is it about the dog walks that you're interested in?'

'I don't have time to explain now,' Helen said quickly, wanting to spare the boy further upset. 'But I do need to know where he goes. What's his route?'

The teenager was becoming more agitated with each passing minute, clearly keen to help but powerless to do so.

'I don't know.'

'Archie, it's really important.'

'Honestly, I've no idea. We were never allowed to go with

him. It was just the pair of them. I know they headed out back, ducked into the woods, but beyond that... Perhaps you could talk to some of the dog walkers, they might know.'

'We haven't got time for that...'

As Helen spoke, her eyes drifted to Willow, who lay curled up by the utility room door, looking up at Helen with mournful eyes.

'Does she have a tracker on her? Anything that might help us trace your dad's movements?'

But Archie was already shaking his head.

'Dad didn't want one. She's chipped of course, but that's it.'

Helen cursed inwardly, determined not to take it out on an innocent boy, but her frustration was near boiling point. Desperately, she cast her mind back, picturing the dog and his master haring through the woods together, happy and carefree. Then, as another thought landed, she turned her attention to the dog once more.

'Does your dad put a lead on Willow when he takes her out?'

This question seemed to trouble Archie, but he quickly replied.

'No. He always took it with him, but I never saw him actually put it on Willow, not *once.*'

Now it was Helen's turn to look up, surprised by the boy's bitter tone. She was about to push further, but Archie got in before her, adding bitterly:

'She was the only member of the family who *wasn't* in chains.'

Chapter 110

The back door swung open and Helen burst out, followed closely by Willow, with a flustered Archie Reynolds bringing up the rear. Helen hurried to the rear gate, sliding the bolt across and throwing it open. Willow obligingly trotted out, pursued by her companions, before making her way down a narrow track to the woodlands beyond.

Helen dogged her heels, praying that her plan might work. She was suddenly possessed by the sense that time was critical, that the margin for error was diminishing second by second, that everything now hung on this last desperate throw of the dice. The whippet climbed a steep path, Helen straining to keep up with her unwitting guide, but as she crested the summit, the dog paused, turning to face Archie, whilst seating herself on the cool earth.

'What now?' Helen demanded.

'I've no idea,' Archie blustered. 'Maybe she wants a treat or something?'

Concerned, Helen dug in her pockets, eventually finding a half-eaten packet of shortbread that she'd picked up at some dreary conference. The remaining biscuit was probably stale, but Willow didn't seem to care, swallowing it in one gulp.

'Good girl, now let's go ...'

Helen didn't really know what she was doing. Barring a short period when she was a small child, she'd never owned a dog. But her words seemed to have the desired effect, Willow resuming her walk, darting fast down a nearby path, nose to the ground. Relieved, Helen set off after her, Archie just behind, both proceeding in hushed silence.

For ten minutes, they weaved their way through the woods, cutting down half-hidden paths, before dropping onto a well-trodden bridleway. With each step, Helen felt her hopes rising, praying that the dog wouldn't tire or lose interest. For the first time in this most troubling of cases, someone was helping her, leading her, even if it was only a dog. Helen felt sure that if Reynolds had used the dog walks as a cover to visit his captives, then the dog would stick to the same path, muscle memory and routine ensuring she stayed on track.

Sure enough, they soon left the wood, dropping down a steep path onto the streets of Midanbury. Once again, Willow hesitated, the advent of cars and pedestrians giving her pause for thought.

'Come on, girl. Don't stop now,' Helen pleaded, marching past the dog down the street, encouraging her to follow.

The whippet duly obliged, soon overtaking Helen, before turning right at the top of the street. Helen kept pace with her, convinced that the end was in sight. She had no idea what that might mean – for her, for Naomi and Mia, for Reynolds – but now she simply longed to bring this disturbing case to a close.

Willow strode on, gracefully avoiding passers-by. She too seemed to be on a mission, sticking to the back streets as she glided along, before suddenly turning down a scruffy side road that eventually led to a derelict building, surrounded by a heavy chain-link fence. The gate was padlocked, but the dog did not break stride, darting to her left and nipping in through a hole in the fence, to access the site beyond. Helen followed suit, dropping down onto her knees and scrabbling through the gap. As she did so, she felt the jagged metal fence edge tear along the top of her scalp, but suppressing a cry of pain, she pressed on. Archie was only seconds behind her, arriving by her side as Helen realized where they were.

'Bloody hell.'

In front of them was a four-storey building that was as dilapidated as it was depressing. It had been fenced off from the public and was now swathed in notices, warning fly-tippers and squatters to steer clear, but they couldn't conceal the tired sign that still hung above the main entrance. Southampton Children's Home.

Helen stared at the crumbling edifice, once a boisterous, anarchic place, now a lifeless shell, scarcely believing that she hadn't thought of this before. David Reynolds had spent several years here, following his abandonment by his parents, and the place had continued to grow and prosper right up until 2019, when it was mothballed because it had turned out to have dangerous cladding. James Peters, in his position on Hampshire County Council, would have known there were no plans to develop it, that it would receive no official visitors. And did this choice of venue please Reynolds too? A chance for him to inflict terrible suffering on those weaker than himself, in the very place he had endured such an awful time?

Stepping towards the building, Helen was not surprised when the front security light flicked on, the sensor having picked up her movement. Clearly the building still had electricity, despite being vacant for several years. Convinced now that she was in the right place, Helen marched up to the main entrance, only to find the doors padlocked shut. Eyeing them for a minute, frustrated, annoyed, Helen took two steps back, before launching her boot at the door. It rattled and groaned, but stood firm, despite the large dent in it. So Helen tried again, then again, before the door finally burst open, laying the way clear for her.

Turning to a startled Archie, she commanded:

'Stay here!'

'Why? Where are y—'

But the rest of the question was lost on Helen, as she sprinted into the gloomy building.

Chapter III

She raced forwards, her eyes scanning the shadowy rooms in front of her. It was almost certain that the crumbling building was deserted, but Helen slid her baton from her pocket, extending it to its full length. She had no idea what she was getting herself into, whether any of Reynolds' co-conspirators were still at large, so it wouldn't do to take chances.

She kept up a swift pace, hurrying through the dusty reception area and into a large side room. This had presumably once been a recreation room, ripped posters of football players and WWF wrestlers hanging apologetically on the wall, but was devoid of life today. The musty smell of decay was overpowering, but clamping a hand over her mouth, Helen pressed on, returning to the corridor. She ran on, darting her head into another empty room, a dormitory of some kind, before hurrying on. On the cusp of entering a third room, however, she paused. Opposite her was a door that in days gone by had had additional security, two padlock fixtures in addition to the standard lock. The former were now unused, but the door appeared to be locked, the metal tongue visible in its mooring. More intriguingly still, the handle to this aged door seemed entirely free of dust, unlike everything else in this decaying shell. Hurrying over to it, Helen beat on the door, pounding it with her hand.

'Naomi? Mia? Can you hear me?'

Pausing, she listened intently, but no response came.

'I'm a police officer. I'm here to help you. Can you hear me?'

Helen's plea was greeted with silence. She didn't like to think what that meant, so stepping back, she threw herself at the door, her shoulder smashing into the decaying wood. It gave way instantly, the door virtually coming off its hinges, revealing a staircase that headed down into the darkness. Gathering herself, Helen illuminated the torch on her phone and hurried down, baton raised in anticipation of attack.

Her progress was swift and Helen soon found herself in a dusty basement. Emerging into the room, she scanned it feverishly, determined not to be ambushed in this grim hole, but to her disappointment as much as her relief, she was alone. Breathing heavily, Helen ran a critical eye over the room. Was this the awful basement in which Naomi had been attacked? Her pulse was pumping, her brain whirring, it was hard to focus, but as Helen took in her surroundings, she slowly recognized details that convinced her that this *was* the place. A rusting water pipe running along one of the walls, a missing brick in the wall just beneath it, and a discarded builder's spade, which had seemed a jarring and bizarre component in Reynolds' horrific video footage.

But if this was the place, where was Naomi? Where was Mia? Had they been brought here, abused, then spirited away? If so, where? It was possible that they were lying, bound and helpless, in an upstairs dormitory. But why would their captors take them up there, when they would be much better concealed down here? Was it too cold? Too airless? Helen hoped that she had hit upon the reason, that a desire to keep them alive might have caused their captors to move the girls elsewhere. But there was another possible explanation for the girls' absence here, one Helen didn't really want to contemplate.

'Naomi? Mia? If you can hear me, please shout out. You're quite safe…'

But Helen's desperate plea echoed off the walls, before slowly dying away. She was quite alone in this hellish place. She had got here too late.

Chapter *112*

Was it real? Or was she dreaming? Naomi couldn't tell. Swathed in total darkness, she was almost tempted to believe that she was already dead, that she'd descended into some bottomless hell that was no different to the prison she'd been incarcerated in. And yet something was telling her that that this was no idle fantasy, that she *was* still in the land of the living, that the faint noise she could hear *was* real.

Gasping, desperate, Naomi tried to push herself up onto her hands and knees. Straining, she managed to raise her head off the ground long enough to pick up a muffled cry, before her arms gave out and she fell down again, her cheek connecting sharply with the hard floor. The shock was extreme, the pain intense, and she was tempted to dissolve into tears, but she swallowed down her distress, convinced now that someone was close by. Someone who could help her, save her even. Such an outcome seemed impossible, fanciful, but...

There it was again. Quieter still this time, but definitely a human voice, possibly even a woman's voice, calling out her name. Who could it be? Her mother? A police officer? And what did it mean? Had her abductor been captured? Had he confessed? But even as hope surged through the floored captive, the cries seemed to die out, silence reigning in her fetid tomb once more. Maybe she was imagining it, maybe this was one last, wild hallucination before death, but if there was the slightest chance that this was real, that a potential saviour was on the other side of that wall, Naomi had to try.

Opening her mouth, she bellowed, bellowed for all she was worth... but all that came out was a dry, feeble wheeze. Her body was failing her, her mouth bone dry, her throat parched and there was not an ounce of oxygen in this suffocating space, no air that she could suck into her lungs. Terrified, she tried again.

'Help!'

But her pitiful cry was no more than a whisper, barely audible to her, let alone anyone else. At the crucial moment, her body had been found wanting. She tried one last time to find some energy, some volume from somewhere, but she knew it was hopeless now. Settling back down on the floor, she leaned her head against the cold pipe and started to cry. It was too little, too late.

This was the end.

Chapter 113

Helen sprinted back up the stairs, taking them two at a time. Having found nothing in the basement, she was determined not to waste another second in this nasty place. She had been convinced that this was the girls' prison, because of Reynolds' past association with it, because it fell under the purview of James Peters at the local council, but clearly she had been wrong, letting her imagination run away with her. She had gambled and lost, with potentially profound consequences for Naomi Watson and Mia Davies. Following a blind hunch, she had wasted precious time, the one commodity they didn't have.

Willing herself to believe that all was not lost, she raced on, upping her speed. There were dozens of other properties on Charlie's long list of council properties that needed to be investigated. Helen couldn't hope to cover them all by herself, but in her mind's eye that was exactly what she wanted to do, bursting into boarded-up buildings, kicking down doors, until she eventually found the missing girls. She knew this was a hopeless fantasy, but she was desperate, riven with fears for their safety, convinced that she had messed up, that she had broken her promise to Sheila Watson, that she had failed.

Fighting back angry tears, Helen drove on, finally cresting the staircase, before sliding out into the corridor. Without breaking stride, she now changed direction, sprinting towards the front door, towards a bemused-looking Archie Reynolds loitering outside. She would have to leave him here, to offer explanations later, as there was no time for delay. She needed to get to the next location on their list ASAP, with no regard for the normal protocols. Tugging her radio from her pocket, she slid to a halt by the front door, pressing down hard on the call button. Breathless, agonized, she prepared to radio in, but as she brought the radio to her lips, she paused.

What was that noise? Lowering her radio, Helen scanned around the gloomy corridor, convinced she'd heard something. She darted a look at Archie, but he remained quiet, looking at her with an air of pure bewilderment. There it was again. This decrepit building had been as silent as the grave since she got here, only her own pointless activities disturbing the peace, but now she could definitely hear something. It wasn't a cry, nor a scream. It wasn't even someone appealing for help. No, it was a high-pitched, repetitive sound. A strange, metallic noise.

Tink, tink, tink.

There it was again. It didn't sound mechanical, and the uneven rhythm made it sound human rather than a defect in the building. But where was it coming from? Helen span round, desperately searching for signs of life, but found nothing. The corridors were empty, the building deserted, so where...?

Tink, tink, tink.

The sound seemed louder now, more desperate, drawing Helen's attention back to the basement stairwell. Hastening towards it, Helen suddenly found what she was looking for, a solid metal water pipe that led up from the basement before diverting away towards the street. Crouching down, Helen felt a shot of adrenaline surge through her – the sound was coming from the pipe, an insistent, repetitive rhythm, beaten out in desperation.

Was it possible that Naomi was here? That was she still *alive*?

Chapter 114

Clutching the cold-water pipe with one hand, Naomi continued to beat out her desperate SOS. Exhausted, floored, the fading teenager knew this was her last hope, her final chance of making contact with her rescuers. Unable to shout, unable to move, she had curled herself up into a ball, preparing for the end. As her last act, she had kissed her eternity ring, her beloved keepsake, wanting to feel close to her mother in her final minutes, and as she felt the soft metal touch her lips, an idea struck her. She was leaning against the metal pipe already, as she had done so many times during the past few days, loving its solidity. All she had to do now was pivot her body slightly, then rap out her desperate rhythm on the hard metal.

Convinced that all was lost, the loud, percussive noise suddenly gave Naomi new strength. Swathed in darkness, smothered by a terrible silence, it felt amazing to fill this awful, airless place with sound, her strident, repetitive rhythm bouncing off the brickwork. She didn't know if it would make any difference, whether she was already too late, but she was determined to go down fighting. This was her last chance to cheat a slow, painful death.

Chapter 115

Crashing back into the basement, Helen skidded to a halt in the middle of the room. She was now convinced that Naomi and Mia were hidden in this awful building, that somehow the answer to the riddle at the heart of this troubling case lay here, but where?

Once more, Helen strained to hear, exhilarated to discover that the repetitive sound continued to ring out. The water pipe that emerged above, however, was no longer visible, which made no sense. It clearly came down here and someone was obviously banging on it, so...

Marching forwards, Helen ran her hand over the side wall nearest the stairs, beating her hand against it. It made sense that the pipe must be concealed somewhere, boxed in perhaps, but the wall felt solid, the brickwork secure. Reaching the far wall, however, Helen paused. This area *had* been plastered over and, pressing the wall with her fingers now, Helen was surprised to find that the plasterwork was springy and fresh. This building hadn't been touched in years, so why had someone redecorated down here? It had dust on it, perhaps kicked up to conceal the repair work, but this was a recent job, no question. Someone had done this in the last day or two. But why? What did this wall conceal?'

'Naomi?'

Opening up her lungs, Helen screamed out her name. Instantly, she got a response, the metallic noise growing in both volume and urgency. Now Helen was scratching urgently at the plasterwork, as she ran her fingers over the surface. Great clumps of plaster seemed to fall away, having barely set, and now she hit something. Pausing, Helen leaned in, to discover that there was a join down the middle of the wall. Using her index finger, she ran her nail down from top to bottom, revealing the full seam. What was this then? Some kind of access point? A hinged door even?

Taking a step back, Helen gathered herself, then threw her foot at the door. Her boot connected hard with the chipboard, the whole wall seeming to shake and quiver in front of her. Energized, exhilarated, Helen attacked the wall again, her boot slamming into it, denting the surface badly.

'Stand back, Naomi, I'm coming in.'

Once more Helen charged at the wall, kicking out at it with all her might. This time her foot went straight through, sending a cloud of plaster dust high into the air. Retrieving her boot, Helen now thrust her hands through the small hole she'd made, tugging at the surrounding plasterboard. Great chunks came off in her hand, opening up a large, round fissure. Now she paused, breathless and exhilarated, ripping out her phone and firing the torch beam inside. The response was immediate, surprising and wonderful, the bedraggled, blinking face of Naomi Watson appearing out of the darkness, pressing herself into the light.

And now all composure deserted Helen. Sinking to her knees, with tears in her eyes, she pulled the gaunt teenager to her, enfolding her in a hug. The desperate captive collapsed into her arms, sobbing out her anguish and relief. Helen pulled her close, more relieved than she could say that she had found the missing girl alive. Stroking her hair, clinging onto her fiercely, Helen pressed her lips to the shaking girl's ear, as she whispered.

'Come on, Naomi. Let's get you home.'

Epilogue

Chapter 116

The two figures walked down the corridor in silence. Helen had made this journey many times during her long career, but never had she felt as hollow as she did this morning. Two days had passed since Naomi's dramatic rescue and, following a spell in hospital, the recuperating teen was now returning home with her mother, to rest and heal. But there would be no such happy ending for Mia Davies.

Ashen, uncertain, Christopher Davies was focusing hard on putting one foot in front of the other, as they moved slowly down the lifeless corridor. He was visibly shaking, overwhelmed by sadness and grief. After months of torturing himself over where his daughter might be, he had his answer, but it was not the one he'd prayed for. Reaching the mortuary doors, he paused now, as if unwilling to confront the final reality.

'It's OK, Christopher. It's just Mia in there,' Helen said quietly, laying a hand on his arm. 'Your daughter, who looks as beautiful, as peaceful, as she ever did. Go to her now.'

The distraught father still looked uncertain, so Helen continued.

'I'm not sure how you left things with Mia, but it's important you see her now. This is your chance to say goodbye.'

This seemed to bolster him and Christopher took a step

forward, standing tall as the mortuary assistants buzzed them in. Helen took the bereaved father's arm and two minutes later they were standing in front of the gurney. Taking his cue from Helen, the mortuary assistant lifted the sheet, turning it back to reveal Mia's head and shoulders.

Immediately, Christopher gasped. But it was not an exclamation of horror, but rather one of recognition. He'd imagined all sorts of desecrations and indignities, yet here she was, his Mia. Thinner, her features sharper, but still striking, with her long flowing hair, her porcelain skin, her beatific expression.

'Mia, Mia...' he whispered.

His eyes were brimming, but not with tears of anguish. These were tears of love.

'I didn't think we'd ever see her again...'

Helen nodded, grateful that Mia's dad could take some comfort from reconnecting with her daughter. The full weight of Mia's suffering, her appalling ordeal, would make itself felt over the ensuing weeks and months, but the opportunity to sweep his daughter up into the family's embrace once more seemed to afford him some solace.

Helen stepped away, giving her companion some privacy as he whispered to his lost girl. It was part of Helen's job to reunite families, to bring together the living and the dead, but she still found it gut-wrenching. Naomi had been saved, Reynolds imprisoned, but the whole case had left Helen feeling agitated and unsettled. The disgraced police officer continued to deny any involvement in these awful crimes, refusing to acknowledge that he'd even met the girls, let alone harmed them. A long and difficult legal process lay ahead, but for Helen that would be the easy bit. She was determined to bring Reynolds to book, to ensure he never set foot on the streets ever again, but she knew that his permanent incarceration would provide little comfort.

Nothing about this complex investigation sat right with Helen: Reynolds' arrogance and entitlement, the Force's wilful blindness to his crimes, and, worst of all, the devastation he'd wreaked on those poor girls. Naomi would survive thanks to her own strength and the determined love of her mother. Mia would not, her family having to lay her to rest now and find what peace they could.

And what of the families of Shanice Lloyd and Laura White? With Reynolds refusing to co-operate, to admit his wrongdoing, it was possible their bodies would never be found, that their loved ones would never be able to grieve, to love, to let go. Where was the justice in that? Where was the closure? The Lloyd family, the White family, would be haunted by what might have happened to them, where their girls might now be lying, alone and unprotected, prey to scavengers, to decay. It was too awful to contemplate, a fate worse than death, a slow drip, drip of agony and grief, but Helen had to face up to it, to acknowledge that she had brought a dangerous criminal to book, but had failed to deliver justice.

'She looks so pretty, doesn't she?'

Helen looked up to see Christopher Davies smiling through tears. Lowering her gaze to the teenager, Helen nodded sadly.

'She had so much to live for,' Mia's dad continued. 'She was so clever, so beautiful, so funny, so ... Mia. We argued all the time, but I never stopped loving her. I think she felt that I was angry with her for running off, but that wasn't true. I'd never have turned her away, closed my door to her. I'd always have welcomed her back. Why couldn't she see that?'

And now sadness seemed to steal over the grieving dad, as he added:

'Why didn't she just come *home*?'

She slid the key into the lock and turned it briskly, pushing the door open. Sheila Watson had been warned that the press might cause problems, but hadn't expected so many journalists to be camped out on their doorstep, waiting for mother and daughter to return from hospital, like vultures circling a wounded animal. Grasping her fragile daughter by the arm, Sheila had batted them aside, handing out a few choice words as she shepherded Naomi towards the front door. As they hurried inside, Sheila turned on the press pack once more, offering a parting shot:

'You've got five minutes to clear off or I'll do you all for trespass. Got that?'

Shutting the door firmly, Sheila ushered her daughter into the living room, settling her down on the sofa. Almost immediately, Sheila's phone started trilling, the doorbell app singing out its familiar melody, but she turned it off quickly, killing the intrusion, before crossing to the living room and closing the curtains. Out of the corner of her eye, Sheila saw her daughter flinch, clearly troubled by being plunged into darkness, so she hurried over to the doorway, punching on the ceiling lights, before switching on a couple of table lamps. It was overkill so early in the morning, but she could see it helped Naomi relax, so as far as Sheila was concerned, these lights could remain on night and day. Anything to make her precious daughter feel safe.

Seating herself next to Naomi, Sheila was quick to break the silence, determined to keep the mood upbeat.

'So, work have told me I can take off as long as I need. That's nice, isn't it?'

Naomi managed a wan smile, but seemed pleased.

'Which means that it's just the two of us. We can hunker down here, watch crap TV and slob about. Doesn't get any better than that, does it?'

Another smile and a brief nod of the head, the effort of which seemed to cost Naomi, who was still very weak.

'I've got all your favourites,' Sheila continued warmly, gesturing to the array of treats on the coffee table. 'Chocolate Hobnobs, Jammie Dodgers, Jaffa Cakes. We're going to eat ourselves fat and I for one am going to enjoy doing so. Fancy something now...?'

She picked up the plate offering, her a Mini Roll.

Looking apologetic, Naomi replied, 'Maybe later. I don't feel very hungry.'

Her voice was still cracked and reedy, her throat nastily inflamed following her ordeal. The sound was so pathetic, so fragile, it broke Sheila's heart, but she refused to buckle, keeping up her cheerful patter.

'No problem at all. We've got all the time in the world, love.'

Never had these words been more true. Sheila was so grateful, so relieved to have her little girl home again that she intended to make the most of every second together. No opportunity would be wasted or spurned, they would seize life by the scruff of the neck now, them against the world. Despite her anguish, despite her sorrow, Sheila was resolved to be zealous in pursuit of happiness, to embrace the future with confidence. Naomi, however, didn't seem to share her zeal, turning to her mother now with an uncertain, tearful expression.

'I'm sorry, Mum. I'm so sorry for everything I've put you through ...'

Naomi had clearly been building up to this, feeling she needed to speak, but Sheila wouldn't accept any apologies from her daughter.

'You've nothing to apologize for, my love,' Sheila replied forcefully, pulling her daughter into a hug. 'You're the one who's suffered, not me ...'

Unbidden, images of Naomi's ordeal, of that horrible cell, of that disgusting man, arrowed their way into Sheila's brain, but she pushed them angrily away. What Naomi had been through beggared belief, it was like a living nightmare, and Sheila refused to go there.

'All that's in the past,' she continued assertively. 'We've wiped the slate clean – the arguments, Darren, the whole lot. None of it matters. To be honest, it never did. Whatever we said to each other, whatever we did, all I ever wanted was *this*. You and me together, in our little house, safe and sound ...'

Her words hit home, Naomi's gaze taking in the familiar contours of their pristine living room, the bunch of freshly picked forget-me-nots gracing the mantelpiece, before collapsing into her mother's embrace and sobbing deeply. For Sheila this afforded some relief, her daughter relaxing, letting her defences drop as she finally realized that she was safe, that her nightmare was over. Pulling her closer still, Sheila entwined her fingers with her daughter's, locking them together.

'For better or worse, this is it now, love. I've got you back. I've got you home. And I'm never *ever* going to let you go again. You're stuck with me now, kid ...'

Unexpectedly, Naomi laughed through her tears, nodding

contentedly as her tears gradually subsided. Sheila said nothing, exhausted but deeply relieved, cherishing their togetherness once more. Squeezing her daughter's hand, she felt their eternity rings touch each other, as they remained locked together in an embrace of pure love.

Chapter 118

'I would like to start by offering my profound and sincere apologies to the families of Naomi Watson, Mia Davies, Shanice Lloyd and Laura White. Hampshire Police let them down, just as they let down the many other young women and girls who were targeted by PC David Reynolds during his time as an officer on this force.'

Chief Superintendent Rebecca Holmes was working hard to appear penitent, but the atmosphere in the room was hostile, the assembled journalists determined to call her to account for a catastrophic failure of safeguarding and leadership. Helen felt it too, indeed she shared their fury, her gaze singling out Emilia Garanita, who was primed to strike. Part of Helen was tempted to join in, to castigate the station chief, but that was obviously out of the question. So instead she swallowed her anger, listening with interest as Holmes continued.

'We obviously have a long road to go down to recover public trust, to reassure the good people of this city that they can have confidence in the men and women of this force, whose job it is to keep the public safe from harm. We will work night and day, *I* will work night and day, to ensure that we learn from the mistakes of the past and that the officers who are lucky enough to serve the people of Southampton are worthy of their trust and respect.'

Helen winced, aggravated by the mention of the past, as if Reynolds' offending belonged to an era before Holmes' clumsy intervention, but kept her counsel. She was aware that Emilia Garanita's gaze had drifted towards her, perhaps expecting dissent. But there was no way Helen was going to open the wound still wider by a public act of rebellion.

'Today is a moment of reckoning for Hampshire Police, a wake-up call. We must learn some painful lessons, take our medicine. The world is changing and we must change with it. I'd like to go on record to thank those brave women who felt able to come forward to tell us of David Reynolds' crimes. Without them the full extent of Reynolds' offending might never have come to light. I applaud them for their courage and their strength.'

That, at least, they could agree on. If it hadn't been for the bravery of women like Tara Bridges, and the half a dozen others who'd subsequently come forward after her, Reynolds' secretive, sickening reign of terror might never have been revealed. For all that, however, for all that Holmes' words seemed honest, empathetic and apologetic, Helen could sense a 'but' coming, as if this very public act of contrition was only skin-deep.

'Our job now is to acknowledge their suffering, applaud their courage and learn from their experience. We as a force must do better, must institute real change, to ensure that nothing like this ever happens again...'

Holmes seemed to be warming to the occasion now, almost enjoying the carefully scripted lines given to her by Media Liaison.

'That is our collective mission, our collective resolve. And I've no doubt that we will rise to the challenge for the simple reason that the vast majority of men and women who wear the uniform of Hampshire Police are good, loyal, dedicated public servants. David Reynolds was a rogue officer, secretive and shrewd, who hid his depravity from those closest to him.'

Helen could feel her hackles rising, surprised to find herself taking a step forward, as if wanting to throw herself bodily into the fray.

'The leadership of this force is sound, its systems and protocols are sound,' Holmes continued. 'Its officers are sound. But historic failings in the management of beat officers like David Reynolds, a misguided sense of loyalty to an experienced and well-liked police constable, a concern to avoid reputational damage, led to this appalling sequence of events. That stops today. I will not let that happen on my watch. And I will personally lead the process of change.'

Holmes was visibly puffing herself up with each phrase. Helen could hardly credit it. Here was a woman who had committed *all* these misdemeanours – protecting Reynolds, gaslighting Helen, trying to bury the whole sorry story – championing herself as the instigator of the change, a beacon of light in the darkness.

'My prime responsibility is to this force, but more than that, it is to the people of this great city, so today I make this pledge. I will protect the rights of women and girls everywhere. I will ensure that everyone wearing the badge is upright, honest and trustworthy. I will ensure that the awful case of PC David Reynolds is a one-off, you have my word on that.'

She stared out at the assembled faces, determine, triumphant, before adding:

'Now, as I'm sure you'll understand, I have a lot of work to do, but I do have time for a few questions.'

Looking over Emilia Garanita's head, Holmes pointed to a friendly journalist at the back of the room. Livid, Helen didn't linger to hear the question, moving away fast towards the door. She had come here hoping to hear news of real change, a shift in the whole culture at Southampton Central, perhaps even a resignation speech from the woman who had done so much to stymie her investigation into PC David Reynolds. But instead, she had witnessed a masterclass in obfuscation and avoidance, culminating in a kind of warped victory parade. Normally, Helen stuck these things out, determined to show loyalty to the people, the institution, she had served for over thirty years, but today she couldn't stomach it.

She was sick of Holmes. She was sick of the lies. She was sick of this place.

Chapter 119

David Reynolds kept his head down, his eyes to the gantry floor, but he could still feel their hatred, their anger, their rage. The two days he'd spent in the custody cell at Southampton Central had been bad enough, former colleagues staring at him with unconcealed distaste, but setting foot inside Winchester Prison, home to numerous violent, unhinged men who would tear him apart as soon as look at him, was something else entirely. Reynolds knew his arrival at the Cat A prison would have been well heralded, malicious colleagues and screws sharing the identity of the new inmate with the prison's inhabitants, ensuring that the disgraced officer received the warmest of receptions. Reynolds had been expecting this, but even so, the avalanche of abuse, vitriol and spittle that rained down on him now was shocking.

'Hurry up, Reynolds, don't dawdle.'

Reynolds didn't need telling twice, responding to the warden's demand, keen to be away from this place as soon as possible. He had no cause to be in this wing – he was on remand, whereas the inmates of this hideous outpost were serving long sentences – and it enraged him that he should be paraded for their pleasure. Perhaps it was just a decent distraction, a bit of entertainment for the violent thugs who spent twenty-three hours of the day in a tiny cell. But Reynolds suspected something else, something more sinister was at play here, the screws ensuring every vicious half-wit who dreamed of scalping a former police officer could take a good look at him, thereby marking his card, perhaps even signing his death warrant. Loath though he was to admit it, Reynolds knew that there could be no higher accolade for a violent lifer than doing in a former police officer accused of sexual offences against minors. Even now, he could hear the vile slurs cascading down on to him – nonce, paedo, pig. Every one of them cut through him, shredding his nerves, and now he just wanted to be away from their vengeful presence, out of sight, out of mind.

Buzzing open the security door, the screw thrust him roughly into the next wing and instantly the cacophony died away. Relieved, Reynolds hurried on, before the warden tugged on his arm, bringing him to an abrupt halt.

'This is it. Your home from home...'

The door opened to reveal a tiny, cramped cell, smeared with the graffiti of despair and filled with the malodorous smell of the overflowing toilet.

'Enjoy,' the screw laughed, shoving him inside and slamming the door.

He *would* enjoy it, despite the grimness of his new circumstances. Reynolds *would* enjoy this respite, this brief moment of safety. But he knew his reprieve would be brief. They would come for him sure enough, the only question was where and when. Would it be a shiv in the belly whilst he took a shower? A rock in a sock in the exercise yard? Or would they slip into his cell as he slept, insensible and powerless to defend himself against their bloodlust?

For so long, Reynolds had been in charge, in control, toying with other people's lives. But now it was his turn to suffer, to

449

be afraid. He was trapped, with nowhere to run, with only violence and degradation to come. This was it then, this was his reckoning.

It was *his* turn to enter Hell.

Chapter 120

She burst through the doors, striding out into the autumn sunlight. Having made up her mind, Helen wanted to be as far away from Southampton Central as possible, marching fast to her Kawasaki. But as she neared her bike, she heard a familiar voice ring out behind her. Slowing, Helen turned to find Charlie approaching, breathless and concerned.

'Is everything OK?' she demanded. 'You shot out of the press conference like you were on fire.'

'I couldn't bear to listen to another word,' Helen replied brusquely. 'Holmes is washing her hands of the whole thing, whilst simultaneously using this whole disaster to polish her CV. It's disgusting, it's immoral...'

'Well, I won't argue with that,' Charlie conceded, pulling a grim face. 'It *is* outrageous, maddening... but publicly walking out like that isn't going to help your cause, *our* cause...'

'And what cause is that, Charlie?' Helen countered bitterly.

'To shake up this place, to change things, to make everyone feel safe again...'

'And you *really* think that's going to happen, do you?'

This time Charlie said nothing, taken aback by the strength of Helen's fervour.

'Holmes, the police commissioner, the powers-that-be, they

451

don't want to embrace real change because that would mean admitting that the whole thing is rotten. Yes, there are good officers, scores of them, but there are also lazy, arrogant, entitled, criminal officers who are protected, even promoted, by the system. You'd have to tear the whole thing up and start again if you wanted to make a difference, and they're never going to do that...'

Helen gestured dismissively at the upper floors of the towering limestone building.

'...because that would mean undermining, destroying, the very system that has got them to the top. So what if you have to lie and fudge and sweep all manner of wrongdoing under the carpet? As long as their promotions and pensions are safe, what do they care?'

'So what now, then?' Charlie hit back, angry and unnerved. 'You can't lead this team, can't help our new officers to grow, can't do your job if you're constantly railing against the regime...'

'I couldn't agree more,' Helen confirmed. 'Which is why I've just resigned.'

For a moment, Charlie was speechless, her mouth opening in shock. 'You can't be serious?'

'Deadly. I couldn't communicate my decision directly to Holmes, as she was *busy*, but I emailed my resignation letter to her office just now. I'm done here.'

'Helen, please, don't do anything rash. You're too important to this place...'

'But it isn't important to *me* anymore. Not the way it is now. I've given my whole life to this place...'

Helen faltered, ambushed by emotion, a lump rising in her throat.

'Because I believed in the fight, because I believed in what we do. But I can't go on like this, when we are undermined and compromised at every turn. This job is my life, was my life, but to these people it's just a game.'

Charlie stared at her imploringly, but Helen wasn't for moving.

'And it's a game I'm not prepared to play anymore, Charlie. I'm out.'

Helen turned away to conceal her emotion, angry with herself, with Holmes, with life, for forcing her to walk out on her friend like this. But her mind was made up, so snatching up her helmet, she mounted her Kawasaki.

'So that's it, is it?'

Charlie was tearful, but indignant too.

'After all those years, taking the hits and getting up again, taking the fight to the bad guys, protecting the weak and the vulnerable. After everything you've done, the knocks you've taken, the scars you've earned, the good you've done, you're just going to walk away?'

Helen stared at her deputy, but didn't respond, knowing she needed to take what was coming to her.

'You of all people know how important it is to keep struggling, to keep fighting, to never give in. How many times have you pulled me back from the brink, made me carry on when all I wanted to do was walk away. And you were right every time, because I would never have forgiven myself if I'd thrown in the towel.'

'That's not what this is, Charlie.'

'Isn't it?' her deputy countered forcefully. 'Because that's what it looks like.'

'That's not fair. I've given everything, but I've nothing left in the tank. I can't fight an entire system.'

'I get that, I really do. I know you've done more for this place, for this city, than anyone before or after you. And I know it seems thankless at times. That the responsibility placed on you, the task allotted to you, is Herculean. Dangerous, gruelling, shattering, sometimes even thankless, but it *has* to be done. Otherwise, people suffer. Otherwise, people *die*. It's an impossible job, Helen, I know that, I really do. But if not you, then *who?*'

For a moment, neither woman spoke, Charlie staring at her old friend, passionate, disappointed, sad. Then, shaking her head, Charlie retreated, marching back into the station lobby. Unnerved, angry, Helen fired up the engine. This was it then. All she had to do was ease back the throttle and she would be free and clear, Southampton Central a receding speck in her mirrors. One tug of the wrist and all the pain, the agony and disappointment of the past, would be behind her. It was time to decide. Should she heed Charlie's heartfelt plea? Return to the fray?

Or had she finally reached the end of the road?

Credits

M.J. Arlidge and Orion Fiction would like to thank everyone at Orion who worked on the publication of *Forget Me Not*.

Agent
Hellie Ogden

Editorial
Emad Akhtar
Sarah O'Hara
Millie Prestidge

Copy-editor
Clare Wallis

Proofreader
John Garth

Editorial Management
Jane Hughes
Charlie Panayiotou
Tamara Morriss

Audio
Paul Stark
Louise Richardson
Georgina Cutler

Contracts
Dan Herron
Ellie Bowker
Alyx Hurst

Finance
Nick Gibson
Jasdip Nandra
Sue Baker
Tom Costello

Inventory
Jo Jacobs
Dan Stevens

455

Design
Nick Shah
Joanna Ridley
Helen Ewing

Production
Ruth Sharvell
Katie Horrocks

Sales
Jen Wilson
Victoria Laws
Esther Waters
Toluwalope Ayo-Ajala
Group Sales teams across
   Digital, Field, International
   and Non-Trade

Operations
Group Sales Operations team

Marketing
Lindsay Terrell
Helena Fouracre

Publicity
Leanne Oliver
Ellen Turner

Rights
Rebecca Folland
Tara Hiatt
Ben Fowler
Alice Cottrell
Marie Henckel